Pra

THE OTHER ME

"Mind bending and emotional . . . a taut psychological thriller with a twisted question at its core: Would you be willing to lose a life you love in order to gain something you thought was lost forever?"

—Julie Clark, *New York Times* bestselling author of *The Last Flight*

"The definition of 'unputdownable' . . . this is one of the most innovative thrillers I've read in a long, long time."

—Samantha Downing, *USA Today* bestselling author of *My Lovely Wife*

"Breathtaking, inventive, and irresistible. . . . Who hasn't wondered what alternate versions of their lives might look like? . . . As relatable as it is suspenseful, cleverly exploring adulthood, identity, and shifting realities. A knockout debut."

—Margarita Montimore, *USA Today* bestselling author of
Oona Out of Order

"Perhaps this book's greatest pleasure—and there are many to choose from—is the way Jeng leads the reader down one road, then makes a sharp right turn and heads off in a new direction. *The Other Me* is not what it seems to be, and Kelly's story is not going to end where you think it will. This is Jeng's first novel, and it immediately establishes her as a writer to watch very closely."

—*Booklist*

"Like both *Black Mirror* and *Russian Doll*, Sarah Zachrich Jeng's *The Other Me* resists categorization, blending the impossible with the probable with the downright plausible."   —*NPR*

"Jeng's novel intricately weaves together two worlds and makes the reader question throughout whether the narrator is a victim of her own mind or something more sinister. In her premiere novel, Jeng builds a unique narrative, complete with compelling characters and continued suspense at every turn. *The Other Me* is not one to be missed and will keep you on the edge of your seat until the very end." —Criminal Element

"Both a suspenseful psychological thriller and an astute reinvention of the time travel narrative." —CrimeReads

"A *Black Mirror*—esque rabbit hole." —PopSugar

"Well-written and engaging . . . recommended for fans of Blake Crouch and anyone interested in the concept of alternative lives." —*Mystery & Suspense Magazine*

"*The Other Me* is an electrifying sci-fi thriller. It's *Sliding Doors* mixed with quite a bit of toxic masculinity, constantly grappling with ideas like fate vs. free will as well as woulds vs. coulds vs. *shoulds*." —Hypable

"Jeng's debut is a page-turner with well-developed characters . . . a good pick for fans of modern women's fiction about controlling one's destiny." —*Library Journal*

ALSO BY SARAH ZACHRICH JENG

The Other Me

WHEN

I'M

HER

SARAH ZACHRICH JENG

BERKLEY
NEW YORK

BERKLEY
An imprint of Penguin Random House LLC
penguinrandomhouse.com

Library of Congress Cataloging-in-Publication Data

Names: Jeng, Sarah Zachrich, author.
Title: When I'm her / Sarah Zachrich Jeng.
Other titles: When I am her
Description: First edition. | New York : Berkley, 2024.
Identifiers: LCCN 2023031110 (print) | LCCN 2023031111 (ebook) |
ISBN 9780593334515 (trade paperback) | ISBN 9780593334539 (ebook)
Subjects: LCSH: Body swapping--Fiction. | LCGFT: Thrillers (Fiction) | Novels.
Classification: LCC PS3610.E5235 W44 2024 (print) | LCC PS3610.E5235 (ebook) |
DDC 813/.6--dc23/eng/20230714
LC record available at https://lccn.loc.gov/2023031110
LC ebook record available at https://lccn.loc.gov/2023031111

First Edition: March 2024

Printed in the United States of America
1st Printing

Title page art: Silhouette © Rytis Bernotas / Shutterstock
Book design by Alison Cnockaert

For Steph

I think I could turn into you if I really tried.

—*Persona*

AUTHOR'S NOTE

Content Warning: This book deals with emotionally difficult topics, including physical violence, gun violence, sexual assault, domestic violence, gaslighting, and drug use. Any readers who believe that such content may upset them or trigger traumatic memories are encouraged to consider their emotional well-being when deciding whether to continue reading.

HALLOWEEN,
SEVEN YEARS AGO

The rain falls in cold needles. It smears the girls' makeup, plasters their cheap polyester dresses to their backs. It makes a dull roar on the rooftop of the house from which they run.

Despite their shivering, they don't turn back for shelter.

The shorter of the pair, in black, hugs herself as she races up the sidewalk. Her head is bowed, hair pasted to her cheeks with rain. Neither rain nor hair can hide her tears.

The taller girl, in a white slip dress that is quickly becoming see-through, trots to catch up. She left her shoes behind in the flight from the party, and the pavement is cold under her feet. The remains of a flower crown hang askew in her long red hair. Her cheeks shimmer with fugitive bits of glitter in the glare from a streetlamp.

"E, wait up," she calls.

The girl in black stumbles to a halt. In appearance, she is her friend's opposite. A head shorter, blunt-cut hair a dirty blond instead of rich auburn. Petite where the other is statuesque, sharp faced instead of serene. Yet there is a thread between them, a resemblance that runs beneath any conscious comparison.

The redhead sets a hand between her friend's shoulder blades.

"He's dead," the blonde spits, as if being touched knocks the words loose.

"Was he?"

"Pretty sure."

Both girls flinch as a gaggle of partyers runs past, laughing madly, their costumes drenched.

"I feel like I'm going to throw up."

"No one saw," the redhead says. "We got out before anyone saw us."

She curls her arm around the other young woman's shoulders. They could be any pair of girlfriends, comforting and being comforted after one of the usual disasters that happen at parties. They are not.

The redhead's name is Elizabeth, but it is not Elizabeth who looks through her wide blue eyes.

Girls become one another all the time, when they're close enough. They copy clothes and hairstyles, pick up one another's mannerisms and turns of phrase, riff back and forth in long message threads until it's as though their thoughts originate from a combined brain. These two, Elizabeth and Mary, have simply taken it a step further.

Tonight, Elizabeth is in Mary's body, and Mary is in Elizabeth's.

It's not the first time they've done this, or the fiftieth. But for Mary, every time is new and thrilling.

After a moment she says, "We should go home. We need to get . . . back."

The blonde barks out a laugh through her tears. "Are you sure you want to come back, Mary?" She glances up, mascara-smudged eyes catching her friend's.

Mary freezes. Is the truth that obvious? It's always been just for fun, this thing they do, but she feels more at home in Elizabeth's body than in her own. She's only ever wanted to be Elizabeth. The tall, gorgeous rose gold one. The one everybody wants.

Things got out of hand tonight. What if Elizabeth decides being Mary isn't fun anymore?

Mary shakes the thought away. She can't start spiraling now. She has to make sure they both get out of this.

"It'll be okay," she says, to herself as much as to her friend.

"I know." Elizabeth has stopped crying, only a slight tremble in her voice betraying any upset. Her expression is calm. It's uncanny how Mary can discern Elizabeth's innate confidence, a quality she has always envied, behind her own foxlike features.

Unless the calm is really shock, and Elizabeth will fall apart once they're safe in the dorm. She certainly doesn't look sad. But then, it's not as if either of them will miss Garrett.

Mary wonders if anyone will.

The blip of a siren a block away makes them jump. Blue and red lights dance between the houses. The police are arriving, and the ambulance, just in case it isn't too late. Elizabeth is the first to move, putting distance between herself and the mess they've left behind. Mary follows. Relief flows through her, cool and sweet, at the thought that Elizabeth is back in control. That Mary doesn't have to be the one to fix this.

More than that, tonight can't be the last time. She can't stand the thought of going through life without ever being Elizabeth again.

1

MARY

NOW

I've just left my apartment, the cold hitting me like a snowball to the face, when Detective Johns appears.

I was never charged in connection with what happened that Halloween, but attempted murder doesn't have a statute of limitations. It kills me that I didn't see this coming.

As a child I hated when my parents said to "go play in the snow," because unsupervised time with other children never went well for me. It was only a matter of time until someone—often my brother, two years older and big enough that I could have fit stacked inside him like a matryoshka doll—would hold me down and force a handful of snow down my collar. Johns' attack is just as sudden, if more subtle. When he falls into step with me, I'm so startled, my worn boots slide out from under me on the icy sidewalk.

He grabs my elbow. "Watch yourself, now. Those slips and falls can really mess you up."

Did he just *wink*?

I jerk my arm from his grasp, too rattled to pretend I don't recognize him.

"Good to see you, Mary," he says. "It's been a while."

Seven years. Anthony Johns was the lead detective, a bald Black man with hunched shoulders who spoke in a deep, soothing voice. His voice is still soothing. His presence outside my building, not so much.

He smiles slightly. In contrast to my mismatched layers, his only outerwear is a black topcoat, unbuttoned to reveal the badge clipped to his belt. No hat shelters the shiny dome of his head from the cutting wind, yet he seems perfectly comfortable. Maybe the prospect of a new break in an old case is what warms him.

"What do you want?" I say.

"Every bit as direct as I remember." His tone is fond, as if he never told me I had nothing to gain by being a bitch. "Are you aware Garrett Deegan died a few months back?"

"Of an overdose."

The news made the rounds through Elizabeth's social media circles, people acting their asses off about what a great guy Garrett had been. How much they would miss him. How they'd had no idea of the demons he was battling.

Please. The only battles Garrett ever fought were against people with a fraction of his power. In my opinion, he lived a lot longer than he should have.

I don't say that to Johns, because I'm not stupid. Garrett's parents placed the blame for his near death—and subsequent decline into addiction—squarely on me. They are rich and powerful, so this makes life difficult. I'm not looking to make it unbearable.

Johns taps his chin. "Did you know illicit drug deaths are treated as homicides?" He plainly does not expect an answer. "Part of my investigation consists of just talking to people who knew the victim."

The victim. Just talking, my ass. "I haven't spoken to Garrett in years." I wasn't allowed to speak to him, even if I'd wanted to.

Johns' voice sharpens. "But you know how he died."

My mouth opens, to say what, I don't know. That I saw it on

the internet, but Garrett wasn't the one I was spying on? Yeah, that wouldn't sound suspicious at all.

I snap my mouth shut. I of all people should know it's never a good idea to talk to the police.

Johns is blocking the way back to my building. I'm afraid that if I get on the bus that's pulling up next to us, he'll board it along with me.

"Do you have a minute to talk? In your apartment, maybe? Sure be a lot more comfortable than out here." Now he shivers, but we both know it's a performance. I'm already shaking my head. "Come on, now, Mary. I've just got a couple things I need you to clear up. You don't want to have to come up to the precinct and piss away half your day, do you?"

My chest tightens, lips going numb as the blood drains from my face. I've never been great at thinking on my feet. The bus pulls away, and there's that escape gone, along with any hope of being on time for my newest crappy job.

"Mary?"

I whirl around, narrowly avoiding a face-plant situation, though this time Johns doesn't bother to help me. Behind us is Miguel, who lives in my building. Great. He's holding his phone vertically. I am so, so glad that my humiliation will be fodder for his @OBEPhDLife channel or whatever the fuck he has. Everyone's got a presence, no matter how obscure, and they're all just waiting for their viral moment.

But his eyes are narrowed in Johns' direction. He asks me, "Everything okay here?"

Johns puts on a warm but insincere smile. "Well, that's up to Ms. Burke—"

"Is she free to go?"

Johns glances at me, then at the phone, and for the first time seems less than in control. "You don't have permission to record—"

"I don't need it. We're on a public street. Is she under arrest?" Miguel's tone remains pleasant; it's the words that are incendiary.

Johns makes eye contact with me. "You should get your side of the story on the record before it comes to that."

"My side of the story? I don't have a story. I didn't have anything to do with it." I'm intentionally vague, because Miguel already knows more than he needs to about my sordid history.

"Then you've got nothing to worry about," Johns says. "You *want* to put this to bed, Mary, and now's the time."

He holds my eye. I try not to look away, but after a moment that feels much longer than it probably is, I have to.

Miguel's phone, and Miguel behind it, continues to bear witness.

Johns sighs. He brings out a card and extends it to me between two leather-gloved fingers.

"Give me a call when you get a minute. Among other things, I've got Garrett's people wondering where you were the night he passed, and I'm sure you want to allay that interest as soon as possible."

If he's trying to intimidate me, it absolutely works. Wordlessly, I accept the card, because that's how I push the detective out of my life for a little longer. Glancing at it, I see he works here in the city now. It's a common enough pipeline from the town where I went to college.

Where Elizabeth and I went to college.

"You planning any travel? Going home for the holidays?"

I don't imagine the mocking note in his voice. That particular trip hasn't happened for a long time. I shake my head, avoiding his eyes.

"Good. Let me know if you decide to leave town. Then I won't have to come after you."

Johns throws Miguel one last, irritated glance before striding off in his wing tips. Miguel and I watch him go, hoping he'll slip and fall on his ass. Or I'm hoping it, anyway.

Miguel puts his phone away and turns to me, which is my cue to scuttle back through the building doors and hopefully up the stairs before he gets a chance to ask any questions. I've decided I'm not going in to work. Under-the-table cleaning and call-center jobs aren't the easiest to get, but they aren't the hardest, and I don't need any more proof that leaving my apartment today was a bad idea.

Maybe staying here was the bad idea. I should have moved across the country years ago; then I wouldn't be in this mess.

But if I'd moved, I wouldn't live in the same city as Elizabeth.

"Mary, hold up!"

I can't flagrantly be a bitch, not when Miguel saved me out there. I stop in front of the mailboxes, most of which have broken locks, and sweep at least a week's worth of bills, payday-loan circulars, and whatever else into my bag.

"Thanks for stepping in," I say. "I think he had me confused with someone else, but cops never believe you when you tell them that."

Miguel's shaking his head while he grabs his own mail. "I hate how they throw their weight around." Usually he speaks in a mild drawl, but now his tone is sharp with indignation, which reminds me why he's the only person in this building I talk to voluntarily. We're not friends. I've never gotten the hang of making those, with that one unfortunate exception. Still, we've bonded somewhat over the fact that we're both from small, shitty towns, his in Florida and mine farther north.

"By the way," he says, "I've been meaning to say sorry about what happened with the job at the lab. Were you able to get your other job back?"

"No, but it's fine."

"Ah shit. I mean, I feel bad. We got your hopes up, and then——"

I make a cutting motion with my hand. "Forget it. Not your fault."

He rocks back on his heels, eyes on the floor; he's still troubled. Not much either of us can do about it, though, is there? "For the record," he says, "Dr. Ofori and I thought you were perfect for it. Just because the Deegans are donors doesn't mean they should have a say in staffing."

But they do. And the last thing Garrett's parents want is for me, the person who ruined their son's life, to have any security. The job wasn't fancy—glorified receptionist in a university research lab—but it offered that much, plus a possible alternate path to the goal I've been working toward. Failing at, rather.

That chance is gone now, and I'm still right where Brian and Rosemary Deegan want me. Scraping a living, looking over my shoulder.

I pretend to be absorbed in my phone so I won't have to make any more awkward conversation with Miguel, who murmurs a farewell and moves on to the stairs.

I'm worried. Johns might not have had enough to arrest me just now, but I've had the look in his eyes directed at me before. The look of a cop who's found his perp. I barely slipped his net last time, and that's got to have pissed him off.

It's always been a vendetta for the Deegans. And now their son isn't just broken; he's dead.

I have no idea what I was doing on the night of Garrett Deegan's alleged overdose. I'm not even sure which night it was—if the rumors are true, he wasn't actually found until a couple of days after the fact, when the housekeeper let herself in and encountered a little more than the usual post-party cleanup. Even if I could come up with an alibi, I'm not sure that would be enough against people who own a private jet and a couple of members of Congress.

I got the blame for Garrett's "accident" in college, and now I'm under suspicion in his "accidental" death. I know what a frame job looks like. This won't end well for me.

At root, this isn't the Deegans' fault. As shitty and destructive as they are, I can almost understand where they're coming from. First rule of the woods: don't fuck with mama bear's cub. Also, trying to fight them would be about as effective as using my bare fists against a grizzly's claws.

Elizabeth is the one who did this to me.

If I try, I can bring up a sense memory of rain pelting my head and shoulders, wet polyester sticking to my skin. The bone-deep chill from that night. We kept shivering long after we'd gotten back to the dorm. Elizabeth told me everything would be fine, but she lied.

And unlike the Deegans, she's not so high up that I can't take her down.

2

MARY

NOW

As soon as I get upstairs, I scroll down Elizabeth's profile. It's my daily—all right, multiple-times-daily—ritual: watching her flourish while I struggle.

There's a new post, a photo of her and Nate posed in front of their meticulously decorated Christmas tree, laughing into each other's faces. They're both so beautiful, it's easier to focus on them in pieces. White teeth, soft sweaters. Nate's shapely fingers tangled in the ends of Elizabeth's long red hair. The caption is some treacly bullshit about the importance of a sense of humor in marriage. She posted it two hours ago and there are already more than five hundred comments.

I switch apps and, for the fiftieth time, watch the tree-trimming video she posted last week. I've got every word memorized, the pitch of their laughter burned on my brain. Their voices echo from my phone's tiny speaker against the bare walls of my apartment, making the space seem emptier. I scrub backward so I can listen to Nate sing the first few bars of "Chestnuts Roasting on an Open Fire" one more time. I watch his mouth until Elizabeth adorably stuffs a cookie into it.

The video has twenty-something thousand comments, most

in the vein of *OMG U GUYS ARE GOALS!!!!*, and it makes me want to throw up. Still, I scroll down to my own cartoonishly effusive comment, left from a fake account right after the video was first posted. Elizabeth, or her lackey, has acknowledged it with a heart. I switch back to her new post and leave a similar comment there.

The response (*Thank you so much!! *sparkly heart emoji**) comes so quickly, I wonder if she's got some kind of answer bot set up, but I still get an unwelcome squirt of dopamine at being acknowledged by the great, the amazing, the perfect @bethybeth.

We met at the beginning of freshman year, matched as room-mates, immediately inseparable. I'd never had that happen before. Other girls in my hometown had formed friendships as easily as breathing, but I'd always been a loner. Not by choice; it was as if everyone else was in on some secret from which I remained cut off, unable to understand a language they'd known since birth.

Yet, inexplicably, Elizabeth chose me. She scooped me up and, for a time, transformed my life. I transformed hers too. What would have happened to our friendship if it hadn't been for me? It was already starting to have run its course by the end of our first term, but I couldn't let it go.

A part of me has missed her every day since it ended.

No. I haven't missed *her*. I've missed *being* her. Speaking in her voice, walking around with her confident stride, having people look at me like I mattered. Life isn't fair; people aren't fair. That won't ever change. The rich get richer. The manipulative manipu-late. Advantages accrue in one direction. And in this world, the right face can get you a hell of a long way, which is one reason I've been trying to take Elizabeth's for years.

What I want most is to shape a life of ease and comfort. To re-gain the sense of stability and belonging I felt for a brief golden period.

Elizabeth destroyed my chances of ever finding that again for myself. She got me expelled from college, ruined my future, and put me in the crosshairs of one of the wealthiest couples in the country. She abandoned and betrayed me when she was supposed to be my best friend.

That's the other reason I'm determined to become her: because then she'll be me. She'll finally have to pay for what she did.

My phone screen goes black. Dead. Funny how time floats by unnoticed when I'm in Bethybeth World.

I plug the phone in, then turn to my bag and dump junk mail onto the scuffed coffee table I scavenged from an alley last summer. Amid the bills and advertisements, there's a flattish box the size of my hand. It's got my address on it but no name, no return address, and at first I think it must be some kind of creative ask for donations. Misdirected, obviously. I almost throw it out before my curiosity gets the better of me, making me open the outer wrapping.

Inside, the box is gift wrapped. A narrow ribbon sheds glitter on my fingers. The edges of the paper are tucked in neatly.

This makes me even more sure the package can't be for me. There's no one in my life who would have sent it; surely not my family, who doesn't even do cards, let alone presents. Yet a fugitive excitement fizzes inside me.

I reach for the end of the ribbon, then hesitate.

I have enemies, powerful ones. The Deegans have never moved outside the law before—have never had to—but would they? I honestly don't know. I would, if it were someone I loved who'd died.

Bracing for shocks, I inspect the package from all sides. No smudges or powder, no weird vibrations. With care, I remove the ribbon and pry up one folded-over end of the wrapping. Nothing explodes, so I keep going until the box is open on the table.

It's for me, all right.

———

I STARE AT what's in the box. Fireworks should be going off in my chest. I should be dancing in triumph around the room, my socks catching on the splintered oak floors. I should be shouting, *Booya! Coming for you, bitch!* I've never yelled *Booya!* in my life, but if there was ever an occasion, this is it.

Instead, I'm numb.

After a long time—a minute, two minutes, five—a curl of something spirals up in my stomach like smoke. A twist of emotions that blend together until I can't tell what I'm feeling. Satisfaction? Elation? Terror? All of those, and more. What I feel doesn't really matter, though, because it's not the time for feelings anymore. It's time for action.

On the table, in that box, is the very thing I've been seeking. For seven years I've been trying and failing to buy, build, or steal it. And now someone has goddamn fucking *mailed* it to me.

The one thing I need to take everything Elizabeth has and make it my own.

I stand, feeling like I'm in a dream, and retrieve a shoebox from a glass-fronted cabinet built into one wall of my studio. *Great bones,* the agent had said while showing me the place, referring to the built-ins and wooden floors, not the mismatched fixtures and grimy layers of lead paint.

Inside the shoebox sits a smaller box and some hand tools: a micro screwdriver set, a soldering iron, a coil of solder. From the small box, I remove a device that looks a little like a smartwatch but isn't one. I've taken it apart and put it back together countless times over the years, and its casing is marred with scratches and hairline cracks. It looks especially battered next to its pristine twin. My gift from some unknown person.

Someone has sent me a second Empathyzer.

3

Elizabeth's not in their room. Mary finds her holding court in the dining hall. She wonders if she will be acknowledged today, with the others there. A while back, when she brought up the way Elizabeth sometimes pretends not to see Mary when she's with her other friends, Elizabeth gave a tense laugh and said, "What are you talking about? I don't *pretend* not to see you. I *don't* see you. I'm *talking* to people. Jeez, Mebs, paranoid much?"

Today, Elizabeth perks up as Mary approaches their table. "Mebs!" She waves her over. Mary is honored that Elizabeth has seen fit to grant her a nickname, based on her initials—M.E.B.— but could do without the aesthetics of the name itself. It sounds like something you'd call a pet.

As usual, she sits in silence while everyone else talks. Gaby is the only one who even nods at her, and they immediately turn back to the conversation, which is at a point where Mary can't quite pick up the thread but would break it if she asked any questions. Elizabeth has been building her circle since fall—a creative, hedonistic, deeply intimidating bunch—and in the beginning she made sure to include Mary, but lately she hasn't been making as much of an effort. Mary just doesn't *click* with the rest of them like she does with E.

Elizabeth seems in no rush to get away, though she must know what Mary's presence means. When Tochi says they should all go for Froyo, Mary takes out her phone and sends a text.

I got them.

On the table, Elizabeth's phone lights up. E doesn't even glance at it. Mary sends another text.

Do you really want frozen yogurt right now?

Mary is so focused on Elizabeth and her inattention that she doesn't see Katarina looking at her—not until she senses the other girl's gaze. Ensconced in the chair to Elizabeth's left, Katarina drops her eyes from Mary's face to Elizabeth's lit-up screen, brazenly reading.

Elizabeth finally notices she has messages. Her brow furrows delicately as she types out a reply.

Got what?

Mary stifles a groan. She's risked her internship—the springboard to a career that will keep her from ever having to return in humiliation to her depressing hometown—and Elizabeth can't even be bothered to *remember*. She'd been so intrigued when Mary had told her about the device Confluence was working on, NDA be damned. Mary hadn't gotten her attention like that in months.

She begged Mary to "borrow" a pair, just over a weekend, to see if they'd work for *them*. It sounded so fun! "Well," she'd amended, casting her eye over Mary, "I'm not sure *fun* is the word. But *interesting*."

In Elizabeth's sheltered but ever-expanding world, being *interesting* is the most valuable quality anything can have.

At first Mary said no. So many good reasons to say no! But by the time Elizabeth talked her into *possibly* trying to sneak a couple of the devices out of the lab, she had realized being persuaded was what she'd hoped for all along. She needed to make herself *interesting* enough to revive their flagging friendship.

Mary never had a real friend before Elizabeth. They shouldn't *be* friends: Elizabeth is exactly the kind of girl who, back in Mary's hometown, used to make her life miserable for sport. Only recently has Mary realized the role she truly plays. A project, a pet. And that's fine, except Elizabeth is tiring of her. They still talk in the room, haven't yet reached the point of excruciating politeness or barely concealed hostility, but whenever they're in public together Mary can sense Elizabeth's desire to shake her off like a stubborn cold.

Mary doesn't want to be shaken off. And she sure isn't going to let E blow her off for *Froyo*.

She texts Elizabeth again.

> Those things we were talking about. Don't you
> want to find out if they work?

Comprehension dawns on Elizabeth's face. Mary's heart swells with hope.

"Did you and Mary get drugs without us?" Katarina asks, making Mary want to throw a butter knife at her. She has mastered a tone Mary loathes, that makes it sound like she's joking when she isn't.

Elizabeth rises in a cloud of laughter and jasmine perfume. "K, if we had drugs, you'd be the first to know." She leans down and drops a kiss on Katarina's curly head like a queen conferring a blessing, then blows one to the rest of the group. "We gotta go study for bio. Love you, babies!"

It takes five minutes for Elizabeth and her friends to finish their farewell ritual, but no one asks any more questions about what she and Mary are up to. The mention of studying short-circuits any curiosity, even in Katarina. They've never been that interested in Mary anyway. A girl who studies all the time, with a boring haircut and no tattoos. A girl who can barely carry on a conversation, who fades into the background, yet whose presence makes people uncomfortable.

Mary would have liked to be one of their group. For a while it almost felt like she was. Then she realized kindness—or the absence of overt cruelty—wasn't the same as being friends.

Oh well. If she can't have a squad, she can still have Elizabeth.

In their room, Elizabeth turns to her. "So? Let's see them." She has the kind of face that makes her excellent at projecting mild interest when she's actually bored out of her mind, but right now she looks sharp, intense. Her curiosity a mirror of Mary's on the day she found out what the Empathyzer was meant to do.

———

SHE'D BEEN AN intern at Confluence Innovations for two hours and no one had told her what she was supposed to be doing, but Mary was used to people ignoring her.

She'd signed all the paperwork, including a nondisclosure agreement that made it sound like they'd be within their rights to take her out back and shoot her if she violated it. She figured it was fine to poke around.

The labs and offices were behind a locked door her badge didn't open, and IT hadn't shown up to give her network access, so she scouted out the open-concept bullpen where a harried receptionist had shown her to her temporary workstation. Nearby, a guy her age worked at a standing desk. She peeked over his shoulder at what looked like a design for a brochure jammed with infographics and ambitious claims.

"Cool, huh?" he said. He stepped aside so Mary could read the copy: *Traditional couples and family therapy fails because it can't create real empathy. The Empathyzer lets you literally walk around in another person's shoes.*

"I'm Garrett," the guy said. "Marketing." Mary took a closer look at him. He was tall and well built, attractive if you were into the future-state-senator vibe. Mary wasn't. And she definitely wasn't into the quick up-and-down glance he gave her.

"Isn't it 'walk a mile in someone else's shoes'?" she asked.

"What?"

"The phrase. It's not 'walk around in another person's shoes.' It's 'walk a mile in someone else's shoes.'"

Garrett's expression soured. "You want to write this?"

"I'm research, not marketing."

"But you're obviously so much better at copywriting."

"I was just . . . never mind." Mary stepped back. She'd made a blunder. Feeling Garrett's eyes on her, she went back to her own computer, where she found a chat message from IT saying she should be able to access network files now. On the shared drive she found a spec sheet for the Empathyzer. Reading it, she felt something between disbelief and deep gratitude to have landed where she had.

The Empathyzer came in pairs, each device used by one member of a dyad. A couple, for instance, or a parent and child, who were having relationship problems. The Empathyzers deployed focused electrical impulses to synchronize the brain wave frequencies of those two people, creating a "consciousness-exchange pathway" to "facilitate radical perspective taking." Buried in jargon, Mary untangled the truth: when two devices were activated, the people using them could switch consciousness with each other. Swap bodies.

The door to the labs burst open, startling her. A tall, well-coiffed white woman shot out and propelled herself across the polished concrete floor. Mary recognized her instantly: Gloria Faculak, Confluence Innovations' CEO. Starry-eyed at the prospect of working for a woman founder, Mary had done research on her.

Garrett took a step away from his standing desk. "Hey, Aunt Gloria!" His voice bounced across the bullpen. Heads turned.

"I've got a meeting, Gar!" She didn't slow down.

He trotted after her. "Can I sit in?"

"Maybe next time." Despite three-inch heels, she ran full tilt through the glass doors that led into the front lobby.

So that was how Garrett had snagged his job. He turned back, shoulders sagging, and it was Mary's bad luck that she happened to make eye contact. His college-lacrosse-player-handsome features twisted into a scowl. "What?"

Great. She'd pissed off the boss's nephew. "Nothing," she said, dropping her eyes. "It must be cool to have your aunt run a start-up."

"It is, actually." He leaned closer, lowering his voice. "You want to get her attention, stick with me."

Mary did want to get Gloria's attention. Confluence was valued in the hundreds of millions, and there were plans to open a manufacturing facility and counseling center in Silicon Valley. A female CEO would be more focused than a man on promoting future women scientists. Mary had believed scoring a slot at Confluence meant she was truly on her way.

The reality turned out to be less exalted, as Mary found out once she was finally given something to do.

————

SINCE THAT FIRST day, Mary has mostly been stuck with busy-work. Only in the last month has she gotten past the locked door to the labs.

During this time, her main task has been to sit in front of a computer that has never been connected to the internet and comb through user-trial data to flag "outliers" for removal from the final results. The deeper she gets, the more she suspects these "outliers" aren't so much bad data as instances in which the Empathyzer didn't work as expected, meaning the participants didn't make it into each other's bodies.

She's supposed to throw out only the instances in which the device had no effect at all: no altered brain activity, no reported change in the participant's state of consciousness. Yet aren't trials meant to test effectiveness? If a device does nothing, shouldn't that be noted instead of ignored?

Because according to her calculations, depending on which "outliers" are left in the results, the Empathyzer has a success rate somewhere between nine and forty-five percent.

Garrett set her up with the work. Mary can't help but notice his aunt has given him an awful lot of responsibility in a short time, and he's become Mary's de facto supervisor even though that makes no sense. When he showed Mary what she'd be doing, he made sure to emphasize that it was a monkey's job, basically clicking a button over and over.

Mary's been vacillating over what she should do. She needs to keep her internship if she wants to get anywhere; it's not as if she could find a new one at this point in the year. It doesn't actually *hurt* anyone if the Empathyzer isn't effective. It's not a medical de- vice, because calling it that would trigger government regulation. The final marketing copy calls it *a proprietary technology that will revolu- tionize the couples and family counseling space, and with it, our most important human relationships.*

She can imagine Garrett's reaction if she shared her reserva- tions with him. She doesn't know who else she could talk to. For a STEM start-up, Confluence doesn't have a culture that seems very focused on scientific inquiry.

She's settled on the decision that it's not her job to bring these things up. She's a cog in the machine, as she's been told in so many little ways since fall. Surely someone higher up will flag these problems before the Empathyzer gets to market.

Being treated like she doesn't matter makes her feel a lot better about borrowing the company's tech.

When she brings the Empathyzers out of her bag to show Elizabeth, she repeats the same thing she said when she first told her about the devices. "Like I said, there's no guarantee they'll work for us."

Elizabeth waves a hand, as though Mary's words are mosquitoes. "I thought they'd *look* cooler," she says, frowning. She runs a fingertip over the cheap black silicone wristband, the polymer casing with CONFLUENCE molded along the edge. It's true that the Empathyzers are plain; they look like off-brand fitness trackers from a big-box store.

"They're prototypes," Mary says. "Looking cool comes later." But her stomach sinks. Elizabeth's already disappointed. She'll be really unimpressed when the Empathyzers don't work. Mary will look like a liar no matter how carefully she has managed expectations. And, more than likely, she'll lose the only friend she's ever had.

Elizabeth claims one of the devices and powers it on. Mary glances at the remaining Empathyzer, still on the desk. She feels a sudden powerful aversion to touching it.

"What happens if they find out you took these?" Elizabeth sounds mildly curious rather than concerned.

Mary will be fired, obviously. Blacklisted from the industry, sued for violating Confluence's draconian nondisclosure agreement, possibly charged with corporate espionage. Her actual intent seems harmless against the consequences.

She could never imagine her previous self taking such a risk.

That girl knew something was missing from her life, but she had no idea how lonely she was, the yawning depth of it. Mary doesn't want to be that lonely ever again.

"I wouldn't want you to get in trouble," Elizabeth says.

Mary looks her in the eye. "I won't."

4

MARY

NOW

Elizabeth's routine is always changing, but she and her friends go to the same brunch place every week.

It's a cavernous room full of long community tables arranged in rows, currently jammed with trust-fund babies easing their hangovers with Bloody Marys and huevos rancheros. The layout is perfect for my purposes: not a sheltering booth to be seen. All I have to do is stay out of Elizabeth's direct sight line and wait until she's downed a few mimosas, then sneak past her chair and slip the Empathyzer into her bag. That will put the device in close enough proximity to her brain for the transfer to work.

Lurking by the bar, I play the same scenarios that ran through my head during my sleepless night. What if Elizabeth recognizes me? What if she finds the Empathyzer after I've planted it on her? What if some change in our brain chemistry over the past seven years means the devices won't work for us anymore?

Or what if there's something wrong with the new Empathyzer? I'm not a trusting person at the best of times, so it's made me a smidge paranoid, having the most important piece of my revenge puzzle fall into my hands literally gift wrapped. I'd be more cautious about using it, but Johns and his homicide investigation have me backed against a wall. There's no way in hell I'm going to prison. Not when I have the means to avoid it.

Elizabeth posted her check-in half an hour ago. If I don't move soon, she'll be gone and I'll have to wait until next week. I might be arrested before next week.

I make my way toward her table, pulling a slouchy black beanie over my hair. I'm wearing no-prescription glasses from a drugstore, and a comically oversize University of Nebraska sweatshirt I borrowed from my building's laundry room.

Not quite *borrowed*, since I don't plan to be back—ever—to replace it. But whoever it belongs to should have fetched their clothes from the dryer in a timely fucking fashion.

The disguise won't fool Elizabeth if she looks at me closely, but I'm counting on her self-absorption and my own tendency to fade into the background. My old Empathyzer is on my wrist, and I clutch the new one in my sweaty palm.

My heart slams against my ribs as I dodge a loaded-down server and a toddler who's screeching and staggering like he's gotten into the prosecco. Slipping into the narrow walkway between Elizabeth's table and the next, I have to remind myself not to stare so she won't feel my gaze.

The closer I get, the more unhinged this whole idea seems. It won't work. My shitty luck virtually ensures that. But desperation, fully ripened rage, and a childish sense of fairness keep me going. Justice needs to be done, and I'm the only one who can do it.

Around me voices spiral, happy and drunk; we're well into bottomless-mimosa time. In contrast, I feel sharp enough to cut. I hold my breath as I approach Elizabeth's chair. Her bag hangs unguarded over the back. She's talking animatedly to the woman across from her, whom I recognize as Brianna, part of the revolving cast of besties who slide down Elizabeth's feed. Focused on their conversation, Elizabeth doesn't see my hand descend to the open top of her yellow calfskin tote. No one sees. I let the Empathyzer drop.

Gone now.

Someone at the next table scoots their chair backward, pushing me right into Elizabeth, which knocks her into the table. She cries out as her mimosa flute topples. Naturally, it spills away from her. That's the kind of luck *she* has.

While she scrambles for napkins, I avert my face and speed down the row. "*Excuse* you," she snits in my direction. Her laser glare burns a circle on my back. She'll recognize me any second. *Mebs? What are you doing here?* I'll be found out, my plans ruined before the end of phase one.

But when she calls out, it's only to get a waiter to wipe up the mess and fetch her another mimosa.

I stop at the end of the row. Elizabeth's beaming at the server, unpleasantness firmly in the past. Just like I am, in her eyes.

She deserves to have her life taken away.

I make my way to the alley behind the restaurant, legs shaking with adrenaline.

This is as far as I'm comfortable going. Technically I can be as far away as a few miles, but a transfer comes with side effects that intensify with distance. At least for me; Elizabeth would never admit to being bothered by them. Plus, the longer I wait, the greater the chance that Elizabeth will find the Empathyzer in her bag. If she gets rid of it or turns it off, all my planning will have been for nothing.

I'm willing to bet she's never seen this side of her favorite brunch spot, with its reeking trash bins and mounds of gray snow. She might not even recognize where she is. The less chance of her finding me right away, the better. But I know Elizabeth: she won't want to confront me in public.

My stomach flutters with anticipation as I activate the Empathyzer. This is it: either the transfer will take, or it won't and I'll have hit a definitive dead end.

The device makes no obvious sound or vibration. Still, I sense a subsonic hum as it locks onto its mate in the restaurant, and my vision wobbles in time with my racing pulse. The energy in the air shifts, causing the hair on my arms to stand up. A strenuous kind of sensitivity sets in, a hyperawareness of my body that makes me struggle for breath.

It's just like I remember.

My heartbeat slows in relief. Also familiar is the dialed-in feeling—like frequencies aligning—as the pathway is created for my consciousness to travel into Elizabeth's body and hers into mine. I can feel the point of no return when the transfer takes.

Elizabeth will feel it too, but it's too late for her to do anything. The rush of triumph carries me through the part we used to call *the shrinkdown*.

I didn't really believe it would work, but I'm doing it. I've *done* it.

A smile spreads over my face as my consciousness expands. A bubble of euphoria rises, escaping in a loud laugh.

Then I'm looking across the table at Brianna, who's staring at me in shock.

5

"Isn't it weird that a wristband can put you in someone else's body?" Elizabeth has strapped her Empathyzer onto her wrist and is poking at the screen. "Go ahead, put yours on. I want to try them."

Mary starts to explain again that the Empathyzers are unlikely to work for them, and Elizabeth tosses coppery hair over her shoulder as she rolls her eyes. "You'll never get anything you want unless you learn to think more positively, Mebs. We're like sisters. We know everything about each other. If these things work for anyone, they'll work for us."

Maybe she's right. On more than one occasion, the darkness of a shared room—plus a few too many vodka shots—has inspired them to share things about themselves that no one else knows. She's told Elizabeth how she lost her virginity to a friend of her brother's (who kept a toothpick in the corner of his mouth the entire time) because she thought she'd never have sex otherwise. In turn, Elizabeth has talked about her overprotective evangelical Christian parents and her plans to leave the church as soon as she can support herself. She doesn't buy that having premarital sex makes you a chewed-up piece of gum, but she still worries that having had three partners in five months means she'll never be able to love anyone.

There is a sense of pride in being the confidant. Mary is certain Elizabeth would never admit these things to Katarina, whose mother was taking her to queer and feminist protest marches before she could walk.

"Maybe using them will help you figure out how to make them better." Elizabeth focuses on the screen of the Empathyzer, as if unaware of how shrewdly she's pushing Mary's buttons.

Mary imagines herself saving the Empathyzer instead of hiding its failures. Gloria would definitely notice that.

Then she remembers what happened the last time she tried to volunteer one of her ideas. It was at Campfire, the ten-minute period Gloria sets aside for staff input at the end of every all-hands meeting. Mary's days of going through data had sparked something in her brain, and the lab director wasn't responding to her emails, so Campfire it was.

She spent the meeting going over her notes, mentally practicing her pitch. She didn't notice Garrett peeking at her notebook until he raised his hand alongside hers.

Of course Gloria called on him first. "I was thinking," he said, widening his stance in his chair so his thigh rubbed against Mary's, "what if instead of a wrist wearable, we made the Empathyzer a transcranial headset? I'm no scientist, but wouldn't that capture brain waves more precisely?"

Heat flamed through Mary's body. It was all she could do to keep from yelling out in the meeting.

Gloria nodded thoughtfully. "That's one idea to consider in the next round of prototyping. Thank you, Garrett." Her gaze moved to Mary, whose hand hovered, forgotten, at her shoulder. "Did you have something, uh . . . ? I'm so sorry. Remind me of your name?"

Mary couldn't even come up with an excuse. "Not this week. Sorry." She looked away, straight into Garrett's shit-eating grin.

He made eye contact with her and mouthed the word *thanks*.

In her and Elizabeth's room, Mary swallows an echo of the nausea she felt that day. "They can't ever find out I've used them myself."

"You'll figure out a way to frame what you tell them so they don't suspect. They'll think you're so brilliant, you came up with it on your own. Because you are brilliant. You know that, right?"

Mary doesn't know why she's suddenly so hesitant; this is what she wanted, a way to keep her and Elizabeth close. A way to know what it's like to be her.

She turns her Empathyzer on, but the smooth polymer and silicone feel unpleasantly warm, like a snake that's been sitting in the sun. She sets it back on the desk.

"Why do you want to do this so bad anyway? Being me sounds that exciting?" She affects a jesting tone, because come on. Who would want to be Mary when they could be Elizabeth?

"Are you kidding? How many people can say they've been in someone else's *body*?" Elizabeth moves into the center of the room and takes a deep breath, as if she's waiting to receive a shot. "Do we both have to push something at the same time, or . . . ?"

Mary's stomach roils. She's not special; she just happens to hold the key to an experience Elizabeth wants. *We're like sisters.* Sure. "It only takes one to initiate a transfer."

Elizabeth quickly figures out how to progress through the menus. The prototype's interface is simple; bells and whistles come later. "You ready?" she asks, without glancing up.

Mary's Empathyzer is still on the desk. She doesn't want to touch it. "No, I need to put mine on—"

Elizabeth presses *YES*.

———

IT'S LIKE DYING.

Mary's conscious mind will forget the fear over the weeks and months to come, as the transfers become routine. But some part of her will always retain this memory and shrink from it.

She doesn't actually know what dying is like, but this is how she has always imagined it. Becoming acutely, painfully aware of every small thing your body is doing, just before you leave it and become nothingness.

She can feel every molecule of air that hits her skin, shifting the tiny hairs, drying the sclerae of her eyes. She can feel blood cells beating through her veins. The minute creaking of her skeleton as it holds her upright. Electrical impulses traveling between the neurons in her brain, making everything else happen, forming thoughts into words and pictures. How strange is that: That a lump of flesh can make art? That it creates reality, moment by moment, for the being that owns it?

Her mind struggles to take conscious control of her involuntary functions, like when someone carrying a stack of boxes trips at the top of a flight of stairs and automatically, foolishly, reaches for the falling items rather than keeping their balance.

It's too much. Somewhere inside, a tiny, gleeful voice is crying, *Holy shit it's working we're doing it*, but existential terror drowns it out. Excitement takes a distant second to the growing certainty that they've made a terrible mistake.

Something is wrong. If they survive this, and if it ever ends, she and Elizabeth will both come out missing some vital piece of themselves. Maybe it won't end; maybe they'll stay trapped in this half-changed state, like a human falling into a black hole would fall for eternity. And it will be Mary's fault.

People weren't meant to be anyone but who they are.

She feels herself reducing, shrinking down and down and down, and the most frightening thing is that she's relieved. She *wants* not to be anymore. Now she knows what people mean when they say *Her troubles are over* about someone who has died. She's becoming a tiny marble of nothingness dropping into a sea of it, and there's nothing she can do to stop it. At least when it's done she won't have to worry about making herself breathe anymore.

Then, as quickly as she compressed, she's expanding. Outward, outward, for seconds and forever. When it's done, she's standing on Elizabeth's purple rug in the center of their room, looking at herself in the chair.

6

MARY (ELIZABETH)

NOW

Brianna closes her mouth with a snap. "O . . . *kay*," she says.

Brianna has glowing brown skin and an impeccable twist out, chartreuse eye shadow that matches her nail color, and over a million followers. She posts her experiences traveling the world as a Black woman, while trying to attend as many Florence + the Machine shows as possible. Right now, she's eyeing me like I just said her next trip should be to Wisconsin to check out the cheese museum.

For a long second I'm frozen, thinking the impossible has happened and I've transported my *physical* self here in Elizabeth's place. That would certainly account for the stares of bemusement from around the table.

I look down at my hands, which are graceful and manicured. I use them to grab the hair that falls in lush waves nearly to my waist. My hands, my hair. The laugh that just came out of *my* mouth was Elizabeth's. I *am* her.

And it's going to be fine—everything will be fine—but right now I am fully in the grip of transfer side effects.

"Sorry, what did you say?" I ask Brianna through a haze of drifting points of light.

"*Wellll* . . . I was talking about how I rode by a sixteen-car pileup on the highway . . . and then you started laughing."

"Oh shit!" I have to power off Elizabeth's Empathyzer before she can get her bearings and transfer back. I twist around and grope through her bag. The wristband drops further into its depths, eluding me. Finally I get a hand on it and hold down the button.

"You feeling all right, E?" asks the round-faced, curly-haired white woman next to me. "You look a little shaky."

How did I not recognize Katarina before? She's one of the few people from college whom Elizabeth still sees, which isn't surprising, considering how ever present she was back then. Like a bad smell, she hung around.

Right now, there's a cloud of noxious brown gas obscuring her face that I'm pretty sure isn't actually there. Nevertheless, I don't want to breathe it in.

"I'm fine. I'll get you another drink." I turn away, ostensibly to scan the room. There's no sign of a tiny, furious dirty-blond-haired woman in a Cornhuskers sweatshirt. I made a bet that Elizabeth wouldn't want to make a scene, and so far it looks like I was right.

A server makes eye contact and comes over. Waitstaff charming is one of Elizabeth's superpowers, and this poor guy's blushing through his artful stubble as I order a round from him.

Our drinks arrive in record time. "The waiter whisperer," Katarina mutters, smiling, as she raises her fresh Bellini for a sip. I wish I could have ordered poison put into her drink. Not to *kill* her, just to mimic a nasty GI infection with immediate effect. Making Katarina shit herself at brunch would be immensely satisfying.

She told the police Garrett and I were fighting that night. That we hated each other, in fact. And she swore Elizabeth had been at her side for the entire party, which all three of us knew was bullshit. Even before that, I could tell she resented the bond Elizabeth and I shared. She showed it in snarky little comments, in the way she'd "forget" to invite me along to things. Katarina was never any friend of mine.

But right now, she loves me. The whole table does. Interacting with people is easier when I'm Elizabeth. I'm not sure if it's because I get a confidence boost or others respond to me more positively, but it's been that way from the beginning. I'm never at a loss for words when I'm her.

The haze from my transfer side effects is fading already. I still feel a little unbalanced, but that's diminishing as well. I'll slip into Elizabeth's life like it's a warm bath.

I banter with her friends—Brianna, Chrissy, even fucking Katarina—and I sip my mimosa and devour my avocado-cucumber salad, and it's the best time I've had in years.

Chrissy is recounting her most recent bad date. She's divorced, in her forties, a refugee from the mommy-blog era. Blond and Botoxed, transparently staying relevant by riding the coattails of younger influencers like Elizabeth and Brianna, but I can hardly hold that against her.

"I keep saying I'm not going to have sex with guys in their twenties anymore, and the next thing I know, I'm getting eaten out on a mattress on the floor. Again." She sighs theatrically. "But my god, trying to *talk* to this man was like pulling teeth. It was either fuck him or give up and go home. I still can't decide if he was even hot. At least this one had *sheets* on his bed."

We're all giggling, Brianna wiping away actual tears. Chrissy smirks. "There's something about a guy with tattoos, though. Artistic bad boys just do it for me."

I've never been into bad boys of any description. Give me someone sweet and uncomplicated who lets me know exactly how he feels. Someone loving and supportive. I think of Nate singing in Elizabeth's tree-trimming video. His barely-there laugh lines.

He's *my* husband now. The thought causes my stomach to do a pleasurable little flip.

Chrissy's attention shifts to me. "Your photographer? With the pretty eyes and the full sleeves? He can't be more than twenty-five, but I'd go home with him in a heartbeat. What was his name, again?"

My fingertips go cold. Elizabeth always tags this person when she posts photos he's taken of her, but I can't remember his handle, let alone his name.

Chrissy snaps her fingers. "Lorne! I knew it was a grandpa name. I wonder if he washes *his* sheets." She pops her eyes at me. Heat floods my face. I grope for my glass of water and gulp half of it.

"She's blushing!" Katarina lets out a witchy giggle. "Stop, Chrissy, you're offending her delicate sensibilities." But in her gaze there's an avid curiosity I don't like.

Oh god. What if *she* sent me the Empathyzer?

She's spent plenty of time in Elizabeth's house, and she never met a medicine cabinet she wouldn't rifle through. It's not improbable that she found Elizabeth's Empathyzer in some drawer or closet and slipped it into her purse.

She didn't believe the wristbands worked. She thought Elizabeth and I were messing with her, needling her with how close we were. But she's the one who remained Elizabeth's friend through the years.

What better way to rub her victory in than to send me the symbol of Elizabeth's and my shattered bond?

Katarina grins tipsily. "Your face, E. If you had pearls on right now, you'd be clutching them."

Joke's on her, because she isn't going to be Elizabeth Jordan's bestie much longer. I give her Elizabeth's most beatific, most terrifying smile. "Are you saying I'm a prude?"

Katarina makes a face like she knows she fucked up somewhere, but she isn't sure where. "No. That's not what I meant."

"So you think I'm judgmental. That I would judge my friend for doing what she wants with who she wants." I look at Chrissy. "No judgment at all, by the way."

"None taken," she says, somewhere between questioning and gleeful. Maybe Katarina's not her favorite person either.

I turn back to Katarina. "I get it. Making fun of other people is a way to cover up your own insecurities, and I know you've got a lot of them."

Our group goes dead silent, the kind of silence that spreads to the people near us until they're listening too.

Anger ripples over Katarina's face like she might call me out. I dare her. I fucking *dare* her.

Then her expression clears and she fixes me with pleading eyes. "Elizabeth, I'm sorry. I didn't mean to . . ." She trails off, seeming to realize how little her intent means to me. I should be kinder; if she did send me the Empathyzer, she's done me the biggest favor of my life.

But I can't find any pity for her in my heart.

"Let me get this brunch for you, K." I take out Elizabeth's wallet and signal the waiter, who speeds over like I've got him on a leash.

Across from me, Chrissy and Brianna look leery, but not mutinous. "The three of us should try somewhere new next time, don't you think?" I say to them. "We'll talk about it in the group text."

Chrissy is first to nod.

7

ELIZABETH (MARY)

NOW

It's been years since her last transfer, but even caught off guard, Elizabeth recognizes what's happening. She snatches one last breath before the shrinkdown.

Then she's standing outside behind a trash bin.

Her feet are freezing. Hands too. She looks down at blunt, unpainted fingernails.

She's had these hands before.

Her legs turn rubbery and she stumbles, then sprawls forward onto the filthy pavement. Pain explodes in her kneecaps and the heels of her hands as they hit the ground. The cold makes everything tender. Tears well up in her eyes.

Blinking them back, she smiles hard to stimulate the release of positivity hormones, a trick she learned long ago. "Pull it together," she mutters to herself, startling at the sound of her changed voice. She lurches to her feet and walks in circles until the pain retreats to a manageable level.

There's an Empathyzer on her wrist. Elizabeth checks to see if it has a mate in range, but it doesn't; Mary will have powered off the one she used.

So. Mary's made her move. Now Elizabeth needs to make hers, as quickly and efficiently as possible.

She takes in her surroundings. An alley crowded with trash bins, the blacktop slick around a stinking grease-disposal container. Gray-black snow edges the pavement. Down the way, a man in cook's whites squats outside a metal door. He smokes a cigarette and studiously avoids looking in her direction.

If this was as far as Mary went before transferring, she didn't expect a confrontation. Elizabeth almost wants to give her one. She's been anticipating something like this, but she's surprised by how betrayed she feels.

Stomping up to the table, guns blazing, could only end badly. Elizabeth is now Mary, for whom things rarely go well. She's out here in a freezing, garbage-scented alley, alone, in the wrong body, because she has no choice.

Angry tears well up. She blinks them away, but more are right behind them, threatening to swamp her.

"Stop it," she snaps, her voice attracting a furtive glance from the smoking cook. He stubs out his cigarette and goes inside.

She knows how to bide her time. She's been doing it since she was a teenager, and she can do it now. Let Mary have her fun. It won't last long.

She might be alone, underprepared, and under-resourced, but if Mary—or anyone else—thinks Elizabeth will sit back and allow them to destroy the life she's built without a fight, they are very much mistaken.

ONCE SHE'S MADE her way from the alley to the nearest street, she knows where she is, but has little idea where she's going. Her assets are meager. A couple of keys on a plain key ring. A wallet containing Mary's ID—recently renewed, so the address should be current—a debit card, a transit card, and four limp dollar bills.

A phone Elizabeth can't get into because there's no biometric un-lock. She tries a few PINs, none of which work. The phone is some-thing she'll need to figure out.

She still feels unsteady, but stronger than when she first arrived in Mary's body. She never suffered the more severe side effects Mary complained of, like hallucinations and fainting, or the hang-over afterward. She can handle this.

She zips up her coat, the same forlorn parka Mary wore in col-lege. Tragically unstylish, painfully shy Mary, who was so grateful when Elizabeth wanted to be her friend. Being looked up to is a high like nothing else. That was something that initially attracted her to Mary, and it's one reason she does what she does now.

Would anyone believe it's not about the money? People think her job is shallow and meaningless, that she's little better than a scam artist, but she loves her work. It's fun and creative, and she enjoys connecting with people, giving them little shots of joy. She's happy to share the best version of her life so they can escape theirs for a little while. Also, always focusing on the next thing is an effective way to keep from dwelling on the past.

Mary once said she felt like Elizabeth was the only person who saw her. There was power, and a sense of accomplishment, in be-ing the one who could navigate Mary's acid remarks and silences.

A bus pulls up, belching fumes and noise that bring Elizabeth forcibly back to the present. The driver doesn't even glance up as Elizabeth swipes Mary's transit card. She holds the strap directly behind him and asks with a smile whether he knows how she can get to the street she wants. She's used to taking rideshares, and only now does she reflect on how dependent this makes her. The posi-tion it puts her in, not knowing how to get around her own city.

The driver's eyes flick to hers in the rearview mirror, then back to the road. "Transit map's online, you wanna use your phone."

"My phone's—"

The automatic voice announcing the next stop drowns out the

rest of her sentence, and then the driver is occupied, or pretends to be, with opening the doors and supervising boarding. New riders nudge Elizabeth down the aisle. Once the bus continues on its juddering way, she's too far back to ask again.

Obviously, the driver would have responded differently if Elizabeth were her normal self and not small and mousy and wearing a deflated old coat. Sudden tears press against the backs of her eyelids, but she holds her eyes wide open until they pass. She's not going to cry on a bus.

She steers her thoughts to the days ahead and how she'll accomplish what she needs to. Privilege has made her soft. Without resources, she'll have to be flexible. Be willing to ask for help.

She turns to a woman sitting nearby who, luckily, is happy to pull up the directions on her phone. The woman even takes a pen and notepad from her voluminous purse and writes down the routes and transfers Elizabeth needs.

"How long you in town for?" the woman asks. She looks motherly in a comfortable way, the opposite of Elizabeth's own mother.

It seems impolite to admit she lives here. Elizabeth says she's visiting a friend.

The woman frowns. "Your friend should be taking better care of you."

"She actually doesn't know I'm here yet," Elizabeth says. "I'm going to surprise her."

8

MARY (ELIZABETH)

NOW

For the first part of the ride to Elizabeth's, I'm buzzing from what I've done to Katarina. I can almost hear the *ping* of Brianna and Chrissy unfollowing her basic-bitch social media accounts. They'll spread the news of her excommunication via their group chats and DM buddies, and Katarina's boozy yoga classes will suddenly become a lot less popular.

The rush fades quickly, though. Katarina texts me with another apology, and blocking her number doesn't feel nearly as satisfying as it should. I'm just running the same kind of mean-girl ostracization campaign I was on the receiving end of in high school.

But I don't have time to dwell, because I've arrived.

Elizabeth lives in a central yet peaceful neighborhood, on a street planted with maples that would cast the sidewalks in deep shade if it weren't the dead of winter. Now, in December, bare branches claw the low skies. I pick my way around snowdrifts that have iced over.

Elizabeth's house is a beacon against the gloom. A narrow slice of blond brick and glass, it's been rehabbed down to the bones and is unrecognizable from its century-old former self. She and Nate didn't do any of the work themselves, but that didn't stop them from posing with his-and-hers sledgehammers during the in-progress phase. I'd actually cracked a smile at her wild-eyed grin in the photo—it seemed like a breach in her polished surface. A peek into the Elizabeth I'd known.

My stomach jumps at the thought of Nate, and not only with anticipation. I feel as though I've got a handle on their dynamic, but not every nuance and inside joke is public. I'll have to stay on my toes.

The front door unlocks with a keypad. It's fine; I was expecting to hit little hurdles like this. I try Elizabeth's birth date, then Nate's, and I'm about to put in their anniversary when the door suddenly opens inward. I jump back, startled.

"I didn't mean to scare you!" cries the woman who opened the door, her hand going to her chest. She's a few years older than I am and wears leggings and a T-shirt that says ROE 73. Her other hand rests on the handle of a vacuum with its cord wrapped up.

"Svitlana! Hi." Elizabeth's cleaner has a nonprivate social me-dia account where she posts anti-Putin memes and pictures of chubby, interchangeable nieces and nephews. "How was Marko's birthday party?"

My last-minute scroll down her profile last night was to gather dirt on her employer more than small-talk fodder. But when Svit-lana's face lights up, I'm glad I took the time.

"It went really well! And thank you for the biodegradable bal-loons. They were a big hit." She goes on about how much food there was while I'm putting away my boots and coat. The entry-way of Elizabeth's house gives on an open-plan living/dining area, with a floating staircase ascending the wall by the front door. The room is bigger than my entire apartment and flooded with natural light despite the cloudy skies.

A Chihuahua trots up to me, ears pricked. This is Jumbo,

whose antics feature prominently in Elizabeth's Furry Friend Friday stories. I half expect him to start yapping, alerted by some doggy sixth sense that I'm not his mistress. He only whines, his tail wagging so fast, it's a blur. I crouch to stroke his silky, bony head, and he claws at my ankle until I pick him up.

"I am done," Svitlana says. "Do you want me to do the alarm system on my way out? Arm it?"

"That would be great." Over the next few days I'll need to glean countless codes and passwords. I know some of Elizabeth's biographical information, the kinds of things that show up in secret questions, but that won't be enough by itself.

I discreetly watch over Svitlana's shoulder while she punches in the alarm system's code. It's not any number sequence I recognize, which just shows how lucky I was to catch Svitlana before she left.

Hopefully my luck will hold. But it has to; I'm Elizabeth now.

PICKING UP THE minutiae of Elizabeth's life is the easy part. The real challenge will be making it my own.

I have ideas, dreams for my new life, but I haven't worked out the details. Though I'm not a superstitious person, I couldn't bring myself to tempt fate again. In college, I had my next ten years planned to the minute. I had leveraged my talent for math and science into a scholarship at a small but well-regarded private university; I majored in bioengineering, the highest-ranked STEM program there. I still had to take out loans, but they were an investment in my future. I would graduate summa cum laude, with experience through my internship at Confluence and undergraduate research, and gain admission to a prestigious graduate program. This would be followed by a postdoc, then a tenure-track position at a large research university. Whether I loved what I was doing was irrelevant. I was good at it, so it was my way up and out.

Now those aspirations feel like someone else's, someone who no longer exists.

Since I received the Empathyzer, my plans have gone off so smoothly, I'm almost suspicious. Before I can focus on my future, I need to make sure I'm safe.

Elizabeth telling someone what I've done could be a problem, even if no one believes her. She might also work against me in other ways. There must be something I can do to tip the balance against her, like she and Katarina did to me back in college. Now "Mary Burke" really is guilty of something. I could call Johns and tell him I have new information about what happened to Garrett. Make sure Elizabeth gets what's coming to her. Yet something inside me shrinks from actively trying to get my old body sent to prison.

I'll start by shoring up my position here. I've done as much research as I could from a distance. I know Elizabeth's friends, her family, and all of her colleagues and employees who have online presences, from her agent to the dog walker. I've learned her tastes, her sense of humor, the rhythm of her days.

But being here, in her house, shows me how little I know.

I move through the living room with a sense of vertigo at occupying a space I've seen only in photographs and videos. Despite the straight, clean lines and the expensive art on the walls, it's welcoming, with a soft rug and arrangements of fresh flowers everywhere. The glow of the Christmas tree, as well as a crowd of holiday cards on the mantel, make it downright nostalgic. I run my hand over a stylized bronze statuette of a rearing horse on the sofa table. It's one of the few items I recognize: Elizabeth unearthed it in a thrift store on one of our bargain shopping trips. I can't believe she still has it, but it looks like it belongs here.

I walk farther into the house, stroking Jumbo's head. I should find Elizabeth's laptop and change the passwords I couldn't get to from her phone. Biometric unlock has been my friend today, but it'll make things inconvenient if she manages to lock me out of any crucial accounts.

I look around long enough to determine that the laptop is probably in Elizabeth's room, but instead of heading upstairs I find myself drawn toward the door that leads to the lower level. Down there is a converted rec room Nate and Elizabeth refer to with no discernible irony as the man cave.

I never truly knew Nate in college. We spoke a few dozen times at most, surface-level conversations about classes, mostly, but that didn't stop me from daydreaming about him. Stupid, fanciful scenarios, like him failing organic chemistry and enlisting me as his emergency tutor, falling for me over our functional group tables. Even then, I was aware that my crush was an obstacle to our forming a real connection. I got so tongue-tied around him, there was no way I could have shown him my true self.

The basement stairs are enclosed and carpeted. My stocking feet make no sound as I descend. Svitlana didn't mention whether Nate was home, and I tense at the thought of coming face-to-face with him.

But the room is empty. It's a low-ceilinged space that runs almost the length of the house, shrouded in dimness except for thin light straining from a glass-paneled walk-out door at the far end. I flip all three light switches, and recessed fixtures cast sharp cones of illumination straight down.

There's a regulation pool table, a bar, and an entire wall clad in rugged natural stone that must be an absolute bitch to clean. A sectional in rich brown leather faces a wall-mounted flat-screen flanked by framed, signed movie posters. The space reeks of masculine luxury, but feels strangely impersonal. The aesthetic seems almost like Nate's fraternity membership back in college: something adopted out of a need to fit in or travel under the radar.

I swivel around to find an executive desk wedged into the corner next to the stairs. It's covered in papers, obviously off-limits to Svitlana. This is where I'll find the real Nate.

I sift through the mess as discreetly as I can. I'm not sure what I'm looking for. A journal that bares Nate's innermost thoughts? I find the normal detritus of a busy, not particularly tidy man with a full life. Nate is a bit of a dilettante; he's done some freelance reviewing and he worked at a gallery for a while, but film is his first and most enduring love. He recently started an independent production company with a friend. It goes without saying that Elizabeth's success allows him the freedom to follow his dreams.

A large red envelope catches my eye from the recycling bin next to the desk. It's been opened, and is addressed in slanting black writing to *Mr. + Mrs. Nathaniel Jordan* from *Mr. + Mrs. Brian Deegan.* Yikes.

Why would Garrett's parents send Elizabeth and Nate a card? Nate and Garrett weren't especially close in college, even though they belonged to the same fraternity. The Deegans must be the kind of people who have hundreds of people on their list.

I take out a card showing a Nativity scene, heavy with gold foil. The inside is filled with the same slanting writing. I check the signature: Rosemary Deegan. Of course she'd be the one to write out the holiday cards, then not even put her own name on the envelope.

Dear Nate,

Merry Christmas to you + your beautiful wife. As we approach the season for the first time without our precious son, I want to assure you we will always remember what a friend + <u>brother</u> [brother is underlined three times] *you were to him. You shone the light that gave us a pathway to follow in that dark time, + we are so close to seeing that bear fruit . . .*

Ugh. Rosemary won't be winning any literary awards—that's for sure.

I hear a long, low creak overhead, followed by the sound of footsteps coming downstairs.

My heart bursts into a gallop. The envelope is addressed to me— sort of—but I'm snooping in Nate's things. My body goes tense with irrational panic, my hands shaking as I try to stuff the card back into the envelope. I'm still holding it when Nate emerges from the stairwell.

9

"Holy shit," Elizabeth-as-Mary says.

She sounds like Mary, yet she doesn't. A voice filtered through the bones and cartilage of the head sounds different than sound waves in the air. Yet it's not like the times Mary has heard her own voice recorded. There's a distinction, almost too subtle to pick up, in the way Elizabeth speaks with Mary's mouth.

Mary looks down at her hands, at moisturized skin and manicured nails that are currently a violent green. Those can't really be attached to *her*. Except when she jabs the painted thumbnail under the pinkie nail on the same hand, the shot of pain makes her gasp.

"Holy *shit*!" Elizabeth bounds over to the full-length mirror on the back of her closet door and takes herself in. She must feel different if she's just sworn twice in a row. She and Mary grin madly at each other and Mary thinks, *How about that? I am prettier when I smile.* Prettier, not prettiest. Now Mary is the tall, lovely one and Elizabeth is small and unremarkable.

Already the memories of her panic during the transfer, that desperate feeling of *wrongness*, are fading.

She doesn't want to be herself ever again.

"Gah! It's so weird!" Elizabeth laughs, a saw-toothed noise that flies out of her mouth on wings. Mary can see it: a tiny black bird. She laughs and hers is a bird too, a yellow one. Of course Elizabeth's laugh would be bright colored.

Hallucinations, usually visual; occasional auditory/olfactory. Mary remembers the other side effects she read in the trial data. *Fainting; racing thoughts/mania; memory lapses; clumsiness or sudden temporary inability to control physical movements; (rarely) derealization, dissociation, and/or psychosis.*

Psychosis?

"Do you feel strange at all?" she asks Elizabeth-as-her.

"When I look at myself in the mirror and it's not me? Uh, yeah."

"Okay, dumb question." Their voices still take on a visual manifestation, but now they look more like colored smoke than fully formed creatures. Mary takes deep breaths, in and out. *Most side effects diminish within minutes, although some subjects report experiencing them intermittently throughout the session.*

"It was freaky when we were in the middle of it. I felt like I was shrinking down to nothing." Elizabeth shudders. "I wondered if I was going to make it back."

"What about now, though? Are you seeing or hearing anything that's not there?"

Elizabeth looks at her with concern. "No. Why? Are you?"

Mary nods.

"Do you want to swap back?" Elizabeth has clasped her hands behind her, as though trying to hide the Empathyzer on her wrist. The smoke wreathing her face is bruise colored.

"I'll be okay in a minute."

Elizabeth brightens. Her dark smoke turns a vivid aqua, then dissipates with an audible *pop*.

And Mary realizes: Elizabeth doesn't want to be herself again either. Not yet.

––––––

THEY GO TO the taco truck at the student union because Elizabeth wants to try cilantro without it tasting like soap.

During the walk, Mary concentrates on acclimating to her longer limbs and higher center of gravity. Elizabeth's clumsy too. When she trips over a crack in the sidewalk, Mary reaches out to steady her.

"I'm fine," Elizabeth says. "You just worry about not breaking *my* bones." She smiles, and Mary swallows the sharp reply that rises to her lips.

The union's dining area is full of students eating and mingling and studying, the kind of unstructured social setting that usually makes Mary twitchy. As Elizabeth, she feels equal to it. She can meet the eyes of strangers and return their smiles.

Once they've finished eating, Elizabeth says, "What should we do next? I want to—"

Her eyes drift over Mary's shoulder.

Mary turns, following Elizabeth's gaze to a pack of guys who have just walked in. Most of them wear shirts or hats from their fraternity, one of the more exalted ones on campus. They rarely let freshman girls into their parties—naturally Elizabeth has been angling for an invite all year.

"Shit," Mary mutters when she sees who's part of the group.

Garrett Deegan's head swivels as if he can hear her. He zeroes in on Elizabeth, who he of course thinks is Mary, then oozes over to their table.

"Ladies." But he looks only at Mary, in Elizabeth's body. She's never had a man stare at her like this before. His gaze crawls over her like a rat with grease on its paws.

"Mary," he says, "who's your friend?"

The pause lasts just long enough to get awkward before Elizabeth jumps in and introduces her.

"Elizabeth." He draws out the sibilants so they grate on Mary's spine. "I can't believe I haven't seen you around before. I'm Garrett. Deegan." He holds out his hand for her to shake like they're at a board meeting.

Elizabeth lets out a loud, fake laugh, especially jarring in Mary's voice. "Oh! *Garrett!* I'm always telling *Elizabeth* how much I enjoy working with you."

Mary can't work out whether the awkwardness is natural—Elizabeth taking on Mary's personality traits along with her appearance—or if she's role-playing. Troubling thought.

She does know Elizabeth wouldn't fawn over Garrett like this if she knew what he'd done at work today.

———

EARLIER, MARY WAS in the prototype storage room, having completed the first phase of her plan: "checking out" a pair of Empathyzers in the system.

Dyads whose in-lab trials had been unsuccessful were encouraged to try the Empathyzers in a more comfortable environment. The two wristbands Mary had checked out had supposedly gone home with Tami and Petra Janssen-Villalobos, a married couple who hadn't been able to make a transfer work, but were still listed as active study participants. Mary didn't normally keep track of the loans—she was too busy cooking data—but she had access to the system.

Phase two: snag the Empathyzers. She had just removed the checked-out pair from their drawer and slipped them into a carrying case when she heard footsteps in the hall.

It was after five and she didn't have an excuse to be in the storage room, but there'd been no opportunity to come in alone earlier in the day. Her hand shot out and flicked off the light.

Instantly, she realized her mistake. The room was small, its walls lined with drawers. Nowhere to hide. If she was discovered, she'd have to explain why she was skulking in the dark.

Voices filtered through the closed door, one of them unmistakably Garrett's. Her stomach sank. He'd love nothing better than to get her fired. Or worse, hold this over her.

The other voice was a woman's—Gloria's? Sweat broke out on Mary's forehead. If the CEO caught her, Mary would be lucky if firing were all that happened.

A sense of unreality washed over her. What the hell was she *doing*? Risking her internship, her future.

"Why are we back here?" The woman's voice was lighter than Gloria's, younger. She sounded like Jessica, one of the lab associates. Mary had never spoken to her, both because of the unspoken hierarchy in the lab and because Jessica was not the kind of person who usually noticed Mary. They were both blond and petite, but that was where the resemblance ended.

"You wanted to show me something?" Jessica said. She and Garrett had stopped right outside the door.

"Come in here for a second," Garrett said. The door handle dipped. Mary shrank uselessly against the drawers, heart beating through her chest.

There was a long pause.

Then Jessica said, "Look, Garrett, I'm not sure it would be appro—"

"There's no rule against it. It's not like I'm your supervisor."

"But we're *at* work."

The door handle pointed at the floor, the door unlatched. All Garrett had to do was pull, and Mary would be exposed.

"Jess." Garrett's voice was silky. "I can do whatever I want here."

Jessica tittered uncomfortably, the kind of sound that comes out when all of your options are bad. "I just don't think— No! Don't touch me!"

The door handle sprang back to its resting place with a clunk.

"Jesus, calm down," Garrett said. "What is *wrong* with you?"

"I won't report this if you leave me alone from now on." Jessica sounded close to tears, her voice fading as she moved down the hall.

"What would you report? Nothing happened. Good luck reporting *nothing*!" He shouted it like a schoolyard taunt. "Uptight bitch," he muttered, loudly enough for Jessica to hear if she was still listening.

———

ELIZABETH CLEARS HER throat. "Isn't that right, E?" She sends a death glare across the table.

Mary has no idea what Elizabeth's talking about. She's been staring at Garrett like he's the headlights and she's the doe.

Oh, hell no. She's not scared of this asshole. She's Elizabeth now, with Elizabeth's soft power.

"Deegan," she says. "Deegan. Like on the new School of Public Policy building?"

His smile deepens. "That's the one."

"Shouldn't you be going to Harvard or somewhere? Or wouldn't they let your parents buy you a spot?"

He eyes her with confusion. Her words are combative, but her expression hasn't changed from Elizabeth's neutral-pleasant mask.

Then he breaks into laughter. "I can tell I'm gonna have to watch you."

He looks ready to sit down at their table. If he tries, what Mary says won't be so easy for him to pass off as a joke.

Fortunately, his phone rings. He takes it out, looks at it, and rolls his eyes. "My little sister. I have to take this, or she'll keep calling me. See you ladies around." He makes a gesture that's something between a finger gun and a salute, then strolls off, lifting his phone to his ear. "'Sup, uggo? That prefect giving you shit again?"

"What the hell was that?" Elizabeth hisses. She's still scowling, an expression she refers to as Mary's ABF (active bitch face) because there's nothing "resting" about it. "We've been trying to get into one of their parties all year. He probably would've asked us if you could've been sweet for two minutes."

Mary can't believe it. Even without hearing what happened between Garrett and Jessica, Elizabeth should know why Mary would have trouble being civil to him.

Then she sees Elizabeth's wrist. With a surge of dread, she grabs it. "You didn't take off your Empathyzer before we came out."

"Was I supposed to?"

"Yes! Do you not understand what *secret* means?"

"I thought we needed to keep them on to stay in each other's—"

"Of course we don't! They aren't *magic*. They create a pathway. You don't need to wear them anymore after you've transferred." She stops and thinks. "I guess you don't even have to be wearing them *to* transfer. I hadn't put mine on when you initiated. Apparently, proximity is enough to—"

"Okay, I get it."

"I would think it would have been obvious."

"We can't all be supersmart scientists." Elizabeth sounds defensive. And envious, like she's the only one who's allowed to be special.

"So you've had it on this whole time. What if Garrett had seen it?"

Now Elizabeth looks chastened. "Sorry."

Mary sighs. "It's okay. I'm pretty sure he was distracted by my boobs."

"You mean *my* boobs." Smirking, Elizabeth takes off her wristband and slips it into her pocket.

"Be careful with that."

Elizabeth blanches. "Right. If one got lost, we'd be stuck like this forever, wouldn't we?"

For Mary, that thought isn't as unsettling as it should be.

"So, what *are* we going to do tonight?" Elizabeth settles back in her seat, blowing dirty-blond strands of hair out of her face. "Should we find a party?"

"You actually want to go to a party like this?" As her, Mary means.

"I'll get ready first. Girl, I'm gonna dress you up like a doll."

It makes sense. They've been doing the same social round since fall, and at first Elizabeth found it new and exciting, but the shine has worn off. She's looking for ways to shake things up.

Which means Mary has a golden opportunity to be the one person she idolizes above all other human beings. Deep down, Mary knows Elizabeth is just a normal girl, a girl like her. Yet she has a fey quality, even more compelling than her beauty, that makes it a special thing to catch her attention. Just once, Mary wants to put someone under her spell.

Someone besides Garrett Deegan.

"Garrett wasn't bothering you, was he?" says a boy—a man— who has appeared at their table with the stealth and suddenness of a fairy king. He looks like one too, or would if he were wearing a tunic and flower crown instead of a rumpled button-down shirt and jeans.

"I just wanted to check in." He smiles and Mary feels a soft-focus film slipping over her brain. "Garrett can be a little bit of a lion stalking the veldt where women are concerned."

Oh, Mary thinks, and hardly anything else. The boy's face— she keeps thinking of him as a boy even though he must be their age or older, because his clean-shaven features have such a freshly chiseled look—has wiped her mind almost completely clear of its internal monologue.

He takes her befuddlement in stride. "I'm Nate," he says.

"Mary." Her voice comes from far away.

Elizabeth coughs, loudly.

"I mean, *this* is Mary. My friend. Mary." She lets out a giggle that sounds nothing like either her or Elizabeth.

Nate doesn't take his eyes from her face. "And what's your name?" He's in the chair next to hers, though she doesn't remember asking him to sit.

"Elizabeth."

His easy smile is everything beautiful in the world. "It's nice to meet you, Elizabeth."

Then something clicks in her brain and she can *talk*, in a way she's never able to talk to guys, particularly ones she finds attractive. She's relaxed, coherent. Charming, even. It's like someone else is talking through her.

Nate is Garrett's "brother," though he's conspicuously absent any fraternity wear. He tells them he's a sophomore majoring in marketing. He asks Mary what her major is, and she tells him Elizabeth's. It gives her a thrill to watch him practically ignore Elizabeth, and to see Elizabeth *notice* he's ignoring her. She doesn't like it one bit: her mouth becomes a slash, then a prune.

Her displeasure seems to ease when he invites them to a party at his fraternity house that night. Clearly he'll make an exception to the no-freshmen policy for a hot redhead and her friend.

Elizabeth jumps back into the conversation to accept. "We'll be there," she purrs, and Mary has the sudden urge to grab a handful of her dirty-blond hair and yank as hard as she can.

Nate glances around the emptied-out dining area. "Looks like I got left. Can I walk with you two?"

On the sidewalk, Elizabeth takes the spot between him and Mary. When someone approaches going the other way, Mary is forced to drop behind. The same thing happens whenever she, Elizabeth, and Katarina walk together.

Annoyed, Mary wonders what Elizabeth's playing at. Can't she ever let Mary have a sliver of attention?

Elizabeth's telling Nate all about herself. About *Mary*, Mary realizes when she hears the name of her own hometown. Elizabeth laughs at something Nate says, and it sounds so strange, an amalgam of Elizabeth's own self-conscious trill and Mary's minimal "Hah!" Nate laughs in response, and their two laughs fly in tandem through the cold, dark air on black wings. They swoop around Mary, confusing her, smacking the back of her head—

"Elizabeth?"

She's lying on something cold and hard. *Oh, the ground.* Nate's face, etched with concern, swims above her.

"So beautiful," Mary mumbles.

He gives her an uncertain smile. "You fainted. How are you feeling? Can you sit up?" He helps Mary to a nearby bench.

"Don't *scare* me like that," Elizabeth says, plopping down beside her with a nervous chuckle.

"I'm all right. I just need to sit for a second."

Nate ends up escorting them to their room. Mary almost dies of embarrassment when she sees a ratty bra hanging over the back of her desk chair. Elizabeth whips it into the hamper while Nate's looking the other way. She and Nate converse in hushed voices by the door before he leaves.

Elizabeth's grinning as she drops into a chair. "That was expert level," she says. "Fainting? Arousing his protective instincts?"

Mary hears a dull boom that sounds like furniture falling over in the next room. Elizabeth doesn't react.

"That wasn't an act. That was . . ." What it *felt* like was if sounds took on physical form and kicked her in the head. The case studies she read described the Empathyzer's side effects as mild, but it shouldn't surprise her that Confluence downplayed the negative.

"You're a dumbass, though. Are you trying to get him to like you or me?"

Mary's thoughts move slowly. It never occurred to her that Nate could be into her real self, that little chipmunk Mary Burke. It's practically a law of nature that guys like Nate match with girls like Elizabeth.

But what if . . . ?

"I've got you covered. I got his digits." Elizabeth holds up Mary's phone. "You are into him, right? I could tell by the way you could hardly look at him."

Mary shrugs, staring at the floor.

"Your face! It's so red right now. I can't believe you actually like someone. Oh! Mebs!" Elizabeth gasps. "I just had the best idea. I can talk to him more. As you. Get him to like me. I mean you."

Hope soars, then crashes. "No."

"Why not? You could pick up where I left off."

"It's not that easy."

"What's so hard about it?"

Mary can't explain. When she's herself around someone she wants to impress, her mind empties of words. She hates having Elizabeth see how inept she is.

Elizabeth takes the Empathyzer out of her pocket and hands it to Mary. "So, plan B. We transfer back before we go to the party, and you make a move on him when you're both drunk. He'll be into it."

Mary ignores the implied insult. "I don't think I can handle a party tonight." Especially not as herself. "You go, though. I need to finalize my plan of how we're going to keep these things without getting caught." She lifts the device in her hand.

Elizabeth brightens. "You liked it? Even with all the weirdness?"

It's been the most exhilarating experience of Mary's life, regardless of side effects and the tension with Garrett. If she hadn't been Elizabeth when she met Nate, she wouldn't feel this sense of something exciting waiting just around the corner.

"Did *you* like it?" Mary asks. That's the real question. She can't be Elizabeth without Elizabeth's consent.

Elizabeth breaks into a smile so wide, it makes Mary's face look almost beautiful. "I already can't wait to do it again."

10

MARY (ELIZABETH)

NOW

Nate startles when he sees me standing by his desk.

"Babe! I didn't know you were home." A smile slips over his face, then decays into confusion as his eyes drop to the card in my hands, half-crumpled into its envelope. "Whatcha got?"

I can't come up with an intelligent answer. My brain is buzzing too loudly from being in Nate's presence. He moves closer and his smell—something woody and masculine—rolls over me. My lungs constrict. I'm used to seeing him in two dimensions. A cologne ad, a distant idol for me to inspect at my leisure. His physicality is overwhelming.

His eyes are liquid and deep, nearly black. They're focused on me. I realize what he's about to do a second before it happens.

He leans in and presses his lips to mine, and I almost pass out.

Scent. Warmth, pressure, smooth skin. His breath slips over my lips like a caress. He brands me, claims me. I'm his. Oh my god, he's *mine*.

I used to fantasize about this on nights when I couldn't sleep, back in college and later, when I needed something to distract me from my furious ruminations. This was the story I told myself: that there could be a reality where Nate Jordan chose me.

The kiss is over almost as soon as it's begun. If a prosaic, years-married hello kiss leaves me breathless, how am I going to handle anything beyond that?

Shoving the thought aside, I say, "I was going to put this card on the mantel with the others."

He frowns. "Did you read what she wrote?"

"Garrett's mom? No." I don't know why I lie. "I mean, I saw it was from her, but I didn't—"

"She needs to let go," Nate says. "They're acting like he's some kind of victim, but he did it to himself. You remember Fourth of July? How out of control he was? I got DMs from people for days, asking why I hosted predatory men at my parties."

Nate's brows draw down in anger. Warmth for him wells up in me. *He* doesn't blame me—Mary-me—for Garrett's drug problem or his death.

But then he says, "Instead of telling them my wife was the one who insisted on inviting him, I groveled. So you're welcome. And if it won't mess up your aesthetic too much, I'd just as soon not have to look at *this* every time I walk through my living room." He plucks the card out of my hand, tears it in quarters, and spikes it back into the recycling bin.

I blink, surprised at both his vehemence and the fact of *Elizabeth* inviting Garrett to her house. "I didn't know you felt that way about Garrett."

"Then you haven't been listening to me very well. But what else is new?"

He starts to turn away, but I catch his arm. "I'm sorry. If I haven't listened to you before. I promise I'll be better from now on."

For a moment his face remains hard, set in lines of resentment.

But he must see my sincerity, because his eyes soften. "Okay. Thank you. I didn't really mean that."

But he did; I saw his frustration. Elizabeth must be as terrible a wife as she is a friend.

———

THAT NIGHT, ELIZABETH is scheduled to attend an influencer party on the south end of the city. Her assistant, Hailey, comes over to help me get ready.

Having an assistant, even part-time, is a relatively new thing for Elizabeth. A few months ago she made a long, confessional post about how she'd been feeling burned out and listless but was still reluctant to say no to things. *I'm putting out into the universe that I need help!* she wrote. Apparently her "manifestation" worked, because on the heels of that post came an account of Hailey dropping into her life like some kind of super-organized fairy godmother.

I've been curious to meet Hailey. She doesn't have any social accounts that I could find. Believe me—I've tried. The person who handles so much of Elizabeth's adulting would be a potential gold mine of information. Apart from Nate, Hailey probably knows the most about Elizabeth's daily life and the person behind the persona.

And Elizabeth trusts her: she lets herself in using her own keypad code. When the door opens I almost jump out of my skin, thinking it's going to be a haggard and furious Elizabeth in my body.

But the woman who strolls into my house is in her early twenties, dressed in black, her dark hair in a messy bun. "You're not dressed yet?" she says, seeing me. For a second she looks annoyed, but then a blank professional mask slides down. She leads me upstairs, where I'm happy to let her take control of my getting-ready process. I got overwhelmed just peeking into Elizabeth's dressing room earlier. Hailey picks my outfit (which I'm apparently contractually obligated to wear tonight), does my makeup, and styles my hair in a loose braided crown.

"You look amazing," she says when she's done. "Artistic, without being intimidating."

"We wouldn't want to intimidate anyone," I joke.

She doesn't crack a smile. I had thought, based on Elizabeth's breezy mentions of Hailey in her posts, that they had more of a "girlfriends" relationship. I'll have to be careful not to arouse her suspicions, but I'm even more intrigued now that I've met her. *She* doesn't seem intimidated by Elizabeth at all.

"Could we go over the, um, itinerary?" I have no idea what's in store this evening. I could be giving a speech, for all I know.

To my relief, Hailey doesn't seem surprised that I need a reminder. She rattles off language about content creation and hashtags, more than I can take in at once, but it's clear I'm not meant to do much more than show up, be seen having a good time, and let Hailey take some off-the-cuff pictures and videos and post them on my accounts. I'm supposedly the creator, but all I have to do tonight is exist as my beautiful self.

Nate has made himself scarce during the primping, but now he knocks on the dressing room door. "Am I allowed in? I come bearing drinks." He's brought a lacquered tray with three heavily garnished glasses set just so, which reminds me of his brief obsession with mixology a couple of years back. For weeks, he posted nothing but photos of cocktails whose recipes involved things like homemade tinctures and ice that was specially frozen to come out perfectly clear.

"I can't drink tonight," Hailey says. "I'm DD."

"Which is why I made you a mocktail."

"Aw, you're the sweetest!"

As we chat and sip, I attempt to work out Nate and Hailey's dynamic. She's not flirty with him, exactly, but she affects a playfulness that makes her professionalism with Elizabeth stand out in higher relief. Yet her shoulders hold more tension since he came into the room, and her smiles look strained.

Maybe she's got a crush on him. She wouldn't be the first.

Hailey is the one who gathers our glasses onto the tray to take downstairs. "I'll be ready whenever you are," she says, and leaves. A moment later, I hear water running in the kitchen.

Nate nudges the dressing room door closed. He didn't take as long as me to get ready, but he obviously put in some effort. He wears dark gray jeans and a jacket that's fitted to show off his shoulders, over an open-collared shirt. His hair is tamed with product. He looks so good I'm afraid to touch him.

"Pregame snack?" He brings a tiny plastic bag of white powder out of his pocket. "Got it from your photographer, so we know it's good. Or it is if he ever wants to take pictures of you again."

It's not as if I've never done drugs as Elizabeth before, but it seems unwise on my first night after so long. I'm already feeling the alcohol.

"I'm okay," I say.

"Really? Is there something I should know?" There's surprise in his eyes, and an attentiveness I don't like. Is it out of character for Elizabeth not to partake?

What if he knows about the Empathyzers? Elizabeth might have shared the whole story with her husband. He could be making the connection right now.

"About what?" I ask, my throat dry.

"About where Lorne gets his shit from." His lips twitch upward in a faint smile, but his eyes are as cold as leftover coffee.

I find myself reaching for the bag. "Not at all." I do a couple of key bumps, letting the majority of the powder fall back into the bag instead of snorting it. Still, my blood races, from the coke or adrenaline.

Or just from being near Nate. His warm hand slides over my

arm, raising goose bumps. He smells so good. I wonder what he'd do if I burrowed my nose into his neck. *Fuck it.* I do just that.

He stiffens—just for an instant—then relaxes, catching me around the waist. Tingling sensations emanate from where we touch. "You are full of surprises tonight," he says, so softly that his throat barely vibrates under my lips.

11

ELIZABETH (MARY)

NOW

Each week Elizabeth Jordan, popularly known as @bethybeth, does four hours of resistance training, three thirty-minute HIIT workouts, and two hour-long spin classes, plus at least two yoga or Pilates classes and as much light-to-medium-intensity cardio as she can fit in. Give or take.

Mary Burke apparently does no exercise at all, apart from climbing the stairs in her building. Elizabeth's panting by the time she crests the fourth floor.

At least the exertion has warmed her up. The hall is unheated, and Mary's studio apartment, once Elizabeth lets herself in, isn't much warmer. The space takes a glance to explore. Twin bed tucked into a nun's cell of an alcove; sad kitchenette; scuffed wooden floor and dingy walls. The only things differentiating this place from a cheap hotel room are the stack of library-bound thrillers by the bed and an absolute doorstop of a laptop on the coffee table.

But Mary never was much of a nester. In college, Elizabeth's side of their room was plastered with art prints and photos of her with her friends from high school, putting her values and personality on display, while Mary's walls remained as blank as the face she showed the world.

Elizabeth is swamped by a physical longing for her own house, where she has arranged her spaces for maximum comfort and visual harmony. Her bedroom, with its tufted headboard and cloud-like down comforter. Her dressing room with its mirrored vanity and trays of perfume and skin care bottles, her gallery wall of travel photos. She's in them all; many were taken by Nate in the early days, when he was obsessed with capturing her image everywhere they went. It got a little annoying, to be honest, always having a camera in her face, though she laughed it off. Now she'd give up a lot to go back to that time. She'd have a few things to tell her younger self.

Her eyes sting and her breathing hitches, so she goes into the bathroom (mildewed tile, *harrowing* fluorescent light) and palms water over her face. No need to worry about ruining her makeup; Mary doesn't wear any. She straightens, facing the mirror. Mary's serious eyes stare back, blue like Elizabeth's own but dimmer. Mary's sharp features and poreless skin. Mary's limp dishwater-blond hair and thin-lipped mouth, just beginning to be lined with discontent.

A plain face at a glance, but Elizabeth saw its potential from the first. Mary had to be persuaded to care about her looks. Elizabeth envied her that indifference, because it underlined the fact that Mary had options other than capitalizing on being pretty. It's always been an uphill struggle for Elizabeth to convince people she has a brain.

Sighing, she switches off the light and goes back into the main room. It doesn't matter how awful this place is, because she doesn't plan on being here long.

It's time to get started. She sits on the sagging couch and opens the laptop, and is shocked to find she doesn't even have to guess at the password. Mary still uses the same one she had in college.

This part might actually be easy.

A knock startles her. Closing the laptop, she approaches the door warily; the building's probably full of sketchy characters.

"Who is it?"

"It's me! Miguel."

There's no peephole, so Elizabeth opens the door with the chain on. A guy around her age stands in the hall. Dark hair, glasses, runner's build, very tall. Everyone's tall when she's Mary. Six two? Six three? Will an inch matter if she needs to describe him to the police?

"Hey." He gives her an awkward little wave.

His hair and beard could use a trim, but he looks harmless enough. Under his unzipped parka, he wears a lanyard with a university ID attached. MIGUEL HIDALGO-MONTES, it reads. OFORI LAB.

"I just wanted to check on you," he says, and he does sound legitimately concerned, not at all like the type of person who might murder her slowly over a period of days. "I haven't seen you since . . . you know. I wanted to make sure you were okay."

"I'm okay," Elizabeth says.

His eyes narrow like he can tell she's thinking about shutting the door in his face. She wonders what he is to Mary. Are they friends? Dating? Surely not dating.

"I've got a friend who works in legal aid—if you wanted to talk to a lawyer. I can give you her number."

Why would Mary need a lawyer? Miguel must sense her anxiety, because he says, "Are you sure everything's all right? I don't mean to be intrusive—I'm just getting a vibe off you . . . Is it okay if I come in?"

A vibe. Elizabeth almost laughs. This does something to her face that makes Miguel look even more concerned, and the last thing she needs is him freaking out and calling in a welfare check or something. She undoes the chain.

Miguel blinks when he sees her in full. Mary's never been much for elaborate grooming rituals, but she must look bad even for her.

"See," she says, smiling, "I'm fine."

He seems taken aback, and she realizes too late that Mary

wouldn't have smiled. His reaction is all the proof Elizabeth needs that he knows her.

They look at each other, awkwardly.

"I'm gonna make you some tea." He sounds relieved, like he has hit upon the solution to a sticky problem.

"I don't even know if I have tea," she blurts, but he finds a box in the kitchenette's single cabinet. Knowing Mary, the tea is expired.

"Have a seat." He gestures toward her own couch. In her own apartment. Well, Mary's. But it's comforting to be told what to do, even if it's just *Sit down and let me make you a hot beverage.*

Soon he brings over two mugs and sits on the couch with her, there being no chairs in the apartment. He leaves a few feet of space between them.

Elizabeth curls her hands around her warm mug, trying not to stare too obviously at Mary's laptop. "Thanks."

"You seemed like you could use it."

The way he looks at her is an examination, but his eyes are kind. Elizabeth's too overwhelmed to fill the silence with chitchat, like she normally would. He doesn't seem to mind. His presence is oddly restful.

"I spoke to Dr. Ofori about you trying an OBE. She said, under the circumstances, it would be better if you weren't seen in the lab. Makes me want to swipe some VR goggles and try it here."

Elizabeth wonders what "circumstances" would make Miguel's face darken like it just did, and wants to ask what a *nobeyee* is. But clearly she's supposed to know already.

"We could do that, if you want." He speaks casually, but there's a tension in the way he glances at her, a bloom on his cheeks. It makes Elizabeth notice he's cute. Not the type she'd usually go for; she prefers her men to look disheveled on purpose.

But is he . . . hitting on her? She stiffens. He can't be proposing some kind of sex thing, can he? Not if it's something done in a lab, unless it's *that* kind of lab. He remains a respectful distance away on the couch, and another glance at his university lanyard yields no clues.

It's probably innocent. Her instincts have been primed by too many unwanted dick pics.

"Or not," he says, looking away.

"Let me think about it," she hedges.

"Sure. You know where to find me." He pops to his feet and carries his mug to the sink.

Elizabeth worries she's offended him somehow. This happens every time she asserts a boundary: the fear that she's gone too far, misinterpreted the situation. Alienated someone who could help her.

She meets him at the door. "I'm sorry," she says, laying her hand lightly on his arm. He looks down at it, surprised. Mary's not a toucher.

"Nothing to be sorry about," he says.

Elizabeth starts to pull her hand away, then changes her mind. What does she have to gain by behaving like Mary would? She smiles. "Remind me which apartment you're in?" She's not even a hundred percent sure they're neighbors.

But it turns out her guess was right. He's two floors down.

"You seem different." Smiling, he shakes his head as if to clear it. "Take care of yourself, Mary."

As soon as the door is closed and locked behind him, she wakes up Mary's laptop again. The tea Miguel made for her has gone cold, but she drinks it anyway; she'll be up for a while yet, going through every folder with a fine-tooth comb. So much to do, and the first thing she looks up is the Ofori Lab's website.

Out-of-body experiences. OBE, not *nobeyee*. *That's* what Miguel studies. It makes sense that Mary would be interested, given her circumstances. That she'd explore other avenues for leaving herself behind once her efforts at getting another Empathyzer had failed.

Elizabeth takes Mary's Empathyzer off her wrist and inspects it. It's battered, like it's been taken apart and messed with. Of course Mary would have studied it. Tried to replicate it. She'd even visited the former CEO of Confluence: Garrett, snickering, had told Elizabeth about the restraining order his family had taken out.

Elizabeth was right in thinking Mary would stop at nothing to be her again.

But for how long? Elizabeth's instincts prickle, and for the first time she wonders why Mary didn't care enough to change the password on her laptop.

Probably because she has everything backed up somewhere else, like the phone Elizabeth can't get access to. That's all it is. Mary has always been malleable, biddable, willing to do what Elizabeth wants. There isn't any reason for that to change. Mary will move in whatever direction Elizabeth pushes her.

For now, Elizabeth needs to take advantage of the temporary—*temporary!*—position in which she finds herself. She turns her attention to Mary's laptop and gets to work.

12

It's the first time they've transferred since spring. As Mary emerges from the shrinkdown into Elizabeth's body, she feels a sense of clicking into the right slot. She is exactly where—who—she's meant to be.

"You okay?" Elizabeth asks.

Mary stays sprawled on the rug with her eyes closed. "Waiting for the dizziness to pass."

"You still get dizzy, huh?"

She's not *that* dizzy, not with their having been in the same room when they transferred, but she enjoys the pull of gravity on her more substantial body. She is here. She has weight.

Elizabeth flips through Mary's closet like a little girl playing dress-up. "Well, whenever you're ready. Katarina and them are going to be there soon." "There" is a pizza joint near the fine arts building where the servers don't check ID.

By the time Elizabeth's dressed, Mary's mild side effects have passed.

She sits up and watches Elizabeth do her makeup, a winged eye Mary has never been able to master. Then they go out into the evening. The air tastes fresh as an apple. The colors—green of grass and trees and ivy, red-gold of sunset-washed brick—burst against Mary's eyes. Everything is more vivid when she's Elizabeth. The campus and the surrounding streets are full of students, and their faces look friendly instead of indifferent or judgmental. Mary's blood quickens with anticipation.

"Wow! I've missed this." Elizabeth looks around. Mary knows she doesn't mean being back at school.

She asked Elizabeth once what she even got out of the transfers. Mary understands why *she* wants to be *Elizabeth*: Who wouldn't? It's well worth the side effects, which are manageable as long as she and Elizabeth are no more than a few hundred yards apart when they transfer. Their first outing was the only time things got scary. Mary figures her brain needed to adjust.

Elizabeth doesn't even get the racing thoughts or blink-and-you-miss-them hallucinations, which is just her luck. Nor does she experience the hours-long malaise that descends on Mary once she's back in her own body. On those hangover days, Mary tucks herself away in her loft bed and swipes through the pictures of their adventures, and sometimes she can't tell if it's her or Elizabeth she's looking at. It's unsettling how much satisfaction this gives her. When she's herself, she sometimes feels like she doesn't exist at all.

She's glad Elizabeth doesn't have side effects. The less friction involved in the experience for her, the better. Mary even worried that she'd broken the spell when she brought up Elizabeth's reasons for wanting to inhabit her. That Elizabeth would say, *You know what? You're right! It does suck being you. I'm done.*

But her answer was a surprise. "Everyone's always looking at me," she said. "Watching me. Wanting things. Expecting me to be a certain way. Especially now that I'm getting more followers. It's nice to have a break from that and just *be*." She was in her own body, so her smile looked soft and kind, belying what she said next. "Plus, when I'm you, I can be a bitch and nobody cares."

Mary never feels bitchy when she's Elizabeth. It turns out having people treat you well does make you nicer.

But she believed Elizabeth's explanation until spring. Until Zeke. That episode showed her another reason Elizabeth liked being Mary: because she got to play puppet master with Mary's life.

As they'd figured out the natural laws of what they were doing, they'd also set rules for themselves. No sex while transferred, obviously, and Elizabeth warned Mary not to "impersonate" her on her social media accounts, because she wanted to be "authentic."

It would never have occurred to Mary to forbid Elizabeth from meddling with her relationships. It had never occurred to her that she'd *have* a relationship.

She hadn't even liked Zeke that much. They'd gone out a handful of times, and Elizabeth was right that he was kind of a loser. He certainly couldn't compare to Nate, whom Mary had never gotten up the courage to text. But he wasn't a bad person. No matter what, it should have been up to Mary whether she wanted to keep seeing him.

Or when and how she wanted to cut him loose. Elizabeth had been needlessly cruel, asking him to meet her, then telling him to his face that a guy who worked in a bowling alley wasn't good enough for her. Mary learned about it only after he hadn't texted in a couple of days and she found his number blocked on her phone.

She'd blown up. Elizabeth had said they shouldn't use the Empathyzers anymore if Mary was going to get so mad about an honest mistake.

"I thought I was doing you a favor," Elizabeth said. After that, she refused to transfer for the rest of the year.

Maybe she wasn't trying to teach Mary a lesson, but Mary learned it. Having to be only herself, when she'd been used to flitting between bodies several times a week, was like wearing an itchy, too-small sweater. It was even worse not knowing if she'd ever escape again.

Or if Elizabeth even still wanted to be friends. She didn't answer Mary's texts for all of June.

In desperation, to distract herself from her dread of returning to school friendless, Mary began to write about the past year.

At first, she structured the entries like the personal reports the research participants at Confluence turned in. She simply typed up what details she could remember about each time she and Elizabeth had used the Empathyzers. But soon, emotion began to leak into the accounts. The feeling of power that rushed through her when she was Elizabeth. The sense of violation mixed with possibility when she watched Elizabeth-as-her, in a short skirt Mary would never wear, trade banter with a cute guy.

The journaling cut both ways. Writing the entries was cathartic. It let her escape home for a little while; neither her parents nor her brother had changed for the better during the last year. It let her relive better times. But it also made her miss Elizabeth—and *being* Elizabeth—even more.

Eventually, she swallowed her pride. You were right about Zeke. I'm sorry I got so pissed.

When Elizabeth texted back, two days later, she didn't acknowledge Mary's apology. She complained about the mission trip she'd just gotten back from, to the Caribbean during one of the hottest months of the year. Literal hell, she messaged.

Mary was just glad they were talking. Neither she nor Elizabeth brought up Zeke again. But privately, even after Mary came around to being relieved that she hadn't had to break up with him herself, she held on to a kernel of distrust.

It refused to dissipate until they arrived back on campus and Elizabeth said, "Are you going to get your Empathyzer out or what?"

Now that Mary's inhabiting her better self, she can let that last bit of resentment go.

She grins at her best friend. "I've missed this too."

When they arrive at the patio of Roygbiv's Pizza she feels the intoxicating sense of attention locking on to her. A split second of total silence, like everyone's thinking, *She's here. Now the story can begin.*

"Elizabeth!" Katarina beckons her to a table in the corner where the crew from last year is sitting, already a couple of pitchers in. They're all living together in a house, one Elizabeth couldn't join because her parents wanted her in the dorms, where they were under the impression she'd be supervised more closely than in off-campus housing. Mary's not complaining, since it means she gets to room with her friend again.

"Hi, Mary," Gaby says to Elizabeth. The two of them chat about classes while Mary orders more beer for the table on E's dime. She appreciates that Elizabeth, when she's Mary, doesn't fade completely. She carries some of her charisma with her, which smooths the way for Mary when she's herself again. A halo effect.

The late-summer light bends and softens and fades. String lights pop on overhead. Pizzas are eaten; pitchers are ordered and emptied. In Elizabeth's taller body, Mary can drink more without getting out of control, but she paces herself since they're going out later. Sips one beer, then a second.

Elizabeth's tolerance moves in the opposite direction, yet Mary watches her drink glass after glass. Her smiles become constant and sloppy.

Katarina's getting a little sloppy herself. She nudges Mary. "The house is *amaaaazing*. It's already *so* much better than the dorms. We have a *patio*. We have a *fireplace*."

"You told me that," Mary says shortly. The house was all Katarina talked about last spring, when she was trying to get Elizabeth to sign the lease.

"We're going to have so many parties. Wait! We should have a party tonight!"

"No one'll come. There are already a bunch of parties going on," Tochi says.

"Okay, but definitely next weekend. E, you have to live with us next year. You *have* to. Tell your parents it's not the 1950s anymore. You don't want to spend all four years of college in a little dorm room, with a little—"

Katarina's bloodshot gaze wanders across the table to Elizabeth, who glares back through Mary's narrowed eyes.

Is this the moment? Mary has tried to let her know what a snake in the grass Katarina is, but Elizabeth acts like she's blowing things out of proportion. Will she see it now?

Katarina leans closer, murmuring in Mary's ear. "*She's* not invited."

"Careful what you say to her, K." Elizabeth's voice rings out, only a little slurred. "She's not who you think she is."

Now she swings her gaze to Mary. She grins, wider than Mary ever does, showing crooked bottom teeth.

Elizabeth understands the need for secrecy. Mary's impressed it upon her often enough. She has to appreciate the seriousness—

"She's Mary," Elizabeth says, her laugh a bolt of black lightning Mary feels rather than sees. "And I'm Elizabeth." She pushes up her sleeve to reveal the Empathyzer's silicone wristband. "This thing lets us swap bodies with each other. She stole a pair from work last year, and we've been using them ever since."

There's an instant of silence. Mary can't even close her eyes to avoid watching the end of her life break across every face at the table. Even if she swears them to secrecy, they'll tell people. People will tell other people. And it'll get back to the *wrong* people. It always does.

Gaby bursts out laughing. "Oh my god," they say. "That's precious. Good one, Mary."

Tochi and Syd laugh too, and finally Katarina, and Mary realizes their silence was from confusion rather than shock. Mary Burke is not known for her jokes.

Elizabeth hasn't broken eye contact with Mary. She's still got that sly grin on her face. "What, you don't believe me? We're doing cutting-edge work up in that place. Cutting-edge, I tell you."

That makes them all crack up even more. Mary has to say something, join in. Nip this in the bud. "Are we that desperate for attention, Mebs?" Her smile feels fake, but she strikes the right tone of amused disinterest.

"Yeah, try therapy," Katarina says.

"Who needs therapy when you've got alcohol?" Tochi empties the last pitcher into his glass. The conversation moves on.

Mary waits for Elizabeth to go to the bathroom and follows her. "What the hell was that?"

Elizabeth smiles at her in the mirror. "Why are you so pissed?"

"Why are you so irresponsible? Telling them about the Empathyzers? *Showing* them? You're not even supposed to be bringing it out."

"I knew they wouldn't believe me. I wanted to show you it wasn't a big deal. And oh, look! It wasn't!" Elizabeth leans forward to check that her eyeliner is still perfect.

"Confluence isn't exactly low profile in this town."

"And everyone knows they're a big fat fraud. So you don't need to worry about anyone believing the Empathyzers work."

"I'll still get in trouble if it comes out that I have them."

Chagrin flickers across Elizabeth's face, as though she hadn't thought of that. "It's not going to come out. It was just a joke. Everyone's wasted. They've probably already forgotten about it, if you don't make it a big deal."

Elizabeth's attitude makes Mary want to shake her, but at the same time, she hopes she's right.

THAT NIGHT, THEY go to a party at Nate's fraternity. As soon as they walk in, Mary becomes hyperaware of every other body in the space around her. The rooms on the main floor are dark, full of rented club lights and music like a giant's heartbeat, but Mary will recognize him. She knows the tilt of his head, the slope of his shoulders.

They shared a class last spring, a gender studies elective in which she spent so much time watching him instead of the lecturer that she barely scraped out an A minus. Mary had only taken it to fulfill her social science requirement, but Nate was fully invested. His comments about toxic masculinity and the insidiousness of gender roles made him the darling of the cishet women in class. A man who was smoking hot *and* feminist? The field was crowded, and Mary didn't have a chance. As herself, she didn't exchange ten words with him all semester.

But as Elizabeth, she could seek him out when they found themselves at the same parties. She could talk to him, soak up the interest in his eyes. She'd never do anything more. Because of her and Elizabeth's rules, and because part of her prefers him this way, kept safely in daydreams. Noble and untouchable and unable to disappoint her.

One of her favorite things to do while transferred is to flirt with guys who would never look twice at her normally, making them think they'll get somewhere, then ruthlessly shoot them down. In their faces she sees every boy in middle school who stuffed fake love notes in her backpack. Every high school classmate who looked past her like she wasn't there.

A likely candidate weaves up now, in a Greek-lettered baseball cap he'll still be wearing ten years from now to cover up his male pattern baldness. He offers a sloppy grin and a red plastic cup half full of foam. Leaning close, he yells something unintelligible in her ear.

She manages not to recoil, takes the cup, and pretends to sip. As if she'd drink anything from the hands of these men.

He leans in again. "I said, what's your name?"

"Katarina!" She gives him Elizabeth's smile and watches his eyes wander over her body. Over his shoulder, something catches her attention. The angle of a jaw, the curve of a smile. *Nate.* Her heart picks up speed.

"It was really unpleasant to meet you!" She squeezes past her grinning suitor, who clearly hasn't heard a word she's said.

Nate's talking to someone, a short woman hidden behind him until now. It's Elizabeth. Elizabeth in Mary's body. Smiling, tossing her dirty-blond hair, *flirting*.

As Mary watches, Elizabeth goes up on tiptoe to speak to him, her hand on his shoulder. He bends his head to listen, close enough that he could feel the caress of her breath. Everything inside Mary goes quiet. The quiet of a sniper before taking a shot.

Elizabeth's gaze shifts and she meets Mary's eyes. Mary sees triumph, not contrition. *Watch me do what you can't. Watch me do what you won't dare.*

A hand slides around Mary's midsection, making her jump. She turns to see Garrett Deegan's smug mug inches from hers. "Hey, you. Long time no see," he says. "Want a beer?"

"Got one." She lifts her decoy cup. She sees Garrett, like Nate, at parties. He's impossible to avoid.

His hand curls more tightly, squeezing her hip. His breath is hot on her ear. "You look," he says, "like a girl who needs to have some fun."

Last year, as Elizabeth, Mary tolerated him because she worried that if she didn't, it would blow back on her real self at Confluence. This year she's in a stronger position, having been promoted to an actual staff position from her internship. She isn't naive enough to think this makes her invulnerable, but it gives her some protection. Confluence has had a lot of people resign.

And after the summer she's had, she's in no mood to put up with Garrett's bullshit. "Every time we talk, I feel like you're hitting on me."

"I mean, you're superhot." He smiles like he expects this crumb of praise to make her fall to her knees in front of him.

"Haven't you heard that if you want to get with someone, their friends are who you need to impress?"

"Sure."

"Mary's my best friend," she says.

"So?"

"So you're a total dick to her."

"Okay. So you're saying if I'm nice to Mary—"

"Let's not even finish that sentence. It's never gonna happen, Garrett. Never. Going. To happen." She shoves her cup into his chest. He catches it clumsily. The dawning outrage on his face as she walks away is well worth having come to this disappointing party.

Mary can't tell him what she thinks of him, but Elizabeth can.

Later, she finds Elizabeth dancing in a group. She looks like she hiked up a mountain and loved every minute of it: eyeliner fuzzed around the edges, hair plastered to her face with sweat.

"Mebs!" Elizabeth pulls her into a drunken hug. "Oops. Shit." She looks around theatrically, but no one heard her slip. "Hey! Guess who I saw earlier! Your crush!"

Mary takes her aside, holding her still with hands on her shoulders. "I know. I saw you talking to him."

"Just to help. I was helping because *you*"—she pokes Mary in the sternum—"won't help yourself. You won't even talk to him. You just *staaare* at him, like . . ." She assumes a moony, dopey expression. "That's why I had to get rid of Zeke for you. Because I knew you'd always wonder. Do you have any idea how frustrating it is being friends with someone who gets in her own way as much as you do?"

Mary opens her mouth, but Elizabeth's not interested in what she has to say. She breaks Mary's hold and spins away, back into the heaving crowd.

13

MARY (ELIZABETH)

NOW

Somewhere on the south side of the city, Nate and I climb the front steps of an imposing greystone mansion. Inside, almost every interior wall has been removed, creating a huge space teeming with influencers and minor celebrities, colored LEDs, and logos. So many logos.

I scan the room, pretending to check out the displays of skin care products and branded cocktail mixers. I see plenty of petite blond women, but none who look like me.

If Elizabeth wants to ambush me, this would be a good place for it. She could cause a scene by playing an obsessed follower, or present some version of the truth that we used to be friends.

Or she could plant an Empathyzer on me and transfer back.

I shake the thought away. If I couldn't get my hands on a second Empathyzer in seven years of searching, there's no way she can find one in a matter of hours. The device I dropped into her tote at brunch is turned off, tucked under a tube of lipstick and a pack of gum in my clutch. I'll find a more permanent hiding place, but for now it seems safest to keep it on me.

Nate rubs the back of my neck, kneading warmth into my body. "You're tense tonight."

There's a drink in my hand, one that Nate or one of the professionally unobtrusive servers put there, and I down it before remembering how many intoxicants I've already had. Alcohol generally intensifies the side effects of a transfer. That's one reason I didn't drink much in college, once Elizabeth and I started using the Empathyzers. In certain circumstances, I would begin to feel as though I were dissolving into my surroundings. Like I was ceasing to exist.

There isn't much danger of that tonight. I can't take ten steps without someone stopping to talk to me, to embrace me and kiss my cheeks and exclaim about how gorgeous I look. As Elizabeth, I bask in the attention. Even though people ask me questions I don't know the answers to, such as where Nate's and my first big trip of the new year will be. "You'll have to wait for the pictures!" I say airily.

"We thought about heading to Costa Rica for the holidays," Nate says, slipping an arm around my waist, "but there's nothing like Christmas in the city, just the two of us."

I'm glad we won't be making an extended visit to either Nate's parents' or Elizabeth's. My entire body flushes hot at the thought of the two of us nestled together in Elizabeth's sponsor-provided breathable goose-down bedding.

Hailey is with us, taking pictures on her phone and holding swag bags, and I turn to her. "What about you, Hailey? Are you going home for the holidays?"

Everyone looks taken aback, as though I've spoken to one of the chairs. Hailey, with a sad little smile that makes my chest tighten, shakes her head. "My family doesn't really celebrate." Clearly not keen to discuss why, she ushers us into yet another photo-op nook.

She snaps photo after photo, telling me where to stand and which parts of my outfit to accentuate. It would get tiresome if not for Nate. He dotes on me; there's no other word for it. He makes sure I always have a drink in hand or a small bite to nibble on. When he's not fetching me food or libations, he's touching me. A hand resting on my elbow or the small of my back. An arm around my waist. His lips, shiveringly, brushing the sensitive spot under my ear.

Anticipation—or unease—swells inside me at the thought of what might happen later, when we're alone. Any moral qualms I have about what I'm doing are because of Nate, because I'm deceiving him. Elizabeth deserves this; he doesn't. He thinks I'm his wife, and I'm not. But I can be. I will be.

My goal has never been to live Elizabeth's life exactly the way she would. I'm becoming her, but a better version of her. The body is only the first step. My inner transformation might be slower, but it will happen, like a caterpillar dissolving and reforming itself inside its chrysalis. Being with Nate is a necessary part of that metamorphosis. I won't push things, though. I'll follow his lead.

Surely at some point he'll understand, on some level, that his wife is different. I hope he thinks it's a change for the better.

"Should we head upstairs?" Hailey asks. "The installations will make for some cool backdrops."

Nate leans down to speak into my ear. "We could find somewhere private up there. But not too private."

"Do you want to leak a video of us making out?" I raise an eyebrow, daring him, and my stomach jumps at the spark in his eyes.

"Wouldn't be the worst idea."

After two—or is it three?—signature cocktails, I have a bit of trouble on the stairs in my four-inch heels. Nate's guiding arm is strong and steady. We follow the people in front of us into a tunnel of light, thousands and thousands of tiny bulbs affixed to mirrored walls in arches and dripping branch shapes. They seem to undulate as they fade from white to blue to magenta to purple, extending forever in the mirrored walls. The space is full of light, but the people around me, even my own reflection, are nothing but shadows.

My mouth goes dry.

"It's like a Kusama piece!" someone yells over a pounding beat. Their voice sounds disembodied, stripped of depth by the throbbing of the bass. I see one of the shadows move the wrong way— the opposite way we are all moving, and differently. We meander; the thing I saw *darted*. I turn my head to follow it.

"All right?" Nate asks me.

"Fine." I shouldn't be hallucinating, not hours after a transfer, though Elizabeth and I were a fairly large distance apart. Plus, I've had too much to drink, and that coke earlier.

The light tunnel spits us into a darkened room. A tall man in black emerges from the shadows, his face and hands like floating white puppets against the darkness. "Stand here," he says, nudging me into position a few feet in front of the intersection of two angled walls.

For a stretched moment, nothing happens. Then the angled walls explode in light.

Geometries rush at me, red and black and white lines forming triangles and quadrangles. A trick of perspective opens a three-dimensional portal that looks ready to swallow me whole. I flinch, but nothing touches me except light. Bands of harsh color play on the rapt faces around me.

The lines shift direction, receding, and I breathe a little easier. Then they come in sideways, as sharply pointed as the knife you don't see. Droplets of sweat spring up on my skin. I can't get a breath. My self is being sliced up, smaller and smaller and smaller, until I disappear into the black spaces between the red and white, darker than the darkness in the room. It's nothing like an Empathyzer-enabled transfer, but I grab my wrist to make sure a device hasn't been placed there without my knowledge.

It wouldn't need to be on my wrist, though. I know that perfectly well. And although Elizabeth might not be able to get hold of another one, maybe whoever sent me the Empathyzer did.

I need to get out of here. I stumble into the hall, away from the light tunnel. Wrench off my cursed high heels. A back staircase winds down to a kitchen bustling with caterers. It's too loud, too bright. I can't breathe. I turn away, finding a door to the outside.

In the alley, I pat myself down. I go through my clutch, shake the back of my dress, plunge my hands into my cleavage. Shove my fingers through Elizabeth's hair, destroying the braided crown Hailey made. The only Empathyzer I find is the one I brought with me.

The door opens. Nate steps out, scanning the alley, his face tight with concern. His shoulders relax when he sees me. "What was that, back there?"

My feelings are a stew of relief mixed with dread. Nate came after me. There's someone *to* come after me. My new life hasn't been snatched away. But something happened to me that I can't explain.

"You're shivering." Nate takes off his jacket and drapes it around my shoulders. I breathe in his scent. My feet are wet and freezing, so I shove them back into my shoes.

Nate's messing with his phone. "Hailey says she's grabbing our coats."

Nate's warmth fades from his jacket quickly, and cold seeps into my skin. "Should we go back in and meet her?"

"I don't want people seeing you like this." The sharpness in his voice, as though I've embarrassed him, pulls me up short.

I didn't think I'd made that big of a scene.

Hailey comes out through the back door, carrying my and Nate's coats along with half a dozen swag bags. "Do you want to wait inside while I get the car?" she asks.

"We'll walk," Nate says. The balls of my feet shriek in protest, but I don't love the idea of freezing here for another twenty minutes.

I limp down sidewalks treacherous with melted-and-refrozen

snow, my toes feeling like they're about to snap off. Nate, so courtly with his assistance back at the party, now seems to offer it almost grudgingly. I strain for a glimpse of his champagne-colored luxury SUV.

"It's right around the next corner," Hailey says over her shoulder, as we make slow progress up a side street. "Ah, here we go—"

Her voice drains away.

"What the fuck?" Nate drops my arm and bounds forward, leaving me to get along as best I can. Alarm spirals inside my chest when I see what has him so agitated.

Spray-painted on the hood of the car in foot-high letters, the color of dried blood under the streetlamp, is one word.

CONFESS

14

ELIZABETH (MARY)

NOW

Elizabeth sits up with a gasp, gray dawn barely illuminating the room. For a second, she has no idea where she is. Then memories snap into place.

Her involuntary transfer to a stinking alley. The indifferent bus driver. The kind neighbor. The dark, cold night.

She was dreaming she'd been kidnapped. Nate was the detective searching for her, while somehow still her husband too. He found her, but refused to believe who she was.

I'm Elizabeth, she told him over and over, crying tears of frustration. *I'm your wife!*

She slept on the couch, wrapped in a blanket she now pulls tight around her shoulders. The floor is icy through her socks. There's a thermostat, but adjusting it doesn't have any effect.

The Empathyzer's screen is unresponsive, its battery dead. It accepts Mary's phone charger. The phone must be nearly as old as the Empathyzer, because it will open only with a PIN. Based on the documents she deleted from the laptop and Mary's cloud storage, it's vital that she see what's on that phone. She attempts a few more codes, none of which work.

Taking a break from the phone, she wakes the laptop and tries logging into her own socials. She can't. *Those* passwords, Mary changed.

Elizabeth swallows down a surge of panic. She feels as though she's stepped out over a drop, confident that something will catch her, and it hasn't. Yet.

Her optimistic outlook has never failed her. And, she reminds herself, it's not as if she had much choice. The truth of what happened in college cannot come out. She had to risk her life in order to save it.

So far, it doesn't look as though Mary is using her new position to make any public mischief. Elizabeth watches a video of herself and Nate from the party last night. Bathed in colored light, a smiling Nate spins her in a waltzlike turn. The Elizabeth on the screen looks at Nate like all of her princess dreams have come true.

Elizabeth has a sudden, vivid imagining of Mary in her exact place on this couch, watching Elizabeth and Nate on a screen together, her face full of longing. She'll get to live her dream for a little longer while the real Elizabeth does what's necessary. The first step is almost complete; the next is when her real test will come.

And Mary's illusions will be shattered soon enough.

Back to the phone. It's a black box, a roadblock. Elizabeth goes over the apartment thoroughly, looking for telltale slips of paper. In a drawer, there's a business card for Detective Anthony Johns, the name sending a shock of recognition through her. Detective Johns talking to Mary can't mean anything good.

Is that why Mary had asked Miguel about out-of-body experiences? To eavesdrop without being seen, find out what Johns has on her?

Elizabeth read on the Ofori Lab's website that the CIA used to conduct experiments with what they called "remote viewing." Nowadays, the website says, psychologists research OBEs for insight on consciousness of the self, not to develop spying techniques.

But that doesn't mean Mary wouldn't pursue it with that goal. Maybe she meant to spy on Elizabeth herself, not Johns. If Mary wants to wreak havoc on her life, she's welcome to try. But the threat is all the more reason for Elizabeth to wrap up this phase of her plan so she can move on to the next, as painful as that will be.

If Mary approached Miguel about his research, maybe she asked for help with other things too. He'd certainly seemed open to giving it last night. Every lead is worth following if it'll get Elizabeth home and out of that detective's sights.

It's still early, and academics are notorious for being night owls. Elizabeth takes her time getting ready. She hasn't forgotten Miguel's look of not-unpleasant surprise when she touched his arm last night.

The familiar motions soothe her, even though the face is different and Mary's makeup collection leaves much to be desired. Elizabeth's lucky to find a tube of tacky mascara. Her efforts with her hair go better. She starts out trimming Mary's split ends and somehow winds up with choppy layers, but it's surprisingly flattering. Mary's small features set off the hungry, androgynous look nicely. Her cheekbones look sharper, her eyes brighter. Elizabeth showers and puts on black jeans and a button-down shirt, the most stylish outfit she can assemble from Mary's closet of despair.

Before she knocks on Miguel's door, she stretches her face into a huge fake smile, squeezing her eyes shut, then widening them. As soon as her knuckles hit wood, she lets the smile drop. Her expression will be neutral but softer, more pleasant, than Mary's usual face.

Miguel opens the door with an electric toothbrush in hand. His features lift in the same kind of surprise as last night.

"Hi. You're busy, aren't you?" She says it this way specifically so he'll have to contradict her.

"Not at all. Come on in. You want coffee?"

"Oh my gosh, that sounds amazing." She's gushing, and that's weird, but she'd just about murder somebody for one of Nate's two-shot lattes right now. There was nothing in Mary's kitchen-ette except instant oatmeal and those dusty tea bags.

Miguel gives her another look like he did last night that tells her he's noticed her un-Mary-like behavior. "I like the haircut," he says over his shoulder as she follows him to the rear of the apart-ment. His place is bigger than Mary's, a one-bedroom with a living room and separate, albeit tiny, kitchen. It's homier too: art on the walls, a bookshelf with books, thriving houseplants. He measures out grounds into a French press and starts an electric kettle.

"I thought you already had coffee made," Elizabeth says. "I didn't realize you'd have to do all this." Of course not everyone has a cof-fee machine that grinds its own beans and brews at the touch of a button. Miguel's process looks like less work than Nate's, which involves detachable plastic tubing and steamed milk, but she still feels she's imposing.

"It's no trouble."

"But you probably have to get to work."

"Mary," he says, "it's no trouble."

What's wrong with her? She doesn't usually get uncomfortable when people put themselves out for her. And clearly, he doesn't mind. He turns the oven on and takes a glass container out of the refrigerator. "Cinnamon rolls," he says. "They just need a few min-utes to heat up."

"Are you kidding? You don't have to . . . Wait, are those home-made?" A divine scent of yeast and cinnamon rises in the air.

He shrugs. "I like to bake. It's stress relief."

Nate's good in the kitchen too. Knowing a man who cooks is a thirst object, he developed his prowess specifically to appeal to Elizabeth's followers. Not that he's ever admitted that out loud.

She pushes her husband out of her mind. "Why do you need stress relief?"

"School and career stuff, mostly. Getting a PhD in the social sciences is not the express train to security you'd think it is." The corner of his mouth kicks up. "But I can go in whenever I want most days, which is nice when you want to have a leisurely breakfast with your neighbor."

He places the cinnamon rolls on a baking sheet and slides them into the oven. Then he leans back, propping himself against the counter. Elizabeth's eyes catch on his hands. They're attractive—long, graceful fingers; short, clean nails—and just veiny enough to look strong. She's always appreciated men's hands. Nate—

She bites the inside of her cheek, then feels Miguel's attention on her as though he can sense her turmoil. What does he see?

Mary. He sees Mary. Who will soon be back in her own body, while Elizabeth is home taking care of business.

"I know why you're here," Miguel says.

"You do?"

"You want your flash drive back, don't you?"

She has to work to hide her surprise. She thought he was going to bring up out-of-body experiences. "Yes," she says, "but there's no hurry."

They eat at a two-person table shoved next to the window in the living room. Elizabeth has her cinnamon roll slathered in icing; back in college, not worrying about calories was one of the things she enjoyed most about being Mary. She pops the last bite into her mouth with a groan of pleasure.

Miguel looks away a beat too late. The sudden tension in the air might be awkwardness, but her instincts—which are rarely wrong where male attraction is concerned—say no.

Pretending not to notice, she delicately licks a bit of icing off her finger. She's doing Mary a favor, really. Leaving her a little present for when she gets back.

Then she remembers what happened the last time she did Mary this kind of favor, and her stomach tightens.

Miguel's phone vibrates with a text. He ignores it until three more arrive in quick succession. "Sorry. It's my sister." He looks at his phone quizzically, then turns it so Elizabeth can see. "Do you have any idea what this means?" It's a meme she recognizes, one that's been making the rounds.

"None," she lies.

"She's always sending me random stuff like this. She's really into internet culture and influencers and all that, and I try to roll with it even though I don't understand half of it."

Elizabeth laughs. "I can't even use my phone right now. I think I accidentally changed the PIN and locked myself out. You don't know how to fix that, do you?"

"You could, um . . . what's it called?" He snaps his fingers. "Factory reset it."

Elizabeth wants to slap her own forehead. "Of course! That's exactly what I need to do."

"You'll lose all your data, though, I think."

Even better. "The price of stupidity."

He laughs at that, and Elizabeth is surprised at the warmth that wells up inside her. He uses his phone to look up how to reset hers. When she manages to sign in with a new PIN, she crows in triumph. Mary's apps are gone, along with her messages and, of course, any files. A clean slate.

"Let me get your drive before I forget." Miguel disappears into his bedroom and comes out less than a minute later, handing her a rather ancient-looking memory stick.

"It's been sitting in my sock drawer," he says. "I haven't looked at it."

If that's true, then Mary's trust in him wasn't misplaced. She doesn't trust easily. And Elizabeth never would've known about it if he hadn't said something.

"You gonna tell me why you wanted me to hold on to it?"

Elizabeth wishes she knew that herself. She assumes the drive contains copies of what was on the laptop. And Mary's giving it to Miguel shows foresight.

That doesn't mean she knows everything. She could have predicted what Elizabeth would do when she found herself in Mary's body. Still, a sense of urgency pushes Elizabeth to stand.

"Guess that's a no," Miguel says, but mildly. "Mystery Mary."

Elizabeth plays into it with a faint smile. "I could tell you, but I'd have to kill you."

"You could try." There's that amused quirk of his lips, paired with a focus in his eyes that sharpens her awareness of the way they glow amber in the rare winter sunlight pouring through the window. The way they are clear, where Nate's are opaque.

He walks her to the door. "Thanks for your help," she says, "and for breakfast. It was really nice."

That sounds uninspired, hardly the impression she'd prefer to leave. But it's not as if she'll ever see him again.

15

Since the party, Garrett's been insufferable at work. Mary deals with it by remembering the look on his face when "Elizabeth" rejected him. And reminding herself that while his pouting and power trips are annoying, they don't make any difference to her future.

She's more worried Confluence will sink and pull her down with it. Two weeks into the semester, an exposé about the start-up was published on a niche but well-respected tech journalism site. The writer had interviewed multiple former employees, sources who remained anonymous because they were violating their NDAs to talk to him. They spoke truths that were well-known to Mary—that Confluence has been fudging experimental data to make a product that barely works seem more effective—as well as some that were new, like the shadowy origins of the company's funding.

The legitimate investors have launched an investigation and are trying to get Gloria Faculak removed as CEO. While this is obviously a disaster, Mary can't afford to leave a paid position. If she quits now, it's unlikely she'll find any comparable experience, paid or unpaid, until next fall. A year without experience will put her behind. Falling behind will take her out of the running for the best grad school programs. A mediocre grad school program will lower her chances of getting a tenure-track position. She sees few options but to hope she can make it to the next step before the company collapses, and that Confluence doesn't prove to be a black mark on her CV.

She's already preparing her "Working there taught me what not to do" line for interviews.

One day, she watches through the glass wall of the conference room as the executive leadership team meets with a crisis PR firm.

"They wanted me to sit in," Garrett says, materializing beside her. He's been doing that a lot lately. "As soon as I graduate I'll be promoted to VP of communications."

If the company lasts that long. Mary almost believes him, though. So many staffers have left that the remainder have risen quickly, which is another reason she stays.

"Shouldn't you be working instead of fucking off?" As usual he stands too close, his arm pressing against her shoulder. "Word to the wise: those crisis-management hacks don't come cheap. We're going to have to cut some deadweight."

Mary tenses at the implicit threat. The smell of Garrett's aftershave, the same brand a particularly tenacious bully of hers wore in high school, oozes up her nose.

"Hey, how's Elizabeth these days?" he asks. "It's funny. Whenever I see you outside of work, you're with her. Tweedledum and Tweedledee."

"We're roommates." What's funny is his bringing up Elizabeth like this. Or is it? The theft of the Empathyzers is a skittering rat in Mary's mind. She's even thought about deleting the transfer journal that she's continued to write in since summer. Elizabeth doesn't know about it; it's just for Mary.

Mary's not a sentimental person, but getting rid of it feels like too great a loss.

"You're such an odd couple," Garrett says. "I mean, Elizabeth's a smokeshow, and you . . . Well, I guess you're not bad when you put in a little effort, but I hardly ever see you smile."

He taps his chin thoughtfully. "Though there have been a few times . . . when I saw her at our back-to-school party, she wasn't friendly at all. Like she was a different person."

Mary goes still. She keeps her face blank, as blank as Elizabeth's.

He can't know. Maybe he *suspects*; Elizabeth hasn't always been discreet, and he saw something, heard something. He's trying to get Mary to break.

"You're not *actually* a couple, are you? That'd be a waste." He leans closer, and she feels the humidity of his breath in her ear. "You ever thought about doing a threesome?"

Mary's gasp hisses between her teeth. Garrett chuckles.

She clenches her jaw. Antagonizing him would only make matters worse. "We're just friends."

Just doesn't seem like a word to apply to what she and Elizabeth have.

"If you ever do, let me know." He reaches out and palms Mary's neck just above her collar, his hand fever hot.

She manages not to flinch.

"I've got a feeling you two have a pretty good handle on each other's needs—you know what I'm saying? And I'm someone you want to keep on your side." He gives her neck a squeeze, then walks away.

———

"DID HE ACTUALLY accuse you of stealing them?" Elizabeth asks after Mary comes home freaking out.

"No. But he implied it, and said it would be in my best interest to keep him on my side." Tired of pacing, Mary drops into a chair.

"Which apparently involves letting him watch us have sex with each other."

Elizabeth snorts. "I doubt he'd be happy with just watching." She peers over the side of her loft bed. Her hair is tousled, but in a sexy way, like Jane Birkin fresh from a roll in the hay with Serge Gainsbourg. "Maybe this is a sign you should quit."

"I can't. I need the money. I need this on my CV." And quitting would be letting Garrett win. She wishes, bitterly, that she'd found a way to join forces with Jessica after he crossed the line with her. The two of them telling the same story might have been enough to create some doubt. There have probably been others too.

Mary wonders if Jessica, who quit soon after that, is one of those anonymous sources from the article. If so, good for her.

"You can't report him?"

"And have him accuse me of stealing company property?"

"Oh. Right."

"Maybe next time I'm you I'll charm a couple of guys into kicking his ass." Mary's only half joking. "Or—if only I could get some kind of leverage on him. Maybe I could try to record him sexually harassing me."

"That's not going to go very far in this world," Elizabeth says. "What you need is to catch him acting like the clown he is. Guys like that, their worst fear is being laughed at."

Then her eyes widen and her mouth pops open. "Oh, oh! Mebs!" She claps her hands in glee. "I have an idea."

MARY DOESN'T BELIEVE Garrett will show until he texts her from outside their dorm. Fifteen minutes after the transfer and she's still seeing trails, but the side effects should calm down soon. It's mostly nerves.

It feels right that she's doing this as Elizabeth. Being Elizabeth gives her the confidence she'll need to pull this off, while being Mary helps Elizabeth get in touch with her inner bitch.

Garrett looks relieved when she opens the street door for him, as though he didn't quite believe she was serious. He's flushed, like he's nervous or has been pregaming. As soon as he's inside, he reaches for her, trying to pull her to him.

She steps back. "Don't get impatient." To soften the rebuke, she gives him Elizabeth's most promising smile.

His greed makes her even more certain. Humiliation is the only way to get through to him. After tonight, he'll associate Mary and Elizabeth with humiliation for the rest of his life. And he won't be inclined to mess with either of them.

"I brought a handle of vodka," Garrett says. "That should help loosen you up."

His shit-eating grin falters when he sees the setup in their room. "I didn't know you were going to video this."

"Is that okay? We won't share it with anyone. We just like to have it for . . . ourselves." Mary lowers her head, letting Elizabeth's long hair curtain her face, and smiles demurely. Inside, she's on edge. This is where the whole plan could break down. She *told* Elizabeth they should video him secretly, but E insisted it was better this way.

Elizabeth, adjusting the angle of her phone on the tripod, has dialed in Mary's bitchiest bitch face. "Let's be clear," she says. "This doesn't mean I like you."

He laughs. "You hate that you want me, don't you."

Her eyes narrow. "Take off your shirt."

"Damn, girl, let me take a shot first." He gets the vodka out of his backpack, and his hands tremble slightly as he pours shots for the three of them. While he's tugging his polo over his head, Mary dumps her vodka into the potted pothos on their windowsill, sending it a silent apology. She needs a clear head.

Garrett's gym-sculpted physique is admittedly impressive. It's almost believable that someone like Elizabeth would want him. Mary's gorge rises at the thought of them together, let alone him touching *her*, but she swallows it. "Sit," she says, motioning toward the desk chair positioned in the crosshairs of the phone's camera. Elizabeth even got out the ring light.

Mary holds up a pair of silk scarves and assumes Elizabeth's most kittenish expression. "We want to tie you up. Is that okay?"

He chuckles. "You girls are freaks, huh?"

"We can't have you jumping on us and ripping our clothes off. I promise you won't feel left out." She lets her eyes flick downward to the rising bulge in his khakis.

"Do what you've gotta do." His eyes have gone hazy, and Mary allows herself a second of amazement at how easy this is, how right Elizabeth was. All they have to do is play to Garrett's basic-ass fantasies.

It'll get trickier once he stops cooperating. With that in mind, she makes the knots tight enough that he can't escape easily, pinioning his arms to the back of the chair. Then she steps out of frame and starts the recording.

"Consent is important to us, so we won't touch you anywhere you don't explicitly say is fine." Mary takes a breath. The steadiness of Elizabeth's voice coming from her own throat gives her confidence. "Actually, we prefer *enthusiastic* consent. Can you give us that?"

"Just undo my pants already." Garrett lolls back in the chair, as much as the knots will let him without hyperextending his shoulders, and spreads his knees, his movements loose. He was definitely drinking before he came here, though he's far from wasted. A guy like Garrett puts away ten beers on a quiet night.

"Not yet."

He blinks, twice, and a line appears between his brows. Mary begins to enjoy herself.

"Garrett Deegan, Garrett Deegan. What do you want us to do

with you, Garrett?" The words are an invitation, but she makes her voice cold.

"Whatever your wicked little brains can dream up."

"We're going to need you to be more specific. Like I said, we're very fussy about consent."

Garrett shifts in his seat. "Look, I'm just gonna say it. I think the whole thing where you have to ask before you touch every little body part is dumb. As far as I'm concerned, once you've entered into a situation, you're up for just about anything."

"That's a dangerous thing to say to someone who's got you tied to a chair half naked."

The briefest flash of unease moves over his face. "If I want you to stop, I'll say so. Now, are you ladies gonna take off *your* clothes, or what?"

"You want us to get naked?"

"Uh, yeah, it wouldn't hurt."

"After that, what then? Do you want us to kiss?"

He starts to look less impatient and more aroused. "Yeah."

"You want us to touch each other for you? Writhe around on the floor and talk about how much we want your cock? How does that sound?"

"Sounds hot." He's breathing hard, pupils dilated. "I'm fucking ready."

"I can see that." Mary casts an amused glance at his crotch.

"You like that, baby? It's for you."

Elizabeth, who until now has hung back in the way Mary normally would, scoffs. Garrett turns his smirk toward her. "Maybe there'll be enough left over for you."

Elizabeth steps toward him, taking care to stay out of the frame. "So, you get a text from a woman who can barely stand to be in the same room with you, inviting you to a threesome with her and her friend, and you trust it? I think that's funny."

He stiffens for an instant, then laughs.

"Right. You're just jealous that everyone wants her instead of you. You can't throw a rock on this campus without hitting a guy who'd give his left nut to fuck Elizabeth."

Elizabeth goes still, her borrowed features abstracted, as though Garrett's words have sent her somewhere else for a second. Then she smiles in a way that makes cold water trickle through Mary's insides.

It's a good thing they don't plan to hurt him.

Elizabeth slips Mary's phone out of her pocket and reads, pitching her voice low in mockery. "'Hey. That sounds hot. I knew you swung that way.'" It's Garrett's reply to Mary's invite.

"What are you doing?" Garrett asks.

"Setting the mood."

"Oh. Excellent." But he looks uncertain.

Elizabeth continues reading. "'I don't want to come between you girls, but I'm happy to come between you.' Wow. The word-play is . . ." She kisses her fingertips. "And then he puts a winky face. And *water droplets*. Could you be any more of a cliché?"

Garrett's face darkens. "All right, I see what this is. You ladies have had your fun."

Elizabeth laughs. "I'm just messing with you, *Gar*. This is like foreplay for us."

"Foreplay?" Incredibly, hope dawns on his face again. "So when's the real shit start?"

Something draws tight in Mary, making her forget who she's supposed to be. "You really think things will always go your way, don't you? I guess it makes sense, when you've had everything handed to you."

"Look, I'm not sure this whole negging bit's doing it for me, so—"

"You've never had to earn a single thing in your life," Mary goes on. "College. A job you use as your personal playground. Maybe you're the reason all the women there quit. I bet Jessica was far from the only one you pushed out."

"I didn't push her out. I was trying to have some fun and she decided to take it seriously." It's as if he's forgotten there's a camera recording his every word. "Wait, how do *you* know her?"

Oh shit.

Mary turns to Elizabeth, who looks as lost for words as Mary would be in her place, but recovers more quickly. "You think women don't talk to each other? Elizabeth's my best friend. She knows everything. I've told her what a pathetic shit you are."

Garrett turns the color of old brick. "Untie me," he says hoarsely. "Untie me *now.*"

Watching him struggle against his bonds, Mary gets a surge of the satisfaction she was hoping for. "Doesn't feel so great when you're the one who's powerless, does it?"

Garrett stops moving. "Fine. I'm a pig. Is that what you want me to say?"

"I don't think he can please us," Mary says to Elizabeth. "I don't think he's capable of it."

"That's okay. We've got enough." Elizabeth stops the recording and takes her phone off the tripod.

Mary can see the instant Garrett remembers all of this has been recorded. He leaps the chair forward, but only ends up almost tipping over onto his face.

"Careful, there, sport," Elizabeth says. "We'll untie you in a minute. Just uploading this real quick."

"Uploading?!" he yelps.

"Just to the cloud drive," Mary says soothingly. "We're not going to show anyone yet."

He flops back in defeat. "How much do you want?" He's speaking to Elizabeth, who he thinks is Mary.

It irks Mary that he thinks she'd resort to simple blackmail. "We don't want your money. We want you to stop being a creep. Stay out of Mary's way at work."

"Actually, you know what?" Elizabeth looms over Garrett, as much as she can. "I want you to do me another favor."

Mary gives her a sharp look. Elizabeth's departing from their plan, which is to gain a measure of control over Garrett. The video will make him tamp down his excesses, but it'll also deter him from going to Gloria if he does have suspicions about the Empathyzers.

"Your aunt. A letter of recommendation from her has to be pretty valuable, right? Get her to write me one."

Garrett looks confused. "For what? Is there a certain program you're trying to get into, or . . . ?"

Elizabeth shrugs, and Mary suppresses a wince. "I'll get you the details later. You'll do it for me when I ask you, though. This video only gets more embarrassing as it ages. Should we send it to Katarina?" She turns to Mary. "In case he gets squirrelly when we untie him?"

"No," Mary says. "Katarina can't keep a secret for shit."

"I'll be good," Garrett promises.

When Mary has undone the scarves, he doesn't even stop to put on his shirt before he runs out the door.

Mary collapses into the chair he just vacated. He's no longer her problem; she's free of him. Thanks to Elizabeth, he might even be forced to help her rise in the world. So why does she feel this sense of dread?

Elizabeth's silently breaking down the tripod and light stand. Mary would have thought she'd be crowing. "What's wrong?"

"Nothing."

"Are you sure?"

"Yes." Elizabeth lays the collapsed tripod on the floor, then climbs into her own loft bed, still in Mary's body.

"E," Mary says.

Elizabeth's voice comes from deep in her loft, disembodied.

"Just . . . the way he was looking at you. At my body. What he said about every guy wanting to . . . They're all like that, aren't they? Maybe not as bad as him, but they see me as this sex doll. Like I'm not even a person. Just a body."

Mary doesn't know what men are like. Her experience is so limited. But it's obvious how they look at Elizabeth. She'd thought Elizabeth had come to terms with it, since she's been turning it to her advantage the whole time Mary's known her.

The disillusionment in her tone strikes to Mary's core. She'd like to be able to say Elizabeth's wrong, but she's never been able to lie for shit. "They wouldn't know what to do with you if they had you."

"I thought it would be different once I got out of my parents' house. That I'd be the one making the rules. And it's so much better to have control over my life. I know I have style. I'm photogenic. I can make that into something, I'm trying to. But I thought I'd find someone who *sees* me, you know?"

"You will," Mary says. "Everyone loves you."

"What is it about me that they love? It's different for you. Your brain will open doors. You don't need people to love you."

Mary flinches. But Elizabeth doesn't say anything else.

16

MARY (ELIZABETH)

NOW

Jumbo's high frantic barks pull me from a dream of falling.

I'm exhausted, achy; I need several more hours of sleep. My mind is sluggish. I could be having transfer side effects—though I feel more like I used to after I moved back into my own body—or it could be a run-of-the-mill hangover.

Last night I spent the ride home in a haze. The main thing I remember is Nate joking nervously that someone must be trying to convince Hailey to go back to Mass. Hailey didn't seem amused.

Rolling over, I pull the pillow over my head, but Jumbo's noise goes right through it. Just when he's subsided to whining and scratching at the bedroom door, the front doorbell goes, setting off another round of angry yapping. The doorbell must have been what got him riled up in the first place. Which probably means no one else is here to answer it.

That doesn't mean *I* have to answer it.

The doorbell rings again, followed by a firm, determined knocking that sends Jumbo into paroxysms. "For fuck's *sake*, dog," I moan. Whoever's down there obviously isn't going away. I drag myself upright, tie a robe over Elizabeth's silk pajamas, and shuffle downstairs. The double-paned glass in the door reveals a uniformed police officer on the porch.

I freeze. But he can see me too. He makes eye contact, raises a hand.

I make myself breathe slowly, in and out through the nose, but I can barely feel the last three steps under my bare feet.

Confess. No one believes Elizabeth Jordan is guilty of anything. The thought swings through my mind that maybe this cop is here to investigate what *I've* done. Somehow he knows who I really am, how I've gained possession of stolen electronic devices and used them to steal something much more important.

Impossible. Only one other person knows what I've done. Actually, two: Elizabeth, and whoever sent me the Empathyzer.

I force a smile as I open the door. "Good morning!"

"Closer to afternoon, actually," the cop says. Jumbo barrels onto the front porch and stops six inches away from him, yapping furiously.

"Well, who's this?" The cop crouches, reaching out to pet him. "You a guard dog, little guy? You are, aren't— Ow!" He recoils, hand going to his mouth. "He *bit* me!"

"I'm so sorry." I manage to scoop Jumbo into my arms, where he vibrates with low growls. "Do you need a bandage?"

"Doesn't look like he broke the skin. You mind if I come in and wash my hands?"

This might be a technique to gain entry. Antagonize the dog to bite, then make a stink if the owner is reluctant to let you in the house. But this officer doesn't seem crafty; he looks like what would come up in an image search for *beat cop*. In his thirties, with a round, pink face on an undersize buzz-cut head. Whatever his aims, I have little choice but to show him the way to the kitchen.

I shut Jumbo behind the door to Nate's man cave, where he tries to scratch the wood to pieces.

"Nate Jordan's your husband, I'm assuming?" the cop asks as he dries his hands.

I look at him blankly. Is *Nate* being accused of something?

Confess.

"The one who made the call," the cop prompts. "About a vehicle being vandalized?"

"Oh," I say. "Of course." Though I don't know why the police would be in my house asking about it.

The cop gives me a look like he's concerned for my mental health. "Can I . . . see the vehicle?"

"Oh. Yes. I'm sorry, I'm just . . ." I let out a shaky breath, too flustered to feign calm. "It's been a long couple of days."

"I can imagine, ma'am." His face stays neutral.

Coats hang on hooks by the back door. I shrug one over my robe and step into boots that look like an old pair of Nate's, then lead the officer across the backyard to the detached garage.

"I don't know why anyone would do this to us." It feels important to establish that we're innocent victims.

"Probably just kids, ma'am," the cop says, but I have my doubts. Did Nate tell the police *what* was written on the car?

Confess. Confess to what? This kind of vandalism seems calculated to unsettle its target, without having to be specific. Everyone's guilty of something, no matter how small. And we were unsettled last night, all three of us.

But I didn't see any other cars with paint on them. If it was just kids, they would have gone down the whole street. More likely it was someone who recognized Nate's SUV, who knows him and Elizabeth. Or who knows me. Someone with a grudge; someone who has had their most precious possession ripped away without warning.

If spray paint on a car is all Elizabeth's got, then I can handle it. Easily.

The garage is windowless, but I can see without having to turn the light on that it's empty. I'm stumped, staring into the dark space as if Nate's SUV and Elizabeth's luxury crossover will materialize there.

"I don't know where the car is," I tell the cop. I fumble my phone from the pocket of my robe to ask Nate, wherever he is.

Just then, a message comes in from Hailey. Dropped off Nate's car at detailer's an hour ago. It won't be done for a few hours—can I run some errands or do you need it back the second it's done?

I text her back, too shocked to be diplomatic. You're having the paint removed?? Nate called the cops. There's an officer here to look at the car.

Dots bounce on the screen for almost a minute before her reply comes in. You told me to get it cleaned. Last night

I did? I have no memory of it. I look at the cop. "Apparently there's been a miscommunication. My assistant is having the paint cleaned off as we speak."

"Oh. That doesn't make my job any easier." He does everything but roll his eyes.

Back in the house, he goes through a cursory list of questions— Did I see anyone lurking around the car when we discovered it spray-painted? Did we take pictures of the damage? Do I know of anyone who might be inclined to vandalize my husband's vehicle for any reason?—but it's clear he considers the "investigation" all but finished. He's standing to leave, thanking me for my time, when the back door opens and Nate steps in.

"Hey, babe, where's my c—— Oh. Thanks for coming," he says to the cop. "Did you get a look at the damage?"

"I did not," the cop says. "The evidence is at the detailer's."

"What?"

Quickly, I explain what happened with Hailey. "She must have misunderstood me. But you could have told us you were going to call the police."

"I would think it'd be obvious."

The cop goes through his questions with Nate. When he gets to the one about whether Nate has any enemies, Nate scowls.

"I haven't done anything to deserve this. I'm the victim here. Maybe you all need to do your jobs better if I can't even park on a street in this city without—"

"Nate." I lay a hand on his arm. He looks as though he'd like to shake it off, but restrains himself.

"It's an unusual thing for someone to write," the cop says. "Usually we get tags, slurs, stuff like that."

"I have no idea why someone would spray paint 'confess' on the hood of my car. I don't know what to tell you."

The cop closes the cover on his tablet with a snap. "Yessir. We'll be in touch."

As soon as the door closes on him, Nate heads to the man cave. Jumbo runs out the door when he opens it.

Nate groans. "Oh, come on, Elizabeth! I've *asked* you not to let that dog down there. I bet you a hundred bucks he peed in the corner. If he has, you're cleaning it up."

My temper flares. "What was I supposed to do, let him use that cop as a chew toy? Why did you even call the police?"

"Are you kidding? You want to brush this off? One of your stalkers did this. You know it's true."

"What happened to someone trying to get Hailey to go to church?" And how did Nate know she was Catholic, anyway?

"That was a joke. Look, you wanted this career. *You* couldn't live without the attention, and now we both have to deal with the fallout."

How can he say that when Elizabeth's career is what makes their perfect life possible?

His eyes narrow. "Unless it's not just a stalker. How about it? Do you have anything you want to tell me?"

That fastens my mouth shut. I've got so much to hide, I can barely keep track of it all.

His face softens, turning him back to the lovely, loving husband I've watched for years. "You know what? We're both reading too much into this. It was probably random. Some asshole got a good laugh at our expense. But no one got hurt, and aside from the detailing, it didn't cost us anything."

I wish I could believe that. But remembering the suspicion in Nate's eyes a moment ago, I'm not so sure.

———

NATE HAS AN afternoon meeting with his friend Declan, the one he's trying to make films with, and after that he has plans to go out for drinks with the guys. He and Elizabeth pride themselves on not being one of those joined-at-the-hip couples; their independence is what makes them work so well.

Hailey hasn't come by with his car yet, so I tell him to take mine, like he did when he went to the gym this morning. He's dressed more casually than he was for the event last night, but his Henley—sleeves pushed up to reveal lean-muscled forearms—makes him look every bit as appealing.

I'm at the dining room table, responding to comments on the pictures Hailey posted last night. As Nate bends down to brush my cheek with his lips, I pull in a dizzying breath of his scent.

"What are you doing tonight?" he asks.

There's nothing on Elizabeth's calendar, and Hailey hasn't alerted me to any commitments. "I think I'll stay in. Take a bath, have some wine, read a trashy book."

"Probably a good idea after last night." His brow knits. "You sure you'll be all right on your own?"

"I'm looking forward to having some me time. Get out of here. Have fun." I'm brave enough to pull him down for one more kiss.

I don't know if I'll ever get to a point where that doesn't make fireworks go off inside me. This time he gives it a little tongue, which might as well set off a bomb in my chest cavity. As he pulls back, his eyes catch mine and widen at what he sees in them.

"Babe," he whispers, wondering.

I almost think he's not about to go anywhere. That instead, we'll throw off our clothes and make use of the sheepskin rug under the Christmas tree. I'm not sure I'm ready for that.

But he just kisses me once more, hard, then leaves.

I wasn't lying: I *am* looking forward to some time alone. I knew the first few days would be taxing, but I didn't predict how much. And being alone here is different from being alone in my shitty apartment.

In the shower in my apartment, I can touch two freezing tile walls without fully stretching out my arms. Elizabeth's tub is large enough to bathe a Great Dane. As the sky darkens toward early twilight, I run a bath and pour myself a second glass of Rioja gran reserva.

Jumbo wants nothing to do with the water. He trots back and forth worriedly at the threshold between bathroom and bedroom.

"In or out, dog. I'm not leaving the door open."

He whines.

"Okay, out, then." He's still audible with the door closed, but I can muffle the noise by sinking under the bubbles. I let out every bit of my breath and feel some of my stress go with it.

Why would Elizabeth bother spray-painting Nate's car when she could simply walk into her house at any time? Why *hasn't* she walked into her house?

Because it's not hers, as far as the world is concerned. The police are notoriously inept at protecting human beings from harm, but they're efficient at removing undesirables from property where they don't belong. Especially if one of those undesirables is a

105-pound woman whose only weapons are spite and an obsolete wearable device. If I called 911 and said someone like that had broken in and refused to leave, they'd be here in ten minutes.

So what's her plan? She must have one. Elizabeth wouldn't sit back and take what I've hit her with. She must have a way in.

I sit up in the bath, swearing as water sloshes over the side and onto the floor.

Nate. Nate is her way in.

How could I have overlooked it? Of course she'll try to get to him. He's her husband, her support, the one who sleeps beside her and brews her lattes and buys her tulips in December. The one person who knows her well enough that he might recognize her even in another body. She might have told him what she and I got up to back in college. He might have believed her.

And here I've been acting strange and not like "myself." What if he knows I'm an impostor?

Just then, I notice how quiet it is. It takes me a moment to realize it's because Jumbo is no longer whining outside the bathroom door.

Piercing beeps drift up from downstairs. Someone's inputting a code to unlock the door.

Did I arm the security system after Nate left?

I hurry out of the bath and wrap Elizabeth's robe around myself without drying off. Leaving wet footprints on the wooden floor, I ease into the hall just in time to hear the outer door closing.

I freeze. I should grab a vase, a candlestick, something to defend myself. My phone, at the very least.

Jumbo's not barking. Someone below mutters high-pitched nonsense to him, which loosens the tension in my jaw. Of course! It's just Hailey. She was going to drop off Nate's car after she ran errands.

Pulling the robe around myself more securely, I head down. As I descend each step, the ceiling of the ground floor moves a little higher in my vision, revealing more of the floor below, and the person who has entered.

Black boots. Black jeans. Black jacket. A tattooed hand scratching Jumbo behind his ears. A face I've never seen before, its lower half shadowed in dark scruff.

There's a strange man in my house.

17

In the weeks after the video, Mary barely sees Garrett. He's leaving her alone like she ordered him to, but she can't shake her sense of impending disaster.

She's outside the Confluence building, having made a visit to the coffee cart, when he cozies up next to her on a bench. "So," he says, "are you Mary today, or Elizabeth?"

She remembers to breathe. It's oddly comforting to see the worst arrive. Instead of fearing that Garrett knows her secret, she can deal with the reality that he does.

He smirks at the look on her face, forestalling any thoughts she might have of bluffing her way out. Leaning in, he lowers his voice, even though there's no one else around. "I did have my suspicions. And then *Elizabeth* was so uptight about Jessica, and *you* demanded that letter of recommendation without knowing what you wanted it for. It really clicked for me that night.

"So I looked at the device checkout logs, then had a little chat with Petra Janssen-Villalobos. Nice lady. She was surprised to learn her dogs had apparently chewed up two Empathyzer prototypes beyond repair."

He stretches his arm along the back of the bench behind Mary's shoulders. "I wondered where you were getting all those ideas about how to improve the Empathyzers. I gotta tell you, Aunt Gloria's impressed. Be a shame if she found out you'd stolen from her company."

He shifts his arm forward. Mary sits up, away from his touch, but he just chuckles and leans closer.

"Naturally she'll fire your ass. You can kiss any hopes of working in bioengineering goodbye. Oh shit, you've got a scholarship, don't you?" He tsks. "Pretty sure the student code of conduct says something about thievery. Even if you don't get expelled, I hope you took out a shitload of student loans."

Mary's lips feel numb. "We'll post the video if you say anything."

"Yeah, about that. Holding me against my will? Making false accusations? Post that shit and I'll ruin you. Both of you. Do you have a team of lawyers looking out for your family's interests?" He knows the answer to that. "I didn't think so."

She looks down, wishing she could throw her coffee in his smug face. "What do you want?" He must want something, or he would have gone to Gloria already.

"Do you ever let Elizabeth come into work as you?"

"No." As if she'd tell him if she did. But work is the one thing she holds sacrosanct.

The silence pulls tight between them. "What's the boiling point of nitrogen?" he asks.

"Seventy-seven kelvin. Why?" Then she realizes why. The moment before he speaks again feels endless.

"I want some action with Elizabeth," he says. "I want you to make that happen."

Her stomach clenches. "You can't be serious."

"Don't be such a prude. We'll meet up at my house's Halloween party. You can get nice and drunk first. All you have to do is lie there."

If his face looked punchable before, it's practically got a target painted on it now. "You want me to make out with you while I'm in Elizabeth's body."

He sniffs. "I want to fuck her."

Bile rises, stinging, in her throat. "That's gross. That's . . ." She swallows. "That's *rape*."

"It's not rape if you let me. She never needs to find out about it."

"What? No. It is. You're—— What is *wrong* with you?"

His eyes narrow. "I didn't appreciate the way you two treated me when I came over."

"So this is what, revenge?" Mary almost laughs at the sheer pettiness.

He shrugs. "You can help me out, or you can lose everything. I know what I'd pick. Think about it. Halloween night, baby. Or I go to Aunt Gloria on November first." He curls his arm around and squeezes her shoulder, then gets up and walks away.

———

MARY REMEMBERS, LAST November first, walking by Garrett and Nate's fraternity after their annual Halloween blowout. Marveling at the amount of trash strewn over every inch of the lawn. Beer bottles, pizza boxes, bits of costumes. Enough red plastic cups to stack to the roof. A black lace bra discarded six feet from the sidewalk.

She hadn't been invited then, but this year things are different. Elizabeth flits around their room chattering about what they'll wear, oblivious to Mary's gloom.

Finally it seems to sink in. "What're you typing away on so studiously?" Imitating Mary's frown of concentration, Elizabeth peers at her screen.

Mary slams her laptop shut. She still can't bring herself to delete the journal. The laptop is password protected anyway, and no one can force her to unlock it. She has a vague hope that if Garrett does go to Gloria, Mary's observations about the Empathyzer will have enough value to save her.

Elizabeth's smile is impish. "I saw the word *Empathyzer*. What are you writing?"

Mary sighs. Elizabeth will keep pushing until Mary tells her. "Just a description of our last transfer."

"Like a journal? Look at you, being all creative and introspective."

"It's not that!" Somehow her putting herself into it, rather than its being research, makes it more embarrassing. "I'm just . . . trying to figure out what makes them work for us."

"Mm-hmm."

Right then, Mary almost tells Elizabeth about Garrett's threat and the deal he offered. But then she'd have to admit she didn't shoot it down immediately. Telling him *No* would send him straight to Gloria, but Elizabeth might not understand that.

Elizabeth chuckles. "We're such a pair. Even when we're having fun, we're working."

They're not the same, though. All Elizabeth does is take the life she'd be living anyway and put it online, where more and more strangers are watching every day. Mary doesn't have that option.

If she does what Garrett wants, she can never call herself anything but Elizabeth's enemy. But if she wants to have a future, she can't *not* do it.

She imagines moving back home, to her parents' speaking silences and her brother's relentless put-downs. Her parents were neutral on college as long as they didn't have to pay for it, but Brandon will be gleeful at her crashing and burning. How long will it take before she's guilted into helping out in the flower shop, hopeless as she is at it? Or Brandon will get her a job at the shipping warehouse where he works, and she'll be stuck owing him a favor. She'll never get free again.

Garrett wants Elizabeth's body, but that's not the real allure for him. His true aim is dominance, degradation. He wants to crush Mary as much as Elizabeth, force her to do something that disgusts her. Humiliate the two women who joined forces to make him feel powerless for once, and drive them apart in the process.

It's working already. *It was Elizabeth's idea to video him. It was her idea to take the Empathyzers in the first place.* Those thoughts are poison. Mary cannot plant the idea of her betrayal in Elizabeth's head, not when it's so close to being real.

And the last time she confided in Elizabeth about Garrett, it only made things worse. She has to solve this on her own.

———

SATURDAY, THEY GO with Katarina to rave night at one of the few clubs downtown that cater to underage students, since Mary doesn't have a fake ID. The irony is not lost on her, when she can literally become someone else. Not that it matters when Katarina can get them whatever they want. Mary doesn't love doing drugs when she and Elizabeth are transferred—they tend to make the day-after hangover worse—but she thought it might help her forget. The pills tonight have a speedy, aggressive edge, though, increasing her paranoia.

Katarina sticks by her side like a babysitter. From the edge of the room, Mary can see the bounce of her own blond head out on the floor, the flash of her teeth as Elizabeth beams at strangers in a way she herself never does. A guy who could fit two of Mary inside his body holds her loosely from behind, grinding his pelvis on her back, and Elizabeth appears to be loving it.

"She's having a good time for once! Must be the drugs."

Katarina shouts into Mary's ear to be heard over the pounding music. She has never mentioned the night, over a month ago now, when Elizabeth showed her friends the Empathyzers and blurted out the truth as if it were a joke. But that doesn't mean Katarina, or one of the others, hasn't mentioned it to someone else. The rumor could have easily made its way to Garrett.

"Looks like she's over Nate!" Katarina laughs. Everything seems to be moving more slowly than usual, except for people's voices, which sound high-pitched and frenetic. "I don't get the point of pining for someone and not talking to them!"

Mary feels a stab of hurt at the realization that Elizabeth must have told Katarina about her crush. It's hardly a state secret, yet she feels betrayed.

"I'm gonna go dance." Katarina follows her onto the floor, but out there they don't have to talk.

Later, having lost track of Elizabeth, she goes into the bathroom and finds her sitting on the floor with her back against the wall. She hopes fervently that there was nothing in those pills that will send her to the ER. "Elizabeth," she hisses, crouching down and taking her chin in her hand.

Elizabeth responds, thank god, her eyes opening, a red-lipsticked smile smearing across her face. "Hey," she says. "You're me."

Katarina comes in. "Wow, someone's having too much fun."

"My legs got tired," Elizabeth slurs. Her head lolls to one side, her eyes falling shut. "I'm so tired."

"No passing out in the bathroom," Katarina snaps. She gets water from the sink on her hands and slaps it onto Elizabeth's cheeks. "Wakey, wakey!"

They haul Elizabeth to her feet and out into the night. Revived by the chilly air, Elizabeth is able to walk on her own. "I'm fine, you bitches," she says, batting away their hands and staggering ahead. "I don't know why you're making me go home this early."

"This walk's going to be easier when you don't have to go all the way to the dorm," Katarina says to Mary.

"What do you mean?"

"Next semester? When you're living with us?" Katarina sounds matter-of-fact. Like they're discussing something she and Elizabeth already agreed upon.

"Keep your voice down," Mary says, as a test. "I haven't told her yet."

Katarina follows Mary's gaze to Elizabeth's diminutive, stumbling figure. "Ahh, she won't remember. I don't blame you for putting off telling her, though. Mary's so clingy with you. You know she's going to flip her shit."

18

MARY (ELIZABETH)

NOW

I don't have the breath to scream, but I must make some kind of noise. The man at the bottom of the stairs looks up from where he's crouched petting my dog.

He smiles, open and sunny, like a little boy seeing someone whose presence he has craved for a long time.

"Hey, you." He stands and walks toward me. I catalog details to relate in the police report later, if there is a later. White male, early twenties, wearing all black, including a black beanie. A day's growth of facial hair. Eyes a striking shade of hazel, turned down at the inner corners. They fix on me with unnerving intensity. He's not tall; with me on the bottom step, he's shorter. But he's strong enough to wrap his arms around my waist and lift me down to his level with no difficulty. His jacket is cold from outside.

He telegraphs what he's going to do, but it's still a shock when he kisses me. The heat of his mouth, the wetness of his tongue plunging between my lips. His hands tighten on my waist.

"No!" Reflexively, I push away from him, stumbling back. He stumbles too.

"He's not here, is he? I thought this was his going-out night." The man sneers, but sends a furtive glance through the doorway to the kitchen behind me as if he's afraid Nate will come out swinging.

What is happening?

The man carefully sets his black backpack on the couch, then takes off his beanie and jacket, revealing a fitted T-shirt—also black—and two full sleeves of tattoos that extend onto his hands. His hair is bleached white-blond with roots the same color as his stubble, a style he's almost good-looking enough to transcend.

His unsettling light eyes shift back to me, flicking down my barely covered body and back up to my face. "I thought it was time for us to start talking again." He doesn't look like talking is what's on his mind. "I missed you, Beth."

The tattoos are tripping a recent memory. Who was I just talking about tattoos with? Chrissy. *Your photographer? With the pretty eyes and the full sleeves? I'd go home with him in a heartbeat.*

This is no attack. And this man is no stranger. Chrissy's knowing smile has a new context.

He's Elizabeth's dirty secret. Lorne, her photographer, but not *just* her photographer. Not much of a secret, either. It's such a cliché.

The thought of her cheating on Nate makes me want to throw up.

Lorne grabs my hand and draws me toward the stairs. "Haven't you missed me too? I keep thinking about the time I had you in your bed. You were so—"

"You have to leave." I pull free and back away.

His brows draw together. "Why? How long do we have before he comes back?"

"No, this isn't . . . We're not . . ." I motion between us.

"You want me to take photographs? Make it legit? I'm gonna need a deposit first." Grinning, he embraces me, his hand sliding inside my robe. I make a broken sound and skirt the couch to put it between us.

At last he seems to get that something is wrong. His face darkens. "Are you mad because I came over without you summoning me? You only want your little dog to come when you whistle for him? I'm not a dog, Beth."

"I know we're 'putting a pause on things.'" He does air quotes as his voice rises to a mocking falsetto. "But it's been a long fuckin' pause."

Too late, I realize I've fenced myself in between him, the couch, and the Christmas tree in the corner. He advances on me. "You can't just keep fucking me when you want revenge on your husband."

"What did you say?"

"We both know that's what it is. And that was okay for a while, but . . . come on." He takes hold of my elbows, gazing into my eyes. "When are we going to— This is stupid. I love you. I know you love me. When are we going to be together for real?"

I can't hide my shock, or my repulsion. I pull away.

His face twists and he steps back, hand rising to cup the back of his neck. As he does, his shirt pulls up and I see the holster at his waist. The sour taste of fear fills my mouth.

Lorne sees how appalled I am. It would be hard to miss. He holds his hands up, glaring at me like I've confirmed his worst expectations. "Oh, right. You're too good for me," he says in a soft, mocking voice. "I knew it. I knew you'd never leave him."

I feel faint. Just because he hasn't gone for the gun doesn't mean he won't.

"We're done. Don't text me again." He watches my face to see how his words land.

"I'm sorry I can't give you what you want." I'm not sorry, not particularly, but I'll say it if it gets him out of here.

He huffs out a bitter chuckle. "Yeah, me too." Turning away, he scoops up his things, not bothering to put on his jacket. I'm frozen, afraid any move I make will keep him from leaving.

At the door he pauses. I hold my breath, ready to bolt if he turns back.

"You never did thank me for solving your problem," he says.

I don't know what he means, and I don't care. He stalks out into the cold, his jacket and backpack in his arms.

As soon as the door slams behind him, I collapse onto the couch.

Slowly, my heart rate and breathing return to normal. My mind is tripping over the contradictions. Elizabeth, having an affair. With a guy like *that*. He's good-looking, but I don't see anything about him that would justify her risking her marriage and her reputation.

You can't just keep fucking me when you want revenge on your husband. Revenge for what?

Nate wouldn't cheat on her. No, Lorne must mean something else. Elizabeth likes having people dance to her tune, and maybe Nate has stopped dancing fast enough.

But she loves him. Doesn't she? No one else had ever conquered her the way he did, or at least that's what it looked like. I've watched their love story unfold online like a modern-day fairy tale, and it shatters me to see the proof that it's nothing but fiction after all.

Yet I also feel vindicated. Elizabeth had everything, and this just goes to show how little she deserved it.

———

AFTER LORNE'S VISIT, the tap of a tree branch on the window sounds like knuckles. The trundle of a winter-fat squirrel through rotted leaves morphs into stealthy footsteps. I don't feel safe even with the security system armed. What if Elizabeth gave Lorne the code to that too? I don't have the master code to change it; nor can I reset the door's unlock codes.

I text Nate. How was your meeting?

I can see he's read the message, but he doesn't answer it for ten minutes. Great! Really fruitful. At dinner now

I hesitate over my next one, torn between my desire not to nag and my need for connection. Any idea when you'll be home?

This time the gap is shorter, but I still die a little bit in it. I've overstepped. I'm being clingy, needy. And, given Elizabeth's behavior, hypocritical.

Is everything ok? Do you need me there?

Relief pours through me with his response. I want to say, *Yes, I need you. Come home to me.* When he gets here, I'll take him upstairs and make myself his wife for real. I'll wipe away the transgressions of the past and try to forget I was ever anyone besides Elizabeth Jordan.

But am I imagining a long-suffering tone? In his delay, if not the words themselves?

I don't want to be like the other Elizabeth, with her sense of entitlement. I want to be a good partner. That means not ruining Nate's night out with his friends.

Nah, I text him. Have a good time. I'll see you when you get in

Then I type, Love you! and send it before I can change my mind.

The dots bounce for a good thirty seconds, as though he's typing and deleting. Finally the reply comes through. I might be late. I'll crash in the man cave if I am, I know you need your sleep for tomorrow

My disappointment barely has time to register before he sends one last text.

And no, you don't need to worry about me being hungover.

I stare at the period at the end of his message. I wait for something more, an *I love you* or even *Sweet dreams*, but it never comes.

19

ELIZABETH (MARY)

NOW

Elizabeth remembers the street where Nate and Declan's fledgling production company has its office, but has to look up the address. She hasn't spent enough time in this part of the city to know it well. It started as industrial docklands in the early part of the previous century, but a hundred years later has gentrified to loft condos and shops that sell kombucha and e-bikes.

Her walk from the nearest train stop takes her past a canal that makes an excellent place to dispose of a small, unwanted electronic device. When no one's looking she flips the flash drive into it. The water's absorbed worse pollutants in its time.

The temperature drops as the sun sinks behind a layer of cloud. Elizabeth's not wearing a coat, Mary's tired brown parka being decidedly unsuitable for her purposes, and the wind goes right through her black polyester blazer. She doesn't have to wait long—she's timed her arrival well—but her whole body feels numb by the time Nate emerges from the building with his partner.

She's not prepared for the emotions that well up at the sight of him. She expected to feel nervous, but a wave of homesickness and heartache threatens to submerge her. She fights down the lump in her throat and draws farther into the doorway where she's been lurking, pretending to be interested in the flyers posted in the window. She wants to choose her moment.

Nate and Declan stand talking for ages. Finally, they do a mutual shoulder clap and split up: Declan walking toward Elizabeth's hidey-hole, Nate in the opposite direction. Elizabeth has to hustle so she won't lose him.

Declan, who usually treats her with smarmy charm, doesn't spare a glance as she scurries by. It gives her a few seconds of doubt; she remembers the bus driver. She's a dull penny, not a diamond.

But there's only one person she needs to fascinate, and she has reason to believe she can get Nate's attention in her current guise.

She's right behind him now, close enough to see the five-o'clock shadow emerging on his jaw, and his ears flushing pink from the cold. She just needs an opening. She sees one when he takes his phone out, his steps slowing as he bends his head to the screen.

Coming up on his left, she glances at him, then away, then back as if in surprise.

"Nate Jordan?" she says. "Is that you?"

The face he turns to her is blank with nonrecognition. Fear freezes her. What was she thinking? Of course he doesn't remember her. Mary was never anything to him.

"It's Mary Burke. From college."

His expression shifts, warming. "Mary! Of course. Wow, it's been years!" His eyes trace her from head to feet. "You look great. I'm so glad."

He gives her a small grimace, a tacit acknowledgment of Mary's downfall.

She pushes past the discomfort. "You look great too. I can't believe we ran into each other like this!"

"I didn't even know you lived in the city. What have you—"

"I was just about to go grab a drink . . . Are you doing anything right now?"

"Oh." He glances down at his phone. Elizabeth's heart squeezes in panic. Her one chance, and she's already lost him.

No. She can't think this way. She steps closer, tilting her head up to smile at him. "I'd love to catch up." She pulls her lower lip between her teeth and watches him follow the movement with his eyes. She hopes she's sparking the right memory.

His hand drops, sliding his phone into his back pocket. "You know what? That sounds like fun. I know a great little cocktail bar right up here—unless you had someplace else in mind."

She spreads her hands. "I'll follow your lead."

Nate has to send a few texts along their way—business, he claims—but Elizabeth has his undivided attention once they arrive at the bar. It's a strange sensation, being the object of a Nate Jordan charm offensive again. Memories from her former life float up, his younger face overlaid with the one he has now. They'd reconnected a couple of years after graduation, when he spilled a piña colada on her at a club. He apologized profusely once he realized who she was. They ended up talking, then dancing, then kissing as the liquid stiffened the front of her dress into a sticky mat.

The next day a box from a local designer boutique showed up at her apartment, along with a note: *Replacing what I ruined. NJ.* The dress inside looked nothing like the one she'd worn at the club, like nothing she would have chosen for herself, but it fit her perfectly.

Still, a high-handed move. She made a post telling the story of the previous night and the handsome "stranger" who'd figured in it, and she took a poll: Was it creepy of "N" to buy her the dress, or romantic?

The post went viral, catapulting her over a follower milestone. The verdict: "Romantic AF" by a good twenty percent margin, though some of the comments specified *Only if he's hot.* Less than a month later, she and Nate were exclusive.

She's never asked him who that piña colada was for.

Tonight he orders his drink of choice, Scotch neat. "Mary, get this one, you'll love it," he says, pointing to a cocktail on the list, and she does love it. It's got a touch of sweetness, with an alcoholic bite that warns her of its potency.

Under the dim pendant light over their booth, his lashes cast spidery shadows onto his cheeks. "I admired you when we were in school. You weren't afraid to show people how smart you were. You didn't care what anyone thought." He looks up and his eyes flash onyx.

She could fall into those eyes, the dark depths of them. She has before. A smile touches his lips, as though he can sense what she's thinking. "I always thought that was sexy," he says.

Without asking, he orders another round for them both. More of that high-handedness, the kind attractive men can get away with. Elizabeth's stomach churns, but she sips her drink. She's so close to gaining the clarity she needs, bitter as it tastes. This is what she knew, deep down, that she needed to do.

He asks her questions about herself, and acts like her responses are wise and fascinating. Neither of them mentions Elizabeth's name. Nate doesn't wear a wedding band, since he got spooked after reading an article about ring avulsion a couple of years back. He'd said it wasn't a piece of metal that makes a marriage; the real tie was in their hearts. She'd accepted that at the time.

His eyes grow hotter, his mouth looser. Elizabeth's heart is trying to come up her throat and plop into her glass, but he's smooth enough for them both. He probably dismisses her skittishness as Mary's lack of social grace.

After the third drink, he pays, also without consulting her. As they walk out of the bar, his palm finds the small of her back. A few doors down, he pulls her into the dark vestibule of a boutique that's closed for the night, and backs her against the locked door. Elizabeth feels like her body is out of her control, a satellite in planetary orbit.

Heat pours off him. He breathes into her ear, "We didn't run into each other by accident, did we?" The warm fingers spreading through her stomach close into a fist. But then his lips meet her neck, his hands sliding into her hair. His body molds to hers, warming her in the cold.

"I know you feel this. What's between us." He presses his tongue to a spot under her ear, a move she recognizes. It wakes her up a little, despite the ripples of pleasure it sends through her body. She's trembling when his mouth brushes, then captures, hers. Wanting it, wanting more. Hating that she still wants it.

Moments later, he says, "You want to go somewhere? I'm parked nearby."

The feelings gushing through her are cut off neatly, as though with a heated blade. "I'm not having sex in your car."

Nate chuckles at her tartness. He thinks she's Mary, and a certain amount of bitchiness is in character. "I meant we could drive somewhere. Or go to my office."

Elizabeth's been to his and Declan's office. The idea of getting naked on that red velvet monstrosity of a couch—especially knowing Nate has almost certainly brought other women there—makes her tongue shrivel in her mouth. She disentangles herself from him, ducking under the arm caging her against the shop door.

Got what you need, huh? says a sardonic voice in her head, one that sounds suspiciously like Mary's.

"I have a confession to make," she says. "I know you're married. And who your wife is."

His mouth purses in a W, as if to deny, or justify. Elizabeth rushes on before he can speak.

"I wanted to get back at her. Because of the way she treated me when we were in school. I wanted to take something that was hers, even if it was just for a night."

He's listening now, eyes flat and unreadable in the dark.

"But it wouldn't be right to do that to you. I don't want to be the reason you cheat on your wife. I don't want to break up your marriage. I'm sorry."

She wonders if he'll buy that Mary is this naive. If he thinks she's still the same Mary he knew seven years ago. She turns away, but he doesn't let her get more than a few steps.

"Hey." He takes her arm, turning her around. "It's okay. We can be together. She doesn't have to know."

He's looking at her with the corner of his mouth tipped up, mischief in his dark eyes. A look that promises pleasure and gives her permission to pursue it, to hell with what's *right*. She's never seen anything she hates so much. She wants to scream at him, tell him exactly what she thinks of him.

But that has to wait until she's herself again.

He takes out his phone. "Give me your number."

She can tell he won't take no for an answer, but she doesn't remember the number to Mary's phone. She takes it out of her pocket. "Give me yours," she says.

He does, and refrains from asking her to text him right away so he'll have hers. He's confident enough to believe Mary's moral qualms will melt away. He moves closer, but instead of coming in for a kiss he murmurs into her ear, "I still think about you. My little witch."

He caresses her cheek with his warm hand, and then he's gone.

She walks to the train in a daze. Nate has always had a talent for spinning a fairy tale in which they're the only two people who matter. He's let her be the main character, while he plays the supporting love interest.

She's known for a while that the tale was a false one. But until now, she hadn't *felt* it. Hadn't experienced it from the point of view that would give her, if not objectivity, a more truthful perspective.

Now she knows. Nate will tell that story to anyone.

20

MARY (ELIZABETH)

NOW

By the time Hailey texts, letting me know Nate's car is ready and she'll drop it off within the hour, I've convinced myself that Lorne will sneak back into my house before the sun comes up again if I don't find a way to lock him out. It makes no sense, but I can't stop feeling his hands under my robe. And I can't rid myself of the crawling sense that I'm being watched.

The design of Elizabeth's house doesn't help. Why did she think floor-to-ceiling windows were a good idea? Then I remember: she puts everything online. She wouldn't care about living in a fishbowl.

The darkness outside is swallowing, alive. Anything could be in it.

I text Hailey back asking if she has the master codes for the door locks and alarm system. I don't explain why I need them; to the extent that I care what she thinks by now, I tell myself that in any given situation most people will come to the simplest conclusion. Hailey will think I'm a flaky airhead who forgot her own master codes.

She texts back that she can reset whatever I need when she gets here. And that she's on her way, which is the only thing that keeps me from responding in a panic that I need those codes *now*.

I'll ask her in person to write them down for me, so she can't misinterpret my instructions.

Sooner than I expect, the back door keypad beeps. In the living room, I freeze. What if it's Lorne? I should have insisted Hailey send me the codes. No—I should have grabbed a knife from the kitchen.

But it's not Lorne. Or Hailey.

The smell alerts me. I wouldn't normally notice it, because I smell it every day, or used to. It surrounded me, especially after laundry day. The fake-lavender perfume of cheap laundry detergent. In this elegant house full of expensive scents, it sticks out like dog shit. With the slam of the back door, it wafts from the kitchen into the living room.

I leap to my feet, watching the pass-through, knowing whom I'm about to see.

She stops, framed in the archway, fists clenched and jaw set.

Not me. Elizabeth.

She's here.

――――――

LOOKING AT ELIZABETH in my body is like looking at any other person—mundane—yet surreal. In college, I almost got used to seeing my own physical presence from the outside. Evaluating it. It wasn't at all like looking into a mirror.

Now it feels new all over again.

We face off across the living room. I can feel my pulse in my neck.

The tip of her nose is bright red. Her eyes are puffy and bloodshot and rimmed with smudged mascara. The remnants of cheap lipstick stain her lips a raw-meat pink.

She looks terrible. Though I don't hate what she's done with my hair.

My mood takes a sudden turn into glee. She must be having such a bad time, and I get to enjoy it. "I got your little message," I say. "I'm not confessing shit. I'm not the one who has something to hide."

She walks forward, leaving a trail of wet boot prints on the floor. Halfway across the room she stumbles, barely catching herself.

I take in her flushed face. "Are you drunk?"

She shakes her head—out of bemusement more than denial, it seems. Jumbo chooses that moment to zip out from underneath the couch. Barking frantically, the dog makes little feints at her, then darts to safety behind me.

Her face crumples, making me feel sorry for her against my will. It's a reflex, an echo left over from when I cared about her feelings. When I had someone whose feelings I cared about.

But now I have lots of friends. I have a *husband*, no thanks to Elizabeth. Pity won't get me anywhere.

I pick Jumbo up and he quiets, other than an isolated yip or two. She watches my hand stroking his head. *And your little dog too.* I do feel a tiny bit wicked-witchy, but damn it, I've earned this.

"How are you settling in?" I ask, injecting into my tone a lightness that I hope infuriates her. I want her to be as filled with rage as I've been for seven years, and to feel every bit as powerless. "I know it's not what you're used to, but you'll adjust.

"If you came here to ask me for money, you can go fuck yourself. I'm still paying off student loans for the degree I never got to finish. Though actually, those are your loans now. Next payment's due January first. You're welcome for the heads-up."

Her eyes widen, her mouth opening as if she's about to speak, but I refuse to let her before I've said my piece. She barged into my house. She can damn well listen to me.

"You brought this on yourself," I say. "Everything that's happening to you right now, everything you've lost—it's only what you deserve. You stole my future. It's only fair I should take yours."

That felt amazing.

But she doesn't look angry; she looks sad. "I can't believe you gave up," she says. "You could have gone back to school. The Mary I remember would have. You were always so ambitious."

It enrages me to hear her dismiss the obvious. "I gave up on school because it was useless to do anything else! With an expulsion on my transcript, I probably could've gotten into a third-tier air-conditioning-repair training program. And been kicked out of *that* because Garrett's parents own the training school's parent company or something."

"You could have moved. They don't have that much influence everywhere."

I won't say I stayed because of her. "Even after you'd fucked up my life beyond repair, it wasn't enough. You had to swoop in and *marry* the one guy I ever really liked. If that isn't some next-level betrayal, I don't know what is."

She sways on her feet as though my words have hit her hard, but her mask of composure comes down fast. "Have you been having fun?" The wistful note in her voice surprises me. "It's kind of like old times, isn't it?"

"Not even a little bit."

Instantly, she rearranges her expression into my patented active bitch face. It didn't take much to dissolve her fake nostalgia.

"Where is it?" she asks.

I know exactly what she's talking about. "Where's what?"

"Where. Is. It?"

"I don't have any idea what you could be referring to, *Mary*."

She laughs, actually laughs, at me. Like I'm too pathetic to deal with. Then she lifts her left arm and pushes up her sleeve, showing me the device on her wrist. The janky, taken-apart-and-put-back-together-more-times-than-I-can-count Empathyzer I left her with.

"You know very well I'm talking about my Empathyzer." She lowers her arm and looks me in the eye. "The one I sent you."

21

The weekend before Halloween, Elizabeth and Mary go shopping for costumes.

"What do you mean, you want to go as yourself?" Elizabeth demands. A vertical line appears between her brows, giving Mary a sudden vision of how she will look decades in the future, with frown lines marring her ethereal beauty. Except on Elizabeth, wrinkles will look like character, not damage.

She and Mary are flipping through an overstuffed rack at their favorite thrift shop. Elizabeth pulls out a dress, holds it up, scrunches her nose, puts it back.

"We'll already be in costume. Isn't that enough?" Mary picks out a green lamé jumpsuit. "This might be good for yours."

"I want you to be a fairy queen, not a wood sprite from 1972."

Before now, Mary hadn't even questioned that Elizabeth planned *both* their costumes. "Can't we go to a party like normal people for once?"

"Do you really think you'll have any fun if you're not me?" Elizabeth answers her own question. "No. You'll stand in a corner and stare at people and be miserable the whole night." The *And I'm not going to babysit you* goes unspoken.

Mary gets a flash of last fall, before the Empathyzers. Elizabeth would drag her out, then straight up abandon her if she so much as grimaced at the taste of cheap beer.

"We can't keep doing this forever." Mary lowers her voice. "The devices won't last that long. Or . . ." *Or you'll get sick of it. Maybe you already have.*

She's tried a dozen times to bring up Elizabeth's move and chickened out every time. What she doesn't know is why. Why would Elizabeth abandon her? What did she do to deserve it? The questions fill her mouth like bitter liquid. Like her knowledge of Garrett's plans.

"Well, I assume they'll last through Halloween." Right then, Elizabeth's hand lands on a dress of glittering white and silver. When she raises it to her shoulder, it looks like it'll hit somewhere between midthigh and right below the ass. "Oh, this is perfect. Don't you think?"

Mary has a premonition of herself trying to hold the dress down while Garrett hikes it up. She swallows bile. "How much is it?"

Elizabeth checks the tag. "It's not bad. I've got it. Now we just need to find you a slutty witch costume."

Mary trails her down the rack, words bubbling up behind her lips. If Elizabeth would *tell* her she's moving out, that would be something. But she keeps acting like everything is normal.

Just like Mary's trying to do.

She wants so badly to lay down that burden. Tell Elizabeth what Garrett said, let her come up with some deliciously diabolical big-picture scheme to defeat him. Mary will handle the details.

But it'll backfire somehow, and Mary will be the one to lose everything. And she won't be able to hide how long she kept this knowledge to herself.

How does she know Elizabeth hasn't used *her* body to fuck someone? They have rules, but that doesn't mean those rules are always followed. Elizabeth obviously has no problem keeping secrets.

If Mary gave in to Garrett, her reasons for doing so would be selfish, but understandable. She'd be saving her own life. Her own future. It's increasingly obvious that she's the only one truly looking out for herself.

They find a black slip dress and, wonder of wonders so close to Halloween, a witch's hat. On the way to the checkout, Elizabeth stops by the housewares area, which usually holds nothing more alluring than rickety picture frames. "This is cool," she says, running her hand over a bronze statuette of a rearing horse. She picks it up to look at the sticker on the bottom. "It's five bucks. I'm buying it."

"Where will you put it?" Mary asks. Their room isn't exactly bristling with empty shelves.

"I'll find somewhere."

The eighty-year-old house where Katarina and the others live has built-in shelves in every room, decorated with flea market bric-a-brac and old books. The horse statuette would fit right in.

"Elizabeth," Mary says. But Elizabeth is smiling and charming the cashier as she takes out her credit card, all her attention focused on the world before her.

22

MARY (ELIZABETH)

NOW

My brain short-circuits. Elizabeth sent me the Empathyzer? *Elizabeth?*

"Why?"

The question comes out on a forced breath, as though I've been kicked in the gut. I see the ghost of glitter on my fingers. The same feeling echoes inside me as when I pried up the corner of the wrapping paper. A sense that what was in that box would divide my life into *before* and *after*.

Like meeting Elizabeth had done.

Like what happened on Halloween night just over a year later.

I'd thought of these as pendulum swings from fortune to disaster. Making a friend: good. Being expelled from school: bad.

I questioned the second Empathyzer's falling into my hands, but not too much. It was just the pendulum swinging back. I'd had so much shitty luck in my life that I was past due for a break. But there would have been no *befores*, no *afters*, if not for Elizabeth. No rise, but no fall either. And whatever happens now? That's an *after* too.

Elizabeth wears a small smile of quiet amusement, one I've seen many times on both her faces.

"I knew you wouldn't be able to resist using it," she says. "I knew you'd tried to get your hands on another Empathyzer."

I don't know how she knows this, but it wouldn't have been that hard to find out. Trying to locate or build a new Empathyzer over the years, I've approached everyone I could find from Confluence. I even went to Gloria. It was nothing but a series of dead ends.

I walk past Elizabeth to the sofa and sit heavily. Jumbo squirms in my arms until I let him down, then runs to settle himself under the Christmas tree, side-eyeing Elizabeth and her outstretched hand.

"Why would you want to be me? Especially now." That's what I can't wrap my head around. Is she *slumming*?

Elizabeth sits sideways on the couch, facing me like we're on a talk show. "You probably won't believe me, but I do miss you. I miss our friendship. What we had was special. I bet that's why the Empathyzers work for us. Don't you ever think about that?"

"You're right. I don't believe you."

My shock and disbelief curdle into anger. Who does she think she is to manipulate me and not even tell the truth about why?

Her shoulders drop. "Okay, fine. I needed to find out something. I needed to be you to do it. And I figured if I asked for your help, you'd tell me to get lost."

"So you do know what you did."

"I wanted to help you, you know. You didn't make yourself easy to find, but I tried to email you after you left school. I called your parents, sent them money."

They've never mentioned it to me. Not that we talk much—especially about that time. But if they accepted Elizabeth's payoff, that's their business.

"I can help you now," she says. "I *want* to help you. But it's time for us to go home."

I let out a short bark of a laugh. "Are you serious?"

She regards me from my own dark blue eyes. "You have your own life to live, and so do I. We should transfer back tonight. Where's my Empathyzer?"

In her tone there's a quiet confidence that makes rage pulse in my temples. She thinks I'll roll over for her because that was our dynamic for our entire relationship.

She's about to find out how wrong she is.

"It's gone," I say.

She blanches, which gives me a jolt of pure satisfaction. "Gone where?"

"Gone. I destroyed it." I try not to think too hard about the actual location of Elizabeth's Empathyzer, which I shoved into a small box deep in one of this house's many closets.

"What?" She's on her feet, her face drained of color. "What were you thinking?"

I drink in her distress like the shots of flavored vodka we used to take in our room. "I thought, since you were so careless with my life, you could live it yourself."

"You think you can *become* me? Permanently?"

"I don't *think* I can. I have." Like I told her, what was hers is mine now. It doesn't matter whether she acknowledges the wrong she did me, whether she feels sorry. Justice needed to be served, and now it has been.

"You don't want to do this, Mary. If you *knew*—"

"Shouldn't we start calling each other by our right names?"

I can't resist gloating. Elizabeth might have been pulling my strings all along, but now that I'm aware of it, I won't be jerked around anymore. Now the control is all on my side, and I mean to hold on to it.

She collapses onto the couch and drops her head into her hands. Then she looks up, as though she's had a flash of insight. "This is about Nate, isn't it? You want Nate."

"It's not like you deserve him." And then, angrily because she's started to laugh, I say, "I know about your fuck buddy. He came by today. Walked right in the door and started manhandling me."

Something like contrition passes over her face. But then she says, "You don't know anywhere near as much as you think you do."

She closes her eyes, steepling her hands at her mouth, then seems to decide something.

"Do you know where my husband is right now?"

My husband, I want to correct her, but I hold back. Pettiness is the refuge of the powerless. I hold the power here.

"Let me guess what he told you. Guys' night." She lets out a bitter chuckle. "He lied. An hour ago he was at a bar with me, trying to get me to go somewhere and have sex with him. And just to be clear, he thought I was you."

"Stop lying."

"I'm not. He's been cheating on me for months. Probably longer than that."

"You're so full of shit." Why would Nate go for me when he has her? She's so transparent, trying to make her life look spoiled so I'll give it back.

"It's strange when you start seeing someone and you realize this is it. Your big love story." She speaks so quietly, I have to lean in to hear. "Especially when you've never felt that way about anyone before. That was what it was like for me with Nate. For a long time, I was willing to put up with anything to hold on to him."

The pain in her eyes comes dangerously close to stirring my sympathy, so I look away with a snort of disgust. "Big love story? You're screwing your photographer!"

"I don't have to explain myself to you. You wouldn't understand anyway." Her face shows a flicker of anger, then smooths to a placid blank. She has to make more of an effort with my features, which default to sullenness. Even so, I feel like I'm seeing the old, superior Elizabeth, who always knew more than me.

"I couldn't make myself believe what Nate was." She touches the Empathyzer on her wrist. "So I decided I'd become you, then see what he'd do with someone who he'd already—" She stops, staring at her hands. She's cut my hair, but ignored my nails; they're as ragged as ever. "Until tonight, I really did hope it wasn't as bad as I thought. That I was blowing things out of proportion. You have no idea how convincing he can be." She takes in a breath, lets it out in a huff. "But now I know. *Really* know. And if you're hoping to somehow be with him through me, just know that you'll never have anything real with him."

She plays the wronged wife believably. But even if what she's saying is true, she cheated on him too. And something's off. She said herself that she knows how badly I wanted to become her. Why would she have handed me her life, taking the risk that I wouldn't give it back? There are easier ways to catch your husband cheating.

"Look at this," she says, getting my phone out and showing me her contacts list with Nate's number in it.

"This doesn't prove anything except you have your husband's number memorized."

"Fine. You want more proof? I'll get you proof. You'll see." She punches in a message and sends it.

"I'm not here just because I want Nate. I want everything you have." I lean toward her, looking her in the eye, making sure she understands what I say next. "Taking it away from you is the point."

She blinks. Then, to my frustration, her eyes crinkle with amusement. "You don't want my life, Mary. Trust me."

It's the *trust me* that sends me over the edge.

My mind goes blank with rage. When I can think again, I'm on my feet with my phone in my hand. "Get out."

Her mouth slackens. "You can't pull this off. You don't even know—"

"I know enough to get a running start." I got rid of her stalker boyfriend. I have money to throw at any other nasty surprises. And I'd be the worst kind of stupid to put any stock in what she says about Nate. "If you don't leave right now, I'm going to call the police and say a former roommate of mine, who has a history of violence and instability, has broken into my house and won't leave." I remember Detective Johns saying not to leave town without telling him. There's no way in hell Elizabeth would have become me if she'd had any idea it would put her in the crosshairs of a homicide investigation.

I think I'll let that be a surprise.

"I'm sure they'd be interested in hearing about you making threats too. Vandalizing your own husband's car? Classy."

Her eyes widen. "What are you talking about?"

A trickle of unease runs through my insides. But did I really believe she'd admit it?

"Don't act like you don't know. Actually, I don't care. Do your worst. Or just do what you're best at and leave me the fuck alone."

I lift my phone to dial. "You'd better get going before the cops get here."

She stares at me until I actually tap the screen.

"Fine," she says. "You want me to leave? I'll leave."

I'm surprised; I didn't expect her to give up this easily. But people who've never had to deal with adversity tend to crumble at the first hint of it.

At the front door, she stops. "It's funny. I wasn't sure Nate would even go for me while I was you. But you know what he told me? He still thinks about what happened between us that night."

I don't think. I pick up a vase full of lilies from the coffee table and hurl it at her. It shatters against the closing door.

"What the hell?" The voice comes from the kitchen, where the back door is opening.

I'd completely forgotten about Hailey.

She hurries into the room, taking in my heated face and heaving breath, the smashed glass and scattered flowers. "Are you . . . okay?"

"Perfect. But I need to reset every code that would get someone into this house, tonight."

I hold eye contact with her, wondering what I'll say if she presses the issue.

I can see the instant she decides not to. *Rich people,* I practically hear her thinking.

She says, "I'll get a broom."

———

HAILEY CATCHES A rideshare forty minutes later, leaving me alone once again, but I feel safer now that neither Lorne nor Elizabeth can simply walk in.

Elizabeth couldn't have been telling the truth about Nate. I still wish I could see him, feel his kiss before I go to sleep tonight. Lying in bed, I text him with the new door and alarm codes, but don't get a response or a read receipt. I picture him playing wingman to one of his single friends in a pulsating club, or getting sucked into a spirited debate about whether Lars von Trier is overrated. I hold those images in my mind until sleep takes me.

The chirp of my phone pulls me out of a doze. I grope for it, but instead of a text back from Nate, it's a priority DM from an account with the handle @iknowursecrets2554 and no profile photo.

My sleep-fuzzed mind comes into focus when I see what it says.

The only way you'll be safe is if you tell the police
what you've done and let them lock you up. It
doesn't matter who you are. Confess, or
you'll be sorry.

You think you've gotten away with it? You think
you're safe in that glass house?

You're not safe.

23

Elizabeth does both their going-out makeup. First her own, then Mary's after they transfer. Mary watches the refurbishment of her own body from the outside. Elizabeth gives her a dramatic dark red lip and sooty eyes, setting off the requisite pointed hat and a black slip dress cut into artful tatters.

Mary has trouble keeping her gaze from the mirror. Elizabeth has outdone herself. Mary is flower crowned, every inch of exposed skin shimmering with glitter powder. There are a lot of inches; never mind that it's forty degrees outside. Her red hair falls in loose waves. When they walk outside under the full moon, she catches sight of their reflection in a window and they look barely human, barely real.

Every boy they pass, and a few of the girls, looks at Mary in a way she has come to recognize as *hungry*. "Hey, Titania, where you going?" a boy asks. Mary bestows a smile on him, and lets it shrivel when he follows up with a lewd suggestion.

Inside, she's trembling. She clutches her tiny purse in sweaty hands. Everything depends on her remaining calm, following the plan she's made, and having good luck. Elizabeth's luck.

The party has multiple levels. The main floor is the most public, supplied with a keg of the cheapest beer possible. It looks like a decent time: someone has decorated the common room to look like a haunted house, they're playing nineties hip-hop, and people are already making out in corners at eleven thirty. The two upper floors are off-limits to everyone but brothers and their "guests." The basement is the semi-VIP area; at the door a pledge is posted whose job it is to repel girls who fail to meet some arbitrary standard of attractiveness. Mary, Elizabeth, and Katarina, who met them outside, make the cut. They follow a throbbing EDM beat downstairs to the open bar.

Last year when she went to parties as herself, Mary felt assaulted by the blaring music, the strobe lights, the babble of raised voices. But Elizabeth thrives on spontaneity and attention from strangers. Some of that transfers to Mary when she's her.

Elizabeth wanders off almost immediately, her disappearance raising a spike of panic in Mary's stomach. Tonight of all nights, they need to stick together.

Katarina places a restraining hand on Mary's arm. "She'll be fine! Let's get hammered." She tugs Mary toward the bar. *Who's clingy now?* Mary thinks.

Mary nurses a vodka soda, Elizabeth's favorite drink, while Katarina does shots and gets riotously drunk with alarming speed. They dance; guys buzz around like mosquitoes. Katarina encourages them, but Mary shuts them down with a glance. Turning her head, she spies Nate by the stairs across the room. As if called by her gaze, he makes eye contact.

She could go over there. Dance with him. Kiss him, just once.

She's making her way through the tightly packed crowd when a hot, damp hand caresses the exposed upper part of her back.

"Hey there," Garrett says in her ear.

Adrenaline prickles her skin, pushing out through her limbs.

She wants to run. Instead, she smiles. Elizabeth's slow, enigmatic, yet promising smile. The one that turns men into idiots every time.

She'd told him a few days ago at work that Elizabeth had decided she wanted to go to the party in her own body. Mary said she didn't want to push too hard, lest Elizabeth become suspicious, but she had a backup idea. She could still help, because Elizabeth trusted her, but she needed Garrett to get her something.

Garrett said, *All right. I guess we do it the old-fashioned way. It's her I want anyway, not you in an Elizabeth skin suit.*

For once, Mary was glad not to be the object of desire.

Now her nerves are sparking, but her mind is oddly calm. She lets her eyes glaze and the shape of her smile go a little messy. "Hey there yourself." She stumbles against him. He catches her around the waist, the drink in his other hand slanting perilously toward her white dress. "These stupid shoes," she complains.

She looks up at him through her lashes. He's watching her face, still not a hundred percent sure which one she is. She'll show him. One fun, sexy Elizabeth coming right up.

"You're not dancing!" she shouts. She presses her body against his and moves with the music as if she's not disgusted by his very existence.

His fingers dig into her hip. He starts to move with her. "You look really good tonight," he shouts in her ear. "I like the glitter."

"What? You want some glitter?" She opens her clutch, pulls out a little pot of body glitter, and uses her finger to smear some on his forehead. "There. Gorgeous, darling."

It's ridiculously easy to drop the pill, the one Garrett himself gave her to give to Elizabeth, into his cup.

He actually believed she would roofie her best friend for him. Her plan is to wait until he starts to feel the effects, then leave him passed out in his room with his pants down and a "used" condom in the trash. He won't remember what they did—or didn't do—but he's too arrogant to admit it.

She hopes. This plan is running on way too much hope, but it's all she's been able to come up with.

He finishes his drink in two swallows and brandishes his empty cup. "Let's go to the bar."

She nods, clinging to his hand as he leads her away.

Katarina grabs her. Fucking Katarina. Mary forgot all about her. "Where are you guys going?" she says.

Garrett looks at her the way Mary wants to, like she's dog shit on his shoe.

"You need to stay here," Katarina insists. "You're not allowed . . . It's not good to go off with a guy by yourself."

"I'm not gonna hurt her," Garrett says. Is he slurring yet? "We're just getting another drink."

"Bullshit. You're the lion and she's the . . . the whatever. That animal. The gazelle." Katarina moves her hands like she's dog-paddling, presumably to indicate running. It's a little awkward with her holding a drink.

At any other time, Mary would be impressed with her grasp of the situation. She laughs and tries to move off, but Katarina seizes her hand.

"Noooo!" she howls. "Stay here and dance with me."

Mary could grind her teeth in frustration. "I'll be fine, I promise. It's too crowded down here." She swivels her head up to Garrett. "Do you have any alcohol in your room?"

"What kind of host would I be if I didn't?" Garrett tips his head back, looking Katarina up and down. "You can come with us if you want."

Mary says into Katarina's ear, "It's okay! I want to go with him."

"Are you sure? Are you *sure* sure? I'm not letting you go up to his room by yourself."

Mary weighs her options. She could make a scene, which would then be the memory Garrett takes away. Or she could let Katarina tag along and hope he remembers something more pleasant. A witness will complicate matters, but Katarina's not exactly lucid herself. Mary will figure out how to handle her once Garrett's upstairs and semiconscious.

"Okay," she says. "You be my guard gazelle."

Once they're out of the basement, Garrett leads them through the house's less populated areas, a warren of interconnected rooms and hallways. "We'll go up the back stairs," he says. Through the industrial-looking kitchen, there's a back door that sits at the bottom of a long, narrow, enclosed staircase.

Katarina takes a step backward, looking up. "So many stairs."

"So many," Garrett agrees. On the way up he stumbles and falls, laying himself out face down. He almost pulls Mary down with him. For a second she thinks he's passed out, but then he starts to laugh.

"Oh my god, are you okay? Oh god, we're so drunk." Katarina pulls ineffectually at his shirt.

Eventually, they make it to the second-floor landing. "My room's in this floor," Garrett says. "I think."

"Your room's *in* the floor? What are you, a rat? Ratty rat, in the frat?" Katarina giggles. "*Hey-ooo*, I made a rhyme! I'm a poet and didn't—"

"Would you shut the fuck up?" Garrett's definitely slurring. "*On* this floor. *On* it. You know what I fucking mean."

"Dude, simmer down, I was only . . . ugh." Katarina sways on her feet. "Oh shit," she says, clapping a hand to her mouth. "I need to . . . I'm gonna . . ."

"Bathroom's right there." Garrett points. "You puke anywhere but the toilet, you clean it up."

Katarina bolts, and a moment later Mary hears her retching through the open door. A true friend would make sure she's all right. Katarina will get mad at Elizabeth for abandoning her. *Good,* Mary thinks.

Garrett's lips, unpleasantly warm, land on hers. Heavy, alcoholic breath snakes down her throat and into her nose. Mary gasps and wrenches her face away.

"Everything okay?" He watches her narrowly, probably thinking she's too lucid, not pliable enough, to have been drugged. He's acting a little too with-it, himself, for Mary's liking.

"Yeah, you surprised me." Mary garbles her speech deliberately. "Where's your room, again?"

He smiles. "This way."

———

"I SHOULD GO see if K's all right."

In response to her twitch toward the closed door, Garrett's arms tighten around her. "In a little bit."

They aren't lying down yet, but they're on his bed. He kisses her neck. His hands on her are sweaty and purposeful.

Too purposeful. A worm of unease twists in Mary's belly.

"She's going to be sorry to miss this. She does love a threesome." Mary puts a tempting lilt into her voice, trying to draw him away from what's happening with the promise of something better.

"She's yakking. And it's not her I want. God, I'm so fucking in love with you."

Mary huffs a laugh.

"You don't believe me? I would literally kill someone to eat your pussy right now." But his kisses are slowing, his hands growing clumsy. She just has to wait him out.

"You should lie down," she says.

"I don't want to lie down." His voice sharpens alarmingly. He eases her shoulders to the mattress, and Mary lets him, despite the klaxons going off in her brain. "I can't believe I've got you here."

As if he didn't engineer this entire situation through black-mail. *As if Elizabeth would look twice at you,* Mary wants to say, but in-stead she goes limp under his weight.

"It's gonna be okay, Elizabeth. I'm gonna take care of you."

Shouldn't he be less coherent, less *conscious*? It figures that the drugs he gave her wouldn't even work. He sits up. She feels him watching her while she lies with her eyes closed, trying to look inert.

The bed shudders. There's a rustling of clothing and a sound that is unmistakably that of his pants dropping to the floor. He fumbles under her dress, his fingers trying to hook her underwear down over her hips.

She jolts upright, panic cutting off her air.

"It's okay, baby," he soothes, pressing her back down. "Go back to sleep. I've got you." He wants her to be a doll, a corpse, a body for him to work his will on.

"No," she says. "Wait."

"Just let me—"

"Stop it!"

He freezes at the sharpness, the *awareness*, in her voice. His face twists. There's no way this ends without either him being pissed or her being raped.

Mary knows which option she'll take. She slides past him and stands, adjusting her clothes.

"What the fuck is your problem?" He stumbles toward her but falls, pantsless, flat on his face. "What the—the fuck is wrong with me? What did you do?"

Mary backs toward the door. It's locked. She fumbles at the knob, the tiny latch within it, until it turns and the door springs open.

"Elizabeth!" Garrett bellows, reaching for his pants. "Come back here!"

Mary runs. She rounds a corner, then another. She hears Gar-

rett's pursuit, his growling voice and shuffling footsteps, over her
own ragged breaths.

This house is a maze. She can't remember the way back to the
stairs; all she sees are hallways lined with closed doors.

She sprints around another corner. At the end of the hall is a
glowing red exit sign and a propped-open fire door that leads to
the stairs they came up by. But he'll know where she went; he'll
overtake her in the stairwell.

"*Kill* this bitch," he says from somewhere behind. As quietly as
possible, she tries the doors she passes. Locked. Locked. Not even
the bathroom where Katarina went to puke is open, but the next
knob turns. She ducks inside a pitch-black room that smells of
dirty socks and closes the door behind her. Garrett's footfalls lum-
ber by.

Her breath leaks out in a long, shaky draft. She's safe, for now,
as long as he doesn't decide to double back. She needs to find her
way downstairs, grab Elizabeth, and get them both the hell out of
here.

Cracking the door open, she fades back at the sound of Garrett's voice, harsh and echoing, from the stairwell not twenty feet
away.

"You think you're so fucking smart."

There's barely a slur between syllables. He must have a super-
human tolerance. Mary's mistake was in not taking that possibility into account.

"Garrett?" a woman answers, sounding wary.

The voice is Mary's own.

24

ELIZABETH (MARY)

NOW

It was the smell that had gotten to her. People don't notice what their houses smell like while they're living in them, day in and day out. But go on a trip, especially one longer than a few days, and when you come back you're shocked that you could have missed it.

Elizabeth hasn't been gone long in chronological time, but it feels like an age since she walked across her own floorboards. Scent isn't just a sensory perception. It's memory, emotion. Coffee and soap from the kitchen, pine from the Christmas tree, almond from the organic wood polish Svitlana uses. A little bit of dog, despite twice-weekly cleanings. Her own jasmine perfume. Nate's cologne. They all have their own associations, mundane or sharply evocative. The smell of her house had brought tears to her eyes.

That emotional instability was probably why she gave in to the petty urge to needle Mary.

The bus she's riding back to Mary's neighborhood smells like bleach and bad breath. It's hard to believe she was just home. Even harder to believe that a day and a half ago, *she* was the woman in designer loungewear who could have the police at her house in fifteen minutes. She's already losing her identity.

She can't afford to panic. She needs to be more strategic, less reactive. Mary surprised her tonight. If the stakes weren't so high, Elizabeth would be proud of her for showing some backbone.

Her phone vibrates. It's a text from Nate, a nibble on the baited hook she dangled earlier. All she wrote was Hi. It's Mary. His response is more charged.

Hey sexy

She fights tears, the words blurring on the cracked screen. She underestimated how upsetting it would be to have a front-row seat to his hitting on someone else. But the wounds he's given her aren't new. She's so, so tired of the pain of them.

It had been Nate's idea, last spring, to open the marriage. Chrissy had seen him leaving a bar with a woman who looked like she was barely drinking age, and had taken video of it. When Elizabeth confronted him, at first he claimed nothing had happened—he'd just been flirting—and then, when Elizabeth pressed, he swore it had been a lapse, the worst mistake he'd ever made in his life. He'd *cried.*

Elizabeth had been taken aback and—yes—flattered by the storm of emotion he released when he thought he might actually lose her. Between the lines, she read the truth: he wanted more attention. If he didn't get it from her, he'd look elsewhere. She'd been raised to believe that in marriage, the wife accommodates her husband's needs. Her followers' value systems were worlds apart from the one in which she'd grown up, but their discourse about influencer and celebrity drama showed her that they were all too ready to judge the woman for whatever went wrong in a relationship. A divorce would have a real impact on her career.

So when Nate brought up the idea of them seeing other people, she had to consider it.

The thought of sharing her husband made her want to roar like a jealous lioness. But if losing him was the alternative, what could she do? She'd already tried being more present. When she gave up opportunities, he panicked that she'd slip into irrelevance, but if she worked too hard, he said things like *I feel so disconnected from you.* There was no happy medium.

Though she had misgivings, at first it seemed like it might work. It took some of the pressure off; Elizabeth was no longer the only one responsible for making Nate feel like a man. She kept the hurt folded up small inside her heart. Nate was the person she loved most, and even if she wasn't enough for him, she wanted him to be happy.

But *she* wasn't happy, and she wasn't made of stone. Lorne was right there and obviously willing. An open marriage went both ways, supposedly.

When she told Nate about her and Lorne, there was an epic fight, with tears on both sides. The end result was that their marriage once again became monogamous.

Supposedly.

Nate was just discreet enough not to get caught red-handed, and he had an explanation for everything. His phone had died. That woman was an actress he and Declan were considering casting. Why couldn't Elizabeth trust him? Trust was the foundation of a marriage. Didn't he do enough for her? Did she think all the goddamn tap-dancing he did on camera for her followers was because he liked the attention?

Elizabeth *wanted* to believe him. She wanted so badly for him to be the man she needed him to be.

You can convince yourself of anything if you're willing to lie.

Stripping away her self-deception was the point of this exercise. Seeking him out while wearing Mary's face was a test, and he failed.

She ignores the little voice telling her she's broken her own heart for nothing. Mary's harebrained scheme for vengeance has thrown the success of Elizabeth's own plans into doubt.

But Mary can be persuaded. The threats aren't what will sway her; she already knows about them, though Elizabeth was unnerved to hear they've escalated to vandalism. Dwelling on them, however, would only push Mary closer to finding out the main reason Elizabeth sent her the Empathyzer. If Mary learns her precious journals have been erased, she'll never let Elizabeth come back.

No, Mary needs to have her stupid fantasy of Nate destroyed. She needs to be shown, like Elizabeth was shown. Elizabeth will have to keep on breaking her own heart for a little longer.

A bleak, cloudy feeling descends on her as she lets herself into Mary's building. She planned to let herself cry when she got upstairs, but now she's not even sure if she'll be able to.

Miguel's at the mailboxes. She slips past, not having the energy to talk.

"Oh, hey," he says, turning. "Where are you coming from?"

It's painful seeing him when the last time she did, she was smug in her certainty of being home soon.

"Sorry. It's none of my business," he says, looking uncomfortable.

None of this is his fault. With an effort, she relaxes her expression into something approaching friendliness. "It's not that. I've just had a really long day."

He pauses, seeming to weigh something. Then he says, "You hungry?"

She hasn't eaten since the cinnamon rolls this morning, and Mary has no food in her apartment. An unreasonable anger at such poor planning bubbles up in Elizabeth's empty stomach. She would never let a guest go hungry in her home.

"I was just gonna make some fried rice, but I usually have a ton of leftovers. You're welcome to . . ."

"That sounds amazing. Thank you."

His thick brown eyebrows jump. Maybe she should have said no at first, to make sure he meant it.

"I don't want to put you out. I know it's late." Her stomach growls, audible to them both.

He waves a hand. "I'm a night owl. I'd appreciate the company." Maybe he is just being polite, but she's starving.

His apartment is warm, lamplight tinting it gold against the darkness outside, and it lifts the clouds inside her.

"Can I do anything?" She feels bad about imposing on him twice in one day, but she's a little surprised when he puts her to work chopping onions. Nate never lets her help while he's cooking; chopping vegetables is one of the things he says she does wrong.

The thought of Nate makes her close her eyes in pain.

"Are you okay? Did you cut yourself?" Miguel is looking at her with concern.

"No, I'm fine." She needs to talk about something besides herself. "How did you learn to cook?"

"I didn't, until I left home. My mom and aunts tried to teach me when I was a kid, but I was never interested until I actually had to feed myself." He gives a rueful grin. "Takeout gets pretty expensive. And then it was just video tutorials. I still need to get my mom to show me her tamale recipe. I don't get home as often as I'd like."

"Where's home?"

He gives her a strange look, and she realizes too late that this must be something Mary knows already. "Oh right, down South," she says. That much is apparent from the way he draws out his vowels. "My head's been all over the place the last couple of days." This is like working undercover. With amnesia.

"I bet. That cop ever show up to bother you again?"

She remembers Detective Johns' card in the drawer in Mary's apartment. "Not so far."

"Good. I've still got the video on my phone if you need it." He drops a pat of butter in a pan and lets it melt, then cracks two eggs and scrambles them.

Elizabeth's mind seizes on what he said. "Could I . . . see that video?"

"Sure. Just a sec." He removes the scrambled eggs to a plate, then puts in the vegetables and sautés one-handed while he retrieves his phone from his back pocket. He unlocks it and hands it to her as if it holds nothing he'd be ashamed for her to see.

Elizabeth goes into the other room, where the hiss of frying onions won't drown out the sound of the video. By the time she's watched the confrontation between Mary and the detective for the third time, her stomach is in knots.

I've got Garrett's people wondering where you were the night he passed.

Let me know if you decide to leave town.

She zooms in on Johns' face. He looks like he's aged more than seven years. And he looks dead serious about his suspicion that Mary was involved in Garrett's death.

It always comes back to Garrett Deegan. No wonder Mary hates Elizabeth so much. Nobody would be looking at Mary if not for what Elizabeth did that Halloween night.

She has to get back to herself.

Miguel carries out two bowls heaping with fried rice and sets them on the table where they ate this morning. "This is getting to be a habit, us eating together," he jokes.

The food steams, fragrant, but Elizabeth's lost her appetite. Still, she knows how to fake normality. She tries a bite and is surprised when her mouth waters in response. "Oh wow. What did you put in this? You can cook for me anytime."

Maybe it's not the flavor that tempts her as much as the feeling of being taken care of. And for no reason other than that he's kind and he wants to.

Men are never just kind, whispers the part of her that always tells the truth.

She looks up to find him watching her, a hopeful little smile on his face, and she realizes what she just said. How he took it.

Miguel, like every other man she's ever met, wants something from her.

An ally would be useful. Especially now, when she's stuck here, with Detective Johns after her.

Miguel has proven he's willing to help Mary, whether or not he was attracted to her before Elizabeth came onto the scene. She doesn't yet know what else he might be able to do for her, but she needs all the support she can get. She's never had any trouble getting men to bend over backward on her behalf.

She kind of hates that she thinks this way about people— about men—but there it is.

"Are you okay? You looked a little . . ." He grimaces at his phone, which is on the table.

She wonders what he'd say if she told him the truth. That she's stuck in a body that's not her own. That she did it to herself, trying to be clever, but Mary might as well have been the one to set the trap for her. He'd never believe it, no matter what his research area is.

"I just feel so powerless," she says truthfully.

He looks her in the eye. "Well, let me know if there's anything I can do. You don't have to deal with it all by yourself."

Her throat closes up. He must notice, because he starts talking about his plans to fly home to Florida in a few weeks. His whole extended family converges on his mom's house—she's the eldest of the sisters—and December is one of the only times of year when the weather is bearable down there.

They stay on safe subjects for the remainder of the meal, but the whole time Elizabeth's mind is working.

She's grateful to him. She was in despair before he provided her with a meal and conversation and sympathy. Using his interest in her isn't something a good person would do, but: desperate times. She needs a weapon in order to fight. Even if that weapon is just a renewed sense of her own power.

She'll be careful with Miguel, more careful than she was with Lorne. And really, she'd be giving him what he wants. Is that so wrong?

He's finished his food. She's not quite done with hers, but she stands, taking both their bowls. "Don't even think about trying to do the dishes. You cooked, I'll clean."

He leans back in his chair, raising his hands. "Hey, no argument here. Doing dishes is my least favorite thing. That's why everything I cook only needs one pan."

He still does the bulk of the cleanup. Then, gentlemanly, he walks her to the door. He leaves so much space between them that Elizabeth wonders if she misread him. Her perception must be warped from managing so many men with ulterior motives.

"I'm glad you came over," he says, smiling down at her, and the warmth in his eyes renews her hope. "We should, um, do this again." He glances at his feet, hair falling over his forehead. Before she can circle any more in her thoughts, she steps closer, goes up on her toes, and presses her mouth against his.

What surprises her most is that it's not calculation that spurs her, but actual tenderness. He's so *sweet*, with his pleasant half-Southern accent and his direct sentiments, and he's taken her terrible day and turned it into something almost positive.

His mouth is warm and tastes faintly of sesame, with an edge of red pepper. A rush goes through her as if all of her energy is flowing to the places where their bodies touch, where his hands rest on the small of her back and their lips slip softly together.

She shouldn't enjoy a kiss this much, especially in her state of mind. She pictures a valentine heart, splitting along the faint zigzag of a barely healed crack. But then Miguel's hands spread wide to touch as much of her back as possible. She finds herself doing the same thing, holding him closer. With Lorne, her mind never stopped calculating, even as her body responded. There was always that mental voyeur: Nate, angry and hurt like he hurt her.

She got off on that, especially after the open-marriage charade ended.

Now she pushes Nate out of her mind. This kiss is about no one but the two people engaged in it.

Miguel eases back, but she presses forward a little, opening her lips. She lets her tongue slip out and he meets it with his, everything so deliciously reciprocal. No clumsy escalation, no demanding tongue or wandering hands.

Finally, they pull apart. "Um," he says. His eyes look dazed behind his glasses.

"Sorry," she says, not sorry at all. Fireworks are going off inside her; she wonders if he can tell.

"No, it's, uh . . . I wasn't expecting that."

But you hoped, she thinks. There are guys who hide their impatience behind screens of niceness, and then there are men like Miguel, who won't make a move unless they're absolutely sure. Sometimes you have to be the one to go first, but once it's on, it's *on*. They're yours for as long as you want them.

25

MARY (ELIZABETH)

NOW

"Babe? You're not ready."

The voice pulls me from a fitful sleep just deepening after a restless night. I'm confused as to why there's a man in my apartment until I remember who and where I am.

My eyes won't stay open, try as I might to make them. The expensive mattress barely moves as Nate sits on the bed, but it feels like an earthquake. "Babe. We're going to be late."

The edge in his voice brings me closer to full consciousness.

"Okay. Okay," I say, my voice thick with sleep. "What are we doing, again?"

"You could try keeping up with your own calendar for once. What's wrong with you? Did you take a sleeping pill?"

"I . . . no. I'm getting up." I shove myself into a sitting position. I don't recall hearing Nate come in, so either he slept downstairs as promised or got home very late indeed. He still looks more rested than I feel, wearing a cream cable-knit sweater that makes me want to bury my face in his chest. "I'll be ready in fifteen minutes."

Nate runs his eyes over me in perusal. "Take thirty," he says, and stalks from the room.

———

AN HOUR LATER, we're in the gleaming kitchen classroom of a locally owned cookware shop, wearing matching aprons and learning how to bake the perfect sugar cookie.

"You don't want to overmix your batter," says Liv, our college-aged, preternaturally perky instructor. "You might think it's a good idea to beat it 'til every lump's smoothed out, but don't give in to the temptation." She sends Nate a wink on the word *temptation*. I watch his reaction, thrown back to Elizabeth's claim that he's a womanizer, but to my relief he ignores her obvious flirtation.

I can't tell if that's because he's faithful or just in a foul mood. "I've got enough video of this," he snaps. "Let's skip to the cookie cutter part. That and the decorating are going to look the best."

Wilting at his businesslike tone, Liv shuts off the stand mixer. "Of course. We've got dough prechilled in the fridge. I'll just roll it out for you."

While she sets up, Nate adjusts my phone on a tripod. According to Elizabeth's calendar, he and I have a full day of holiday cheer planned, starting with this private baking lesson. In the afternoon is ice-skating in the park. At dusk, we'll take a horse-drawn-carriage ride down Mansion Row to see the light displays. All to create content for sponsor agreements, of course. The theme is "Holiday clichés are good, actually!" and I'm getting paid more for this one day than I would have made cleaning apartments in a month.

That plus getting to spend the entire day with Nate should have me buzzing, if not for my worry over last night.

I stayed up until almost dawn going through Elizabeth's phone and computer. I was sure she'd sent that DM. I didn't know how she got it to land in my priority inbox, or why she would want me to confess to a crime on her behalf, but it couldn't be anyone else. Elizabeth Jordan has no enemies.

A look through her DM history and her email seemed to confirm this. They contained nothing more aggressive than spam and "Hello, pretty lady" overtures.

But then I checked her text messages. I didn't have to scroll back very far before I found the threats.

They came in from a series of unknown numbers, at different intervals—some hours apart, others days—but their gist was the same. I know what you did. I know what you're guilty of. Confess. Try harder, you can make them believe you. The latest came six days before the one last night. The earliest arrived three months ago. That one gave me the biggest shock:

I know it was you on Halloween, Elizabeth.

Someone has been threatening Elizabeth since well before I took over her body. Someone knows it was her that night, not me.

One of the earlier messages mentions me too. Did you know Mary's got enough evidence to take you down? You'd better hope no one listens to her.

So whoever sent these knew I'd been collecting documentation on the Empathyzer. It's not clear if they know about my personal accounts of our transfers, or if they're just trying to spook Elizabeth. It seems strange that they'd only use texts, but Hailey has access to Elizabeth's email and social accounts, so maybe Elizabeth deleted anything incriminating from those places.

"Babe, we're ready," Nate says, jarring me out of my thoughts.

We shoot what Liv assures us is perfect video, showing off the cookie cutters and decorating equipment to best advantage while engaging in sparkling husband-and-wife banter. But Nate's distracted, buried in his phone between takes, and he barely speaks to me unless he's being recorded.

His mood hasn't lifted by the time we make it onto the outdoor ice rink downtown. Mine sinks as well. The sun is out, but the wind cuts across the ice so fiercely, it brings tears to my eyes. The puffer jacket I'm supposed to be photographed in is cute and made of "partially recycled materials," whatever that means, but provides about as much warmth as a plastic bag. Lacing up my skates, I wonder how I'm supposed to look gorgeous with my nose and eyes running and my hair windblown.

Nate looks around. "Is Hailey meeting us here?"

"Was she supposed to?"

"She's your assistant. And I don't see anywhere to set up a tripod, do you? What's going on with you today?"

"I'm sorry. I'll text her."

Nate glides around the ice with athletic grace while we wait for Hailey to respond. I wobble near the edge of the rink, getting lapped by children half my size. I haven't been ice-skating since I was nine, when I chipped a tooth because my brother thought it would be funny to trip me when we played crack the whip.

After ten minutes, Nate scrapes out a hockey stop directly in front of me. "Well, we can't give up this collab. You'll have to call your photographer and see if he can come out on short notice." He spits out the word *photographer* like a curse. Suddenly I'm sure he knows the truth about Elizabeth and Lorne.

And after yesterday, there's no way Lorne will show up for me.

A thought jolts me. What if Lorne sent me that DM? What if he's the one who's been threatening Elizabeth?

It would make sense if she's confided in him at some point, or if he somehow found out. He's got a motive to harass her. I went through several months of texts between them, could trace the heating and cooling of their relationship.

The messages weren't blatant—no sexting or nudes—but many of them set up photo shoots I'm pretty sure were cover for hookups. In the last couple of months, it was mostly Lorne sending and Elizabeth ignoring the messages, or giving brief, tepid responses like *Not today* or *Sorry, that won't work for me.*

Lorne's desperation and resentment were clearly growing with the distance Elizabeth tried to put between them. It didn't occur to me to cross-reference the threats with the times she pushed him away the hardest, but I'll do that as soon as I have the chance.

I don't want it to be Lorne. He's too capable of hurting me.

I take out my phone, planning to fake a call and tell Nate there's no answer, but it's already ringing. Hailey! The screen shows a number instead of her name, but maybe she's calling from some other phone.

"Hello?"

"Ms. Jordan," says a familiar voice, one I've heard more than I cared to in recent days. "Glad I caught you. This is Detective Anthony—"

I don't hear the rest, because my ankles wobble and I crumple to the ground. My phone smacks onto the ice.

"Ms. Jordan? Are you still with me?" Johns says from the speaker.

Nate turns and, seeing I've fallen, skates up with a worried look on his face. Something, some instinct that doesn't want him talking to Johns, makes me scoop up the phone before he can touch it. "How did you get this number?"

"You filed a police report about a vehicle that was vandalized." A pause. "Spray paint on the hood? Is that correct?"

Why would a homicide detective be calling about Nate's car?

I take Nate's offered hand, getting carefully to my feet, and skate to a rink-side bench. By the time I get there, I've taken several cleansing breaths and gotten a tiny bit of perspective. Johns doesn't know who I really am. He is not, in fact, following me like an evil spirit. It's not in my interest to be a bitch.

"Yes," I say. "Sorry. I'm ice-skating and I fell."

"If you're hurt, Ms. Jordan, we can pick this up later—"

"No," I say, struck by the difference in his manner when speaking to someone with money and influence versus someone without. "I'm fine. Go ahead."

"The report says you're not aware of anyone who might have any kind of grudge against you or your husband. Is that right?"

Nate has joined me on the bench and is listening to my side of the conversation, so I try to say as little as possible. "Yes."

"You do know of someone with a grudge?"

"No," I say, flustered. "I meant, yes, that's correct. I'm not aware of anyone."

"So you've got no idea why someone might want to write 'Confess' on your husband's car. No business deals gone wrong? Maybe a woman he got a little too close to on a night out? Is your husband faithful, Ms. Jordan?"

"What?"

"I don't mean to give offense."

Jesus fucking Christ. "Of course he is," I snap. "If you don't have any more questions, I'll—"

"You've employed a photographer named Lorne Gagnon before, is that correct?"

Elizabeth tagged Lorne in the photos he took of her, so I can't very well lie. "Yes. Why?"

"Does he just take your picture, or do you have a social relationship as well?"

Somehow, Johns manages to make *social* sound vulgar.

"We're not friends," I say. "I barely know him."

"But you *were* friends with Garrett Deegan. Or acquaintances, at any rate."

This is moving too fast, in directions I can't predict or interpret. "What does Lorne have to do with Garrett?"

"Are you aware he's a drug dealer?"

"Lorne?"

"Yes. Lorne Gagnon."

"I—no."

"Never had him get you a little something for a night out?"

As if I'd admit that to a cop. I glance at Nate, remembering the coke he had the other night.

"Never."

Johns remains quiet, considering my answers. Or leaving an opening for me to reveal something else.

Finally he says, "Thank you, Ms. Jordan. You've cleared things up for me a great deal. Have a merry Christmas, now." He hangs up, with nothing any clearer that I can see.

Nate's eyes flash. "Who was that, and why were they asking you about that asshole?"

I don't think he'll take it well if I ask him which asshole he meant, so I tell him it was about the car.

"Do they think your photographer did the spray-painting? A little freelance art on the side?" Nate rubs a hand over his lips, stands, almost falls, visibly remembers he's wearing ice skates, and sits back down hard on the bench. "That little shit. I'm gonna kill him."

"Nate, don't—"

"I knew you'd stick up for him." He fixes a blistering glare on me. "Seeing as how you two have history. *Is* it history?"

My heart thrashes in my chest. *Yes* is all I have to say. *Of course it is.* But that would be admitting it happened in the first place. No matter what Elizabeth got up to when she was in this body, I can't bring myself to do that.

Making a small sound of disgust in his throat, Nate unlaces his skates with resentful little jerks. As soon as he has his boots back on, he gets up and walks away without a backward glance.

"Nate!" I try to follow him, but his strides are too long and emphatic for me to have any chance of catching up in my skates. I sink back down on the bench. The sun reached its apex hours ago. As it sinks behind the skyscrapers the temperature drops, but that's not the reason for my shivering. Or my tears.

I can't sit out here freezing and crying. I remove my skates with trembling hands, then find a restaurant nearby where the server looks at me strangely when I order a coffee.

"I could make a pot," she says, smiling. She's young, her short hair dyed blue, with a tattoo of a gemstone-eyed snake winding up her arm.

"You don't need to go to all that trouble." I watch her blush at my smile. Elizabeth's face still has its magic, even puffy and red nosed. "Could I have a glass of . . . oh, whatever red you recommend?"

"My pleasure." She sashays toward the bar. Out the window, there's no sign of Nate, who drove today. I'll have to get a rideshare home.

My stomach sinks when I think of how much work I'll have to do to get back to where we were. What if he doesn't forgive me? Fucking Elizabeth. Fucking Lorne. Why couldn't they have kept it in their pants?

And why did Johns ask me about Lorne right before he mentioned Garrett?

The server comes back with my wine and to tell me the specials. "That sounds good," I say after barely hearing the first one. I don't feel like eating, but I need a reason to sit and let my mind work.

I think back over my conversation with Johns. I'll reread Lorne and Elizabeth's messages, but first I try to remember everything I know about Lorne, every word he said to me when he came to the house.

By the time my food arrives, I have it.

It was right before his parting shot. *We're done,* he said, but the look on his face said different. And after that:

You never did thank me for solving your problem.

It could mean anything. Maybe Elizabeth had a photography-related dilemma. Or the condom broke and he picked up the morning-after pill.

But Garrett died of a fentanyl overdose. Lorne knows how to

get drugs. A man who carries a gun is open to at least the possibility of violence, and the rawness in his eyes whenever he looked at Elizabeth's face told me he'd do anything she asked. Or would have, before yesterday.

There are plenty of reasons Garrett wouldn't be Elizabeth's favorite person. I was shocked last year when I saw pictures of them online, grinning together like the old friends they absolutely weren't. But would she want him dead after all this time? Would she put her lover up to the job? Without more information, it's a stretch to believe.

But she did almost kill him once.

26

Mary's voice—or rather, Elizabeth, *speaking with* Mary's voice—
echoes just like Garrett's, which means Elizabeth is in the stairwell with him. But why would she be there? The upper floors
are forbidden to everyone except fraternity brothers and their
guests.

"You fucked up," Garrett snarls. "You were supposed to drug
her, not me."

Mary's paralysis breaks. She pulls open the door of her hiding
place and runs for the stairs.

"You're the one who's fucking up," Elizabeth says, full of bra-
vado. "We said to leave us alone—"

There's a blur of movement through the doorframe, and a cry.
Then a series of thumps that, sickeningly, can't be anything other
than those of a body falling down the stairs. Silence.

"Oh no," Mary breathes, picturing her own broken body at the
bottom. She runs to the door and exhales in relief when she sees
Elizabeth on the landing, a hand pressed to her mouth.

Elizabeth turns. The expression on her sharp features is not
one of horror or relief, but leftover fury.

It crumbles as Mary watches. "Shit," Elizabeth says through her fingers. "Shit," and she starts to cry.

———

"HE CAN'T BE dead," Elizabeth moans. "He's not dead, is he? I can't look." Her face is buried in the glitter-dusted junction of Mary's neck and shoulder. Mary strokes her short hair.

Garrett lies crumpled by the exit door at the bottom of the long, long stairway. He's not moving.

"He attacked me, Mary. I—I was just trying to push him away, I swear. It was an accident."

Under the circumstances, it seems callous for Mary to remind Elizabeth not to use her name.

You're in shock, says a quiet voice in her head, *and that's normal. But you need to* handle *this.*

"We have to get out of here before anyone sees us." She takes Elizabeth's arm, trying to draw her out of the stairwell and into the hallway. They'll find another way down. The main stairs. Someone might see them, but it's a risk they'll have to take.

Elizabeth, shocked, resists. "We can't just leave him there."

Why not? Mary's about to ask, but Elizabeth doesn't know the extent of his depravity, and Mary can't tell her about it. She can't ever tell her the truth.

"Stay here," Elizabeth says. "You be lookout." Tears are still streaming down her cheeks, but she presses her lips together and heads down the stairs without making a sound.

"Elizabeth!" Mary hisses. "We'll get him help. We'll call from one of those emergency phones outside." But Elizabeth doesn't listen. She leans over him, probably checking for a pulse. Her body blocks his so Mary can't see what she's doing.

Drunken laughter echoes from the kitchen up the stairwell. Elizabeth jumps and sprints back upstairs, shoes clattering. "Go, go!" she whisper-screams, motioning at the fire door, but Mary waits until Elizabeth gains the landing and they can go together. They're halfway down the hall when they hear someone shout, "Oh my god! Did that guy fall down the stairs?"

———

"YOU BELIEVE ME, right?"

They're back in the dorm, back in their own bodies. The room is wrapped in darkness. Elizabeth's voice issues from her loft bed. Mary sits on the floor under the window. The rain taps against the glass, and Mary concentrates on her simple relief that she's no longer out in it.

"You believe it was an accident?" Elizabeth sounds like she might be crying again.

Of course Mary believes her. For Garrett to have run into the woman he thought was responsible for his humiliation, at that exact moment, was nothing more than spectacularly bad luck. Mary-caliber luck.

But she can't get the words out. Elizabeth's secret plans to move out are on her mind. They're not on a level with what happened tonight, but they're a betrayal nonetheless. Proof that Elizabeth has no problem hiding things from her when it's convenient.

That doesn't matter. What matters is that they're friends, and friends stick together in a crisis. The desperate thoughts that went through Mary's mind during their walk home, about not wanting to give up transferring, now seem selfish and petty. Her best friend needs her support. That's the important thing.

She opens her mouth to tell Elizabeth she knows she acted in self-defense. That she's not alone in this.

What comes out is, "Why were you upstairs?"

A short pause. "What?"

"When you ran into Garrett in the stairwell. Were you coming down from the third floor? What were you doing up there?"

Too late, Mary realizes she's opened herself up to the same question. But Elizabeth just says, "I had to pee, and all the downstairs bathrooms had a huge line."

The delivery's a little too pat, the excuse a little too perfect. Mary's intuition waves its feelers, telling her something's off.

Elizabeth says, "I know this could put you in a bad spot if anyone saw. But I'm pretty sure no one did except Garrett. If he's even still . . ."

Mary's stomach drops. It's a testament to the chaos of the night that it didn't even occur to her until now. From a witness's perspective, it wouldn't be Elizabeth who pushed Garrett, but Mary.

"Even if he's okay, he won't remember anything," Elizabeth says quickly. "People forget traumatic experiences all the time, right? Like car crashes. If he does remember, we'll figure something out. I won't let you take the fall, I promise."

"Take the fall," Mary repeats, faintly. "Nice one."

After an instant of shocked silence, Elizabeth starts to giggle. Mary does too. They laugh helplessly until all the tension has leaked out of Mary's body and she slides down the wall, sideways, to lie on the rug. She should go to bed, but she doesn't have the strength to move.

With a final giggle, her laughter expires. There's nothing from Elizabeth's bed but thick silence.

"I believe you," Mary says.

27

MARY (ELIZABETH)

NOW

I leave my server a generous tip. When she picks up my credit card slip she says, "Can I just say, I follow you, and I love your whole thing so much? You're like, peak comfort internet." She makes it sound like Elizabeth's life is a show she watches.

I could summon a rideshare to get home, but my feet take me to the nearest subway stop. Public transit might be grimy and crowded, but I've been dependent on it for years and it's familiar. I need that right now.

On the train, I revisit Elizabeth's text message inbox. I'm not quite ready to discard my theory that Lorne's behind the threats, though I can't find a pattern between his and Elizabeth's ups and downs and the timing of the messages. Nor is there a smoking-gun directive to Lorne from Elizabeth, ordering Garrett's death.

If she asked him to get rid of Garrett, she did it in person.

What if Elizabeth had Lorne kill Garrett with an overdose, and now he's got that to hang over my head? Then I'll really be screwed.

But I still can't find proof that she took such a risk. Once I scroll back to before Garrett died, I find a surprising number of texts between him and Elizabeth, but they don't tell me much. They're similar to her exchanges with Lorne: brief and mainly setting up in-person meetups. Only instead of fake photo shoots they're brunches, happy hours, and Elizabeth's influencer parties. In one, she arranges to help Garrett shop for a gift for his assistant, which sounds innocent until I realize there's no way in hell he was holding down a job at that point in his downward slide.

Were Elizabeth and *Garrett* having an affair?

The train goes around a sharp curve, causing one of the tourists standing next to me to stumble into my shoulder. It knocks some sense into me. There's no way she'd be screwing Garrett Deegan. He repulsed her even before Halloween, and afterward she'd have gone out of her way to avoid him.

It's suspicious that they hung out so frequently in the weeks leading up to his death, especially in situations where it was just the two of them.

Garrett knew Elizabeth and I could inhabit each other. I always assumed he'd never figured out that we had used the Empathyzers that night, and that was one reason it had been so easy for the Deegans to blame me—because he didn't throw any doubt on my guilt. But what if he knew, or suspected, that Elizabeth had been the one who pushed him? What if he told her that, before he met his end?

Elizabeth might have panicked. She might have devised a plan to rid herself of Garrett, then escape the consequences by starting a new life in my body. Joke's on her, right? She never realized I'd end up as the prime suspect, and her visit to the house last night was buyer's remorse.

Except I'm not sure Mary Burke is the prime suspect in Garrett's death anymore. Johns might be getting pressure from Garrett's parents to make whatever arrest he can, and he's following other leads too. And in my head I can't make the idea harmonize, that Elizabeth would give up her entire life out of desperation. She's too in love with herself. Too confident—with reason—that things will always work out in her favor. No. She had a reason for sending the Empathyzer, one besides her little sting operation on Nate, but escape wasn't it.

My train stop is only a few blocks from Elizabeth's house. She gets residential idyll *and* convenience, goddamn her. But as soon as I turn the corner onto her street, I realize my mistake. Every shadow could be an attacker. My boots clatter on the pavement, more loudly as I pick up my pace, and the echo sounds like someone following me. By the time I fling myself into the house, my heart's pounding like it wants to escape my body. I lock the door behind me and lean against it, listening to my own shaking breath.

You think you're safe in that glass house? You're not safe.

———

NATE'S NOT HOME. He hasn't called or texted. Hailey finally responds to the message I sent from the ice rink earlier. She's so sorry; her phone died; does she need to reschedule the carriage ride Nate and I seem to have missed?

I pace, stewing. Before Elizabeth sent me the Empathyzer, she was receiving threats from someone who knew she'd been the one to push Garrett down the stairs on Halloween. The threats started after Garrett died, so they couldn't have been from him. Someone else knew.

Someone else *knows.*

And that person is invested in making sure Elizabeth pays for her sins. Which, since I'm her, means that I'll wind up paying for them yet again.

Why wasn't she scared? I once knew her better than anyone else did. Social media is a performance, but it's hard for me to believe I wouldn't have seen some sign. I was watching her so closely, preparing to slip into her life, and I never suspected.

You're not safe. I wonder if Elizabeth considered the messages empty threats. Maybe I'm overreacting.

But I don't think so. I think the threats are connected to why she sent me the Empathyzer.

My instincts have been wrong before. I find myself wishing I could talk to her. That we could compare notes, figure this out. Be honest with each other for once. But allyship, let alone friendship, is not something we'll ever have again.

28

Elizabeth skips class the day after Halloween. Mary can't. She feels awful—in addition to metabolizing whatever Elizabeth drank last night, she's working through an unusually vicious post-transfer hangover—but if she wants to keep her peerless GPA and her scholarship, she has to show up.

She can't pay much attention to the biomechanics lecture, because two girls in front of her spend the entire period whispering about the goings-on at Garrett's fraternity's house last night.

"It was actually kind of traumatizing," says one of the girls, who has her black hair in two French braids.

"I can imagine," says the other, with blond beach waves.

"I was in the yard and I could hear him screaming all the way out there."

Mary is pretty sure Braids is exaggerating, if not outright lying. There was no screaming. Still, she leans closer, pretending to be absorbed in taking notes.

"I saw him on the stretcher when they were bringing him to the ambulance," Braids goes on. "He wasn't moving. And the cops were questioning *everyone*."

"What did they say happened?" Beach Waves asks.

"I don't know, but they obviously thought something was shady."

"Like someone tried to kill him or something?"

"Or, like, some kind of altercation. His parents are superrich. Maybe someone was trying to—I don't know—extort them or something? I don't even know. But he's in the ICU. I think he's paralyzed." Braids takes a wad of gum from her mouth and absently sticks it to the underside of her desk. "Like, from the neck down. He wasn't moving *at all*. I thought he was dead, to be honest."

After class ends, Mary has to wait for her legs to stop shaking before she can leave the lecture hall.

The cops were questioning everyone.

If anyone saw Mary and Elizabeth, they're both in big trouble.

Mary is walking home when a text comes through on her phone. She scrabbles for it with the thought that Elizabeth might be sending news, but it's from Nate.

Nate Jordan, whose number she's had in her phone since the first night she and Elizabeth transferred, but who has never contacted her until today.

> Hey

Heat floods her face. She doesn't notice she has stopped walking until a girl, staring at her own phone, runs into her from behind.

"You're not the only person on the sidewalk, you know," the girl says, glaring until Mary moves to the grass.

Why would Nate Jordan, for whom she's quietly pined from afar for most of a year, be texting her now? And what is this "Hey" shit? What is *with* guys?

Hey yourself, she types, then backspaces and types Hi.

In the six minutes that follow—she keeps track—she continues toward the dorm while sifting through the possibilities, until an idea occurs that freezes the breath in her lungs. Nate is Garrett's fraternity brother. Even though they don't seem close, he would naturally be upset about Garrett getting injured. He wants more information about what happened. If he's texting *her*, that means he suspects she had something to do with it.

"You need to *move*." A guy bumps her shoulder. She's stopped in the middle of the path again. She goes to stand under a tree.

Did Nate see Elizabeth—see *Mary*—upstairs last night?

She's hyperventilating by the time his next messages come through.

> Last night was fun
>
> I mean, considering. I actually slept through most of the craziness
>
> Did you get caught up in that at all?

Mary lets out her breath. Nate doesn't suspect her.

Or he does, and he's trying to draw her out.

She starts to type a reply but keeps having to delete it. If she mentions Garrett, that makes her look guilty. If she doesn't, it makes her look callous. Finally she settles on I left early, but I heard about what happened with Garrett. Is he going to be ok??

> He's going to need surgery I think? He fractured one of his vertebrae and some ribs and messed up his shoulder pretty bad. Plus he has a concussion. Those stairs are a fucking deathtrap tbh. I feel for the guy. That could have been any one of us being drunk and stupid & unlucky

Despite the litany of injuries, Mary breathes a little easier. It sounds like Garrett's fall is being treated as an accident. If that's the case, it means Garrett hasn't related any memories of what led up to it.

Maybe she and Elizabeth are in the clear.

I feel bad for him too, Mary replies. She doesn't—Garrett deserves every bruise and fracture, as far as she's concerned—but it's the minimum socially acceptable reaction. Her inappropriate brain quickly moves on to what it really wants, which is to seize this opportunity to get closer to Nate.

Her brain's got nothing. She doesn't want to keep talking about Garrett, but changing the subject too abruptly will make her seem like a psychopath.

Another message comes in from Nate. I am sooooo hungover . . . sorry for being so wasted last night

She stares at her screen, confused. She and Nate didn't talk last night. She would have remembered; she stores up their tiniest interactions like treasure.

Then, finally, it hits her. The reason he's texting. She can't believe it took her this long to get it—except she's exhausted and hungover and frightened, so actually she can believe it. Elizabeth must have spoken to him at the party. He's not really reaching out to *Mary* at all.

Annoyance licks at her insides. This is just like Elizabeth: being told no, then doing the thing anyway.

"I *said* I didn't need any help," Mary says out loud. A guy walking by glances at her, then away.

Another text comes in from Nate. In case you couldn't tell, I was very into what was happening

The coldness starts in her stomach and spreads quickly through her limbs. She freezes, as if being still will keep the revelation from shattering her. But she can't stop herself from reading the words that appear on her phone.

That thing where you bit my lip was superhot

You're secretly kind of an animal aren't you?

Nausea breaks over her in a wave and she braces her hand on the tree next to her, leaning over its roots. She spits, but nothing else comes out.

In her other hand, the phone pulses and pulses.

All she can see is Elizabeth. With Nate. In *her* body. Using it.

The trunk of the oak that supports her is three times as big around as her body. It's been here a hundred years, easy. Seen the felling of its companions, the construction of walking paths and buildings, generation after generation of students streaming by. Years of protests and celebrations. It has been a silent witness to innumerable broken hearts. Mary's thoughts don't usually go in such poetic directions, but she fancies she can feel a slow kind of sympathy filtering through the rough bark.

She snatches her hand away and checks the new messages on her phone.

U doing anything later?

You should come over

I'll be more sober this time ☺

The ice holding her in place steams away. Heat flushes her cheeks. She thought Garrett had made her feel powerless, but now she truly knows what violation feels like.

She begins to walk, fast, weaving around people as class change fills the sidewalks, her steps growing bigger and bigger until she's practically running. Like a red line of rage is leading her home.

29

ELIZABETH (MARY)

NOW

It takes two days for Elizabeth to build up her defenses enough to reply to Nate's text. The messages he sends in return make her want to throw up and cry at the same time, but she encourages him. They start up an exchange. The more proof she can gather that her life is hollow at its core, the less Mary will want it.

In theory, anyway.

Nate wants her—wants Mary—to meet him, to finish what they started outside that bar. He's so focused on conquest. If he got what he's after, Elizabeth doubts he'd ever contact her again. She puts him off, keeping her language promising but vague, both to seem more like Mary and because his is obscene enough for both of them.

Sexting with him is bad enough. But the worst part, emotionally, is when she brings up his wife and he says, She won't be a problem. You think this is the first time I've done this?

It's out of character for her husband, this callousness on display. Or maybe she's just never gotten to see this side of him. She's gullible as shit, he goes on. Whenever she gets suspicious I whine about how she doesn't trust me and she calms right down. Then I stroke her ego a little bit and she's good.

It's as though he feels safe to let his resentment out with someone who hates his wife as much as Mary does. Which leads her to believe that Nate must hate her a little bit too.

Try to let him lead you, honey, Elizabeth's mother had said on their wedding day. She'd been worried that Elizabeth, with her success, was upsetting the natural order of things. Maybe she knew more about the nature of men than her daughter had given her credit for.

So . . . what are you wearing? Nate messages, with a winky-face emoji. They've been texting for a few days, and he's started pestering her for nudes.

Cringe, Elizabeth responds, but she adds a smiling eye roll.

Are you naked?

She's got layers on every part of her body, trying to keep warm in Mary's frigid apartment, but she replies, Maybe.

They go back and forth. He sends her a dick pic, and she asks for one with his face in it. He obliges with a smirking selfie, sprawled on the couch in the man cave, dick in hand. He should look stupid—he *does* look stupid—but it still makes a part of her want him in the same old way. She hates that he can do that to her.

But it's more proof.

Elizabeth always planned to excise Nate from her life when she got back. Getting a firsthand look at his cheating was going to give her the push she needed. But now she finds herself examining the rest of her life too.

Being Mary gives her an odd sense of perspective. On one hand, she's gaining an intimate understanding of the importance of money, security, influence. She can barely buy food, and she has no idea how she'll pay Mary's rent if she's still here on January first. She has no defense against Detective Johns, who could show up at any time with an arrest warrant. She misses her work, and the assurance that thousands of people are only as far away as her phone. That they're focused on her, wanting to be like her.

On the other hand, what's the point of work, except to keep her busy and her followers engaged? Engaged in what? She's always thought of her content as a welcome escape for people, but what's it called when someone's whole life is unreal? Madness—that's what.

There's something freeing about not having to think of every moment in her life as potential content. Not having to worry about how people see her.

It's funny that she can hold these two thoughts equally prominent in her mind. *I like not having to worry about what people think* can coexist with *I hate not having strangers love me.* Being Mary must be making her smarter. Or maybe trying so hard to prove to Mary that her life is empty has shown her where its hollow places are.

Her work has given her financial stability and independence, but she's been so focused on moving up in the world that her priorities have gotten skewed. She doesn't even talk to anyone from college anymore, aside from Katarina and Nate. Friends have become content and competitors. They're tools rather than human beings. No wonder Nate thinks it's okay to use her.

E won't always be the one getting all the attention, he texted her the other day, when they were talking about how many times he'd cheated on his wife. She's not as special as she thinks she is. People are going to find that out one day soon.

Mary's phone vibrates with a new message, and Elizabeth steels herself. But it's Miguel, not Nate, asking if she wants to grab dinner at an Indian place in the neighborhood.

She hasn't seen him since their kiss, though she's thought about it enough. Relived it. Relished the memory of his warm mouth on hers, his intuitive grasp of what she wanted. That's exactly why she told him she wasn't feeling well yesterday morning when he texted that he'd made more cinnamon rolls and would be happy to bring some up. Why she tells him she's busy now, though her stomach is growling and there's nothing but oatmeal.

That, and the guilt. He doesn't deserve to be her tool.

As soon as she'd left his apartment, she remembered the words Mary had once flung at her. *He deserves to know who he really hooked up with.*

Miguel thought he was kissing Mary Burke. She keeps trying to justify it to herself: it was just a kiss! He enjoyed it! She didn't even break her and Mary's old rule against having sex while transferred. It wasn't the same as what she'd done with Nate—though Mary blew that out of proportion too.

Every first kiss with someone new is different. With Lorne, it was scorching and desperate. With Miguel, it felt warm and friendly and, above all, safe. Yet it lit a fire inside her that's still burning, even as she tries to ignore it. She's sorry she'll never get another first kiss with him.

Her first kiss with Nate didn't feel safe at all.

———

IT WASN'T PLANNED. She'll go to her grave saying that.

She hadn't gone upstairs to pee, as she later told Mary, but to fix her witch costume. The cheap black dress kept ripping more than she wanted it to. She didn't want to show the world Mary's underwear. Mary didn't have very nice underwear.

The music from the party throbbed through the floor, but the second story was deserted. Still too early for the brothers to start bringing their hookups upstairs, Elizabeth guessed. Wandering the halls, she found a large mirror mounted on a wall. She was fumbling for the safety pins she'd had the foresight to tuck into her bag when she heard a voice behind her.

"Hey! You're not supposed to be up here."

"Aahh!" She whirled around; it was Nate. The tide of adrenaline receded. "Sorry. I was trying to pin my costume, and drunk people kept running into me downstairs, and—"

"I'm just messing with you. Need me to hold your witch hat?"

"That would be helpful." She had to tilt her head up to smile at him. Inches taller even when she was herself, he towered over her now.

She understood why Mary had a crush. He was gorgeous, all cut-glass jawline and long eyelashes. He was dressed as some sort of glam rock pirate, which only heightened his magnetism.

"I've always had a thing for witches," he said. "I used to listen to the Broadway recording of *Wicked* over and over when I was in middle school."

Elizabeth raised an eyebrow. "You were a theater kid?"

"Played Oberon senior year." He made a face. "I should've gotten Puck, but they gave it to a girl."

"Wow." Elizabeth cast about for something to say. She hadn't been allowed to watch secular plays when she lived with her parents—especially not anything about fairies or witchcraft—but she'd seen some of the memes. "So . . . Glinda or Elphaba?"

"Definitely Elphaba. She's more the Platonic ideal of a witch, wouldn't you say?"

Elizabeth giggled, reflecting too late that Mary wouldn't have cracked a smile. She'd have been wooden with terror at being alone with her crush. Not because he was threatening, but because she'd be afraid of choking. And then fear of choking would become a self-fulfilling prophecy.

Elizabeth had never been intimidated by cute boys; they were just people, like everyone else. Nate had clearly had more than a bit to drink, making him loose and smiley.

He moved behind her. "Let me get that for you." She'd been twisting herself into a pretzel trying to access a long rip in the back of her dress.

"Are you sure?" She meant, *Are you sure you're not too drunk?*

"Totally." He set her witch's hat on his own head and tried a cackle, which made her giggle again.

She handed a safety pin over her shoulder. Their eyes met in the mirror, the contact sparking inside of her.

She dropped her gaze as he pinned the tear in her dress. He didn't touch her, but she could feel the warmth of his hands, millimeters from her skin.

"Thanks," she said. He stayed where he was instead of stepping back. She could have turned around and kissed him without doing more than going up on her toes.

Mary had said no.

But she'd vetoed Elizabeth seeking him out and cultivating him on purpose, not seizing a chance that fell into her hands.

Once again she met his slightly unfocused gaze in the mirror. She could feel alcohol working in her too, making her feel like anything might happen, and she could let it, and it would be okay.

She couldn't get a full breath. She let her weight fall back, into his chest. If he stepped away, she'd act like it was just clumsiness, but the fingertips of his right hand lit on the side of her neck. She leaned into the touch, watching his head follow his hand down. His lips traced the path laid out by his fingers.

Her eyes fell shut. Elizabeth could lay the groundwork, and as long as she was honest about what she'd done, Mary would understand. She had to. It wasn't as if she'd ever have made a move herself.

His mouth pressed harder on her neck, his arms coming around her from behind. He sighed into her skin. "You feel good," he murmured as he laid little kisses from her neck to her bare shoulder, moving the strap of her dress aside so he could kiss that place too. It caused a pleasant swoop low in her stomach. He turned her around, tipped her chin up, and kissed her. His mouth was warm and masterful, his hands in her hair just rough enough. The rush of feeling made her gasp.

"This okay?" he asked.

"Yes." The word came out on a breath, before she could think. But it was okay, wasn't it? Kissing was allowed.

Not with him. But she didn't put a stop to it.

"So . . . you want to go up to my room?"

"I don't want to have sex." She wouldn't break the rules.

"Whatever you want."

She had one more test. "Do you know what my name is?"

He laughed. "Elphaba, right?"

She laughed too, but removed his hands from her waist, where they'd migrated. "You don't get to make out with me unless you know my name."

He put his hands back. "Tell me what it is. I won't forget."

"You already did once."

"I won't now. Promise." His hand had moved into her hair again, his teeth closing lightly on her earlobe. She shivered.

And told him Mary's name.

30

"Why did you do it?"

Elizabeth, lying on her loft bed, keeps her eyes glued to her phone. "Do what?" She sounds bored, which makes Mary grit her teeth.

"Come down here."

Now Elizabeth looks at her. "Mebs, I'm tired," she whines.

Mary's fury ratchets up another notch. "If you wanted to fuck Nate Jordan, why didn't you do it as yourself? Why drag me into it?"

Elizabeth sits up too fast and hits her head on the ceiling. With a wince, she raises her hand to the already-forming bruise, hiding her eyes.

"We didn't have sex," she says.

"That's not what the texts I just got from him say!"

"I don't know why he would say that."

"He wants me to go over to his house today and do it again. He was 'very into what was happening.'" Mary does air quotes, her temper rising as she sees the corner of Elizabeth's mouth kick up in a self-satisfied little smirk. "It would be bad enough if you'd done it the normal way. Was this some kind of thrill for you? Proving you could still bag him with the handicap of being me?"

"*No.*" Elizabeth climbs down from the loft and faces Mary. "I'm

telling you the truth. Nate and I didn't have sex. He was too drunk."
She claps her hand over her mouth. "I mean, I was only going to
make out with him anyway. I was doing it for you. I was trying to
help you."

"Please. I bet it was *torture*, hooking up with a cute guy for the
benefit of your ugly friend who never asked for it. In fact, I specifically remember saying I *didn't* want you to do anything like that. I
love how you're trying to twist this into you doing me a favor.
That is so . . . *you*."

"I was going to tell you, but I forgot. With everything."

Mary pushes air through her teeth. "Like you were going to
tell me you're moving out?"

Elizabeth's face goes still.

"I found out from Katarina. When we went to the club a couple
of weeks ago."

"They had a room open up in their house," Elizabeth says. "I
still have to share, but it's half of what the dorm costs."

"Like you need to worry about paying rent."

"I *could* pay it, though. With the sponsorships I've been getting,
I could actually cover it myself. I wouldn't have to be dependent
on my parents. You know I've been wanting to get out from under
them. We'll still be *friends*, Mary. We just won't be living in each
other's laps. We're literally in each other's *bodies* half the time! I
knew you would act like this, that's why I—"

"You told her I liked Nate," Mary says, her voice shaking.

"Why should it be a secret? If you ask me, you've got a few too
many secrets." Elizabeth's eyes harden as if Mary's the one who's
done something wrong.

"I guess now I know what you were doing upstairs last night.
Don't you think he deserves to know who he really hooked up
with?"

Elizabeth goes pale. "He won't believe you if you tell him. No
one will."

"What are you saying?"

Silence falls between them. Cold spreads through Mary's chest as the implication sinks in.

"Don't you dare," she whispers. "Don't you dare try to pin it on me."

Elizabeth's lips tremble. "I'm your *friend*, Mary. I would never."

Mary doesn't believe her.

Rage beats in her temples. She might rise out of her body with it. To ground herself, she walks to the window and places her hand on its cold glass.

She knows how this goes. They went through it after Elizabeth took it upon herself to break things off with Zeke. Mary gets rightfully angry; then Elizabeth freezes her out until Mary comes crawling back and Elizabeth accepts her apology like the gracious fucking queen she is.

Not this time. They're finished.

Elizabeth comes to stand beside her. Out of the corner of her eye, Mary sees her raise her hand, as though she'd touch her, try to smooth things over. Pretend it never happened.

"I used to be so flattered that someone like you would even bother with me."

Elizabeth jerks her hand back at Mary's tone.

"But now I see who you really are. You're jealous because I have something going for me besides being pretty." Mary feels a lightening in her chest as she pokes at Elizabeth's main insecurity. "You can't even own who you are. You have to create this fake person. You'll be pretending for the rest of your life."

Elizabeth barks out a laugh. "You're a good one to talk about pretending. At least I didn't go upstairs with a guy I hate." She takes in the reaction on Mary's face. "Yeah, K said something. What were you doing up there with him?"

"Don't you dare judge me," Mary says. "You don't know anything about it."

"So tell me why you went up there."

That's one thing Mary can't do. She'll never confide in Elizabeth again. "You said everything would be okay. But you were full of shit like always."

"Mebs, I don't know what you're—"

"I should have just let him fuck you." The words are horrible, they aren't true, but it gives Mary a mean thrill to say them. "It would have made things a hell of a lot easier."

Elizabeth's dusting of freckles stands out on her white face. Her hand rises, so fast that Mary thinks she might slap her.

Instead, she whirls around and runs out the door.

NATE GETS PETULANT when Mary won't reply to his texts. He starts with Sooooo are you coming over or what? and ends, two hours and half a dozen unanswered messages later, with OK well have fun dying alone with your cats and your vibrator I guess. I was going to throw you a pity fuck but fuck it.

Mary always knew Nate would never see her as anything but a hookup, if he saw her at all. It still hurts to have it confirmed.

Days go by, and she and Elizabeth don't speak. No one else knows why they're fighting, so naturally they take Elizabeth's side. Once again, Mary is friendless. She knows why Elizabeth's not speaking to her. The way she handled Garrett was unforgivable, and they can't come back from it. But Elizabeth doesn't seem to grasp that her behavior with Nate was just as bad, in its own way.

Mary stays away from their room as much as possible. Surely they can avoid each other until the end of term, and then Elizabeth will move out and it will be as if their friendship never existed.

That's if Mary manages to stay in school. What she'd explain to Elizabeth, if she thought she'd listen, is that she gave up her future to keep Elizabeth safe. Garrett will tell his aunt about the

Empathyzers, if he hasn't already. Mary will lose her job, her scholarship, everything that matters. It's only a matter of time.

She's in the library, running her eyes over the same line in her notes for the tenth time, when Elizabeth pulls out the chair next to hers. The legs scrape over the floor, drawing dirty looks from the people around them.

"They have cameras," Elizabeth whispers. She's breathing hard, as if she ran here. Her hair is wild.

Mary stares at her. "What are you talking about?"

"The frat house! They have security cameras. Video. From Halloween." A stricken look comes over Elizabeth's face. "I have to go." She runs out of the library, leaving her chair pushed away from the table.

That's when Mary's phone rings.

THEY MAKE MARY watch the video so many times, she almost forgets what being there was like.

"Is that you?" Johns asks again, as she enters the frame and crouches next to Garrett, who looks like an oversize doll tossed on the floor. The video is black-and-white, but high-quality enough to see that his eyes are closed. The Mary on the screen leans over him, blocking the camera's view of his body.

The Mary in the room with Johns says, "It looks like me."

More than anything else, she feels numb. The revelation that the fraternity has security cameras mounted inside all the exits, that they have footage of what happened on Halloween, seems like a cosmic joke.

She says, for at least the third time, "He fell by accident."

She's been firm on that part of the story. As far as she knows, they don't have video of the landing from which Garrett fell.

She goes through the litany again. "He was drunk. We ran into each other at the second-floor landing. We were talking, and I guess he didn't realize he was so close to the stairs. He took a step back and fell."

Johns unpauses the video. Maybe they do have footage of her pushing him. Maybe they're letting her hang herself with lies before they trot out the proof with a jazz-hands flourish. *Surprise, you're screwed!*

No, if they had anything like that, they would have led with it. And she might be screwed regardless, but it's not as if Elizabeth meant to hurt him.

It would be nice to have confirmation on that point from Elizabeth herself. It appears, however, that Mary's on her own. She hasn't seen or heard from Elizabeth since she tore out of the library.

"If his fall was accidental, can you explain to me why you didn't summon help right away?"

The Mary on the screen jerks her head up. The security video doesn't have audio, but the real Mary hears that echoing laughter from the kitchen in her memory. She feels the same falling sensation in her stomach as she did that night.

Screen-Mary springs up and runs out of frame, back up the stairs.

"Why did you run when you heard other people approaching?" Johns asks.

"Why do you think?"

"You're telling me Garrett fell, but that's not what he says. I have a mismatch between your two stories. Garrett says you pushed him. He also seems to think you were the one who drugged him. Can you tell me why that is?"

Mary is surprised Garrett would mention that, both because he got her the pill and because it would call his story into question. Maybe he had to explain traces of the drug in his blood. "Why would I drug him?"

"You tell me."

"You think I planned for him to fall down the stairs?"

"Did you?"

"No!"

"But you two didn't like each other very much, did you? Had some tension at work? You resented him being promoted over you? Maybe he threw his weight around, so you thought you'd put him out of commission."

Now the detective is just fishing. "No. We all knew Confluence was probably about to close."

The company did close, abruptly, at the beginning of November. The ongoing fraud investigation is on all the tech-news outlets and has filtered into the mainstream media. A start-up raising hundreds of millions in funding for a product they knew was a dud is hardly unusual, but the sheer audacity of the con has temporarily caught the public imagination. A body-swapping device? Seriously? The *Freaky Friday* memes are rampant.

So no, she hasn't mentioned the Empathyzers, for the same reason she hasn't told the police Garrett attacked her. They'd never believe her.

"Look," Johns says, "I've been talking to people. I know he's not the easiest dude to deal with. Kind of a chauvinist pig? Talks to your chest instead of looking you in the eye?"

"That doesn't mean I wanted to hurt him."

"But you two argued that night."

Mary falls silent. Johns hasn't mentioned this before.

"I have witnesses who say you and Garrett, quote, 'got into a screaming match' on the landing right before he fell."

Mary goes cold, feeling like a hand has grabbed her throat and twisted it.

"Looks like a bell's ringing in there, Mary."

She thinks of Elizabeth promising not to let her take the fall. Of them laughing together. Giving up a future to keep her best friend safe is one thing; losing it because her fake friend threw her under the bus is quite another.

It's on the tip of her tongue that Elizabeth was there, at the top of the stairs. That she was the one who pushed Garrett. Then the full meaning of Johns' statement catches up to her. *Witnesses*, plural. That means Elizabeth not only betrayed her; she colluded with someone to do it.

Katarina. It has to be her. She was in the second-floor bathroom, and she'd say whatever Elizabeth told her to. Because that's what friends do: they protect one another.

Mary knows who will be believed if their stories don't match up. She's already been cast as the villain in this tale.

"Garrett fell by accident," she says, and refuses to tell him anything more.

31

ELIZABETH (MARY)

NOW

Elizabeth paces the apartment to keep warm, socks catching on splinters in the floorboards. She's sick to death of being cold all the time, of eating oatmeal and ramen, of feeling small and invisible and powerless.

She hasn't checked her own socials for days because she hates following her own life from the outside, watching helplessly as Mary steals it all away. No one appears to have noticed. That's the worst part: it makes it seem like nothing she's done, nothing she is, truly matters.

She has a phone full of horny texts from Nate to wave in Mary's face, to show her the flip side of her shiny new life. But it doesn't feel like enough.

Taking it away from you is the point. What if Mary meant what she said? What if she really did destroy the Empathyzer? She'll have changed the lock codes at the house, so Elizabeth can't even search there. Obviously, she underestimated both Mary's abilities and her hatred.

There was a time when she'd thought the messages coming in, the demands that Elizabeth confess to her crimes, might be from Mary. It made objective sense; Mary was the only other person still alive who knew and believed the truth about Halloween. But it didn't make *emotional* sense. Mary wouldn't show her hand like that. And she definitely wouldn't make empty threats.

If Elizabeth had truly believed Mary was the one threatening her, she'd never have given her the chance to inhabit her again, even for a minute.

She happened to be right that it wasn't Mary. Otherwise @bethybeth's confession that she'd caused Garrett's life-ruining "accident" would be trending. But how much has Elizabeth been wrong about? It's clear she never knew Mary as well as she thought she did.

Elizabeth still thinks, quite a lot, about why they became friends. What they needed from each other and what they got. People assumed they were romantically involved, because they spent so much time together. Elizabeth did wonder, after the friendship blew up, if Mary might have been in love with her. A deeply buried crush would fit with the resentment that came spewing out, the polarity switch of strong emotions.

But Mary wanted to *be* Elizabeth more than be with her, even before the Empathyzers came into their lives. She was starved for attention and belonging, but at the same time so prickly that it took a certain touch to make her blossom. Elizabeth liked being the one who had that touch. She had always thought Mary needed just one person who supported and believed in her.

It's seductive to have so much importance in someone's life. To know they'll happily do whatever you say. It's almost like being two people at once.

Elizabeth needs to move past the mindset that soft power will work. She no longer has it, not over Mary. She needs to be willing to get down and dirty, to do some damage. Damage can be repaired. But there are so many possible complications. What if she gets back home and Nate won't go quietly? Why is Lorne trying to squirm back into her life, and why *now*?

She can't think in this place. Letting out a groan, she shrugs into the hated parka, stomps her feet into Mary's boots.

The downstairs lobby is empty except for the smell of cat piss. Or maybe it's not cats, Elizabeth thinks, and a slightly unhinged giggle escapes her as she steps outside.

"Gonna let me in on the joke?" A man in a long black coat ambles up as though he's been waiting for her. Lurking, even.

She ignores him, as she would any random street creeper, but he falls into step with her. "Ms. Burke, I don't know if I'd be laughing if I were in your position."

"Do I know you?" She doesn't bother with politeness. Mary Burke doesn't care if you like her.

"Don't play games with me, Mary."

She looks directly at him for the first time. Her eyes catch on the badge at his belt, then his careworn face, and an electric shock goes through her. It's Detective Johns.

He raises his eyebrows with interest, as though he's clocked her dismay at seeing him. "I was hoping you'd call me, so I wouldn't have to come out here again. I still have some questions for you about Garrett Deegan's death."

"I'm not talking to you without a lawyer," Elizabeth says. Johns almost certainly knows Mary can't afford a decent one, but it's the only bluff she can think of.

Anticipating her move, he blocks the door back into Mary's building. She'd have to shove him to get past. Elizabeth looks around; a few people are walking by, but they're all intent on their own routes. They wouldn't help her anyway. He's a police officer. In this situation, she's the wrongdoer.

"Why would you think you need a lawyer? I haven't accused you of anything yet, Mary."

"You just said you wouldn't be laughing if you were me."

"I want to get your side. It's not even you I'm interested in at this point."

"Is that right."

"When's the last time you were in contact with Elizabeth Jordan?"

Elizabeth freezes just long enough that he can't possibly miss it.

"Recently?" he asks. "After Garrett died?"

"We don't talk anymore." Has Johns been following her? Does he know she went to the house?

"I didn't ask if you were best friends with her. I asked, when was the last time you had contact?"

She tries a shrug, but it's more like a twitch of her shoulders. "I watched one of her videos on the internet the other day." Her voice seems to come from far away, like some other part of herself is conducting the conversation while her mind spins.

The police are after her. The real her.

Does Johns suspect her of having caused Garrett's death? Or does he now believe that Elizabeth was the one who pushed him seven years ago?

She's not naive enough to think she's in the clear as Mary either. She's heard the stories about the police in this city. They'll nab whoever they can get and make the evidence fit, especially when there's a powerful interest—like Garrett's parents—pushing for them to solve the case. They might even be building a narrative that Elizabeth and Mary were in on it together.

"You follow her on social media? That's it?"

"If I'm not under arrest, I'm going to go. Excuse me." She strides up to the door as if she's confident he'll move aside, but her legs feel weak. If he doesn't give ground, she can't touch him. Can't give him an excuse.

At the last second, he allows her entry. She makes sure the door latches behind her so he can't follow her into the building. She makes it into the stairwell before crumpling against the wall, legs rubbery.

She's in real trouble now if she can't get back home. If she were herself, she could retain a lawyer and let them worry about it. But there's a little voice in her head telling her even that might not be good enough if the police find out the truth.

Because Elizabeth Jordan has an excellent reason for wanting Garrett Deegan dead.

32

MARY (ELIZABETH)

NOW

Things are quiet for a few days, but I feel a sense of foreboding, like something is gathering its energy to unleash on me.

Chrissy and I are supposed to meet up for wine and holiday shopping. In the rideshare, I once again go down my list of people close to Elizabeth who could have known or found out the truth about Halloween. Elizabeth herself. Lorne. Katarina. Nate. Garrett's parents. Someone else from college? It could be anyone, really. When I start to wonder if Garrett could have faked his own death, I know it's time to put the problem aside.

The driver drops me off in a formerly industrial area, all vacant lots and broken streetlights. "Here?" he says doubtfully, but there are shapes of people moving through the sullen twilight, all in a single direction, so I get out of the car. My destination is a pop-up hipster craft market in a former warehouse, a place Chrissy suggested. Soon enough the flow of foot traffic leads me there.

Inside, tiny lights twinkle from the exposed ceiling beams and the air is scented with cinnamon and spilled beer. The space is cavernous but overheated, packed shoulder to shoulder, voices and laughter humming against the hard surfaces. Couples sip from compostable cups of beer and wine and wander among stalls selling fair-trade jewelry and small-batch olive oil. Nobody does their real holiday shopping in a place like this. It's a destination in itself, and it seems like half the city is here. I have no idea how I'm going to find Chrissy.

I take out my phone and text her. Then, while I'm waiting, I post a quick video of myself with the market in the background. Comment notifications bubble up, and instead of stress, I feel a little charge of excitement. This job is actually pretty easy, now that I've gotten the knack of it. It's taken me days to realize how little of her true self Elizabeth puts out into the world.

And the thing is, people don't care. They don't need it to be real. They just want it to be pretty. It's seductive, getting paid this much to do something that demands so little of me.

I'm responding to comments in real time, mostly with emojis, when a text comes in from an unknown number.

> You'll never take responsibility, will you? You keep trying to hide, but I know what you did, and I know how rotten you are. Now everyone else will know it too.

Fear stabs through my gut, and I duck my head as if that will fend off an attack. Why did I have to advertise where I was? Anyone could follow me here.

I pick an aisle at random and plunge into the crowd, going against the grain. I'm still clutching my phone, so I feel when it vibrates in my hand.

I pause for a breather next to a stall selling human organs rendered in crochet, anatomically correct except for their smiling cartoon faces. "Hey there," the vendor says, glancing up from her phone. She does a double take, then checks her screen. Her expression lifts. "Hey—"

The last thing I need right now is to get roped into a conversation with one of @bethybeth's adoring fans. I move on as if I haven't heard her, but now I'm paranoid. Gazes slide to meet mine, then away. People glance from their phones to me. Their eyes widen in recognition.

My phone hasn't stopped vibrating, which is odd. Maybe there's something wrong with it. I check it as soon as I reach the end of the aisle. The screen is flooded with notifications.

I open a text from Chrissy. Hey sweetie!! There's a crash on the hwy, traffic completely stopped! I don't think I'll make it . . . sry! Catch you again soon!!!

There's something off about her wording. Too many exclamation points. The notifications popping at the top of my screen come in too fast to monitor: comments, DMs, text messages. Something's happened. Something big. Dread settles in my stomach.

Another text comes in, this one from Hailey, and I grab it, scrolling up to read the thread.

> OK . . . not sure what's happening but we need to get ahead of this

> Do you need me to jump in and crisis manage?

> Pls tell me what you want me to do

She's still typing. Then she stops and the phone rings with a call from her. I answer with the heavy sense that I'm about to get news that will make my life impossible.

"Have you seen this shit?" Hailey yells.

"I'm at the craft market," I tell her.

"You're *out*? Like, with people around?" She sounds horrified. She starts talking about getting as many people as we can to report the platform policy violations.

"Hailey," I say, finally getting a word in. "What's going on?"

There's a long pause. "You haven't seen them?"

"Seen what?"

I hear her take a deep breath. "The photos."

"What photos?"

"Are you sitting down?"

"No, I'm in—"

"Okay, don't panic. Someone posted a bunch of pictures of you. And a couple of videos. Obviously they're fake, but . . ."

She goes on, her voice fading as I lower the phone to do a search for Elizabeth's name.

I have to turn off push notifications before the app will even load. There's a feed, @bethybethexposed. The bio reads And I do mean exposed. NSFW!!

The pictures look like screenshots from an only-halfway-decent webcam, but Elizabeth is clearly recognizable. The top photo shows her sprawled on her back in her own bed. Lorne is face down, but I recognize his bleached hair and tattoos. On his back he has a big, complicated piece featuring some kind of winged creature. A dragon, or a phoenix, with a woman's face.

"Elizabeth? Elizabeth! Can you hear me?"

I hang up on Hailey. I can't deal with her right now, while I'm still taking in the full scope of what's happening. I scroll through picture after picture, all of Lorne and Elizabeth together, all explicit enough to make me cringe. In her bedroom, her living room, her kitchen. I zoom in on one, momentarily ensnared by Elizabeth's expression. There's something beatific about it. She doesn't find Lorne repellent, the way I do.

All the pictures show her face, while Lorne's remains hidden.

Who could have taken these? Who would post them? Only someone who hates Elizabeth as much as I do.

I know how rotten you are.

I look up from my phone. Hundreds of strangers mill around

me, every one of them a potential enemy. When I set out to ruin Elizabeth's life, I didn't know that one of the sweetest rewards would be watching her reaction. If I'd posted these photos, I'd want to see her response. Every cringe. That means whoever did this is probably here with me.

33

In the end, they don't charge Mary with anything. The evidence is circumstantial, the victim's testimony compromised, and Mary hasn't changed her story.

She had hoped Elizabeth would show up for her. Confess her true role, or write a statement in support, or *something*. But since she told Mary about the cameras, it's like she's vanished off the face of the earth.

One day Mary comes home to find Katarina and Tochi carrying two boxes—clearly the last of Elizabeth's things—out of the room. "How did you get in here?" she demands. "What are you doing? Where's Elizabeth?"

Tochi hightails it down the hall. Katarina, more brazen, turns to face Mary. "She's moved out. Don't try to come to the house. We'll call the cops if we see you there."

Mary laughs. Elizabeth's *scared* of her? Please. But that's Mary's last, guilty hope taken away—that Elizabeth is under suspicion too, or her parents snatched her from campus amid the scandal, and that's why she hasn't been able to show up for her best friend.

"Don't get me wrong, Mary. I really hope you get the help you need. But I am heart-attack serious. Stay away." Katarina makes to continue down the hall, but Mary calls after her.

"What did you tell the cops about me?"

Katarina tosses her curls. "About you? Nothing. I didn't see anything. I was in the bathroom with E, holding her hair back while she puked."

"That's what you told them? That she was with you the whole night?"

"I told them the truth." Katarina strides away, haste making the items in her box clank against one another.

The university has lower standards for due process than the police, and with Platinum Circle donors Brian and Rosemary Deegan out for blood, the administration isn't inclined to give Mary the benefit of the doubt. They suspend her and ban her from campus. The bondage video of Garrett, which Mary was foolish enough to back up in her university-sponsored cloud storage, gives them ample excuse to revoke her scholarship for violating the student code of conduct. Though she'd have lost it anyway, since she won't be allowed to take her finals.

While she's packing to move home, Mary has visitors. A middle-aged couple, the woman looking about five years younger than Mary's own mother. The man is a wider, jowlier version of Garrett Deegan.

Mary pauses while stuffing dresses and crop tops she'll never wear again into a duffel bag. "You're Garrett's parents."

Rosemary Deegan—whom Mary has imagined as birdlike and neurasthenic, when she pictured her at all—is surprisingly substantial, a freckled blond woman who looks like she'd be more at home on a softball field than at a charity benefit. She wears no jewelry except a small gold crucifix that winks between her collarbones.

She gives Mary a tight smile. Brian glowers like none of this was his idea.

Mary sees no point in being polite, considering these people were gunning for her to go to prison. "What do you want?"

"Let's have a chat," Rosemary says. "No lawyers, no police. Just us."

Mary looks around for a recording device. Or a sniper. "What about?"

Rosemary sits in a desk chair without asking. Brian goes to stand beside her, putting his hand on her shoulder, taking breaks from glaring at Mary to shoot disdainful little glances around her room. *Yes,* Mary wants to say, *it's a shitty college dorm. I'm not rich. What do you expect?*

"Garrett mentioned you," Rosemary says. "Said you were one of the smartest people he knew at Confluence." Her accent is excessively Midwestern, so it comes out sounding like *Kaahnflewence.* She pauses, seemingly leaving room for Mary to thank her. Mary doesn't.

"So, being such a smart girl," she continues, "you know what's at stake. We looked into you. Your parents have a small business, don't they?"

"A flower shop." Between big-box stores and online delivery, revenue has been declining for years. Funerals keep the shop afloat.

"Ah. How nice. Well, Garrett has a bright future ahead of him. A bright future." Rosemary sighs. "And with what you've done, you've put that in jeopardy."

"It was an accident," Mary says.

"All we want is an apology, hon. Accept responsibility and apologize, and we can put this behind us."

"Apologize to who? You?"

"Well, no. Garrett's the one in a hospital bed."

Catch Mary groveling to that rapist fuck. She knows a trap when she sees one. If she admits any guilt, she'll be all the way screwed instead of most of the way.

"I sympathize with what happened to him," Mary says, gritting her teeth to get that much out. "But like I told the detective—several times—I had nothing to do with him falling. We were talking, and he—"

"Bullshit," Brian bursts out. "You were fighting. Screaming at each other."

"That's not true." Mary struggles to keep her voice calm. "He'd been drinking. People get loud when they've had a few drinks."

"You pushed him! I saw the video. You were about to finish him off, weren't you? If those other kids hadn't come in—"

"Brian!" Rosemary admonishes.

Mary's shaking, and not just because Garrett's father looks as though he'd like to wrap his hands around her throat. The security video had almost overwritten her own perspective of what happened that night. Brian's words bring it back, like she's there again. She's watching Elizabeth go down the long, long stairs to check on Garrett after he fell. She sees the way Elizabeth's shoulders angled as she leaned over him, blocking Mary's view of his body. Elizabeth didn't even try to be quiet when she came back up. Almost as if she wanted to be caught.

Mary hadn't seen what happened just before Garrett fell, but she saw the look on Elizabeth's face afterward. Her own features made unrecognizable by fury.

Mary walks to the door quickly, while her legs will still hold her, and opens it. "I think you should leave."

Brian looks like he'll protest, but then he storms out. Rosemary stops when she's level with Mary. "This is your last chance, hon."

Mary can't hold her gaze. As soon as Rosemary is through the door, Mary slams it shut and locks it. Then she collapses against it and slides down to the floor, trembling.

How did she not see it before?

You didn't see it because you trusted her, a voice in her head says. It's angry but somehow soothing: her most truthful, stripped-down self. *You thought she was your friend. That was stupid.*

Before last year, no one wanted to be Mary Burke's friend. Back home, when new people came to town and she tried to befriend them, they'd hang out for a few days before finding out she was social poison, and then off they'd go to find their real friends. She'd been naive to think things would be different in a new place. *She* was still the same.

That was why she hadn't been able to face the wreck of this friendship. Finally being seen by another person, finally being known, valued—giving that up hurt too much. She'd stolen the Empathyzers to preserve it. She'd kept Garrett's plans from Elizabeth, and her own plans to deal with him, because she was too afraid Elizabeth wouldn't understand.

It turns out she was right.

Elizabeth must have found out somehow; that's all Mary can think. She found out about Garrett's demands, assumed Mary was going along with them, and hatched a plan to get payback. Kill or maim Garrett, then frame Mary for it. It's devastatingly simple.

Yes, the angry voice says. *That's how it happened.*

How else to explain Elizabeth's failure to defend her? If Mary really had planned to help Garrett rape Elizabeth, ruining her life would be justified. Elizabeth didn't trust her to be a real friend. That's what hurts the most, and what makes Mary the angriest.

IT TAKES MONTHS for her to find out what Rosemary meant by her parting statement. Mary has slunk back to her childhood bedroom, which is now piled with storage boxes. She was expelled from school in a hearing that took place in her absence. She figures the Deegans had a hand in that, though it hardly matters. Without her scholarship, it's almost impossible to continue. Just like that, the future she'd planned is over.

Her drive is gone. College and academic achievement were her ticket out of a life in which she felt isolated and misunderstood, her way of sticking it to everyone who had underestimated her. Now she's mired in that life forever, stuck with the people who said she'd never amount to anything.

When both Mary and her parents are served with a lawsuit brought by the Deegans, it drives home how the world works. Her family doesn't have the resources to fight the suit, dubious as it is. Because of the way her parents' business is structured, it ends up being dissolved to go toward the judgment. Thirty years of work down the drain, and for what? They'll be working at shitty jobs for the rest of their lives, and everyone in their small town knows it's Mary's fault.

Her mother and father don't kick her out, but it's obvious they find her presence a discomfort. Every time he sees her, her brother asks when she's going to get a goddamn job already.

She doesn't see the point. A percentage of every dollar she earns for the rest of her days will go to Garrett and his parents, who already have more money than they could ever spend. That debt will never be paid.

Mary has always known that some people are worth more, while others—their dreams, aspirations, struggles—are worth less. There are the lucky and the unlucky, and the fortunate ones have convinced themselves they deserve their fates. It follows, then, that the poor suckers on the bottom deserve theirs too.

It should make her hopeless, and it does. It's also clarifying. This isn't even the worst of what Elizabeth tried to bring about for her.

Mary's feelings toward Elizabeth have been on a seesaw, swinging between heartbreak and anger. Raging one day, sunk in a depression the next. But now, rage wins out. And with it, her drive returns.

It aims in a new direction now. Elizabeth ruined her life; Mary will ruin hers right back.

Along with everything else she hauled back home, she's still got her Empathyzer. While it's charging, she thinks about the mischief she could do as Elizabeth. She could get caught cheating on a test or tell her evangelical parents how much premarital sex she's been having. She could shave Elizabeth's head, get a tattoo on her forehead, punch Katarina in the face. She could murder Garrett.

Then she could slip back into her own body and let Elizabeth deal with the consequences.

The main flaw in her plan is that Elizabeth will be in *her* body at the same time, with the same ability to wreak havoc. But at this point, Mary's got less to lose. And her feeling of jubilation, of *rightness*, tells her that revenge is indeed her new calling. She won't sit and rot in her parents' house. She will take action.

When she turns her wristband on, there aren't any others in range, which is only what she expected. Even if Elizabeth hasn't gotten rid of her Empathyzer, she's hardly dumb enough to keep it turned on. But Mary will find another one. She'll plant it on Elizabeth and make the transfer before Elizabeth knows what's happening. And then the payback will begin.

34

ELIZABETH

FEBRUARY,
ONE YEAR AGO

Garrett didn't have to try hard to find her. The period between New Year's and April was bleak at the best of times, and this was not the best of times. Nate had been distant for months. They'd just returned from a Valentine's trip to Kauai that had been such a disaster, they'd gone the entire ten-hour flight home without speaking. Elizabeth didn't know what was wrong, and Nate wouldn't tell her. She'd been distracting herself by going out practically every night.

She was at an event where she had to appear to be having a good time, and she already regretted showing up when Garrett appeared at her elbow. "Hey!" he yelled in her ear, over the music.

She jumped, then smiled reflexively.

"Awesome to see an old friend." His breath smelled like he'd eaten spoiled meat before gargling with cooking sherry.

She smiled harder. "I thought you were—on a trip!" She'd almost said *in rehab*. She needed to ease up on the cocktails.

His lip curled. "I got homesick."

"Well, we're glad to have you back." She glanced over his shoulder, ready to end the conversation. Garrett and Nate had been in the same fraternity and now lived in the same city, so it would have looked strange if she refused to speak to him, but that didn't mean they had to be best buds.

Not taking the hint, he bolted the rest of his drink and lifted his glass to her. "Can I get you something?"

"Sure! I'm going to switch to the mocktail, though!"

He nodded and weaved off through the crowd, and she hoped he would run into someone else and forget about her. A voice in her head told her she should have asked for bottled water instead of a mixed drink in an open glass, but surely he wouldn't be so stupid as to try anything.

He was back in less than five minutes, like he'd been on a mission. She sipped the drink he'd brought her. Annoyance prickled with the bite of the alcohol. "I told you to get me the mocktail."

He downed half his drink in a gulp; he'd gotten straight whiskey. So much for rehab. "I actually wanted to talk to you in private."

Not a chance, buddy. She looked around for the friends she'd shown up with, or anyone else she knew, but she appeared to be surrounded by indifferent strangers. "I told Nate I'd meet him here," she lied, because men like Garrett would back off only if you reminded them they were horning in on another man's territory. "He gets jealous when he shows up somewhere and can't find me." That was true enough; Nate just didn't like it when *she* did the same.

"Nate might be interested in what I have to say. I don't think you want him to hear it, though. Unless you're more open with him about your college years than I thought."

She didn't like Garrett's tone, or the way he was suddenly eyeing her.

"Let's have a chat," he said. "It'll take five minutes. I promise you'll be glad you did."

Elizabeth doubted that. But she followed him out onto the balcony, which was freezing cold and, accordingly, deserted. He closed the double-paned slider behind them. The event venue was a thirtieth-floor condo, and the city spread out far below in glittering ice chips.

If I were Mary, he wouldn't have dared come out here alone with me. The thought made her smile.

"Nice, isn't it?" he said, grinning back.

"Little cold." Her coat was in coat check; she was dressed for being inside at a hot, crowded party.

"Your nipples hard, eh?" He nudged her. "Hey, I'm just messing with you. The nuns at Catholic school used to make that same face you're making."

"Did you ask them about their nipples?" She tried for a *See? I'm a cool girl* smile, but it felt more like a grimace, her teeth chattering.

"You should be nicer to me." He brushed the back of his hand down her bare arm. Her goose-bumped flesh shrank away from his touch. "Considering what I know about you."

He twisted his hand around and grabbed her arm, hard, positioning his body so no one from the party would be able to see.

"About what you did," he went on, "and who took the blame for it."

Her suddenly dry lips felt stretched over her teeth. "What?"

"You know how many bones I broke when I fell down those stairs?" He let go of her to count on his fingers. "Fractured seventh thoracic vertebra. Three broken ribs. Fractured scapula. Couple of bones in my foot. Small phalanges. What is that, eight? Plus a slipped disc and multiple ligaments in my shoulder blown out, and a grade-three concussion. I still get migraines from that shit. And that's not even counting all the bruises." He showed her his spread fingers. "It won't fit on two hands! I've had four surgeries. I'm in constant pain. Yet I can't get medication for it because I have a *problem*. And they said I was lucky. Does that sound *lucky* to you?"

"I don't know," Elizabeth whispered, dread trickling through her.

He leaned in. "What's that?"

"No." She swallowed, but her mouth was a desert. "It doesn't."

"I don't really remember the fall. A lot of my memories from that night are fuzzy, you know? Or not there at all. But you know what I do remember? The way you were acting before I took you up to my room."

The street below was a river of gold and ruby lights. She wished she were in one of those cars right now, going home to Nate.

"I thought you were drunk and horny, but it took me years to realize that wasn't it. You wanted me to *think* you were drunk and horny. You wanted me to take you upstairs, but not to fuck. You had this grim determination. Like you were about to go off to battle. I'll admit it, I was thinking with my dick, but I can't believe it took me this long to get it.

"That wasn't you at all, was it? It was Mary. So, if Mary was with me . . . then it had to have been you on the stairs. Were you in on it together? It wasn't enough for you to embarrass me, you had to break me too—was that it? Or were you actually trying to kill me?"

She kept her face blank, blank, blank. A pond with a calm surface, reflecting nothing. "I don't know what you're talking about."

"Right. Look, I don't actually care at this point. Nothing can bring me back to the way I was. We can only go forward from where we are, right?"

Oh, for fuck's sake, Elizabeth thought. Garrett Deegan being philosophical was too much. And he was a liar; he cared a lot. That was why they were here.

"My immediate problem is that my parents cut me off when I left rehab. They're still covering my apartment, my cook, the baseline stuff, but as you're aware, I have additional needs. My parents are pretty pissed at me, but I'm sure they'd be interested to hear about someone else being responsible for my fall. Someone who has something worth taking away."

Elizabeth scoffed. "There's no evidence I was involved."

"But there is. Ask your old friend Mary. She's built up quite a trove over the years, from what I've been able to find out. Notes, documents. A bunch of stuff from Confluence. Who knows what else?"

Elizabeth knew what else. She remembered Mary typing away at those journal entries, concentration stitching a line between her thin eyebrows.

"I'm sure that with the right incentive, she'd be more than willing to share. Hell, she wouldn't even need the incentive. You ruined her life, letting her take the fall for you. She's just waiting for someone to listen to her."

Garrett smiled. His face was bloated and reptilian, his youthful good looks gone the way of a corrupt congressman's, but his teeth were still as white and straight as money could make them. "Shame you two don't talk anymore. You were so close in college."

She looked at him. "It's not fair, what your parents did to Mary and her family."

"Oh? Why isn't it fair?"

She glanced away, then gasped in disgust as Garrett's cold lips grazed the side of her neck. Gah, he was like a snake striking. "I wish I could remember if we fucked," he said in her ear.

He stood behind her and slid his hands down her arms. His knuckles pressed against her breasts. "The way I see it is, either you can give me a little, or my parents can take everything. And they will."

She stiffened. *No. No way.*

He laughed. "Calm down, Bethybeth. I don't mean *that*. Drugs and money'll work just fine. I'll let you know what I need."

Moving his hands up to her shoulders, he turned her toward the party. "Let's get you inside before you catch your death."

35

ELIZABETH (MARY)

NOW

Elizabeth doesn't know how long she crouches at the bottom of the stairs in Mary's building. She should go up, get safe behind a locked door, but all those stairs feel like too much. Mary's neighbors pass by, but they barely glance at her. She's grateful for their indifference.

She spreads her fingers to massage her forehead, as if she could press away the spiraling panic. Surely the detective doesn't know about Elizabeth and Garrett's arrangement. He could be speaking with Garrett's friends and associates as a formality. But then why approach Mary, someone Elizabeth hadn't spoken to in years before this week?

What if Johns has talked to Lorne?

Garrett's "requests" had been limited at first. Relatively small amounts of money, easy for Elizabeth to hide or explain away. Once she took up with Lorne, he gave her discounts on what he supplied to Garrett. But Garrett's appetite only increased, and Lorne started asking questions.

She had to tell him something, so she said Garrett had threatened to tell Nate she and Lorne were still seeing each other.

"Maybe that wouldn't be so bad," Lorne had said.

"Maybe what wouldn't be so bad?" They'd been at his place. This was well after her and Nate's open-marriage experiment had ended, and she was all too aware of what a hypocrite she was, getting upset about the things her husband did when she wasn't around.

Lorne shrugged, his bare chest rising and falling under her cheek. "At least then we wouldn't have to sneak around anymore."

Elizabeth sat up, looking down at him. "No. No! Nate finding out would be very bad." Lorne's eyes narrowed; he hated it when she talked to him like he was stupid. "I need to get Garrett off my back." And she needed to make sure he couldn't get to Mary and her stash of documents.

"I could help with that. It's obviously stressing you out." Lorne stroked the back of her arm from tricep to wrist, his touch light, almost ticklish. Elizabeth shivered. Then he switched to the baby voice that made her squirm with secondhand embarrassment. "I don't like it when my Bethy is stressy."

"You know how to get me relaxed." She reached for him, and nothing more was said about Garrett that day.

She was ashamed of herself for being relieved when he died. One of her most pressing problems solved, *poof*, like magic.

It wasn't just the blackmail that made her glad he was gone. It was the way he'd looked at her on the stairs that Halloween night. Mary had drawn blood on his pride, and he wanted to see her broken for it. It never leaves you, seeing your own death in someone's eyes.

"Oh." The voice echoes from the landing above. "Excuse me." Miguel, frozen in the act of descending, wears an almost comical expression of dismay. Of course he's not happy to run into her after the way she brushed him off.

Then he focuses on her face and surges forward like he can't help himself. "Are you okay?"

She starts to tell him she's fine. She's Mary Burke and she doesn't need anyone's help. Pushing people away is what she does. But that fragile, unwilling note of caring in Miguel's voice breaks her. She bursts into tears.

———

TEN MINUTES LATER, she's sitting with a cup of tea in Miguel's living room.

He's in the armchair, pretending to look at his phone. It's his way of making his concern seem less intense, which she appreciates. She's embarrassed about falling apart in front of him.

"I should go," she says. "I don't want to keep you. You were headed out."

"Just to the store. It can wait."

They sit, Elizabeth warming her hands with her mug, Miguel scrolling his phone. After a minute, he speaks.

"Is it that cop? Did he come back?"

She lets out a shaky breath. "Yes. But I can handle it."

He puts his phone down. "Look, it's fine if you just want to be friends, or neighbors, or whatever. I didn't mean to make it weird the other night. But you don't have to deal with everything on your own." He runs a hand through his hair, drawing the strands together at his nape. A gesture of frustration, of embarrassment. Elizabeth wants to take those feelings away.

"You didn't make it weird. I was the one who kissed you, and I shouldn't have."

"Why not?"

So many reasons, and none she can share with him.

She can tell he's intrigued rather than annoyed. When did she get so attuned to his emotions? That's how she's always lived. Homing in on the feelings of those around her, learning how to . . . oh, not *manipulate* them, nothing so mercenary. But Miguel wants to help. He cares.

He says, "If you're concerned about anything on my end, you don't need to be. At all. I was definitely into it." His emphasis, and the fact that he's blushing, make her want to kiss him again.

"I was into it too," she says.

He looks happy, then guarded. "Okay."

He's picked up that her words aren't necessarily an invitation. He doesn't say anything else, letting her get around to it in her own time, her own way, or maybe not at all. Not because he's passive, or engaging in the kind of cat-and-mouse game Nate would play. Because he wants her to be sure before she takes that step. And he still wants Mary even though he knows there's a stain on her past, the stain that's actually Elizabeth's. He doesn't think it defines her.

That patience and acceptance plant wild ideas in her head. Such as: if he knew who she was, she could find out what a second kiss with him feels like.

But that's not the only reason she's thinking of telling him what's really going on with her. He's a researcher in a field many people dismiss as quackery. Even if he doesn't believe her story, he won't say she's crazy or a liar or suddenly remember a pressing engagement elsewhere. He won't make snap judgments, or sit back and do nothing. He'll listen. And he'll help in whatever way he can.

She'd resolved not to use him, but the stakes are higher now, and Miguel will be better able to help if he knows the truth. If he has to become her tool, she might as well make it a pleasant experience for both of them.

"I have to tell you something," she says before she can change her mind.

Miguel sits forward. There's no tension in his hands; they're open, like his face. "Okay."

She takes a deep breath and lets it out. "I'm not who you think I am."

He gets a small, bemused smile on his face, but waits for her to go on.

"I'm not really Mary Burke. I'm someone else. And I'm in trouble."

36

MARY (ELIZABETH)

NOW

I swivel my head from side to side, trying to pick out anyone in the market who seems overly interested. More than one person meets my gaze. Are they concerned about my wild-eyed panic, or drinking it in?

I see smirks, up-and-down looks, words exchanged behind hands. And phones. So many people looking at their phones.

Words float to my ears on the cinnamon-scented air. *I can't believe she'd show her face.* Are they talking about me? Surely Elizabeth's not that famous, but she is local. And the interactions on those posts, already high, were ticking up even as I watched.

I find a wall and lean against it, closing my eyes. As soon as I do, the photos begin a parade through my head. Lorne and Elizabeth were thorough; I'll say that for them. They must have had sex on every horizontal surface in her house, plus a few that weren't.

I need privacy to figure out how to deal with this. But there are people everywhere, their eyes probing and judging, voices breaking into my head. A feeling of being watched crawls up my spine. I can't even unravel the problem of how to get home safely. I force my breaths into a calming pattern, but find myself hyperventilating instead.

This is going to ruin everything. It's exactly the kind of thing I would have done if I'd kept on my original course of destroying Elizabeth's life instead of stealing it.

Someone is much better at revenge than I am. This is a devastating hit: livelihood, reputation, marriage, all gone.

Oh god. *Nate.*

I have to get to him before he sees. Pushing off the wall, I make a beeline toward the exit. I'll summon a rideshare. No—I can't risk the driver's recognizing me. I'll text Hailey to come pick me up. I take out my phone and see that I have a message from Lorne.

Just what I fucking need.

He's sent a photo: Elizabeth in one-quarter profile, the graceful line of her neck descending from her jaw. She's in a dim, cavernous space, warmly lit. It's a beautiful shot.

It takes me a moment to figure out that it's me, here in this market, today.

This u? asks the text Lorne has sent with it.

It was taken from above. I look up reflexively. Nothing but rafters and twinkle lights.

The phone vibrates in my hand. Behind you

I whip around and he's there, wearing a guarded expression and the same all-black ensemble, backpack and all, as when he broke into my house.

Garrett's killer.

"How did you know I was here?" I sound scared. Weak.

Lorne stops moving toward me, as if he senses I'm ready to bolt. "I'm making a promo video for the market . . . I was going over my drone footage and saw you were here. I wasn't creeping on you, I swear."

He doesn't look me in the eye.

I haven't seen or heard a drone since I arrived here. Can drones be programmed? I'm sure they can. It's less likely one could go unnoticed inside Elizabeth's house. Maybe he flew it outside the windows—all that glass—or had a hidden camera. But I'm pretty sure I'm looking at the culprit behind @bethybethexposed.

His gaze flicks to mine, then away. "You've seen them." Not a question: the shock must be all over my face. Is he proud of himself? "Are you okay? Do you need—"

"I don't need anything from you."

He takes a step toward me; I take a step back.

"Have you heard from *him*?"

Nate—he means Nate. I ignore his question and accuse him instead. "You did this."

Lorne smirks. "I thought we did it together." He sidles closer and I shift farther away, bumping up against a divider that separates the main market area from a group of café tables. On the other side, people sit drinking coffee, beer, wine. And, of course, looking at their phones. I don't want their attention on me. I could scream, but it's a choice between fear and humiliation.

"Did you come here to gloat?" I hate the quaver in my voice. I hate that Lorne scares me.

His face screws up in fake confusion. "Who's gloating? I just want to help. I hope you know he's gonna leave you."

"Beth." He leans in, and I've run out of space to get away from him. "What I said the other day, about how I feel—I meant that. I'd never abandon you."

"Nate isn't going to *abandon* me." I'm beginning to see Lorne's strategy. Ruin Elizabeth in the eyes of her husband and her public, erode her supports, then white-knight in and scoop up the damaged goods.

If Elizabeth's damaged goods, then so is he. He's in those pictures too.

Not his face. And he's not the one in an extremely public marriage. *And* men don't get slut-shamed like women do. This asshole's smarter than he looks.

"You really think he'll stay?" His unsettling pale eyes pierce mine. "Now that everyone knows his pristine little princess has been fucking around on him with the dirtbag who gets him his party drugs?" His lip curls. Fear washes over me with the reek of his cologne. What will I do if he grabs me? If he pulls out his gun?

"You think he'll still want you after this? He's going to let you down. But I don't care what anyone says about you. *I* won't let you down. You already know I can be trusted."

He backs off a bit, and I can draw breath. What he says next steals it again.

"A detective came to talk to me."

My lips go numb. "Why?"

"Why do you think?"

"I don't—I don't know—"

Lorne chuckles. I can't blame him; I wouldn't convince a child. "I know you won't let me go down. I know you love me. And I swear to god, I've never been like this about anyone—"

He reaches for me.

"Don't touch me!" I use every inch Elizabeth's high-heeled boots lend me to make myself taller than him. "Leave me alone."

Lorne raises his hands. "You're upset right now. But you'll see."

I push past him into the open, then turn and run toward the bathrooms. Bumping into someone, I push them aside without an apology.

Lorne shouts after me, "You'll see, Beth! And I'll be right here!"

There's a family restroom open. I slam the door behind me, my hands trembling so it takes me two attempts to get it locked. Fortunately it has one of those ridiculously oversize industrial slide bolts. Lorne's not getting in here without a crowbar.

I text Hailey to come pick me up, and she replies that she can be outside in twenty minutes.

I can hunker down for twenty minutes. There are plenty of bathrooms. I consider messaging Nate, but this is not a situation I can explain over text. And there's always the possibility he hasn't seen the photos yet.

Who am I kidding? He'll see them soon enough. Lorne has ruined everything.

I feel tears trickling off my chin. Did I just start, or was I crying the whole time I was talking to him? I hate the thought of showing weakness. The bathroom is out of toilet paper, so I dig in Elizabeth's tote bag for a pack of tissues. There has to be one; she carries everything else in there.

At the bottom of the bag my fingers find something I can't identify. Smooth, square, a little smaller and thinner than a key fob. I bring it out.

It's a location tracking tag.

Rage boils up in me. Taking promo video for the market, my ass. And I know only too well how easy it is to slip a small item into someone's bag.

The rage evaporates, leaving fear in its place. Lorne is dangerous. I don't know if Elizabeth asked him to kill Garrett or he acted on his own, but he obviously considers it a debt to be paid.

How could Elizabeth be so careless? She had everything. It didn't fall into her lap, either; I spent years watching her work for it. But somehow, she managed to make as big a mess of her life as she did of mine.

37

Elizabeth makes herself easy to keep tabs on. She checks in everywhere she goes; she posts on a schedule, at least once a day. Apartment, clothes, travel, puppy, friends. And now, fiancé.

I couldn't be more excited to finally make it official! reads the
caption. Elizabeth and "N" have been dating for months, and Elizabeth has posted tantalizing glimpses—presents he's gotten her,
photos of their hands entwined—but never his face or his full
name, until this morning. She knows how to draw out a reveal.

> Allow me to introduce Nate, aka N! He asked me
> to marry him and I said YES!! Two months from
> now, he'll be my husband!!!

This underneath their engagement photo stream. Mary swipes
through it again, focusing on Nate's face in each picture. He looks
sincere no matter the mood of the photo—laughter, adoration, or
a light smolder. There's no denying it: Nate Jordan is as deeply in
love with @bethybeth as the rest of the world.

Mary has monitored Elizabeth through four years of success.
Her platform grew steadily during college, but she still had to get

a job at a marketing firm after graduation. Her follower count didn't reach the stratosphere until the fateful dress poll the day after she met "N." Or remet him, apparently.

(Mary, using a fake account, had cast her vote for "Creepy." Who buys an expensive dress for someone they barely know?)

Now Mary can put in context the itchy sensation she's gotten whenever Elizabeth has posted about her boyfriend. Now she knows what she was missing: a whirlwind courtship between her former best friend and the one man for whom Mary has ever expressed romantic feelings.

She doesn't know why this news has her so unbalanced. It's not as if Elizabeth respects girl code; she already took a bite out of Nate on that Halloween. And she obviously doesn't give a shit about Mary. In four years, she's never once reached out to apologize.

True, Mary doesn't use email or social media under her real name, and she's never been able to keep a phone turned on for longer than a few months. She works off the books so her wages won't be garnished, and she changes jobs frequently. Even her parents don't know her address, not that they're interested. But it's not as if she's changed her name or left the country. Elizabeth could find her if she really wanted to.

There's a scattered knock at the door to Mary's room. Her roommate bursts in without waiting for an answer; the door hits Mary's mattress on the floor before it can open all the way. "I need that money for the electric bill."

Both her roommates gave up being civil to her months ago. Mary can see the signs: by summer, they'll have kicked her out of this closet they call a bedroom. "I'll have it tomorrow," she lies.

Her roommate sighs theatrically and stomps away, leaving the door ajar.

Mary sits up and pulls on socks. Elizabeth and Nate just checked in at a brunch place downtown. She has to see them together for herself, in person.

She closes her bedroom door, then digs into an old soft-sided suitcase she uses for storage, since she doesn't have a closet. Her Empathyzer from college is in there, along with a device she's spent months building from a universal electronics prototyping kit. She had to save up for almost a year before that to buy the kit online.

There have been iterations before this, but she could never get them to pair with the device from Confluence. It's been difficult fitting revenge around survival.

Today is the day. She'll ruin Elizabeth's life and stop this marriage in one fell swoop. Once she's Elizabeth, she'll break up with Nate. Publicly, explosively, so it can't be taken back. It's perfect: it'll get Nate out of Elizabeth's life *and* piss off her followers and sponsors.

She takes out the prototype. It looks nothing like the Empathyzer. It's not even a wristband, but a rectangular lump of plastic with an LED indicator and a single button. It needs to do only two things: pair and execute.

A notification pops up on Mary's phone that Elizabeth has posted a video of her and Nate. Mary watches, then watches again, as they talk over each other in their eagerness to share their perfect fucking love.

Nausea rolls through her. The perfection of Nate's face makes her chest ache. He looks so happy; should she really ruin that for him? Can she stand to have him, even as someone else, only to give him up?

An idea strikes, as sudden and explosive as lightning. Why give him up at all? Why destroy Elizabeth's life when she can take it for herself?

Mary's never considered killing Elizabeth, no matter how her hatred burns. But to slip into her skin and stay there. To steal everything she's worked for, all the good things she doesn't deserve. Beauty, money, comfort, love. Nate.

Meanwhile, Elizabeth will be stuck being Mary. She'll finally have to pay for what she's done.

It's perfect.

It also cancels out her slight anxiety about Elizabeth having access to Mary's own life and body. What will it matter, if she's not coming back?

She'll have to put on a flawless performance for the people who know Elizabeth best, not just for a short time, but forever. At least in the short term, she'll have to do Elizabeth's job, which she knows is more than just taking pictures and looking pretty. But she doesn't have to keep being an influencer. Once she's embedded in Elizabeth's life, she can shape it however she wants.

A small voice in her mind tells her she should wait, be cautious, think it through. But she doesn't want to wait. She's spent the last four years learning everything she can about her target. She's ready. It's time.

Today is the first day of her new life.

———

SHE GETS OFF the train downtown and shivers as she walks toward the restaurant; after the springtime bout of freezing rain that passed through last night it's colder than she thought. Wind whips through her hoodie. She slides her hand into the kangaroo pocket, cupping the prototype inside.

Her Empathyzer is on her wrist. She still doesn't know exactly how she'll do this. She's added a piece of double-sided tape to the prototype so she can stick it to Elizabeth's back. It's small and light enough to go unnoticed. Or she could simply slip it into Elizabeth's bag or pocket. The risk is that she'll be recognized despite her hood and cheap sunglasses. If that happens she'll have to think on her feet, which isn't what she's best at.

She's ten feet away from the restaurant when the door opens. The smell of coffee and cinnamon puffs out, making Mary's mouth water. A familiar laugh wafts to Mary's ears. The sweet smell becomes sickly, nauseating.

Nate holds the door for Elizabeth as she glides out. She wears a sleek hunter green trench that sets off her auburn hair.

And Nate: in person, he takes Mary's breath away. Dark brows run straight above soulful, long-lashed eyes, and he's grown a neatly trimmed beard he didn't have when they were in school. His hair's artfully messy, tumbling over a green scarf the exact shade of Elizabeth's coat.

He chuckles in response to his fiancé's laugh, his smile conveying the uncomplicated happiness of a man who has everything he wants, as he slips his arm around Elizabeth's waist. It's like he can't stand not to touch her for too long.

The two of them walk toward Mary. She braces for the inevitable recognition, the forced smiles, the pretense that they're merely college friends who fell out of touch.

Or maybe—Mary is shocked by the ache this thought drives into her chest—this will be their reckoning.

She presses a hand to her sternum until the ache goes away. If Elizabeth wanted to apologize, she could have done it a long time ago.

Still, Mary feels a surge of anticipation as Nate's gaze swings to make contact with hers. His eyes widen just enough to tell her she's been seen and recognized. His perception sends a charge sparking through her body to the ends of her fingers, the roots of her hair.

Her lips part, his name on them.

The look stretches between them like a thread about to break. Then he drops his eyes. He turns toward Elizabeth and says something, drawing her attention to him, almost as if he's distracting her deliberately.

They come even with Mary, passing her. Mary stops and stares after them, expecting another glance. A sign. He doesn't look back.

Elizabeth is getting away!

Mary runs after the couple, bringing the prototype out of her pocket. She makes it three steps before she slips on a patch of ice and falls hard onto her hands and knees. Her breath goes out in a whoosh, the pain in her kneecaps catching up a second later.

She lets out a moan. Seeing blood on the icy sidewalk, she lifts her right hand to find a mess of shattered plastic and silicon.

"No." Fragments of the broken circuit board jam into the fleshy bases of her fingers. She brushes them away on her hoodie, leaving bloody smears. Her breathing hitches. "No no no no no." She tries to pick up the scattered bits of her device, but it's beyond salvaging. She'll have to start all over.

Slowly, she gets up. No one offers to help her. She limps away, gnawing the insides of her cheeks to hold back the tears.

38

MARY (ELIZABETH)

NOW

By the time I've gone through all the closets in Elizabeth's house, every purse and pocket, I've found four more trackers. Lorne didn't bury them deeply; either he was rushed and hid them in easily accessible items, or he knows which articles are her favorites.

When Hailey dropped me off, she asked if I was okay going in alone. I told her—in an icy tone worthy of my old self—that I didn't need a babysitter and she should concentrate on handling my out-of-control mentions. If Nate was inside, I didn't want Hailey to witness our fight. She compressed her lips, but didn't say anything else before peeling off in her slightly dented, salt-stained coupe. I shouldn't have been so bitchy; the last thing I need is her quitting in a huff.

Lorne probably put a tracker in Elizabeth's car. I grab her keys and head downstairs, through the empty house. Nate's not home. Hasn't called or texted. That means one of two things: either he hasn't seen the firestorm yet, or he's too angry and disappointed to deal with me.

My stomach turns at the thought of seeing him, but it sinks to my feet at the thought of him *not* coming home.

It isn't fair. I'm not the one who did those things with Lorne.

Why should I have to deal with the fallout? Maybe Elizabeth knew this was coming. Maybe that's the real reason she sent me the Empathyzer.

As I approach the back door, the keypad beeps its unlocking song. The door swings open, and all thoughts of searching Elizabeth's car fly out of my head.

Nate locks eyes with me. My hope that I could be the one to tell him dies.

I don't even know what I would have said. There's no good way to tell a husband his wife has cheated on him in front of the entire world.

He walks past me without a word. I expect him to go straight down to the man cave, to wall himself off. He keeps some clothes down there; he could pack and be gone in minutes.

Instead, he braces his hands on the kitchen counter, his back to me, every line of him stretched tight. I don't know what will happen when that tension breaks.

"Nate—"

"Tell me something." His voice cracks across mine like a ruler on knuckles. "Do you get off on humiliating me? Are you trying to destroy what little credibility I have?"

I swallow. "Those pictures aren't me."

He shakes his head, unbelieving. "Not only have you been screwing that diseased little fuck behind my back; you let him show the whole world."

"I didn't *let* him—" I realize my mistake. "Those aren't me, Nate."

He takes out his phone, jabs at it, and shoves the screen in my face. "You're telling me that's not you. Look at it. Look at it! That's not you?"

"It's not." My throat aches.

"And you had the nerve to— Of course. It's right out of the cheater's playbook. Accuse me of the things you're doing yourself.

Are you trying to make me leave you? I don't think you want that. You need me. You always have. I just don't think you realized how much."

"I do." My voice shakes, guilt soaking into me even though none of this is my fault. His heart is so raw. "I do realize it."

"You know what happens if I don't stand by you, right?" He backs me against the counter. "You never went above a hundred thousand until I was in the picture. How many of those followers will support you now that they know what you are? How many sponsors will stick around? I haven't been your appendage this long for nothing."

I blink, disoriented at the shift in topic. Nate whirls away from me, toward an area where Elizabeth has arranged a few bottles to create a small bar on the counter. His back to me, he fetches two glasses, drops ice into them, and starts mixing something.

"I'm going to tell you how we move forward as a team." His words would lift my hopes if his voice weren't so flat. "But first, I think we could both use a drink."

"I don't really—"

"Have a fucking drink with me, Elizabeth." Anger snaps in his black eyes as he holds out a glass.

I take the fucking drink. It tastes so bitter I almost choke, but I swallow the first sip. The next isn't as bad.

"I don't want a divorce," he says. "I don't want a long, drawn-out period of people talking about my private shit. I don't want Team Nate and Team Bethybeth and *spousal support*."

He takes in a fast, hard breath and lets it out. "You owe me more than that. It could have been me who took off. You should've ended up as my cheerleader, instead of the other way around. But actually, no, I don't think you would've put up with that. You could never handle being anything but the center of attention." He finishes his drink, then plants the glass on the counter so hard, I'm surprised it doesn't shatter. "And you just love having my balls in a decorative bowl on your mantel, don't you?

"Drink your drink, babe. Come on, you're behind."

I gulp obediently, trying not to gag. What the hell did he put in it? But I can already feel the alcohol relaxing me. He takes my glass, puts it on the counter with his, and mixes each of us another.

"We both know you'll be nothing if I leave you, so now you're going to do what I say. The first thing you do is post an apology on your accounts. Make it good. Make it sincere. This needs to be some epic groveling."

My second drink tastes as bad as the first, as bitter as Nate's words. Why is he trying to humiliate me more than I already am? I lower my head in refusal.

"You don't want to take responsibility for your actions?" he says, his voice rough. "You have to confess to be forgiven, Elizabeth."

My head jerks up. He doesn't seem to realize what he's said, the wording he's used. He doesn't realize how he's betrayed himself. Downing his drink in a long swallow, he rants on. "You wanted to be in the spotlight? This is what comes with it."

The phrase could have been a slip of the tongue, a coincidence. He hates me, though. Hates Elizabeth. I can see it in his eyes. I wonder how long it's been there, under the surface. If he hid that, he could have hidden a lot more. Only now can I see the yawning pit where I thought the supports of Elizabeth's life stood.

"What if I don't want to be in the spotlight anymore?"

"You think you can quit?" His voice rises, making me flinch. "How are we supposed to live, Elizabeth?"

How everyone else lives, I think. *How normal people live.*

He steps into my space, and as he does I see Hailey standing inside the back door.

"Sorry!" she yelps. "I just came in! I didn't mean to interrupt! I didn't hear anything!"

The change that comes over Nate's face is unsettling. All his resentment and bitterness are wiped away, leaving a neutral, almost pleasant expression. "Oh good, you're here. Maybe you can convince her to save her career."

He moves toward her. A look that I can't read passes between them.

It's not until he opens the door that I realize he's leaving. "Where are you—"

"You don't get to ask me that anymore." Nate walks out, slamming the door behind him.

Hailey takes me in. "Is everything . . . okay?"

I must look shattered. I gather myself and manage an almost-smile. Hailey's very obviously not interested in my emotions, so I'm not going to blubber all over her. "It's been a long day."

In her own way, Elizabeth is as alone as I ever was.

"I came over to see what else you needed me to do," Hailey says, moving into the kitchen. "I've already gotten them to take down the, um, *explicit* deepfakes, though unfortunately they're dragging their feet about some of the others. And they've left up a lot of the discussions, which as you can imagine are not complimentary."

I wonder if I should tell her the photos aren't fake. Whether it would affect her willingness to work for me. I decide not to; I need all the allies I can get. "Thank you."

"Obviously, I reported the user who posted them. The support tech I messaged with said they're 'investigating' but you know how meaningful that is." She rolls her eyes. "Some of your sponsors have invoked their morality clauses, but your agent managed to talk a few of them off the ledge. And I've taken your accounts private for the time being, until things die down. I guess you can make them public again whenever you want to post that apology. If you decide to go that way."

"That sounds good. Thank you, again." I can hear the exhaustion in my voice.

Then something she said plucks at my brain. "You heard Nate."

"Sorry?" Hailey is bustling around inside the refrigerator and cabinets, more familiar with the contents than I am.

"You heard what he said. About posting an apology. When you came in, you said you didn't hear anything."

She turns red. "I didn't want to make you uncomfortable." Avoiding my eyes, she places a lime on a cutting board and slices it in half, then does the same with a lemon. "You know he's jealous, right?"

"I'd say that's understandable, considering."

"I don't mean of you with someone else. I mean he resents you being more successful than him."

"That's ridiculous. He's always been supportive." Hasn't he? He helped make Elizabeth's career, with his movie-star looks and his romance-hero ways.

Judging by what he said before he left, he knows it too.

Hailey puts ice in a glass. "I'm just telling it like I see it. Following his advice might not be in your best interests."

Why is she trying to drive a wedge between me and Nate? As unpleasant as he's being, the part of me that's been dreaming about him all these years isn't ready to give up yet.

"You don't think I should apologize?"

"It'll just whip people up more. They'll see it as insincere. If those photos *were* real, the only person you'd owe an apology would be your husband."

She glances up and our eyes lock. There's a spark of awareness in hers. What does she know?

"Thank you for your input, but I don't need marriage counseling from you."

"It's not marriage counseling. It's career guidance. Which is my job." She turns away, toward Elizabeth's kitchen bar.

I scoff. This woman comes out of nowhere, and she acts like she's the expert? Elizabeth's been doing this work since Hailey was a teenager. "It's not your job to tell me what to do. It's your job to do what I tell *you*."

Hailey's expression is sour as she hands me a glass full of ice and clear, fizzing liquid. One slice of lime and one of lemon ride on the rim.

"What is this?" I ask.

"A vodka soda. You looked like you could use it. Lemon-lime, just like you like it."

My head is fuzzy from the two drinks Nate practically poured down my throat, but what the hell? I take a swallow and watch Hailey pushing down whatever emotions my rudeness has stirred in her. Usually I can't even see that; she's so professional. Good at hiding her feelings, just like Elizabeth. I guess you'd have to be to work for her.

"I'm going to head out," Hailey says. "Text me if you need anything."

She stops at the door, hand on the knob.

"I've only ever tried to be a friend to you," she says. "You might want to think about how you treat your friends. You're going to need them."

I open my mouth to respond—to apologize—but with a puff of cold air and a slam of the door, she's gone.

39

ELIZABETH (MARY)

NOW

She'll go soon. She will. But the weight of Miguel's arm around her is so satisfying, his chest a heater under her cheek. Their time together measured out by his heartbeats in one ear, the frantic ticking of his watch in the other.

Is this okay? he kept asking earlier. Like he was the one who should be worried about taking advantage. He knows her real name now, but not much else.

Elizabeth, he'd repeated. Slow and speculative, tasting it. She'd been rattled by how much she liked the sound of it in his mouth.

Her name is the biggest piece she's given him of her true self. He wanted to know more, but she deflected with a sad downward glance and a *Can we not talk about it?* He'd gotten this adorable little frown on his face but said she didn't have to tell him anything she didn't feel comfortable with.

Being with someone—with him—has made her feel more anchored in this body. The feeling panics her, like it means she won't be able to leave when she wants to. If it weren't for the police, for the threat that Johns' attention might turn back to Mary, it would almost be easier to stay.

If she were willing to leave her real self behind.

She can hardly fathom that Miguel believed her. With every word, she expected to break through the skin of his acceptance. She stumbled so badly through her explanation of the Empathyzers that she thought for sure he'd narrow his eyes and say, *Okay, I'm going to call some nice men in white coats for you now.*

But he was more fascinated than skeptical, peppering her with technical questions she couldn't answer about how the devices work and the ways in which they manipulate brain waves. Better that, though, than him asking what exactly might motivate Mary to take over Elizabeth's body again after so many years.

When she thanked him for giving her the benefit of the doubt, he shrugged and said his research background helped him to keep an open mind.

"Plus I, um . . ." he said, then blushed.

"You . . . what?" She acted like she had no idea what he was thinking.

He ran a hand through his hair. "Well, I'm attracted to you. And I never was, to Mary. Before. I mean, we were friendly, but I never thought of her in that way. So. That's one difference."

It wasn't difficult to get him into bed after that. Like with the kiss, she made the first move, but he responded. Enthusiastically.

Is she being strategic, winding him into her web, or is she soothing her own ego? She doesn't even have a practical use for Miguel, beyond some amorphous plan of finding out why Mary was interested in out-of-body experiences. Yet her intuition tells her to keep him close.

Chrissy gave her some unsolicited advice once, after she'd started seeing Lorne. *Make sure you're not solving your man problems with another man.* At the time she brushed it off, but Chrissy knew exactly how much Elizabeth didn't want to be in an open marriage.

Is she solving her man problems with another man?

Or is this something else, something real?

It can't be. It's too messy, her heart still raw after Nate. Though in retrospect, she's known her marriage was over for a long time.

Lorne was her true rebound, and look how that turned out. She doesn't want Miguel doing things for her that will get him into trouble.

Gently moving his arm aside, she rolls over, setting her bare feet on the chilly wooden floor.

"Where are you going?" He sounds sleepy and happy, his tone a flirting lilt.

"I should get upstairs."

"Or you could stay." He catches her hand, his eyes soft, though there's something in them that takes her back through the highlights of the past two hours. Her stomach swoops.

He breaks their gaze first, letting her hand go. "I don't want to put any pressure on you. I know things are . . ."

"Weird," she says when he doesn't finish the sentence.

"Yeah."

She really should go. First rule of seduction: leave them wanting more. And the more time she spends with Miguel, the more likely he is to find out the parts of the truth she hasn't told him.

But she finds herself leaning back in, kissing him. His mouth soft at first, then demanding.

She tells herself, *One more kiss, one more, one more.* He's pulling her on top of him, wrapping her in his warmth. She sinks into it. She doesn't think any more about leaving.

40

Late-summer heat descends as soon as Mary gets out of the ride-share, with its cherry-scented air-conditioning. Sweat pops at her hairline; she can smell the long bus ride from the city on herself. She hurries into the artificial chill of a glaringly new two-story building.

The town has built up since she was in college, so much that she barely recognizes it. Most of the new builds are student housing, but this one has a sign announcing it as *Gracious Assisted Living*.

This is her last hope.

A young woman wearing a blue polo shirt stands behind the reception desk. Mary remembers Elizabeth telling her about learning the psychology of color in a branding class she took for her marketing degree. In the mind of the Western consumer, black and red connoted power, sex, sophistication. Green was savings, conservation. If you wanted your brand to whisper trustworthiness and exclusivity, you would use the muted blue of the receptionist's shirt, the carpet, and the logo on the sign of this building.

A fitting choice, considering the one client of this place whom Mary knows.

"Who are you here to see?" the receptionist asks, pushing a tablet across the counter.

"Gloria Faculak." Mary smiles, her lips feeling stretched across her teeth. "I'm her niece."

The receptionist looks her over doubtfully. "You don't look like her niece."

Right. Garrett has an actual sister. Mary tries to summon the entitlement of someone whose relative can afford to live here. "I'm her other niece. By marriage. I live in California, but I'm in town for the week. I thought I'd come visit."

The attitude and her thin explanation must be convincing, because the receptionist lets her sign in without showing ID. She enters herself as Liz Faculak. An attendant leads her through a locked door. "You can get one of us to open it when you're ready to leave," the attendant says. "Please make sure it shuts and latches behind you."

They walk down a wide hallway lined with doors, television sounds drifting from the open ones. The attendant stops at a door decorated with a hand-lettered sign, the name surrounded by drawings of daisies. *GLORIA*.

"Daisies are her favorite," the attendant explains, opening the door. Her voice rises into the register people use with dogs and babies. "Gloria, honey, you got someone here to see you."

The former CEO of Confluence Innovations slumps in a recliner before yet another blaring TV, wearing joggers and a sweatshirt, slippers on her feet. But when she looks up, her gaze is as sharp as ever.

"I can't talk right now," she says. "I've got a meeting in five."

The attendant lowers the volume on the television. "She's been a little confused today," she tells Mary in an undertone.

"I'm a few minutes early," Mary says to Gloria. "I hope that's okay."

Gloria shrugs. "To be on time is to be late."

Mary sits on the edge of a chair. The attendant tells her to press the call button if Gloria needs anything, then reminds her again to make sure the door of the ward locks behind her when she leaves.

"If you leave the door open, they get out," the attendant says darkly. "They wander."

Once she and Mary are alone, Gloria says, "Did you send out the agenda?"

"I forgot, I'm sorry. I only had one thing I needed to talk with you about, though."

Gloria narrows her eyes. "You look a little like my friend Ingrid from high school."

"Oh?" Mary scans the shelves of a credenza behind Gloria's chair. It's probably too much to expect that she would have a spare Empathyzer just lying around in her room, but Mary could get lucky.

"We were best friends. We used to do our hair and go cruising for boys at the mall. I was just a kid then."

Mary stands and moves across the room to inspect the shelves more closely.

"How do you get your hair so much bigger than mine? You've never told me."

"Um. Hair spray?" Mary peers behind an icon of the Madonna and Child on a shelf above the credenza. Nothing there, not even dust.

"You're a bitch," Gloria says. "You're a conniving, boyfriend-stealing slut, do you know that?"

Mary looks up quickly to find Gloria regarding her with a sweet smile.

"I didn't steal your boyfriend," she says. She feels a swell of pity, but then she remembers how Gloria let Garrett do whatever he wanted at Confluence, and how all the senior management except for her were white men. According to the tech press, Gloria's diagnosis is the main reason she's not in prison. "Gloria, I need to ask you something. What happened to the Empathyzer prototypes when Confluence closed? Did you keep any of them?"

Everyone Mary talked to said they were all destroyed. It's possible she and Elizabeth have the last two Empathyzers in existence. But Mary can't believe it. Someone must have held on to one. One of the higher-ups, planning to sell or improve upon the tech. One of the rats who deserted the sinking ship early. *Someone.*

Mary slides the closet door open. Soft clothes hang inside, taking up less than half the available space. Whoever moved Gloria in here didn't let her bring much in the way of personal effects.

"Are the rest of your things in storage?" Mary asks.

"Your hair looks like shit, by the way," Gloria says waspishly. "You should never have gotten it cut."

Mary doesn't know where she'll go next if she strikes out here. She's collected information from every former Confluence staffer she could find, including a trove of experimental data one of them passed her on a flash drive, like they were in some kind of spy thriller. She's used this information in her attempts at reconstructing a prototype, but it's not enough. None of the higher-level people would talk to her. Gloria is her Hail Mary.

"Don't think I don't know about you and my husband either," Gloria snaps. "Some friend you turned out to be."

Sounds of a commotion filter in from the hall. Brisk footsteps, a crash, shouting muffled by the closed door. "I can't believe . . . my *sister!*"

Mary recognizes that voice.

She places her hands on the arms of Gloria's recliner, bending to look directly into her eyes. "Gloria, I need you to be here with me. *Please.* You had a friend who betrayed you. You understand why I need this."

Gloria's eyes focus on Mary briefly, then shift to a point over her shoulder.

Mary moves so she's in line with Gloria's drifting gaze. She wants to shake the information out of her. "Is there another Empathyzer? Where is it?"

Gloria frowns. She looks off to the side, as though she's thinking hard about the question.

"Please. Do you remember? Tell me. Where are the other Empathyzer prototypes?" Mary grabs Gloria's hand in both of hers. It feels soft and a little moist, like someone rubs lotion into it twice a day. She squeezes. The hand is still strong, substantial underneath the soft skin.

Gloria looks down at their joined hands, then up into Mary's face.

She says, "Who the hell are you?"

That's how Rosemary Deegan finds them when she bursts into the room.

———

MARY HAD BEEN galvanized after she saw Elizabeth and Nate together, and especially after their wedding, which they chronicled throughout their online presences.

She *would* find a way to take over Elizabeth's body, permanently. She *would* live the life she'd watched her nemesis enjoy, the life she deserved.

She would have Nate, and all the other good things she'd been missing out on.

But the next prototype she built didn't work at all. The one after that, instead of pairing with her Empathyzer, caught fire and set off the alarm in her new apartment. That was when she decided to pay Gloria a visit.

The restraining order against her is a reminder that she needs to tread carefully. Mary is no longer allowed within five hundred feet of Gloria Faculak—not that the woman was any help—and the last thing she needs is to put Elizabeth's wind up. So she doesn't try to see Elizabeth and Nate again in person, though she still checks their feeds obsessively.

Seeing Gloria in that condition was sobering. Early-onset dementia has any number of causes, but Mary knows that Gloria, as CEO, tried every version of the Empathyzer herself.

Mary has written accounts of all the times she and Elizabeth used the Empathyzers, every exposure to its brain-manipulating capabilities. There are a lot. Is Gloria's future hers, minus the fancy nursing home?

Maybe her repeated failures are a sign that she should give up. For a while, she does.

She thinks about leaving the city. She could start a new life somewhere else, in a place where the Deegans don't control everything. She could focus on something besides Elizabeth and Nate and revenge.

But what would she *do*? She can't get into a decent school. She'll never work any jobs but menial ones, and the Deegans will garnish her wages wherever she goes. Moving is so expensive as to be impossible.

If she's destined to end up like Gloria, it'll be a lot more comfortable if she's in Elizabeth's body, with Elizabeth's resources.

Most of all, she wouldn't know what to do without her desire for revenge to animate her. Elizabeth shouldn't get away with screwing her over. It's that simple.

If she can't find an old prototype, she'll keep trying to build a new one. Her interrupted scientific training is a problem. She can fiddle with her own device, taking it apart and putting it back together. She can dick around with prototype kits and read over her notes until they cease making sense, but what she really needs is education.

She wouldn't have enough money to pay the fees for a community ed electronics class, let alone college tuition, even if she could get admitted. But she quietly sits in on some lectures at the university, picking up what she can. Because she can go unnoticed only in the larger courses, she expands her subject areas from bio-engineering. That's how she ends up shadow auditing a course on parapsychology, the syllabus of which includes a unit on out-of-body experiences.

She sits in the back, and slips out as class ends. Apparently she's not as unobtrusive as she thinks, because one day the TA stops her after the lecture.

"Hey," he says, and her palms start to sweat even though he doesn't act confrontational.

Should she appeal to his sense of intellectual generosity? Or throw something in a corner to create a distraction, then run away?

"Hi," she says, dry mouthed.

The TA cocks his head and narrows his eyes. Mary rises onto the balls of her feet, preparing to flee.

He smiles. "Don't you live in my building?"

MIGUEL IS DISARMINGLY sympathetic about her having sneaked into his lectures. "I don't blame you. College tuition is ridiculous," he says, and gives her carte blanche to sit in for the rest of term, as long as she doesn't get him into trouble.

She decides his course won't help her—it's too theoretical, its focus on redeeming a discredited field of study, and it doesn't give her any actionable knowledge. But Miguel must assume she's more educated than she is. After months of small talk by the mail-boxes and in the laundry room of their building, he asks if she's ever done any administrative work. The lab where he's doing research on OBEs for his PhD is looking to hire an office manager.

"I haven't had many office jobs," Mary says. Those tend not to be the kind that pay under the table.

"You can learn as you go. You're smart and capable."

How would you know? Mary wonders.

"And you seem kinda type A, if you don't mind me saying," he goes on. "That's what we need. Someone organized and self-directed, who won't get involved in drama. You'd be perfect. Think about it."

She does. When the position at the Ofori Lab is posted on the university website, she looks up the hourly wage and realizes she could afford to pay rent even with the Deegans' garnishment order skimming some off the top. The work would be an improvement over scrubbing toilets or dishes.

And maybe out-of-body experiences aren't the dead end she thought they were. She reads up on them, on astral projection. Much of the "research" out there is clearly pseudoscientific garbage. But if she could make it work . . .

It would be stupid for her to break into the home of, say, Confluence's former lab director without reason or a plan. But if she knew ahead of time that he had an Empathyzer squirreled away, the risk would be worth it. If she'd already sent her mind into his house.

She applies for the job. At the interview, Dr. Ofori asks Mary about future plans.

"I'm looking for something long-term," Mary promises. It might be true. She doesn't know how long she might take to perfect the technique of inducing and controlling an OBE, or to find an Empathyzer.

The job offer email causes a burst of elation that doesn't have anything to do with her revenge plans.

It feels like relief. Like an escape, or at least a rest, from the quest she's been on for so long.

Garrett Deegan died recently. That shows there's some justice in the universe. Mary wants Elizabeth to get her comeuppance, and she wants to be the one to give it to her. But she's so tired. Of the effort it takes to keep her resentment at a high boil, and of not being able to move past the most painful time in her life.

For a brief period after Mary accepts the job offer, Elizabeth seems unreal, as though Mary knows her only from the internet.

Then Dr. Ofori emails again. She says she's very sorry, but she won't be able to have Mary work in the Ofori Lab after all. It seems Dr. Ofori's department chair received an angry call from Brian Deegan. He and his wife had previously made a multimillion-dollar gift to the department. They just came back from an extended trip on their yacht—a grief tour of sorts—and what should they see but Mary Burke's name on a list of new hires? Unacceptable.

In a few lines, the future Mary had started building in her mind is ripped away.

There will be no respite for her. What she gets instead is a reminder that she will never succeed in building a new life, not without leaving her old one behind.

So that's what she'll do.

41

MARY (ELIZABETH)

NOW

I've been alone in the house no more than fifteen minutes when something crashes through the front window. A blast of freezing air rolls through the house, raising goose bumps on my skin.

"You're dead, you slut!" a male voice yells, followed by laughter and the sound of running footsteps.

My body moves without thought. I grab a coat, sprint out the back door to the garage, throw myself into Elizabeth's car, and peel out through the alley.

Only when I'm on the main road, surrounded by traffic and lights and people, does the fear catch up with me. I start to shake so badly I can hardly keep the car on the road.

There's only one reason someone—or multiple someones—would have shattered that window: so they could come in and hurt Elizabeth. Hurt me.

I almost rear-end the car in front of me at a red light, which tells me I either need to pull over or calm the fuck down. I haven't driven far enough to feel safe yet, so I try to control my breathing, stay in my lane, and think about my situation logically.

Who would invade Elizabeth's home? Maybe it wasn't even that;

it could have been another instance of vandalism. Teenagers being assholes. A random troll who saw those photos online and found out where she lives, then decided to put a scare into her.

Or it could be a homicidal psycho. It could be Lorne, who's been tracking Elizabeth's location for an unknown period of time. Who might be threatening her. Thinking of him makes me remember I was about to check the car for tracking devices before Nate came home and all hell broke loose.

I should call the cops. Hailey didn't arm the security system on her way out, so they won't show up at the house unless I summon them. But I hesitate, remembering Johns' call. I don't want to speak to him again, and I've had more to drink than I should have before getting behind the wheel. The police might understand my panic reaction, but then again, they might be looking for any excuse to arrest me.

I check the rearview and see dancing trails coming off the headlights behind me. I blink, then blink again, trying to clear my vision.

Nate slipped up with his words earlier. Is *he* the one who's been sending those messages? Does he know about Elizabeth's past with the Empathyzers and Garrett? Maybe after our fight he decided he didn't want to deal with being married *or* divorced, that he'd rather be widowed and take all of what he and Elizabeth built.

Or is it Lorne who knows the truth? I need to make sure he can't find me. I need to search this car.

Looking for a place to pull off the road, I notice the traffic has thinned considerably and the sidewalks are dark and empty. I'm still not familiar with the borders of the neighborhood. I've driven myself into an industrial area of shut-down factories and vacant lots. Perfect places to get jumped.

The shifting in my vision hasn't gone away. Shadows jump and dance around the car, lights glancing off my retinas, causing visual explosions like cheap fireworks. The car drifts, its tires growling in the slush on the side of the road, and I jerk the wheel back to the left.

What is happening to me?

It feels like the effects from a transfer. Dizziness, disorientation, crawling vision. Chattering voices that I know can't be real. But transfer side effects have always diminished within a few hours. I can't still be having them days later.

Or can I? I've never stayed in Elizabeth's body for this long. What if this is the beginning of something more permanent, like what happened to Gloria Faculak?

Ice forms in my stomach, then shatters when I see headlights in the rearview. They close in fast, the car behind me slaloming on the wet road as it rides my bumper, and I realize what's going on. The broken window was a way to get me to panic and leave the house. Now that I'm defenseless, whoever threw that rock will follow me, run me off the road, and scoop me up.

The lights and shadows swell and converge, pulling back when I focus on them. I make a sharp turn to shake off my pursuer and the engine chugs like it's going to stall out, only falling back into rhythm once I'm on a straightaway. The other car sticks on my tail. On the dash glows an amber light I've never noticed before while driving Elizabeth's car, but I think it's been on this whole time. The words next to it squiggle and squirm. By closing one eye, I manage to read them:

LOW FUEL

"Oh, come on!" I thump the steering wheel. Somehow, this is the last straw. Shouldn't Hailey, my *assistant*, have gassed up the car for me sometime in the last few days? Or Nate, since he was driving it?

Annoyance gives me a shot of lucidity. I accelerate, hoping to see an open gas station or even one other human being. I can't tell who's at the wheel of the car behind me, not with my eyes jiggling in their sockets. It's taking all my concentration just to stay on the road.

The fireworks in my peripheral vision have turned into supernovas. The driver behind me honks their horn and the noise blares through my skull, making me scream.

My phone! My phone is in the cup holder. Steering as best I can with one hand, I jab the emergency call button with my thumb. I have to make a few tries before I hit and confirm it. The voice that answers sounds like gibberish, repeating itself over and over. *What is your emergency? Is your emergency what? Your emergency what is? Emergency*

> *Hello*

Your emergency? What is?

Your name?

"Mary," I gasp out. "My name's Mary."

Then I realize what I've said. "No. This is Elizabeth Jordan." My tongue vibrates at supersonic speed every time it touches my teeth. "My window. Somebody broke . . ."

Ma'am, I can't understand you. You'll need to speak clearly.

"They're chasing me!" My tires slide on ice, and I barely manage to steer out of the skid. The phone flies from my hand into infinity.

Is someone there? The voice comes from the floor of the car.

"Help me!" I scream, blinded by the headlights in my rearview.

The car jerks like it's going to vomit, completely out of fuel. There's a gas station ahead. Safety! I pull up next to a pump, the engine dying as the car coasts to a stop.

There's a yellow bag on the pump handle. The lights are off in the glass box between the pumps. No one here. No one to save me.

There are no more voices from the phone on the floor.

The car that's been following me pulls up alongside. I cringe back into my seat, but then straighten up and clench my fists. This asshole might think I'm defenseless, but screw going down without a fight.

A dark-tinted window glides down to reveal a middle-aged white man I've never seen before with frizzy hair poofing out from under a green stocking cap.

He yells at me, "Get off the road, you drunk asshole! I'm calling the cops!" His window goes back up. He roars off.

I sit frozen, the car growing colder. The strip lighting on the overhead canopy is a sickly greenish white, the old bulbs flickering. I can hear them buzzing through the window glass like the ghosts of summer cicadas. The light above me flares and flickers out. The next one over does the same, and the next, until I'm in darkness. The shadows feel hungry.

An idea pops into my mind, as clear as bold black type on a white background. Elizabeth's body is rejecting me. Like a transplanted organ. A foreign object. A disease. I never read about this in the trial data, but I know it has to be true.

I grope at my wrist for the Empathyzer before I remember it's not there. It's deep in a closet in Elizabeth's house, the house that I've stolen, a stolen house embedded in a stolen life. Why did I steal Elizabeth's life? How could I do that to my best friend?

We're not nineteen anymore. No longer friends but enemies. Instead of fury, I feel sadness. A friend is a precious thing. Especially for me, who's had so few.

A bright rectangle lights up on the floor of the car. My phone is ringing. I should answer, but it might be the police. I don't trust them. Why did I call them? They want me to be the one who killed Garrett.

No one will help me. Hailey is mad at me. Nate is mad at me, and also might be trying to hurt me. Elizabeth's friends aren't real friends.

She and I are both alone in this world.

There's one person who has a vested interest in keeping this body alive and unharmed. Slowly, I unfreeze. I bend down to pick up the phone, which has stopped ringing. I send a text.

After a minute that takes an hour, Elizabeth responds.

Where are you?

I send her a location pin.

Be there soon.

She doesn't text me anything further. Maybe she wants to get on my good side so I'll let her transfer back. Or she's making sure her body is okay. It can't be that she cares about me as a person, not when she let me twist in the wind for so many years. But I feel a tiny door opening in my head, letting in a little light. The light is the possibility that I don't have to deal with this on my own anymore.

42

ELIZABETH (MARY)

NOW

It's immediately obvious that Mary is off her face on something.

"Open up, Mary. It's freezing." Elizabeth taps on the window. Inside the car, Mary flinches, the black of her pupils swallowing her irises.

Miguel hefts a full gas can out of the trunk of his car and comes up beside Elizabeth. Maybe this is why her instincts led her to him, so she could come to Mary's rescue this way, put Mary in her debt. She can't afford a rideshare; without Miguel and his car, she would have no way of getting here that didn't involve over an hour on multiple buses. But if she'd known he was going to see her real face, she would never have told him who she was.

Behind the glass, Mary's eyes shift from Elizabeth's face to Miguel's. His expression is grim, but hers slackens with relief. She unlocks the car doors.

"I'll put the gas in," Miguel mutters, going around the side of Elizabeth's car, but not before sending Mary a glare.

His hostility is no surprise. Mary didn't come out well in the version of the story Elizabeth told him. How could she? The bare facts Elizabeth outlined—that Mary planted an Empathyzer on her and transferred, without warning, while she sat at brunch with her friends—make Mary look like a psychopath. Elizabeth softened that impression only slightly with her explanation of their falling-out in college. She'd told him about Garrett's tumble down the stairs, that it was her fault and that Mary had gotten the blame, but she also made it sound like she'd tried much harder than she had to help Mary out afterward. She also didn't tell Miguel she'd been the one to send Mary the second Empathyzer, let alone why.

And she didn't mention Nate at all.

Making herself safe is worth any number of half-truths and concealments. She would have lied about who they were coming to help if she didn't think Miguel would see through it. That doesn't mean she feels good about keeping things from him.

She gets into the car on the passenger side. It's as cold as outside, but at least it's out of the wind. "What happened?"

Mary struggles for breath. Elizabeth looks at her with concern, but no, her first impression was correct. Mary's not having a heart attack in her body. She's just high.

"Mary." She touches Mary's hand. The contact seems to bring Mary into the here and now. "We're here. You're okay. Tell me what happened."

"Someone tried to kill me."

Swear to god, if Mary's just having a bad trip—

"They threw a rock through the window."

The air goes out of Elizabeth's lungs. "What?"

Mary chews her lower lip, which is swollen as if she's been at it already. "Someone came to your house. Threw something through the window. Yelled, 'You're dead.' I ran. For all I know, they're still there."

"You *left*? What about Jumbo?"

Guilt crosses Mary's face. "I forgot about him. E, I think Nate's been—"

The back door of the car opens, letting in a blast of freezing wind as Miguel gets in. Digging her short fingernails into Mary's hand, Elizabeth sends her emergency eye signals. *Don't say anything, don't say anything.* The message gets through: Mary shuts up.

"Try starting it," Miguel says shortly.

The car starts. The fuel needle floats up to a quarter of a tank.

"You'll need to get more gas." His eyes, angry, meet Mary's in the rearview. "You— What's wrong with her?" he asks Elizabeth.

"I'll drive her home," she says.

"No!" Mary shrinks down in her seat. "I can't go back there. You don't get it, E. I mean, shit." Her gaze cuts to Miguel. "Mary."

"I know who you are," he says. Elizabeth gets the feeling he'd spit on the ground if they weren't in her car.

"Why don't you go home?" she says. "I can handle this."

Miguel doesn't look happy with that idea at all. Elizabeth turns around so she's speaking to him face-to-face, not over her shoulder. "Mary and I need to go talk some things out. I'll be fine."

Clearly he wants to argue, but instead he presses his lips together. "Text me when you're done and I'll come get you." Turning a fierce glare on Mary, he leans between the seats. "In case you don't know, what you're doing is really fucked up."

Mary blinks in confusion, but he slams out of the car before she can respond.

———

"WHAT IS THIS place you've brought me to?"

Mary's slurring more now than she was in the car. Her eyes roll in their sockets, like she's alarmed by all the oak paneling.

"I came here with Lorne a few times," Elizabeth says. An all-night karaoke diner, the jukebox stocked with old country-and-western tunes, patronized almost exclusively by white people over fifty-five. Lorne has an ironic streak; plus, they were unlikely to see anyone they knew.

Elizabeth has ordered coffee and full breakfasts for them both from a waitress who looks like Bettie Page with tattoos. On a small stage behind a wooden railing, a sixtyish woman in a tracksuit sings a slow, mournful rendition of "Back in Baby's Arms." The lyrics scroll across the screen behind her. She's a couple of lines behind.

Mary looks around nervously. "What if he comes in now?"

Mary is afraid of Lorne. Elizabeth files that away.

"I don't think he will." She lets a hint of doubt into her voice. Tapping Mary's coffee cup, she says, "Drink this. And your water. What did you take?"

Mary turns depthless pupils on her. "What?"

"What are you *on.* What drugs did you take?"

"Nothing. I didn't take anything. I think your body's rejecting me."

Elizabeth considers just letting Mary believe that.

"I've dealt with transfer side effects before, though. I can get through this, don't you worry."

The music ends, but the tracksuit woman keeps singing into the silence until she's finished what she considers to be enough repetitions of the song's last line. A tall, stooped man comes onstage and starts singing "You Win Again" in a monotone.

Elizabeth sighs. "Mary. This isn't side effects from the transfer. Someone drugged you."

The waitress drops off their food, and Mary looks at her egg-white spinach omelet like she doesn't know what it's for.

"Eat. It'll help you sober up." Elizabeth attacks her own eggs, sausage, and hash browns.

"Nate made me drink a drink. Two drinks." Mary holds up two fingers, then squints at them as if to make sure she has the right number.

"My *husband* drugged you?"

"Not sure he's gonna be your husband for much longer. He's so pissed. You can't blame that one on me. That fuckup's *aaall* yours, baby."

Nerves squiggle through Elizabeth's stomach. "What are you talking about?"

"You don't know?"

Whatever Elizabeth doesn't know is obviously bad news, something Mary should be champing at the bit to deliver. But for some reason she looks hesitant.

Elizabeth's raging appetite curdles. She sets down her fork. "Just tell me."

Mary spends a laborious minute or two bringing something up on her phone. She pushes it across the table to Elizabeth.

The first thing that hits her eyes is Lorne's phoenix tattoo, stretching from shoulder to naked shoulder and down to his lower back.

Then her own face, caught in a private and extremely unflattering moment. Elizabeth hears a small cry of dismay escape her throat.

Her eyes fly to the top of the screen, the header of the app. This is public. Photographs of her and Lorne having sex are public. People can *see* them. See *her*.

"They took the original photos down, but people keep posting screenshots." Mary's voice is soft. Sympathetic, almost.

"Who—how—" Elizabeth feels the heat of shame rise into her face, hears the whispers in her mind. *Worthless*. She sees her youth pastor—the one who used to accidentally on purpose brush against her when no one was looking—holding a chewed-up piece of gum between thumb and forefinger, the wad glistening with saliva. *Is this what you want to be?*

Somewhere outside her bubble of horror, "You Win Again" finishes to scattered applause, more than Patsy Cline got. The stooped man keeps the stage, launching into "Your Cheatin' Heart."

"Could we get some fucking Dolly Parton in here?" Mary mutters.

Elizabeth shakes away her memories of evangelical sex ed. Yes, she did something wrong. She cheated on her husband—that he was doing it too doesn't make it *less* wrong. But the shame she feels has more to do with the fact that these photos show her using her own body for her own pleasure. The comments, which she can't stop herself from scanning, tell her plenty of other people have a problem with it too.

"Lorne posted them," Mary says.

Elizabeth looks up, her mouth falling open. "But he—" Loves her? Is obsessed with her? Her eyes move irresistibly back to the screen. All that naked skin and ink, but not his face. *Her* face in every picture. The comments, split between judgment and titillation.

Horror drains away, leaving a more pragmatic despair. Lorne knows how important her work is to her, and these photos? *Not* consistent with her brand. "He wouldn't do this."

But how does she know what Lorne would or wouldn't do?

It makes an awful kind of sense, especially if Mary angered him with her rejection. Men turn on a dime for less. From worship to throwing you down in the mud.

"The time will come when you'll be blue," the man on the stage intones, his eyes fixed on a point above Elizabeth's head.

Propping her chin on her hand, Mary uses her fork to pick at a wilted spinach leaf. "It figures. You've got all the luck no matter which body you're in. You push a guy down the stairs and my life gets ruined. You have an affair and I have to deal with the guy posting pictures of it."

Elizabeth sees her opportunity, but doesn't want to press it too soon. Dealing with Mary, especially when she's in this state, requires delicacy. Elizabeth's not feeling delicate. She wants to go at that jukebox with a sledgehammer.

If Lorne were here, she'd take his head off.

"Hailey said going to the police wouldn't do any good," Mary says.

"I don't imagine it would. He knew where to hit me. I don't

know how my career's going to recover from this, especially with you driving."

That last bit might have been going too far, but Mary looks thoughtful and a little incredulous. "You actually like your job, don't you?"

"You don't? This can't be easy for you, then." Elizabeth makes a gesture to encompass Mary's physicality.

"It's not that bad. Work's the least of my problems, right?" Mary huffs a laugh. "The whole thing about money not buying happiness? Bullshit. Or I guess being poor's bad enough that having money *feels* like happiness."

"Mary. If you let me transfer back, I promise you'll never have to worry about money again."

Mary meets her eye, and for a second Elizabeth thinks she'll bite.

"But then I wouldn't have my revenge." Mary's mouth curls up, her voice lilting like this is some kind of game to her. Elizabeth knows it's not.

Mary might hate her, but she can still be moved with the right lever. *Nate.*

Elizabeth brings up the message thread between her and Nate on her phone, then slides it across the table. "That's what my husband has been doing," she says. "Sending dick pics to his wife's best friend from college. He doesn't have a leg to stand on, being mad about Lorne."

Mary squints at the screen, the urge to deny written across her face.

"He drugged you," Elizabeth presses. "You have to admit he's up to something." She wishes she knew what.

Mary's shaking her head. Words bubble to Elizabeth's lips, more attempts to convince, but then Mary says, "He wanted me to post a public apology for cheating on him. He was all, *Things are going to change around here! I wear the pants in this couple now!*"

Elizabeth's throat tightens. The drugging must have been part of Nate's attempt to seize control. Put her off-balance, make her doubt her own perceptions. Make her afraid.

What about the rock through the window? Elizabeth's still not sure that actually happened, but something scared the hell out of Mary tonight.

"Did you really get rid of the other Empathyzer?"

Mary sets down her fork and pushes her still-half-full plate aside. "I know what you're doing."

"And? It doesn't change the fact that you're not safe in that house."

Mary's expression of narrow-eyed suspicion remains in place, so Elizabeth pivots. "Detective Johns came by to talk to me earlier."

Mary cackles, drawing a glare from the senior citizens at the next table over. "Ah. Karma."

"He was asking about me. *Me* me."

The smile drops off Mary's face.

Elizabeth lowers her voice. "Garrett knew I was the one who pushed him that night. He was blackmailing me before he died."

Mary's wheels are turning more slowly than usual, but she gets it. "Motive."

"And Lorne——" She stops, realizing something. She has a perfect way to get back at him. The police might not go after him for revenge porn, but they will for murder.

She needs to figure out a way to take him down without getting caught up in his downward slide. And if anyone's good at figuring things out, Mary is.

"What about Lorne?" Mary says.

Elizabeth can see the fear and distaste in her eyes. Lorne's done something worse than posting those pictures, than showing up at the house. Elizabeth can use that.

"Did he know about Halloween too?" Mary asks.

"Lorne? No." Lorne thinks Garrett was blackmailing her because he found out they were still sleeping together after her and Nate's marriage had closed. "But he knew Garrett was a problem for me. Mebs, I think . . ." She makes her voice go faint and trembly. "I think Lorne might have killed Garrett. For me."

Mary doesn't look surprised. She cocks her head, auburn hair flowing over her shoulder. "You didn't put him up to it?"

"What? *No.* Whatever Lorne did, he came up with on his own. I'm just afraid that now he's going to think you're some kind of loose end."

Maybe she's laid it on too thick. Mary closes one eye, fixing her with the other, but eventually nods. Elizabeth lets out her breath.

"You're sure he doesn't know it was you on Halloween?"

Why does Mary think that? "If he does, it's not because I told him."

A lightning bolt of an idea strikes. Elizabeth slaps the table, making the dishes rattle. "What if we could get him to confess to the killing? I could get it on video. Like we did with Garrett. Then we tell him that if anything happens to me—to you—the video will be sent to the police."

Mary thinks about it for a second, then shakes her head. "Why would he tell *you* anything?"

He won't, not to Mary's face. Elizabeth shrugs, like it doesn't matter. "So you do it. I'll coach you on what to say."

This is the trap. Mary will be even less able to pretend with Lorne than she was with Garrett. But she's not safe unless they handle him. They'll have to transfer back.

The logic is airtight. Elizabeth's actually proud of herself.

43

MARY (ELIZABETH)

NOW

It's hard not to be swayed. Elizabeth probably came out of the womb working an angle. She'd be willing to do anything, say anything, to get out of my body and back into her own.

You'll never have to worry about money again. Please.

The waitress comes by and refills our coffee, and a woman with a salon bouffant bigger than her face gets up and starts singing "D-I-V-O-R-C-E." A little on the nose, if you ask me.

When Elizabeth started talking about Lorne, I showed my hand. I couldn't hide how much he creeps me out, and now she knows I'll never be able to handle being close to him.

She's gone quiet. She won't say it; she wants me to think transferring back is my idea.

Being able to see how she's manipulating the situation doesn't give me any magical revelations about how to get around it.

"You're going to have to do better than that," I tell her. Her face falls, but not as far as I'd hoped.

I'm feeling more lucid after two cups of coffee and half an omelet. I'm glad I didn't tell her about the newest threats—they'd only strengthen her case. Though I'm almost positive now that it wasn't Lorne who sent them.

Nate. The poisoner. The cheater, the manipulator, the *bastard.* How could I have been so wrong about him?

I don't want him to get away with what he's done any more than Elizabeth wants Lorne to. But part of me is tempted to play into her hands. Johns seems to have pivoted to her as a suspect. Her life is in shambles. Let her deal with it.

That wouldn't be her paying for what she did to me, though. Once she got back into her own body, she'd hire a lawyer, feed Lorne to the police, divorce Nate, and come out on top like she always does. And where would that leave me? Right back where I started, albeit without the threat of a murder charge hanging over my head.

She must sense what I'm thinking. "You won't be on your own this time. I'll get you a lawyer, help you deal with the Deegans and whatever else."

Her promises are worth less than this crappy coffee. It amazes me that I used to trust her.

"I did try to contact you, after you left school," Elizabeth goes on. "I tried to help."

"I wouldn't have taken your 'help.' I wouldn't even have needed it if not for you."

Elizabeth's eyes go wide and guileless, almost as innocent-looking as they would be in her own face. "You know Garrett's fall was an accident."

"I know you wanted me to think that. But you found out what he was planning, assumed I was helping him, so you decided you'd fuck both of us over." It feels so good to get it out there! Why haven't I done this before?

Elizabeth's face wrinkles in confusion. "Are you still talking about Halloween?"

Jesus, E, try to keep up. "Yes. Just admit it!" I lean over the table. "You found out he was trying to force me to have sex with him in your body. So you planned the whole thing. You went upstairs with Nate, so you'd be in position. You waited for Garrett in the stairwell. You pushed him, then made sure I'd get blamed for it."

Only when I outline the events of that night do I see the holes in my story. How would she have known Garrett would be alone in the stairwell right then, instead of in his room with me?

Elizabeth is speechless. Her already pale face goes an ugly greenish color. She looks like she's about to lose her sausage and eggs.

What a performance.

"Garrett *planned* to . . ." She gulps air. Actual tears well up in her eyes and spill down her cheeks. She gropes for a napkin to blot them, regaining her composure. "He planned to rape me? Why would he think you'd go along with that? Unless . . . He found out you'd stolen the Empathyzers, didn't he? He threatened you."

Elizabeth's a good actress, sure, but her shock and confusion seem sincere.

"I wondered when he'd discovered it," she says. "He cornered me at a party last year, told me he knew it was me on Halloween— but I had no idea he'd known about the Empathyzers so early on."

I have one fragment of solid ground to stand on amid the crumbling of all my assumptions. "You had Katarina tell the cops Garrett and I were fighting. She gave you an alibi."

"I didn't tell Katarina what to say. I was actually mad at her when I found out she'd lied to the police."

"*You* didn't tell them Garrett and I argued?"

"No. I——" Elizabeth frowns. "You think I would set you up?"

"If I'd arranged for you to get raped, I would deserve it."

"But you didn't." She looks at me, double-checking.

"Of course not."

"That's what I thought. Mebs, I would never think you'd do something like that. No matter what he had on you. That's not part of your makeup."

Tears sting my eyes in a surprise attack of emotion. She has that much faith in me? Still?

"Why didn't you tell me?"

I can't take hold of my own reasoning for that anymore. It came down to my not believing in our friendship.

"I had a whole plan to deal with him," I say. "I drugged him so he'd pass out, and I was going to make him think we'd had sex. But he wouldn't . . ." I give a damp chuckle. "He wouldn't fucking pass out." I blink back tears and blow my nose on a napkin.

I need to pull myself together. Even if she didn't set me up, she still let me take the fall.

But then she says, "I tried to confess."

I freeze. There's no way I've heard her right. Her voice is so quiet, and pedal steel is wailing from the jukebox.

"I went to the police first," she goes on. "I showed Detective Johns my Empathyzer. Told him we were transferred that night, that Garrett had threatened me and my pushing him was self-defense. He laughed at me. He said if I wanted to be noble, I needed to think of a more convincing story. So I went to the dean of students' office and told them. I said they should check your computer, because you'd written down every transfer we'd ever done. *They* referred me to counseling in the student health center. But it's all on record.

"Confluence was all over the news for being a fraud, so maybe the university didn't want to remind people of the ties between them. Especially in connection with the 'tragedy' on campus. Or maybe it was just easier to go with the suspect they had on camera."

It's feasible, what she says, especially with Garrett's parents bringing the pressure to punish someone. But believing her would mean that everything I've done over the last seven years was a fool's errand.

"I guess I could have tried harder to make them believe me.

But then I started thinking, *What if they think we planned it together? Then we're both screwed.* I didn't have my own money, not enough for a lawyer. My parents were an inch away from cutting me off at any given time. And this doesn't excuse it, but I was pissed too. I'd gone through this traumatic experience and you were being a giant bitch."

That sounds more like the Elizabeth I know.

She reaches across the table and grabs my hand. I don't even pull away, just look down at our joined hands in surprise.

"I'm so sorry, Mary. I'm sorry that it happened, and that I didn't try harder to keep you from getting in trouble for it, and that you've been paying for it all these years."

An apology. One of the things I've been craving from her; not the most important by a long shot, but significant. A heartfelt acknowledgment of the wrong she did and the way it derailed me. It should give me some small glow of satisfaction, but I only feel empty.

It's not that I don't appreciate her words. I do. But they can't give me back the last seven years of my life.

I pull my hand from hers. "If you really tried to confess, then why did you pay Garrett off? Why were you so worried about the truth coming out?"

"Just because I was ready to be a martyr when I was young and stupid doesn't mean I want to be one now."

I've heard enough. I reach across and grab my car keys from where they sit next to Elizabeth's plate. "Well. Thanks for the apology, and for coming out. But I think I've got everything under control. And I've got this, too." I pick up the bill, relishing any tiny cut I can give her. I know, down to the dollar, what my bank balance was on the day I transferred—you have to, when the slightest miscalculation can drop you into a sinkhole of overdraft fees—and I doubt it's risen since.

"But, Mebs—"

"I always hated that fucking nickname."

Her mouth firms into a line. "You want to deal with my problems by yourself? Be my guest. I've got enough to handle with yours." She slides out of the booth.

"Hey," I say.

She turns back to me, her face closed.

"Try not to fuck my neighbor up too badly. He's a good guy, he doesn't deserve you."

Letting out a snort, Elizabeth walks away.

"Did you tell him you're married?" I yell, but the only answer I get is the bell on the diner's door as it shuts behind her.

44

ELIZABETH (MARY)

NOW

Elizabeth's so annoyed at Mary's stubbornness that she's a block down the street before she remembers she doesn't have a car.

She takes out her phone and texts Miguel, hearing Mary's parting shot in her head. *Did you tell him you're married?*

Maybe she should. She thinks about how, back in college, Mary failed to share that Garrett had forced her into an impossible corner. Everything would have turned out so differently if she'd just trusted Elizabeth with the truth.

This isn't the same. Her and Miguel's whole relationship is based on deception. She has almost no resources; she can't afford to lose his support. Mary—and by extension, Elizabeth's own body, which she still very much plans to transfer into one way or another—is in danger.

What's doing the right thing against losing her identity?

She waits, shivering, for Miguel to text her back. Finally he does, but it's not to tell her he's on his way.

He's sent her a link to the post she made for her and Nate's wedding anniversary. If Miguel scrolled all the way back to June, he's gotten quite the tour of their marriage. The shiny social-media version of it, at least.

Your face looked familiar, he texted along with the link.

Nausea butts at her throat. He's still typing.

My sister had sent me a link to some video you made. She's obsessed with you. His sister who sends him memes, who's into influencers.

I don't want to tell her who you really are.

There's no more. Elizabeth slumps against a brick wall, hardly feeling the wind in her face or the tears it whips from her eyes.

Letting him see her real face was a terrible idea in a string of bad ones.

She starts typing out a reply, then changes her mind and calls him. He's blocked her number.

"Gah!" she screams, but it doesn't satisfy. "Fuck!" That's a little better. She tightens her hand around the phone to keep herself from dashing it against the frozen sidewalk. She can't afford a new one.

Then she uses it to look up how to get back to Mary's on public transit.

———

MIGUEL MUST BE home at this time of night, unless he went out to drown his sorrows, but he's not opening the door.

Her plan is to tell him the whole truth. Confess her entire role in the Empathyzer fiasco. All of her reasons, selfish and altruistic, for the things she's done. Then she'll apologize—a real, legitimate grovel—and hope there's some spark of affection for her left in his heart. There has to be. He's mad and hurt, but she can fix that. This has to be fixable.

She knocks again, not too loud, because she doesn't want his neighbors to come out and see her lurking like some kind of obsessive.

She straightens at the sound of footsteps on the other side of the door. She feels him waiting, can imagine him there. Jaw clenched, hair messy from where he's been running his hands through it. Separated from her by two inches of wood and her lies.

"Miguel," she says, just above a whisper. "Let me explain."

"There's nothing to explain." He speaks at normal volume. He doesn't sound like he's been asleep.

"There is." She swallows the lump in her throat. "Please."

He suspends her in a silence that lasts so long, she wonders if she imagined him coming to the door. If she's imagined their whole relationship, every interaction, his existence.

"Miguel?" she whispers, fearful.

"Please go away, Elizabeth." Polite to the end. She hears the slow tread of his receding steps, then the closing of a door. Probably his bedroom, where she so recently lay warm and contented.

She wants to pound on the door, but she's so tired she's seeing double. Now is not the time to press the issue. She'll get him back; she'll think of something.

The two flights up to Mary's apartment seem steeper than usual. She's never hated any four walls more. This place is a dead end.

Gah, why is she so upset? It's not just Miguel. It's those photos. It's learning what Garrett had planned for her on Halloween. Even after all these years, with Garrett in his grave, it makes her skin crawl.

She's so stupid about men. That's part of why she feels so devastated right now; she'd finally chosen a good one, but it turns out she's not good enough for him.

It's not as if she and Miguel could have had anything lasting. Even without Nate in the picture, Miguel would never fit into her real life. He's far from camera ready, and what's more, he'd never aspire to be. He wouldn't *like* the real her. He'd be baffled by her posturing, her need to have strangers love and admire her.

But there was something there. A seed taking root, the idea

that they would find each other once she was herself again. It's what happens in stories.

But in the real world, he despises her. She thinks of his apartment, its golden light and plump green plants. Mary was right: he doesn't deserve the turmoil she'd bring into his life. And he can't absolve her. Not when Mary brushed off her apology like it meant nothing.

A text comes in. She dives for Mary's phone, but it's not Miguel; it's Nate.

> Enough messing around. Come out and meet me.

> I'm getting ducking divorced. I'll be a free
> man soon

Drunk. And angry, obviously, about the photos and the general state of his life. Elizabeth doesn't need any more proof that he's trash. It's wiser not to engage. She's glad Nate doesn't know where Mary lives.

She turns off notifications. It's not as if Miguel or Mary are going to have a change of heart tonight. But she can't resist checking her texts one more time, to find Nate's sent one last message.

> Ding dong the witch is dead

45

MARY (ELIZABETH)

NOW

A pounding on the front door awakens me.

It's faint, having to travel through floor and walls, but my sleep is light. After I was finally able to drive home last night, I holed up in Nate's man cave. The door at the top of the stairs is solid wood and has a dead bolt that doesn't unlock with a keypad. The one that leads outside does, but it's glass; I'll see anyone trying to come in.

When I got back, I found the front window unbroken. The house seemingly undisturbed.

The way Jumbo acted was the only sign anything was amiss. When I finally found him hiding under the bed upstairs, he wouldn't come to me, even with the temptation of leftover steak. Eventually I gave up and came down to the only place in the house that felt even a little bit safe. I couldn't bring myself to leave again.

Did last night happen? The panicked car chase, the old people in the diner singing country songs, the conversation with Elizabeth. The window, whole, when I could still recall the high-pitched laughter of the man who broke it. Was any of it real?

Nate must not have come home, which is fine, considering my feelings toward him. Except whoever's at the door isn't going away.

Every strike of knuckles on glass sends a spike into my forehead. I've got an absolute bitch of a hangover.

I roll myself off the edge of the couch and struggle to my feet, wrapping an afghan around my shoulders. If it were a murderer, they'd break in instead of knocking, right?

Jumbo's whining at the door. A shadow stands outside. It's fitting that the knocking sounds like a cop's, because it is.

Detective Johns.

The memory of what Elizabeth said last night filters in, that he was asking about her in connection with Garrett's death. *Her* her.

I'm sure I look like shit, and I wish I didn't. I feel like I'm about to need all the armor I can get. I take a deep breath before opening the door.

"Ms. Jordan! Just the person I was hoping to have a chat with." Johns smiles with his square, coffee-stained teeth. I knit my lips together.

Jumbo starts yapping so fiercely, I have to pick him up.

"Can I come in?" Johns asks, then launches into his shivering-and-commenting-on-the-cold routine.

I put a stop to that by stepping out onto the porch and shutting the door behind me. "We can talk out here."

"Are you sure? You want to draw attention? You've already put *on* a little bit of a show, you know what I mean. With those photos," he adds, just in case I didn't catch his drift.

So this is about Lorne, and his association with Elizabeth. I lift my chin and look Johns in the eye. "Are you here to tell me Lorne's going to be prosecuted for posting them?"

"I'm here because of a nine-one-one call that came in last night from your number. From a woman who said her name was Mary, *then* claimed she was Elizabeth Jordan, and that someone was chasing her. Is everything all right here?"

Cold flashes through me that has nothing to do with the temperature. "I didn't call nine-one-one last night."

"How do you explain the call coming from your phone?"

I shrug, Jumbo growling in my arms. "Can't the source of a call be faked? It wasn't me."

"You mind if I take a look at your phone?"

"I don't have it with me."

"I'll wait while you go in and get it."

"I lost it, actually."

"You lost your phone."

"I did. I think it might have been stolen." I hold his gaze. I'm Elizabeth Jordan. I have money; I have resources; I am no one's scapegoat.

Johns looks away first. Except his eyes go straight to my chest, to which he says, "It certainly looks like you and Mr. Gagnon get along well. Partners, you might say."

My throat closes. "Whatever *that* was," I force out, "it's over now. And he did *not* have my permission to—"

"How long have you and your husband been together, Ms. Jordan? You start dating in college?"

Lovely. He's going to shame me for cheating on Nate. "A few years after graduation."

"So he wouldn't have had any reason back then to lie in order to protect you."

"Lie about what?"

"About Mary Burke and Garrett Deegan having a screaming fight right before Garrett took his fall down the stairs."

"*Nate* told you that?" My jaw drops. Nate wouldn't have even heard Elizabeth-as-me and Garrett on the stairs if he'd been passed out drunk in his room as Elizabeth claimed. Why would he lie to get me into trouble? I think of the texts he sent me in the days after Halloween, how insulted he was when I didn't answer him. Could he really be that petty?

Did he sense something off that night, about the woman he thought was me?

"Ms. Jordan, why did you tell me back then that you were the one who pushed Garrett down the stairs? Were you just trying to confuse the matter and save your friend?"

Holy shit. Elizabeth told me the truth.

Johns steps closer. "Or did I miss something?"

I shake my head. "I don't know what you're talking about. It was so long ago, I don't remember."

"You don't remember that night? Or you don't remember telling me about it?"

I back up until my shoulders hit the glass of the door.

Johns' face wrinkles in annoyance. "Well. Maybe you'll remember this. Your boy Lorne—when I talked to him, he said you and Garrett had been on the outs lately. He seemed to think Garrett had something on you, was maybe squeezing you a little bit. So I took another look at Garrett's bank records, and saw he'd received several funds transfers from you in the weeks before he died. Why'd you send him money?"

"I was probably paying him back for brunch or something."

"A thousand dollars at a time is a hell of a lot of money for brunch, Ms. Jordan." He leans closer. "Tell me what was between you and Garrett. I need to eliminate you as a suspect. I've got his parents riding my ass like I'm in the Kentucky Derby." He makes a face like I should sympathize with him, but all I feel is blind panic.

Johns notices. "Or maybe something did happen." His voice goes low and velvety. "Something you never intended. You were complaining to your lover and he misunderstood your intentions. Things got out of hand. You didn't mean for anyone to die. Is that it?"

I can't summon the words to say no. If I could, would it be the truth?

Jumbo, who has gone oddly limp and quiet in my arms, chooses that moment to start convulsing.

46

MARY (ELIZABETH)

NOW

Johns grimaces and jumps to one side as Jumbo projects a stream of brown vomit, narrowly missing his spotless black topcoat and only lightly salt-stained wing tips.

I'm not so lucky. Jumbo convulses once more and puke drips down the blanket wrapped around me, making nausea rise in my throat. But I'm Elizabeth Jordan, dog owner. It's my job to handle this.

And now I have a reason to get out of this conversation.

"He obviously needs to go to the vet." I'm surprised at how calm my voice sounds, when a minute ago I could hardly breathe. I punch in the new code to the door, which has locked automatically behind me, and leave Johns on the porch without a qualm.

I'd almost let him put me under his spell.

My mind dispassionately lists what I need to do, and I follow it. Call the emergency vet. Find Jumbo's pet carrier, wrap his limp little body in a towel, and put him inside. He's trembling, vomiting every few minutes, but still breathing. He looks so miserable that pity overrides my disgust.

The vet's office asked on the phone if he ate anything that might have caused him to become ill, so before I hustle Jumbo out to the car, I take a quick look around. He had free run of the house all night, and I feel awful about that.

In the living room, I find scraps of shiny paper and foil with the wrapped presents under the tree. There's one shred that's large enough for me to read the words on it: DARK CHOCOLATE, EIGHTY PERCENT CACAO. It had been gift wrapped. Jumbo went to town on it.

As I'm stooping to gather up the scraps to take to the vet, I see something under a chair catching the light from the tree. I bend further, reaching for it, and draw my hand back with a gasp. The object is hard, sharp edged.

It's a shard of glass, half as long as my arm.

———

HAILEY MESSAGES ME while I'm at the vet waiting to hear whether Jumbo will be all right. She gives me an update on the measures she's taken to safeguard @bethybeth's reputation. The tone of her texts is distant, with a thin coating of ice. I can't put my finger on it, but she doesn't seem as professional, as respectful, as she did before.

I guess I can see why she'd lose respect. The photos seem almost unimportant with everything else going on. Lorne killing Garrett and implicating Elizabeth. Nate drugging his own wife, and being a linchpin in the case against me all those years ago. The threats, that rock through the window—

Thanks for getting the window fixed so quickly, I text Hailey.

Her answer takes almost a minute to come back, and it's a question mark.

She's definitely being dismissive with me. I fight down the urge to put her in her place. The window that got broken last night, I remind her, as if she should need it. Thanks for getting it repaired

I don't know about any window, she texts back. I haven't been at your house since I left you there

So Nate got it fixed. But he hasn't been home. Plus, I have a feeling the new, unsupportive Nate wouldn't have dealt with a huge hole in our house without at least sending me a couple of angry texts. Unease squirms in my stomach.

Are you sure the window was broken? Hailey texts.

"Of course I'm fucking sure," I mutter, which elicits a sidelong look from the gray-haired man holding a cat carrier on his lap next to me.

Am I, though? I saw a piece of glass on the floor, but I didn't really touch it. It could have been tinsel or foil, and I imagined almost cutting myself on it. The drugs might still be working in my system. They might be responsible for what I thought I saw and heard last night.

You're dead, you slut!

I shiver. I hope it was the drugs. Because the alternative is that I'm hallucinating as a side effect brought on by staying in Elizabeth's body for too long. Or I'm losing my mind from the stress. Or someone is actually trying to kill me.

Another text comes in, this one from Nate. He wants to know where I am.

I'll have to deal with him. Nate on a power trip, Nate sending me threats to keep me afraid, the possibility that Nate knows the truth about Halloween—but for now, I let him sit on *read*, and he can fucking like it.

Elizabeth might help me. She tried to confess after Halloween. She sent my parents money, tried to find me. Maybe I misjudged her, and she wasn't ever as awful and manipulative as I thought. People see what they want to see, even me. I needed her to be the bad guy.

She's no altruist, though, and she's not my friend. She won't lift a finger unless I give her body back.

I thought everything would be simpler once I had her life. I knew I'd have to work to make it my own and fool her loved ones, but at least I'd be the one on top, the one for whom everything magically worked out. But nothing is working out.

Giving up on my revenge feels like such a deep failure. I don't know who I am if I'm not trying to make her pay for hurting me. If I'm not trying to become her.

Does that make me the victim, or the villain?

———

THE VET TELLS me Jumbo will be fine after a few days, but they'd like to keep him overnight. I walk out to Elizabeth's car and get in, but I don't know where to drive it. Maybe I'll do what I should have done from the beginning: disappear. Become not Elizabeth, not Mary, but someone else entirely.

I haven't gone far down this path in my mind before my phone vibrates with a notification. I thought I'd turned them off, but it's a priority DM. It's from a private account with zero followers and no profile photo.

> You see how easily I can get to you? There are
> worse things than a little chocolate and a broken
> window. I'll fuck with you until you're dead, bitch.

The message scares me, but it also makes me furious. How dare someone terrorize me? How dare they bring a defenseless little dog into their vendetta? If it's Nate, that makes it ten times worse.

If it is Nate, that explains why these messages from random accounts keep getting through. He can sign in and approve them.

But I'm still not sure. I message Elizabeth.

> Who else knows what happened on Halloween?

———

IT TAKES THREE minutes for her to reply.

> Oh, so now you want to talk

She sounds so petulant, so much like *me*, that I want to laugh. But I'm too desperate.

> Fucking fuck, E. Someone poisoned your dog last night. I think it's the same person who's been messaging you for the last three months.

> Jumbo's going to be fine btw

Finally, Elizabeth answers.

> No one knew

> Just you and me and Garrett

> They knew you had proof it was me on Halloween. Files etc

> They said even if I hadn't actually murdered him, I was responsible for his death because it was my fault he became an addict

Something about what she's saying is nudging me, hard, but it takes me a minute to figure out why. Then I have it.

Elizabeth needed to become me so she could get to my "proof." Which wouldn't have proven much, just that I was obsessed with the Empathyzers, with Confluence, and with Elizabeth. Unless there was someone who would listen.

I *knew* she hadn't sent me the Empathyzer just so she could catch Nate cheating.

> Did you delete my research? I ask her.

> I had to.

It still doesn't make sense for her to take such a risk in order to cover up the truth, especially given that she tried to confess.

Another message comes in from her. I really wasn't trying to set you up to have to deal with all my problems. I thought you would let me come back

"Who's naive now?" I mutter.

> When I said I didn't want to be a martyr, I meant neither of us should. Garrett's not worth it.

That knocks me back. I leave her on *read* and drive toward her house, only going a few blocks before I realize how stupid I would have to be to spend another night there.

At the next red light, I check to see if Elizabeth's texted anything more. She hasn't, but Chrissy has.

> Are you ok??? Nate's post has us all frantic. Call me sweetie.

I switch apps and find Nate's profile. He has posted a picture of Elizabeth. She's dressed in white in a field of lavender, laughing, a hand to her forehead. It's the kind of photograph you see at someone's memorial service. She looks so beautiful, it makes me ache.

The top line of the caption says MISSING—AT RISK OF SELF-HARM

47

MARY (ELIZABETH)

NOW

My first instinct is to text Nate. I've typed out, WTF? I just took Jumbo to the vet before I stop and think.

Is this another power play, or is Nate responsible for the threats and for Jumbo's illness?

A car honks behind me, making me jump. The light's changed. Instead of going straight, I switch directions, making a right turn across an empty lane.

I call Elizabeth. As soon as she picks up, I say, "Would Nate poison Jumbo?"

"What? No." She pauses. "I mean . . . I don't know. They've never really bonded."

I assume this means Nate finds Jumbo even less charming than I do.

"But he wouldn't . . . Oh, I don't even know anymore. Are you saying *he* sent the threats?"

"That's exactly what I'm saying. Take a look at the post he just made."

A pause. "Wow," Elizabeth says. "This looks like . . ."

"Like he's planning to murder me and make it look like a suicide?" I'm not even joking.

"I was going to say he's trying to make me look unstable." Elizabeth speaks carefully, like she thinks I might be a little unhinged.

"He said he didn't want to get divorced. If you're dead, he gets everything, plus sympathy for being a widower."

After a few beats of silence, she says, "That's a pretty big leap." But I know what Elizabeth sounds like when she's ready to be convinced.

"How about this, then? If you confess to murder and go to prison, then you're out of his way. Or he can divorce you without looking like the asshole."

Some part of me registers that I've switched pronouns, while also driving toward my old part of town.

"I don't know how we could prove that," Elizabeth says.

"You still love him," I say, realizing. "That's why you won't listen to me."

"Mary, I literally gave up my life to prove to myself that he was cheating on me."

"Exactly. You had to go to extreme measures. And I thought you did it so you could get rid of my evidence."

"It was both of those things. I assure you, I know what Nate is capable of."

An idea sparks in my brain. "Is Nate still texting you, thinking you're me?"

Elizabeth sighs. "Yes."

"Well. As the woman whose pants he's trying to get into, you're in a perfect position to make him tell you his plan for getting rid of his wife. On camera."

Elizabeth is quiet for a moment. "Why would I do that for you?"

I let out my breath, frustrated. "Do you really want to let Nate and Lorne get away with their bullshit?"

"Seems to me they already have."

Only now do I notice her tone. Defeated. Depressed. And she's sounded this way for our entire conversation. Are the blahs of no longer being rich and beautiful catching up with her, or is something more going on?

Elizabeth makes a frustrated noise. "Look. My problem with Nate is the same problem you'd have with Lorne. I can't ... I would cave in. I can barely stand to read the texts he sends me. I can't face him again as you."

She's right. If we want to trap these men, we each have to be in the most advantageous position. She's furious with Lorne; I'm livid at Nate. Our anger sharpens us into blades.

To give them what they deserve, we'll need to become ourselves again.

A big part of me rebels against the idea. I've spent so much time and energy on becoming Elizabeth, and giving her up feels like failing. But is the failure in turning from a course that's leading to disaster, or in continuing until I run over the cliff?

"I don't just want to get back at them," Elizabeth says, her voice gaining energy. "I want us to be okay, Mebs. I mean, Mary."

I don't know why I appreciate that little gesture so much, of her correcting herself.

"Both of us," she goes on. "Not just okay. I want us to *thrive*."

Except for that brief period in college, I don't remember a time when I felt comfortable in my own skin. I've spent my whole life trying to escape myself. Now I've succeeded, and look how well that's gone.

I once thought thriving meant living as Elizabeth. But even if her life had been perfect, it wouldn't have been mine. It wouldn't have been me.

Elizabeth must sense that I'm receptive. "I meant it, about finding you a lawyer. Giving you money. I owe you that."

It's not an offer I would have accepted even yesterday, but I'm surprised to find myself considering it. Even more surprised to find myself actually caring how Elizabeth comes out of this.

I still don't know if I can trust her. She has an obvious motive for going along with my plans; she might double-cross me as soon as I give her what she wants. But I don't see any other choice.

"I'm coming over," I tell her. "I'm not agreeing to anything just yet, but we can talk in person." Then I hang up.

She doesn't need to know my decision is already made.

48

ELIZABETH (MARY)

NOW

It's not clear that Mary is serious about transferring back until she produces the Empathyzer from her purse.

Elizabeth's already wearing Mary's, just in case, but she can't believe it's this easy. "You brought it? You knew we were going to do this?"

"I was worried about it getting stolen, so I grabbed it when I took Jumbo to the vet." Mary's tone is nonchalant, but her gaze cuts away too quickly. She's holding back; something has changed her mind about Elizabeth being her enemy. Or at least her *worst* enemy.

The rush of relief takes Elizabeth by surprise. Like nostalgia but stronger, more painful, making her eyes well up and the lining of her nose prickle with tears. It's not because she's getting what she wants. It's because a crack, however small, has opened in the wall between her and Mary.

She had told Mary she missed their friendship, but only now does it sink in how deeply she meant it.

In college, she'd thought they were good for each other. Getting away from her parents and their church had been necessary but had left her feeling adrift. Mary gave her a purpose, a way to help someone who obviously needed acceptance and guidance to live her best, happiest life.

But slowly she realized Mary had things to offer *her* as well, even beyond the admiration Elizabeth needed like air. Her single-minded ambition was inspiring. Once you got to know her she was wickedly funny and unswervingly loyal. She wasn't easy to like, but liking her made Elizabeth feel as though she was in on some exclusive secret. Mary was *her* friend, no one else's.

And even before the Empathyzers came into the mix, Mary seemed to see the version of Elizabeth that was closest to the one that lived in her head. Becoming another person freed Elizabeth to express aspects of herself she'd always kept hidden—the parts of her that didn't smile on command or suffer fools—but Mary also *knew* her in a way that felt vital. She and Mary needed each other, like those symbiotic pairs she'd learned about in biology. The remora and the shark, or the crocodile and the plover.

After Halloween, Elizabeth had learned what her best friend really thought she was. A parasite. Mary hadn't seen her at all. She'd been building a different version of Elizabeth in her head, a stranger.

The wound from that never really healed. Elizabeth covered it, learned to live with it. Almost forgot about it. Her work, her followers and friends, and Nate provided ample distractions. But none of them ever needed her in the same way Mary did.

If the Empathyzers hadn't been in play, she would have found some other way to get rid of those documents and make herself safe without having to inhabit Mary again. But becoming Mary—and letting Mary become her—was the only sure way to force a confrontation between them.

Elizabeth realizes: she's been waiting for a reckoning as much as Mary has.

She never handled it well when Mary rejected her help—whether it was with Zeke, the loser from the bowling alley, or with

Nate. She was still angry at Mary when she got expelled. Maybe that, even more than fear, was why her efforts at atonement were unsuccessful.

But Mary wouldn't pass up a chance to become Elizabeth again. And now that everything's crashing down, Mary has no choice but to work with her. To let Elizabeth be her friend.

Maybe Mary's right; maybe she is manipulative. Maybe she doesn't truly know how to love someone, to see them and let them see her, without hierarchies or power games. No wonder she attracted someone like Nate. But she has to accept her nature and work within it to create the best outcome for both of them. Which means she needs to make sure Mary won't get left behind again.

She clears her throat, sniffling, though the tears have already retreated.

Mary moves right along to the strategizing she's no doubt been doing on her way over here. They decide that once Elizabeth is herself again, she'll get Lorne to admit his role in Garrett's death without tipping him off that she's recording.

"What about Nate?" Elizabeth asks.

"We know he's trying to make you look bad. With all that 'confess' nonsense, he probably wants to frame you for Garrett's death."

Mary looks into Elizabeth's eyes as if to plumb the depths of her mind.

Elizabeth suppresses a sigh. Will she ever be trusted? "I told you, I didn't kill him."

"That works in our favor." Mary's tone is so dry, Elizabeth can't help but smirk. "But we don't know what else Nate might have planned. We need to discredit him." Pacing, Mary twists her long red hair into a knot, then lets it fall around her shoulders. It's something Elizabeth does herself when she's trying to think. She can almost feel the strands between her fingers.

As Mary gets further into her plan, Elizabeth likes what she hears less and less. Finally she bursts out, "This is sketchy. Can't you meet him in public, like I'm doing with Lorne?"

"We need the visual. Lorne's confession only has to convince the police, but Nate's has to convince everyone."

Elizabeth is impressed. Mary's learned a few lessons about the court of public opinion. "So I'll hide somewhere and video you on my phone."

"No. It has to be an environment I can control. We need audio too, and . . ." Mary winces. "The physical aspect. It can't just be him talking."

"You don't have to take on the risk, you know. We could always lawyer up and trust the system."

"Oh, I'll take the fucking risk," Mary snaps. She acts calm, but Elizabeth recognizes the flat rage behind her eyes. "Nate made sure I got blamed for Garrett's fall. He's going to pay for that."

A shiver runs through Elizabeth at the venom in her tone.

"You're not invulnerable either, E. Being in public won't keep Lorne from hurting you if he figures out you're setting him up."

Elizabeth shrugs, trying to project brash determination. "I'll make sure he doesn't figure it out, then. So you don't think it's my fault you got expelled anymore?"

"I believe you did what you could to fix it. Johns confirmed for me that you tried to confess to him."

That's why Mary believes her. "And you know I wasn't trying to hurt you with my, um, recent actions. Right?"

"Which ones? Tricking me into taking over your fucked-up life, or deleting the evidence I'd been compiling for seven years?"

The words are harsh, but there's no bitterness in them. Mary's lipsticked mouth—one of Elizabeth's favorite shades, Missed Connection—curves up. It seems like she's over being deceived, or as over it as she'll ever be. Elizabeth's heart lifts.

Still, it'll take a concrete gesture to build trust. "After we transfer, I'll keep wearing my wristband," Elizabeth says. "I'll keep it turned on. You'll be able to reverse it if I don't hold up my end of the deal. You should move some money now from my bank account into your own. Say"—she reminds herself that money means nothing against getting her identity back—"ten thousand to start?"

Mary frowns. "The Deegans will pounce on a deposit that big."

"The Deegans are going to be so grateful to us for exposing Garrett's real killer that they'll forget all about scooping up your pennies."

Mary looks skeptical, but she goes into the banking app on her phone. "Are you sure about this?" she asks before she confirms the funds transfer. "It's not reversible."

Elizabeth nods, heart pounding. She knows the money isn't the only thing Mary's talking about.

Mary presses the button on her wristband, powering it on. "Okay. You ready?"

Is she sure? Is she ready?

It doesn't matter anymore. It's happening.

———

ELIZABETH DOESN'T EXPERIENCE transfer side effects. Never has. Not the dizziness and hallucinations of being in a foreign body, not the hangover of being back in her own. But bumbling down the hall from Mary's apartment, her limbs too long and her perspective too high up, she's as clumsy and tender as a baby deer.

By the doorway to the stairs, she pauses, using the wall for support. Looking at her manicured hand propped there, she has the surreal feeling of observing her own body from the outside. Is that her hand? Is this her body? Or is the *other* body hers, back inside the apartment?

She slaps the wall. It stings her palm. "Mine," she mutters, and moves on. She doesn't have time for disorientation.

On the stairs, she pauses at the entrance to Miguel's floor. She's been thinking she'll do something big to get him back, but relationships aren't made of grand gestures; they're made of small ones. They're built on steadiness and trust. She doesn't know how to get Miguel's trust back.

She continues downstairs.

Being in her own car again centers her. The heated steering wheel, the clean leather smell of the upholstery. She did miss her creature comforts.

But she can't bring herself to pull away from the curb. The way she left things with Miguel tugs at her mind with tiny, sharp claws. His asking her to leave can't be the last words between them.

He doesn't owe her the chance to apologize, but it's going to tear at her until she does.

She takes out her phone and does a search for his name. The faculty and staff page on the Ofori Lab website is the first result. He's there, his hair neater than usual in his headshot, his smile a little canned but making Elizabeth smile in response. His university email address is next to the picture. She taps it.

By the time she's done typing out her email, she feels hollowed out with exhaustion. But it's there, the whole story. The whole truth.

She goes to tap Send, then remembers with a jolt that university email isn't private. The last thing she needs is to get Miguel into trouble with some overzealous administrator. The case against Mary was strengthened that way, when they found the video of Garrett in her cloud storage.

Elizabeth searches her car for paper. The interior is pristine, not an errant receipt or piece of junk mail to be found. She goes through the glove compartment and cranes her upper body into the back seat. Shoving her hand under the passenger seat, she comes up against a book. It's a planner, with a buttery-smooth leather cover and an expensive pen in the holder. Elizabeth's never seen it before. Nate might have bought it for himself and accidentally left it in her car. The creamy pages are marked with the days of the waning year, but otherwise empty.

It'll work.

Elizabeth fills several pages, front and back, with the words from her email. It's been a long time since she handwrote more than a quick note, and her wrist aches by the time she's done. Tearing out the pages, she stacks and folds them into quarters.

She stops, thinking about her and Mary's plans for Nate and Lorne. The risks are greater than Elizabeth's comfortable with. They didn't discuss getting anyone else involved, but it wouldn't have occurred to Mary. She's so fierce, reluctant to ask for anyone's help. She's gone so long without a safety net. Maybe Elizabeth can give her one.

She writes one last page, tears it out, and folds it into the letter. Then she runs back into the building and up the stairs, and slips the letter under Miguel's door.

His actions are up to him. Maybe he'll tear up the letter unread. Maybe he'll read it, roll his eyes, and go on with his life. But hopefully the story will strike a chord, and Miguel will think Mary is deserving of help. Elizabeth trusts him to do the right thing more than she trusts herself.

49

MARY

NOW

Being myself again *hurts*.

Even though Elizabeth and I were in the same room when we transferred to our own bodies, I'm mired in discomfort. My bones ache, taking me back to sophomore year of college.

I'm back where I started. Ten thousand dollars richer, but that's not much for a whole life.

If I were smart, I'd withdraw that money as soon as the deposit clears and get on a plane. But as with Elizabeth, I can't let Nate escape the consequences of his misdeeds. It's not only about revenge. He'll keep on being a prick if someone doesn't stop him.

Which is why, despite my dragging limbs and pulsing head, I've made all the preparations. I spent a while getting the setup right; it's surprisingly difficult to position a camera so it's hidden yet maintains the desired sight lines. I'm dressed in a spaghetti strap top and the only skirt I own. In the bathroom I found a tube of drugstore lipstick, which Elizabeth must have bought to help her in setting her snare for Nate. In one of his texts, he said it made her/me look like an eighteen-year-old prostitute and he, quote, "wasn't mad about it." Needless to say, I'm looking forward to taking him down.

I've already texted him with my address, saying I'm ready to do some of the things he's been messaging me about. His reply makes me wonder how I ever thought he was a feminist. Or attractive.

A text comes in from Elizabeth. You good?

I reply, Ready.

She sends me a picture of her wrist with the Empathyzer on it, still turned on. She's keeping her end of the bargain.

Nate's knock on the door comes too soon for my heart, which hammers so hard, I can feel it in my fingertips. The second he's in the door, he slams me up against it, thrusting his hand under my shirt and his tongue into my mouth.

I resist the temptation to bite down. "Wait," I say, breathless, and maneuver him to the couch. "Sit."

"What is this?" He's impatient, but he does as I tell him.

"I just want to talk." I sit next to him, my hands folded in my lap.

"I hope you didn't ask me over here to *talk*."

"Why not? I like talking." I give him my best flirtatious look, which isn't saying much. I'm better at this when I'm Elizabeth.

He puts his hand on my leg. "You get off on dirty talk, huh? You liked those messages I sent you?"

"I want to talk about Elizabeth."

His eyes narrow in confusion. I bite my lower lip in a way I hope he'll interpret as coquettish. "It gets me hot when you tell me how much you hate her."

He chuckles. "You've really got a thing for my wife, don't you? Maybe when I get back home, I'll tell her where I was tonight. After those pictures, she can't say shit about it. I'll make her listen to all the details."

His cruelty feels like a punch. It's fortunate that his eyes have dropped to my chest, so he doesn't see the look on my face.

How am I ever going to trust my instincts about anyone again?

"You think you can do whatever you want now?" My voice comes out colder and sharper than it should.

"I *can* do whatever I want." He moves closer, lowering his lips to the join of my neck and shoulder, and I shiver in disgust. "I bet you like it rough," he murmurs. "I can't wait. I want to fucking break you in half."

I push his shoulders. "Wait."

"What is it?" He leans back just enough that his mouth is no longer touching my skin. Deliberately or not, he's letting me know I can't stop him from doing whatever he wants to me.

"You and me. We could take her down."

"Take who down?"

"Elizabeth!"

"Is that what this is about?" He runs a hand through his hair, annoyed. "Why do you hate her so much? It wasn't her fault you got kicked out of school."

If he's the one threatening her, he knows how false that is. This isn't going like it's supposed to. He should be eager to conspire against her. Unless he's confident he's got Elizabeth's fate sealed on his own and doesn't want to involve me.

I've already provoked enough bad behavior to make anyone doubt his word. I hardly need to risk bringing Garrett up. But I want people to know the full story, that he tried to terrorize his wife into confessing to assault, if not murder. And I need to establish, for myself, that he had a hand in my getting expelled.

He crowds me against the arm of the couch, lightly palming the base of my throat, where he must be able to feel my pulse race. "I came over here because you told me to." His voice simmers. His thumb strokes the side of my neck.

I swallow in his grip. "Why did you lie to the police about me?"

"What?" His face is blank. Does he not even remember ruining my life?

"You told them Garrett and I were fighting before he fell down the stairs. But you couldn't have known that. Elizabeth left you passed out in your room."

He takes his hand off me, frowning. "Elizabeth didn't leave me passed out, you did." Nothing but genuine confusion in his eyes. "Right before you pushed Garrett down the stairs."

He doesn't know it was Elizabeth that night.

Which means he's not the one sending the threats.

"They had you on video," he says. "Everyone knew you did it, I just provided a little more certainty."

"But . . . why?" I hate how plaintive my voice sounds, how it makes his mouth curve.

"Garrett wasn't my favorite person, but he was my brother. Brothers stick together. And you . . ." He leans in again, his large body looming over mine. His scent, which used to intoxicate me, clogs my throat. "You were nothing but a fucking tease. Still are."

He palms the back of my head and mashes his lips against mine so hard, I feel his teeth. "Where're you going?" he pants as I struggle. "You've been begging for it since—"

I jerk my head back. "Everything you're doing is being livestreamed to Elizabeth's followers."

He stops. Releases me. Stares at me, his eyes dark pits.

Then he's sweeping everything off the shelving unit that sits opposite the couch. It takes him all of five seconds to find my laptop behind a row of library books, its camera peeking between them. He peers into the screen, his own enraged face broadcast to hundreds of thousands of people.

He turns and hurls the laptop at my head.

Fortunately for me, he's got bad aim. The computer hits the wall and explodes into shards.

Nate's hair is disheveled, his face a mottled red, his teeth bared. I've never seen him look so ugly.

I turn and sprint for the door. I won't make it.

Someone outside starts knocking—pounding—and I'm glad I didn't lock the door after Nate came in. I scream, and the door flies open.

On the other side is the last person I expect to see.

50

ELIZABETH

NOW

Originally, Elizabeth had wanted to watch the livestream of Mary and Nate from somewhere close by, so she could step in if needed. Mary pointed out that this was the only time Nate wouldn't be breathing down Elizabeth's neck, which would give her the opportunity to move on Lorne.

So Elizabeth's not watching the livestream at all. It'll only be a distraction, and she needs her wits about her.

She has arranged to meet Lorne at a dive bar they used to go to, a place that's loud enough to mask their conversation from eavesdroppers but quiet enough to record, and where the bartenders put up with no misbehavior.

She gets ready to leave. A natural face except for long-wearing lip stain in Mulberry Dream. Hair styled in touchable waves. Flat shoes, to cater to Lorne's ego.

Being back in her room makes her miss Jumbo more than she did while she was Mary. The empty house feels too big, too quiet, like it's waiting. The silence emphasizes her isolation. Like Mary, she has no one.

Earlier, she'd inspected the front window in the living room. It didn't look like anyone had attacked it, except maybe Svitlana with some vinegar and newsprint. But then she'd looked further and found a long shard of glass under the chair by the Christmas tree.

Mary wasn't hallucinating. Someone smashed that window. Someone had it repaired.

The sound of the front door's keypad drifts up the stairs into her room, and she tenses.

Maybe Nate enlisted Hailey to spy on her, police her, while he skipped off to play. Sinister thought. Hailey is Elizabeth's employee, but she likes Nate better. Elizabeth's seen them exchanging looks. She's had her suspicions, but ultimately decided peace was more important.

The keypad emits its disappointed "invalid code" tone. Whoever it is—Hailey?—tries again, with the same result. Then they start battering on the door.

Elizabeth's heart bursts into flight. She can hear herself panting, even as she tries to calm her breath. As if it can be heard through double-paned glass.

"Beth!" It's a man's voice, ragged. *Lorne's* voice. "Beth, open the door!"

She could stay hidden, and he'd go away eventually, but then he might not meet her at the bar. Something must have come up to bring him here.

Before she descends the stairs, she sets her phone to record and slips it in her pocket.

Lorne quiets as soon as he sees her through the door. His overbleached hair stands on end, and his stubble is even more scruffy than usual.

"Beth," he says, stepping inside and wrapping her in his arms like she's a beloved stuffed toy he'd left in an airport. The violation she feels is stark. She doesn't want him touching her.

"Are you ready?" he says. "Are you packed?"

"Packed?"

"Yeah. You texted me?" He takes in the look of utter confusion that must be on her face, then shows her a text on his phone.

> It's B. New phone. Cops closing in. We need to leave town. Come now.

She almost blurts out that she didn't send that text. But who did? Anyone could have found out the police talked to her, talked to Lorne.

Telling him will only throw off her plan even more. She'll have to work with what's happening, then find out who's stirring the pot—and why—once Lorne's in custody.

"I figure we can head into Canada," he says. "If we drive through South Dakota, I know a guy who can get us passports. My mom will let us crash with her while we wait for them to be done."

Elizabeth remembers, dimly, that Lorne is originally from South Dakota. She pictures herself in a double-wide trailer on the prairie. Being awkwardly polite with Lorne's mother, whom she has never even bothered to imagine. Becoming trapped, as Lorne undoubtedly wants her to be, with him.

He's grinning as though this is some grand adventure. "You whistled and I came," he says, with a touch of irony.

"It's the least you can do. The detective told me you killed Garrett. He said I made you do it!"

"I didn't need you to make me. That asshole was riding you like a fucking thoroughbred, Beth. He was ruining your life."

Like you did? she almost snaps. The pictures of them flash through her mind, but they aren't the focus. Lorne's so close to saying what she needs him to.

"Besides, I didn't kill him," Lorne says, and Elizabeth could scream in frustration. "He was already doing a fine job of that himself. Nobody put a gun to his head."

Lorne taps his lips with a finger, one side of his mouth rising in an unkind smile. "I may have forgotten to mention his dose wasn't as stepped-on as usual, though. I kinda might have told him the opposite, that he'd need to use a little more."

A surge of triumph makes her heart stutter. This has to be enough. Now she needs to absolve herself as much as possible. "I never asked you to kill him. I didn't want you to."

"But you needed me to. I'll always give you what you need, Beth." His eyes gleam like yellow topaz.

The smart thing would be to spend a few minutes stroking his ego, then send him somewhere else to meet her. Have the police meet him instead. But then he says, "Go pack. I'll get you out of this," and gives her a proprietary little pat on the ass. He has such confidence that she's forgiven him. That she's too desperate to do otherwise. He thinks he's won.

Hatred makes her rational mind blank out. "I'm not going anywhere with you. You think I'd trust you after you posted those pictures?"

The smirk drops off his face. "Wait. You think *I* took those? No. No, I would never."

He looks more upset than when she accused him of murder. It's a little overdone, honestly. "You expect me to believe that? You're a photographer."

"I swear to *god*, Beth, it wasn't me. I would never post nudes of someone. It's against my fucking ethical standards. Even if I did take photographs, they'd just be for my own—"

"So you admit you took pictures," she interrupts, channeling her inner Detective Johns.

"No! If I don't ask you first, that's like, assault. Plus, those were some of the shittiest quality photographs I've ever seen." His face changes, darkens. "I'll show you."

He grabs her arm and yanks her toward the stairs, pulling through her resistance as if she weighs nothing.

Lorne never seemed like a threat to her before. He was easy to control, through his unquenchable desire for her and the distance she maintained between them. His two most important qualities were that he was eager to please and good in bed. Even his carrying a gun was a quirk, an accessory of his night hustle.

Now, seeing the grim line of his mouth, she realizes how wrong she was. She assumed his devotion to her made him safe, instead of the opposite. For the first time, she fears him.

He drags her upstairs, hauling her to her feet when she trips. He doesn't seem to care if he hurts her. "There's a camera somewhere in that bedroom," he snarls. "I'm gonna find it, and when I do you're gonna fucking apologize to me."

She doesn't have the voice to tell him yes or no. In her room, he flings her to the bed. Then he tears the place apart.

51

MARY

NOW

"Hailey?"

I stumble to a stop, causing Nate to crash into me. This pushes me into Elizabeth's assistant, who stands firm in the threshold of my apartment. She doesn't seem inclined to let me leave. "What are *you* doing here?"

Hailey's eyes pass over me in a single, dismissive glance, then flick to Nate. He looks only slightly less pissed than he did right after learning his terrible behavior was being streamed to thousands upon thousands of eyeballs. Which is to say, still extremely pissed, but Hailey's presence has at least divided his attention.

He peppers her with demands, his voice hoarse with panic. "Are you in on this shit? How did you know I was here? Did Elizabeth send you to spy on me?" His face has drained of color except for two bright pink spots high on his chiseled cheekbones.

Hailey develops a small, anticipatory smile at odds with the previous moods I've seen on her: blankly professional, slightly put-upon. Now she looks Machiavellian. It reminds me, forcibly, how much access she has to the private workings of Nate's and Elizabeth's lives.

"I followed you here," she says.

"Hails." Nate's face falls into an expression of disappointment edged with sympathy. "I told you from the start, it couldn't be any more than physical."

She scoffs. "That's not why I followed you. Not everyone is obsessed with you, you know. I only slept with you to mess with your wife." Her assessing gaze flicks to me. I get a cold feeling.

"That was before I realized she already knew what you were up to, so I couldn't really make things worse for her in that way." She laughs. "I saw the livestream. Man, if I were still on the payroll, I'd have my work cut out for me.

"Anyway, I thought you might like to know that the photographer your wife's been fucking? He's at your house right now." Hailey angles her phone toward us. It shows what looks like a security feed of Elizabeth's living room, but Elizabeth doesn't have security cameras inside the house. Does she?

Two figures are in frame. The view is foreshortened, but even on the small screen I recognize both their faces, and Lorne's tattoos as he gesticulates.

"Looks like he's finding out she isn't going to skip town with him after all." She sounds like she's watching a reality show.

On the screen, Lorne grabs Elizabeth. "Oh wow. They're headed upstairs." Hailey taps something on her phone and the image switches to a high-angle shot of Elizabeth's bedroom, the same perspective from which most of the photos of Elizabeth and Lorne were taken.

Nate swears and barrels out the door past Hailey, who jumps out of his way.

On Hailey's screen, a tiny version of Lorne bursts into the room and shoves Elizabeth onto the bed. Then he starts picking things up and throwing them around like he's either searching for something or going absolutely feral.

"It was you," I say to Hailey. "You took those pictures. You posted them online."

Hailey doesn't say anything, but grins in a way that makes her look deranged.

"Why?" I ask. Elizabeth made mistakes, bad ones, and she probably deserves to lose her marriage and her wholesome image. But having seen some of the internet blowback, I'm not sure she deserves *everything* she's getting. "If you had a problem with her having an affair, you could've quit. Or told Nate privately. You didn't have to make the whole world hate her."

She looks at me curiously. "Which one are you right now?"

My breath freezes. "What?"

"Mary or Elizabeth. Which one?"

"You know?" I can't stop myself from asking.

"I suspected when Elizabeth had me change all the codes. I thought you were taking over." She chuckles. "It doesn't matter. By the time I'm done, neither of you will have anywhere to hide. But I'm surprised. I would think you of all people would be president of the Elizabeth Jordan Haters' Club."

"How do— Who *are* you?"

"Gotta go. I set up this fireworks show, and I need to get to the Jordans' so I can watch it in person." She backs out the door, keeping me in her eye line. "Don't bother trying to warn her. I put her phone in airplane mode." Hailey wiggles her own phone, then takes off. By the time I've shoved my feet into my boots, she's gone.

———

WHEN I TRY to text Elizabeth, the message comes back undelivered.

I put on my coat and bring up a rideshare app on my phone. I won't arrive until after Nate and Hailey do, but I need to go over there. I need to warn her—

I *have* a way to warn Elizabeth. Or at least replace her with someone who knows what's coming.

After we transferred back into ourselves, I put away my Empathyzer, but now I take it out and strap it onto my wrist.

Then I hesitate. Transferring from this far away will make me loopy with side effects when I'll need all my wits about me.

Am I really willing to put myself in that kind of danger for Elizabeth? What I did with Nate was risky enough, and now I know I was minimizing it.

But whoever Hailey is, and whatever her reasons, she's out to get both of us. We need to be one step ahead of her. Not behind, like we are now.

I try texting Elizabeth again. Undelivered.

Miguel bursts into my apartment, out of breath.

"Are you all right?" he demands. "I was trying to see where Elizabeth's husband was headed, but he drove off."

I stare at him. "Why are you here? I'm not Elizabeth. She——"

"I know. She wrote to me. Told me your plans, and asked me to monitor the livestream and step in if things got hairy."

"But you hate me," I blurt. He gives me a wry look, but I wasn't imagining the way he acted when he and Elizabeth came to pick me up.

"She told me none of that stuff was your fault, that it was all hers. I'm sorry I was a dick."

"Don't be." I'm surprised Elizabeth would shoulder the blame, especially with someone whose good opinion she values. Then it catches up to me, what Miguel said when he came in. *Elizabeth's husband.* Miguel knows she's married.

Now I'm even more confused. Why would she go out of her way to tell Miguel the whole truth instead of cutting her losses and moving on? The fact that she did makes me more aware of my own obligation to her.

"Do you still care about her?" I ask. He must; she's the reason he's helping me. "She's at her house. That's where Nate's headed, and whatever happens when he gets there, it won't be good."

Miguel goes pale. "We have to go over there."

I know what Elizabeth would want: for Miguel to stay far away from Nate, Lorne, Hailey, and the conflict erupting between them. "I just need you to get me closer."

In his car, I explain who Hailey is and what she's done, though I still have no idea why she'd be gunning for Elizabeth. "Most people are blind to Elizabeth's faults," I say. Miguel doesn't seem to hear me; he's tapping his steering wheel and staring at a red light as if he can turn it green through force of will.

"You do realize she's still married? And that photos were published online of her having sex with a whole other person who she's not married to?" It's not that I want Miguel to think badly of her. It's just irritating, even now, to see someone I think is nice get sucked into her bullshit.

He snaps out of his stress reverie. "Just because I don't want her to get hurt, and I didn't want you to get hurt, doesn't mean I'm okay with the fact that she lied to me."

When the light changes, he accelerates so fast, his tires spin on the icy pavement. The car finally leaps forward, and then he has to steer out of a skid.

Altruism, my ass. Still, there was some fire in his eyes just now. Maybe she won't completely steamroll him. I hope not, because it makes me sad to think the only choice, other than being alone, is between someone you can control and someone who will try to control you.

Miguel's grumbling under his breath. ". . . can't believe I was so . . . god, I'm a dumbass."

"Elizabeth can have that effect on people."

He huffs out a laugh and gives me a quick sidelong glance before returning his eyes to the road. "It's messing with my mind, looking at you and *not* seeing her."

"Is it that obvious?"

"It kind of is. To me, anyway. Maybe it's because I know. I mean, until the other day I thought she was you, and that was pretty weird too. But y'all have been each other for how many days now? And nobody else has noticed."

Hailey did. I try and fail to text Elizabeth a third time.

I calculate how far ahead of us Nate must be. In his heavy SUV with snow tires, he can drive as fast as he wants. Miguel's got a hatchback and has to be more cautious.

"Should we . . . call the police?" I don't mean to sound so reluctant, but Miguel winces and shakes his head, agreeing with me.

"I've honestly never seen a tense situation that was improved by having cops there. And has anyone committed an actual crime? Other than y'all videoing Elizabeth's husband without his knowledge. Who are they going to arrest?"

Up ahead there's an unbroken wall of brake lights, red smears in the darkness. I can't tell whether it's a crash or just traffic and bad roads. I think I see a dancing pattern of blue and red far down the street.

We're still too far away, but this will have to be close enough. I push the sleeve up on my coat so I can see the screen of my Empathyzer. It looks rough after its latest spate of use, coming after years of my periodically taking it apart and putting it back together. In the casing on the back of it I can feel a crack scraping my skin. The screen is slow to respond to my touch. Soon the thing won't be usable at all.

But when I search for paired devices I can see Elizabeth's. She still has it turned on, as promised.

"I'm going to transfer into her," I warn Miguel.

"Wait. You're what? Maybe we should—"

But I'm already gone.

52

ELIZABETH

NOW

Lorne has found a hammer, and the bedroom wall is now pock-marked with holes.

"It's somewhere over here," he mutters. "It has to be. The angle puts it up here. Cameras can be so fucking *tiny* . . ."

Elizabeth's afraid of what he'll do if she tries to leave. She's never seen Lorne this worked up. She doesn't want to end up like the wall.

He drags over her favorite slipper chair to use as a step stool, standing on the five-hundred-dollars-a-yard hummingbird-print upholstery with his dirty boots, and punches a hole high up on the wall. He thrusts his hand into it, his shirt riding up to reveal the holster at his waist.

"There." Satisfaction sharpens his voice. He pulls out a hand covered in drywall dust, something small and glittering held in his fingers. "Ha! See *this!*"

Downstairs, the door slams.

Footsteps pound up the stairs. "Who the *fuck* is in bed with my *wife?*"

Lorne swears and jumps down from the chair, the hammer held high.

Nate takes up the entire doorway. He sends Elizabeth a single burning, hateful look that pins her to the headboard. Then he launches himself at Lorne. They hit the wall hard; the hammer goes flying. Elizabeth ducks, covering her head with her hands.

The men fight, grunting and snarling like dogs. The meaty sounds of fists hitting flesh make Elizabeth want to disappear. Lorne goes for his holster and she screams, "No!"

Her scream distracts Lorne enough for Nate to push him down. They sprawl on the foot of the bed, Lorne's fingers splayed on Nate's chin.

Nate rolls, taking them both to the floor with a thump, and a second later they're on their feet again. The gun is in Lorne's hand. Nate grabs for it. He gets hold of Lorne's wrist and they struggle, the barrel pointing randomly around the room.

Elizabeth slides down to the floor next to the bed. She draws up her feet and tucks in her elbows, making herself small.

She's still wearing her Empathyzer. She could escape, transfer into Mary. It would be wrong, but she'd be safe.

Nate smacks Lorne's wrist against the doorframe, trying to force him to drop the gun. Lorne grips it doggedly. He pushes back. They spin out into the hallway.

Elizabeth's instincts tell her to hide, but whoever wins the fight will come in here and drag her out. She creeps toward the door, needing to know what happens. Nate stumbles past, toward the back of the house, as if he's been pushed. He regains his footing and drives forward. He gives Lorne a hard shove in return.

Lorne launches down the stairs headfirst.

His body floats down as if he's controlling his descent, as though at the bottom he will tuck and roll like a superhero. Instead, he lands with a broken thud.

"Fuck," Nate whispers.

Elizabeth must have made a noise. Nate turns toward her. He looks like he'd forgotten she was there until now.

He takes her arm and draws her, almost gently, out into the hall. She can see Lorne's legs at the base of the stairs, one tangled in the other. The angle of the ceiling blocks her view of his top half, but she can see he's not moving.

Nate looms over her. She always loved that about him, that he was so much taller. She never realized how much of her attraction to him was built on superficialities. His height, his bone structure, the way he smelled. He reaches into a primitive part of her brain that, even now, resists letting go of him.

He smiles. It's his beautiful, shining smile, but with something missing, something wrong.

"Nate." She can't keep the pleading out of her voice.

His fingertips are soft as they stroke her jawline. He is still smiling, but it's muted now, his eyes focused somewhere below hers.

She leans toward him automatically, her face turning up, a flower to the sun. She aches for any bit of warmth he'll give her. How did she think she was going to make him leave? She can't withstand him.

His hand moves up, the pad of his thumb tracing her cheekbone. The heat of him radiates through her. It shivers her like fever, builds up like excitement. Or fear.

She swallows. "I won't—"

He cuts off the promise before she can make it. "I never wanted to hurt you." His voice is soft but implacable. "I just wanted you to disappear."

His hand clamps down on her throat as he slams her back against the wall. He gazes into her eyes; they understand each other perfectly. He knows she saw everything. She knows he is going to end her because of it.

She raises her hands, clawing at his, but blackness is already spreading from the edges of her vision. She feels herself disappearing, like he wanted. She's going

53

MARY (ELIZABETH)

NOW

A monster has me by the throat. Dark smoke wreathes its head, darker than the blackness spreading from the sides of my eyes. I close my eyes to shut out the monster's face, but that makes terrifying pictures jump and writhe in my brain. I can't scream; I can't breathe. I can't—

He's killing you, a voice says in my head. *He is* killing you. *You have to stop this.*

My hands are clumsy at the ends of my too-long arms. I dig my talons into his skin, but I might as well be fighting a hallucination.

Nate floats above me, his face distorted with rage. How did I ever think he was beautiful?

How will he make this look like a suicide?

The terrible pressure on my throat eases. I can breathe again.

I stagger. Dark wings beat in my mind. Nate's blocking the way out. The black smoke of his evil surrounds him, widening his shadow until it takes up the whole stairway.

Window.

My body tenses, getting ready to flee back into the bedroom. It's not my body, it's Elizabeth's. I need to take care of it, because I'm going to give it back.

A green spear of a voice flies up the stairs. "I have Lorne's gun," it says. "You have ten seconds to get down here before I start shooting."

LORNE'S DEAD.

He lies face up, his neck twisted at an angle. Eyes half-open and glazed. It gives me the willies to look at him, so I track his gun instead.

Hailey's gun now.

She looks shaken, especially when she glances down at the body, but she seems comfortable with the gun. She knows how to handle it; she refrains from pointing it randomly around the room. Her finger stays away from the trigger. The threat is implied. The air around her is a noxious yellow-green, the color of vengeance.

Nate and I stand across the body from her. "You don't have to do this, Hails," he says in a talking-her-down-from-the-ledge tone that I, personally, would find infuriating. "This was a misunderstanding. An accident. Give me the—"

"Shut up," she snaps.

Nate glares at her, his black smoke as thick as ever, but he has no power here. Hailey has the power now.

Why did she want it? the voice in my head asks. It's gaining strength, but I was almost a mile away when I transferred. It'll take me a little while to come back up to full lucidity. I'm still shaking too, from Nate's attack. My throat hurts.

Hailey looks at me. "People sure seem to fall down the stairs a lot when you're around, don't they, Elizabeth?"

I squint at her, not knowing if she expects a reply. Her miasma is fading, though trails squiggle in the corners of my vision. I can hear the ground creaking under the house. The creaking sounds like a monster's footsteps in the basement.

I restrain myself from turning my head to listen. I need to get a grip. Hailey doesn't know it's me, and I have to maintain that advantage.

She looks down at Lorne sadly. "He ended up just like my brother." Why would Lorne's death make her sad? Was Lorne her brother? I'm so confused. "Except Garrett took longer to die."

Stunned, I look up. Her eyes are waiting for mine.

"You're Garrett's little sister," I say. My voice cracks from my damaged throat.

She nods. "I used to beg him to let me come visit him at college on weekends, just to escape the awful school my parents sent me to. He'd say I was so ugly, no one would believe I was his real sister." She smiles fondly. "We never went more than a day without texting or calling."

She's serious. The smog around her morphs into nostalgic sparkles.

"He looked out for me, as much as he could. I don't know if you've ever met my parents, but they're pretty big assholes. Do you know how many times my brother went to rehab?"

"I . . . no."

"Nine. Nine times."

I blink. "Oh. I'm sorry."

"You should be. It was all your fault." She advances on me, yellow-green gas rising around her again. But it's faint, and I can think more clearly now. "He was smart, good-looking, charming."

Rich, I think, but stop myself from saying.

"He could have been whatever he wanted. Then *you* pushed him down the stairs. He needed multiple surgeries. Months of physical therapy. He was prescribed a boatload of painkillers to get through all that, and he never really got off them.

"I watched him disintegrate. The last year of his life, our parents amended his trust fund so he couldn't spend all his money on drugs. They wouldn't let him in the house anymore, because he'd steal anything he could get his hands on. He did it to me too, but I let him come over anyway. I couldn't not; he was my *brother*. But you turned him into a shell of a person."

A shell of a deeply shitty person, but I can't say that to his vengeful sister who has me at gunpoint. Hailey and I obviously knew two very different Garretts.

"Do you know what it's like to lose someone while they're still alive?" She meets my eye, and I see there are tears in hers before she blinks them away.

A belated epiphany clears the last of the cobwebs from my mind. "You sent those messages telling me to confess."

"I'm glad you didn't. Now I realize it wouldn't have been enough to make up for you crippling my brother. It's too bad Mary's had to suffer so much in your place, but we'll fix that, won't we? And she deserved it as much as you. It's been fun, fucking with her. Slipping things into her drink. Making her think someone was going to kill her."

I gasp. "*You* broke the window."

"I paid a homeless guy fifty bucks to do it. Told him what to yell. I'm so glad I had cameras in the house! Your *face* when that window smashed in." She laughs. It seems like she's already forgotten who's who, whether I'm Mary in Elizabeth's body or Elizabeth in Elizabeth's body. "And then when you came home and saw it wasn't broken anymore! You thought you were going crazy, didn't you?"

"Did you poison Jumbo too? He's just a little dog."

"But you love him. That's what matters." Her mouth twists. "Everything you care about, I want to take it away."

I shiver, hearing the echo of what I told Elizabeth not long ago in this very room. *Taking it away from you is the point.*

Nate was about to kill me. Why didn't Hailey let him?

The answer dawns on me as she raises the gun. She wants to do it herself.

54

ELIZABETH (MARY)

NOW

Sweet unobstructed oxygen slides into her lungs. She'll never take being able to breathe for granted again.

"Elizabeth? Is that you?"

She looks to her left and Miguel is there. They're in his car, in the dark, a sea of brake lights before them. Her happiness at seeing him pushes every other feeling into irrelevance. She has to touch him to make sure he's real.

He frowns, and she removes her hand from his arm.

Memories rush back of Nate's hands around her throat, Lorne's tangled legs at the bottom of the stairs. "Nate's gotten violent," she says. "Mary's in danger. We need to get over there."

Miguel swears and makes the next turn, threading through side streets. It'll take a while, but at least they're moving.

"What happened at Mary's?" she asks, feeling like her voice should be hoarser. But this isn't the windpipe Nate was trying to crush.

Briefly, Miguel explains the situation. Things with Nate did not go well, though Mary managed to bait him into making an ass of himself on the internet. He rushed home to start a fight with Lorne after Hailey—Hailey? . . . yes, Hailey—showed up and dropped a bombshell.

Hailey posted the photos of Elizabeth and Lorne. Why would she do that?

Elizabeth is afraid to ask Miguel if he looked them up along with her profile. The old voices are in her head, clamoring that of course he doesn't want anything to do with her now, that no good man would. She commands them to shut up. There are bigger things on the line than her supposed virtue.

Mary really must not want Nate to get away with what he's done, if she's willing to put herself in danger to get Elizabeth out of it. Elizabeth can't imagine her other friends doing that. It seems as if even Chrissy, her closest confidant, hasn't done more than send a few sympathetic texts since the photos broke.

Elizabeth would like to think Mary's not acting only out of spite.

She feels oddly comfortable in Mary's skin. It could be because she had barely any time back in her own, or because, like Mary used to say, she's a natural at transfers. Or maybe this is where she's supposed to be.

Miguel's here too, helping her when he has no reason to. "Thank you," she says to him.

"I'm glad you're not hurt." His face remains stony, eyes pointed straight through the windshield, but his mouth softens.

If that's all she gets right now, she'll take it.

———

"OKAY, I THINK *now* might be when we call the cops," Miguel whispers.

Elizabeth holds up a hand for silence. They're at the top of the basement stairs with the door cracked, having entered the house through the man cave. She's trying to listen to what sounds more like an unhinged-villain monologue every second.

"Everything you care about, I want to take it away," Hailey's saying.

Her voice wobbles. Moments ago, sneaking through the yard, Elizabeth saw Hailey through the window with a gun in her hand. She imagines that hand—that gun—wobbling too.

If Mary dies in Elizabeth's body, does she die for real? Does Elizabeth become Mary? She can't allow that to happen. It would be selfish, evil. She's already taken so much away, without meaning to.

From Hailey too. It all makes sense now. The reason Hailey slid into her DMs soon after Garrett died, when Elizabeth was still feeling unsteady and overwhelmed. Elizabeth had been grateful for someone to handle the details. If only she'd done a background check. But Hailey—Hailey Rose, as she'd called herself—would probably have had everything in order.

Hailey Rose Deegan. Garrett's bereaved sister.

"How did you know it wasn't Mary who pushed Garrett?" Mary's voice—*Elizabeth's* voice—trembles as though she's struggling to remain calm.

"I went to the same university. It was a way for me to feel closer to him," Hailey says. "Walking under the same trees, going to class in the same buildings. I'd blamed Mary for ruining his life as much as my parents did. But I worked as a student assistant in the dean of students' office. I looked up Mary's disciplinary records, where there was a note about you coming in and telling an unbelievable story."

"But you believed it," Mary prompts.

"I knew Mary had interned for my aunt's company. I talked to my aunt when she was having a good day. She was able to tell me that just before the company closed, some of the devices they made had gone missing. She never knew who took them. She said she kept expecting some other company to come out with similar tech, but no one ever did."

"That's why you became my assistant? To find out for yourself if I really did it?"

Hailey scoffs. "Oh, I knew you did it. I just needed to get close enough to ruin you. Are you going to try to tell me it was an accident?"

"It *was* an accident."

"Spare me. There was a copy of that video you and Mary made of him in her records. You blackmailed him! Tormented him! Just admit you hated him."

Behind Elizabeth, Miguel mutters, "I'm just gonna make that call," and retreats around the bend in the stairs so the people in the living room won't hear him.

"I did hate him," Elizabeth whispers to herself.

This is her fault. She needs to fix it.

She opens the door just enough to slip out.

"Elizabeth!" Miguel hisses desperately from behind her.

"Stay here," she whispers. And walks out with her hands up.

55

MARY (ELIZABETH)

NOW

"Just admit you hated him." Hailey's hands tighten on the grip of the gun, even as the barrel shakes. "You killed him in the slowest, most painful way possible. That is unforgivable."

"When you won't forgive someone, who do you think it hurts more?"

We jerk our heads toward the kitchen. A woman wearing a parka that dwarfs her small frame, with dishwater blond hair in an angled cut, stands in the pass-through.

"The person you hate? Or yourself?" Elizabeth steps into the room, hands raised. I can see her trembling. A faint, doubtful mist, the color of violets, surrounds her, then fades as I force myself to focus on what I know is real.

The gun. The gun is real. Hailey swings around so it's pointed at Elizabeth. "Stay where you are!"

Elizabeth stops, her gaze shifting to Lorne's body. A mixture of horror and sorrow filters into her expression.

"Is he—" She clears her throat. "Is he dead?"

No one answers.

"Hailey." She meets Hailey's eyes. "Can I cover him up?"

Hailey looks taken aback, as if she wasn't expecting this level of humanity from Mary Burke. She's right to be surprised. As much as Lorne's dead eyes creeped me out, it didn't occur to me to close them for him. A pang of conscience goes through me: for the people who must care about him, if not for Lorne himself.

"You're so full of it," Hailey says to Elizabeth. "You didn't forgive Elizabeth. How could you? She made you take the blame for what she did."

"Elizabeth tried to confess," Elizabeth says. "She wanted to make up for what she did. For years, I refused to let her."

It gives me a crawling feeling of discomfort to hear Elizabeth say these things as though she's me. To know they're true.

Elizabeth turns her gaze on me. "I was too angry. And I had reason to be. I was a good friend to her, the best. But she wasn't there for me when it counted. I lost everything I'd been working toward for so long. I didn't think she even cared.

"But I was wrong about that part. She did care. She does. And she's so, so sorry."

How seamlessly she takes my perspective. The Empathyzers work for their intended purpose sometimes after all.

Before, her apology left me cold. Here, now, it strikes to my heart.

"Can someone explain what the hell is going on?" Nate bursts out.

I shake myself, feeling like I've come out of a dream. "Let her cover Lorne's body," I say to Hailey.

"Fine."

Elizabeth removes her coat and, kneeling, takes Lorne's pulse. She flinches as she touches his skin. "No heartbeat." She lays the coat over his upper body.

I watch Hailey clock the Empathyzer on her wrist, and look from her to me. "Well, *Mary. Elizabeth* can't pay me off like she can with you. And she didn't apologize to *me.*"

She's right; I didn't.

"You got your revenge, though," Elizabeth says. "Her marriage is over. Her career will never be the same."

Nate says, "I don't know what's happening here, but you all better—"

"My brother is dead!" Hailey shouts. "Someone has to pay for that!"

"Lorne killed your brother with an overdose, and now he's dead," Elizabeth says.

"Garrett wouldn't have been on drugs if he hadn't fallen that night!"

"Neither of us meant for him to get hurt," I say. "I know that doesn't really help. It can't bring him back. But I'm sorry you had to lose him."

Hailey's face crumples. "I just wanted the people who wrecked my brother to take responsibility."

I refrain from pointing out that earlier she wanted to make Elizabeth and me suffer. This is a change in tune I can live with. "We will," I say soothingly.

"Both of us will," Elizabeth says, probably not meaning it any more than I did. She gets to her feet. "Hailey, you don't have to do this. Nobody else needs to get hurt." She holds out her hand. "Give me the gun."

Hailey's eyes move from Elizabeth's face to the Empathyzer on her wrist, then down to Lorne's body. Her face hardens.

Elizabeth has miscalculated.

"Why would Lorne kill my brother if not for you?" Hailey says. She aims the gun directly at Elizabeth's chest. At the heart of my body.

That's when Nate lunges for her.

56

MARY (ELIZABETH)

NOW

The gun goes off right as Nate careens into Hailey. Elizabeth drops to her hands and knees. I can't tell if she's been hit. Nate wrests the gun from Hailey easily, then pushes her, hard, into the wall. Stunned, she slides to the floor.

A noise from the kitchen. Nate turns with the gun and fires, his lips shaping the words *Who the fuck are you?* Miguel's in the pass-through, a dark wet bloom on one side of his chest. He falls.

Elizabeth, blood on her shirt, screams and crawls to him. She presses her hands to his chest, where they are quickly covered in blood too.

I'm still taking in the fact that Elizabeth's all right—the visceral relief of seeing my body still alive—when Nate stalks over, hauls her to her feet, and presses the barrel of the gun to her cheek. "Tell me why I shouldn't shoot you."

She struggles, her eyes on Miguel. I take over first aid on him so Elizabeth doesn't wrestle Nate into killing one of us.

"You've been plotting against me this whole time," Nate says to Elizabeth, his teeth gritted. "You sought me out. Invited me to your apartment. It was all a trap, wasn't it?"

A trap he ran into like a kid jumping into a swimming pool in August. He still has no idea Elizabeth isn't me.

"You broke into my house. You and these men." He looks at Lorne, dead, and Miguel, still alive but for who knows how long. "This is my home. I can defend my home."

Miguel's breathing shallowly, his face pale and his eyes closed in pain. Not knowing what else to do, I press my sweater on his chest. I seem to see rot spreading from the wound. The knit soaks through. My dizziness returns.

I reach into my pocket for Elizabeth's phone, but just then Miguel's head lolls to one side. "Hey," I murmur, shaking him. The movement makes him wince, but raises slivers of iris between his eyelids. "Stay awake."

My voice gets Nate's attention. "And Florence fucking Nightingale over here. You care more about helping a burglar than me. Why don't you ever act like you're on my team?" The resentment in his voice makes my gut twist. "Do you have any idea how frustrating it is always being a supporting character in *your* life?"

Spare me the whining of entitled men. Annoyance cuts through my fear and keeps me from crying, or begging. Begging won't stop Nate from doing what he means to do.

He's talking himself into killing us, and if we're going to stay alive, one of us has to get that gun.

I make fleeting eye contact with Elizabeth, then speak to Nate. "What do you do that makes you so interesting?" If I can irritate him, distract him just enough, maybe Elizabeth can grab the gun before he shoots her with it. "Nothing. You playact at making films and cheat on your wife. All you've got going for you is that you're a tall white guy with symmetrical features. You know it, and you can't stand it."

Nate's face twists. "You whore. You would have run off with your *drug dealer* and left me with nothing."

"I wouldn't have," Elizabeth says. He looks down at her, startled, though the gun doesn't move from her cheek.

"I loved you," she goes on. "I wanted to forgive you. Even after it got beyond the point where I could, I still would have treated you fairly."

"What the *hell* is happening right now?" he says.

"It's me," she says. "I'm Elizabeth. *I* ran into you and invited you for a drink. I'm the one you've been texting pictures of your dick. It was me the whole time."

"This is crazy."

"It's true," I say.

Nate looks uncertain. I pop my eyes at Elizabeth, but she doesn't make a move. Hesitant. She needs more motivation.

"What were you trying to pull with that post you made?" I ask. "Saying Elizabeth was missing, that she'd harm herself. Were you planning to kill her?"

"No. A woman dies, the husband's the first person they look at. But if she ends up in the psych ward . . ."

"You would be in control, and Elizabeth would be out of your way."

"Yeah. Too bad that didn't work out. I would have put you away somewhere nice, but now you're about to be killed in a home-invasion robbery."

Laughter startles us all. We all forgot about Hailey, watching and listening.

She gets to her feet, still laughing. "I didn't even need to do anything," she says to Elizabeth. "You married your own revenge. Congratulations." She heads toward the front door in a not-quite-casual saunter.

Nate tracks her with the gun. "Where do you think you're—"

Elizabeth takes her chance to break his hold.

A firecracker *pop* as the gun goes off. Drywall dust puffs from the ceiling. As Nate squeezed the trigger Elizabeth pushed his arms up, keeping the round from hitting Hailey.

The barrel wavers as Nate vacillates between recapturing Elizabeth and taking Hailey out before she can escape. Miguel has slipped into unconsciousness.

Nate's back is to me. My eye lights on the horse statuette on the sofa table. It's the piece Elizabeth found at the thrift store the same day we bought our Halloween costumes. The only thing she kept from college.

Quickly and quietly, I get to my feet. The rearing horse is smooth in my hands, weighty for its size. I swing it as hard as I can at the back of Nate's head.

He goes down on his face. The gun skitters across the floor, where Elizabeth jumps on it. She trembles so badly, she might shoot me by accident. I scurry around beside her.

Zombielike, Nate shakes himself and gets his hands and knees under him. One of his pupils is blown wide; the other is tiny. He crawls toward Elizabeth.

He recognizes her. I can see it in his face. He knows she's his wife. He believes it.

My hands are empty. I look around, frantic, but can't find the statuette. Elizabeth's back is to the wall. Nate slides his foot up. Bent double, he shuffles forward.

Elizabeth raises the gun, shaking. Nate's close enough to reach for her. He'll grab her hands, force them apart, take the gun away.

She squeezes the trigger into his face.

He falls with a shuffling thump I'll hear in my dreams for years, and doesn't move again.

57

MARY (ELIZABETH)

NOW

Blood slides over the hardwood floor in a thick line from Nate's body toward Lorne's. *The house must be slanted,* some detached part of me notes. *Not so perfect after all.*

Elizabeth kneels at Miguel's side, pressing my sweater to his chest. Her shock-blank face is flecked with Nate's blood, her arms covered in Miguel's up to the elbows, sticky with it. I've got blood on my hands too, though not as much of it.

Hailey sits with her back against the front door like her legs have lost all strength. I've packed my own horror away somewhere inside, where I can see it but it can't touch me. It needs to stay there for now; I'm the one responsible for this scene. This is my house.

I feel completely lucid now, and I don't like it.

I call 911. First responders are already on their way. An ambulance arrives and EMTs bundle Miguel into the back. Elizabeth climbs in with him, despite the graze on her torso that has one side of her shirt soaked in blood. "It's fine," she says impatiently, holding a wad of gauze to it.

The uniformed officer lobbing questions at us doesn't want to let her go, but I tell him my attorney is on her way and will represent both of us. I'm impressed at my own authority. Apparently the officer is too, because he doesn't bother to give me any more shit.

Hailey and I are given on-site medical attention and pronounced free of serious physical injuries. The EMT warns me that the finger marks Nate put on my neck will look worse tomorrow. The processing of the scene turns Elizabeth's house into a foreign country. I have no idea what to tell the police, so I don't tell them anything. Hailey's smart enough to keep her mouth shut too. We have to get our stories straight, but I'm in no state to handle it, and being rich has to be good for something.

Elizabeth's lawyer arrives. She's a fiftyish woman dressed like she was on a date and looking mildly annoyed to be pulled away from it. She efficiently shuts down the police questioning, telling the officer that "Mary" and I will give our statements when we're ready.

"Do you need us to take you somewhere?" Hailey asks me. We're down in the man cave, since cops and forensics are swarming over the rest of the house. Her lawyer and mine lean against the pool table, conferring.

Hailey lowers her voice. "Which one are you?"

"Still Mary." Knowing Elizabeth wanted to be with Miguel, I didn't want to transfer without her consent. "I'm going to head to the hospital. But I can drive."

"Thanks for not letting Nate kill me. Tell Elizabeth thanks too."

I was more trying to keep Nate from killing all of us, but it seems unwise to mention that if Hailey's having an epiphany. I nod.

"I know he wasn't perfect." For a second I think she's talking about Nate, but she means Garrett. "I know he gave you a hard time in college. And I believe you now, that it was an accident. I'm going to tell my parents you both saved my life."

I nod again, exhausted. But it's a weight lifted.

"Even if he was a bad person, I still can't help loving him."

I look at her. "Sometimes we can't help loving bad people. It doesn't make us bad." I'm not bullshitting her. It's not who we love that makes us good or bad; it's what we do.

I FIND ELIZABETH in the trauma center's surgical waiting area. She's gotten treatment, exchanging my blood-soaked top for a paper hospital gown worn as a shirt. I should have brought her something to change into. She's washed her hands and face, but there's still blood—hers, Nate's, or Miguel's—stippling her skin.

Seeing me, she motions to the status screen that lists various patients in surgery. "They got him right into the OR." It's a busy night; the room is three-quarters full of people settled in to wait, heads pillowed on coats and feet propped on chairs. "The EMT wouldn't tell me whether she thought he would make it."

I don't know if that bodes ill or if the EMT was just covering her own ass. But Elizabeth looks drawn, her eyes starey. I wouldn't feel right leaving her alone even if Miguel's outlook was good.

"I told him to stay hidden," she says. "He was calling the police. Why did he come rushing out? What was he thinking?"

My first thought is that she's performing her confusion. She's aware of the effect she has on people, and deep down, she must consider Miguel's risking his life to be her due. But I bite back those words. I've spent seven years demonizing Elizabeth. It's time for me to see her not as a manipulating temptress but as a person, with flaws and virtues like everyone else.

So I say, "You'll have to ask him when he's better."

"If he'll talk to me," she sulks. "Detective Johns came by a little while ago."

Adrenaline quavers through my stomach. "What did he say?"

"He tried to get me to say 'Elizabeth' put Lorne up to giving

Garrett adulterated drugs. Didn't seem like his heart was in it."
She shrugs. With Lorne's death, the Deegans can't claim justice
hasn't been served. And I doubt even they could get me or Elizabeth put away without evidence.

"Was my phone recording the whole time?" she asks.

I remember turning it off before I called the police. "Yeah."

"The audio of Hailey's little rant might hold Rosemary and
Brian off if they start to go hard on us again."

I settle back in my chair, prepared for a long vigil. Sitting with
Elizabeth isn't comfortable, exactly. But after what we've been
through, we're more allies than adversaries.

My mind drifts to the future, when all of this will be over except the nightmares. What will we be to each other? Could we ever
be friends again? My goodwill toward her feels fragile, as if a hint
of envy or resentment could shatter it. I imagine she's wary of me
too. But whatever our relationship, what we went through tonight
will knit us together for the rest of our lives.

I believe, now, that Elizabeth was telling the truth when she
said she missed me. Because I miss her too. I've never had someone
who knew me like she did, who had both affection and a use for
my quirks. For all her popularity, I'm not sure she's ever had someone really know her, either. Even me.

"Are you ready to transfer back?" I ask.

Elizabeth looks at me in surprise. "You'd do that?"

"Yeah. I think I've had enough of being you."

She gives a tired smile. "Then I guess there's no point in putting it off. Should we do it right here?"

"I don't think anyone's paying attention to us." I tap the screen
of my Empathyzer to wake it up, and frown when it tells me there
are no others in range. "You've still got yours powered on, right?"

"Yeah, I never turned it"—Elizabeth's voice fades as she takes
a closer look at her wristband—"off."

The Empathyzer on her wrist is clotted with dried blood. It's worked its way into all the little cracks I made over the years, gumming up the exposed circuits. The screen is blank, a dark cast spreading over the lower half like a shadow.

Elizabeth starts to laugh.

My heart—Elizabeth's heart—thrums against my collarbones. "We'll find another one," I say. "There must be someone else at Confluence who stole a pair."

She's still laughing, like she lacks the strength to stop. "Weren't they all . . . destroyed? You spent . . . years . . . looking for one."

"Then I'll figure out how to make one. I'll go back to school . . ."

"Okay." She puts her hand on my arm, more to make me stop talking than to comfort me, I think. "You have to admit, though, it's a little funny." Giggles leak around the edges of her control. Looking at her, I feel the corners of my mouth lifting.

"A little." Finally I laugh too, because it's either that or scream in frustration.

"You should go home," she says. "Get some sleep."

But Elizabeth's house is a crime scene, and I want to see this through, so I stay. We commandeer more chairs and rest as well as we can, until the surgeon comes out and tells us Miguel is going to recover.

58

MARY (ELIZABETH)

SIX MONTHS LATER

Elizabeth's lawyer—my lawyer now—is a miracle worker. She makes everything go away with minimal fuss, arguing that in shooting Mr. Jordan, Ms. Burke was acting to defend herself and three others against a man who had just committed a violent murder. Given the sudden death of Lorne, who caused Garrett's overdose, the investigation into Garrett's death peters out as well.

We use every bit of leverage we gain from the recording of Hailey's confession. The Deegans drop their old judgment claim against me, as well as coughing up a settlement to compensate Elizabeth for the damage the revenge porn caused to her future earning potential. I promptly sign it over to her. Technically, she earned it.

I haven't hired a new assistant, not wanting to give anyone else that much control over my daily life. I can manage things myself, having scaled back @bethybeth's activity to no more than a couple of posts a week. Given her bereavement, the slowdown should be understandable, but I've been shedding dozens of followers a day. It doesn't necessarily look good for her that multiple women have come forward with stories of Nate's borderline abusive behavior toward them. It seems he enjoyed treating his one-night stands like trash. *Not to speak ill of the dead, but dude was a fucking creep* seems to be the consensus, and a sizable minority see his wife as complicit. *They had an open marriage,* people say. *She might have known what he was up to. She had to know. She knew.*

I don't begrudge Nate's victims their right to tell their stories, or their anger, even if they take it out on me. It's not as if he's around to absorb it. I feel less charitable toward the armchair pundits, the lookie-loos and pilers-on. But that's the internet.

Aside from doing a few low-effort activations and living off Elizabeth's savings, I'm drifting. I keep telling myself that soon I'll start on the path to getting Elizabeth and me back to ourselves. Until then, I'm in limbo. I rarely do anything social, even for work, though I've had drinks with Chrissy a few times. She's the only person I've seen lament Lorne's death. "Such a waste," she'll moan after her third skinny margarita. "He was so *pretty.*"

I haven't seen much of Elizabeth, though we text daily. I feel like each of us is wary of meeting for different reasons. Elizabeth might be afraid my longtime hatred will reanimate if we see each other face-to-face. I'm more worried I'll start liking her again.

I already have, without meaning to. I listen to the true-crime podcast she started a couple of months ago, which already has thousands of subscribers and a few big-name sponsors. It's smart and sensitive, and it highlights the stories of people who might otherwise have languished in cold-case obscurity: poor women and women of color, undocumented migrants, sex workers. The common thread is that they were all betrayed by people they trusted. At least a few of those cases have been reopened based on tips from listeners, and every episode raises money for the victims' families. Her voice, speaking into my head every week, brings me back to college, which is still the last time I felt as though I belonged anywhere.

I was right: without hating Elizabeth, I don't know what my purpose is. But unlike me, she's not waiting for her life to start.

———

ON A SUNDAY in June we meet for brunch, but really to discuss the sale of her house. Legally I could unload the place without consulting her, let alone paying her, but I already feel bad enough about my procrastination in finding a new Empathyzer.

I arrive first. It's the kind of golden day that has people waiting hours for a table, but being Elizabeth still has its benefits: the host recognizes me, and I get a table for two on the patio. Elizabeth shows up wearing high-waisted shorts, ankle boots, and a crop top, an outfit that highlights the gamine aesthetic she's got going on. Her blue-streaked, razored pixie cut adds a modicum of edginess, as does a brand-new tattoo on her bicep: a stylized rearing mustang.

"I like the look," I tell her as we exchange loose hugs. I search myself for annoyance about the tattoo, but can't find any.

"Yours too," she says, though her expression betrays a tinge of pity. I've let myself go, if "letting myself go" means not wearing makeup unless I have an event, skipping workouts except for the Brazilian jiu-jitsu classes I've started taking, and dressing in leggings most days.

"Just say what you're thinking," I tell her. "This isn't a look. It's laziness."

She grins. "I always did have to drag you kicking and screaming into a skirt."

"How's everything?" I leave the question open-ended, so she can talk about her podcast or she can talk about whether she, like me, still wakes up sweating and trembling in the middle of the night.

"Pretty good!" she says brightly, and starts going on about some famous-in-true-crime-circles private eye she's interviewing on an upcoming episode. Then, as our drinks arrive, she says, "Miguel and I are talking."

"Oh?" The last update on Miguel, after his recovery, was that he'd told Elizabeth he needed time to process everything. I'd figured it was a polite kiss-off, and good for him. The distance between them increased when she moved out of my old building and into a place with a walk-in closet she could turn into a recording studio.

"Yeah. He texted me about a month ago saying he'd been listening to the pod. I asked him if he wanted to get dinner, and he said okay, and . . . it's been going well, I think." Her cheeks have taken on a slight buoyant blush, which I take to mean it's going even better than she's said.

"So he's over your husband shooting him?"

Her face turns red and she almost spits out her orange juice. "Jeez, Mary."

"I mean, it's a hurdle."

"Sure. But there are only so many times I can apologize. I'm working on my issues in therapy. Trying to treat people like people, not things. Even myself." She grimaces. After a brief lull, during which I sit with my amazement—envy, really—at her ability to forgive herself, the conversation moves on.

We spend the meal nailing down an informal agreement about the house while I wait to see if she'll bring up transferring. It's become like when you owe someone money, and you know they haven't forgotten, but they're too polite to mention it.

So I broach the subject as I'm picking up the bill. "I haven't been able to find anyone else from Confluence who will talk to me." I'm not lying. I made a few half-hearted attempts, thinking people might respond better to my new identity than my old one. No dice.

Elizabeth puts down her glass of orange juice. I noticed she didn't drink any alcohol, though I had a couple of mimosas. "I was thinking."

Then she stops.

"You were thinking?" I prompt.

"What if we left things like they are?"

The walls of the room seem to inhale. "Like . . . you stay in that body and I stay in this one?"

She gives me a tight smile, spreading her hands. "Yes?"

"You *want* to be Mary Burke?" She wants my little life? Though already she's expanded it, further than I ever would have, while I've been collapsing hers down to the smallest possible package.

"It's been a fresh start. I feel like positive things are happening, and I don't want to push my luck. Have you been having any more side effects?"

Nothing worth mentioning. A hallucination every so often, like the breathing walls. Occasionally I wake up confused about who and where I am, but anyone would in my situation. At this point I can hardly separate what might be lingering transfer side effects from my trauma response. Elizabeth, of course, hasn't mentioned having any side effects at all.

The more I learn about Confluence and the fates of some of the people who were the earliest testers of the Empathyzer—there's a higher-than-average incidence of brain disorders—the more concerned I am about Elizabeth's and my futures. But it's not as if we can go back in time and not use the wristbands.

"I heard Gloria Faculak died," Elizabeth says. "Sounded like she declined pretty quickly over the last few months."

Too bad. I had a vague intention to try to contact her, see if I could look through whatever personal effects she might have in storage. Now they're probably all sold off or given away. I picture myself in a thrift shop like the ones Elizabeth and I used to frequent in college, happening on an Empathyzer in a pile of worn-out fitness wearables and defunct gaming consoles.

"Anyway," Elizabeth says, "we don't have to decide right now. It's not as if there's any way for us to transfer back, right?"

I shake my head, feeling like it's wrapped in thick fabric. What she's not mentioning is that the longer we go as each other, the harder it will be to integrate back into ourselves. I've known that for six months. I just haven't done anything about it.

Elizabeth smiles, and I sense she's holding back more persuasive words. "Then take some time to think about it."

OVER THE FOLLOWING days and weeks, I do. Despite (or perhaps because of) its status as a murder house, Elizabeth's place sells quickly. I move into a condo on the river, a shiny new-construction box that provides a comfortable place to exist but not much in the way of inspiration. It does have the advantage of not being the scene of the greatest trauma of my life, and my sleep improves immediately.

I think about getting a cat, but don't. I let Elizabeth take Jumbo back as soon as she moved into a place that allowed pets. He was suspicious of her at first, but soon warmed up.

The @bethybeth account keeps trundling along, my follower count stabilizing at a level well below the previous one, though high enough to attract some sponsorships. The posts I make there feel like I'm still playing dress-up in Elizabeth's life.

For the better part of a decade, Elizabeth has loomed so large that I don't know what to do now that she's been reduced to a normal size in my life. Without even meaning to, she's influenced most of my thoughts and decisions outside of bare survival. And now, yet again, she's in control.

We'll always have a connection: apart from the obvious, we saved each other's lives. We belong to each other. And I think there's a reason the Empathyzers worked for us when they didn't for so many others. We found each other when we most needed to, at the time we most wanted to escape from our old selves. Some of the experimental dyads might have had strong bonds, but they didn't really want to *be* each other. They didn't need it like Elizabeth and I did.

I don't know how to move on. Maybe that's why I've been re-sisting getting back to my old body, because then I'll have to. I've never felt comfortable in my skin; I've always stood outside of my life. It's time for me to start inhabiting it.

Being her, *accepting* being her, might be a way for me to achieve that.

It's not as if it's a hardship. Other people have to get used to new realities, new bodies, all the time. Accidents, disease, even just aging—they can all trap us in new selves we struggle to rec-ognize. I've got it easier than some.

I think about reinventing myself, traveling, moving out of the city. I think about shutting down Elizabeth's accounts and going off the grid, or going back to school. I think about a lot of things. The key is that I have options. And the more I think about it, the more I can't wait to get started.

On a weekday afternoon, I go up to the rooftop garden of my new building. I've started coming up here at this time of day, when I can count on it being deserted. It's tranquil, with sleek furniture and professionally manicured greenery, but today I can see a sum-mer storm approaching, dark clouds pierced with lightning. Soon the wind will be whipping the potted cedars back and forth, rain soaking the outdoor rugs. I'll stay and experience it, even if I risk getting electrocuted.

The clouds sweep toward me as I stand at the railing. I take out my phone and text Elizabeth. My answer is yes.

Almost immediately I see the dancing ellipsis that means she's typing. I imagine a range of possible responses, from excitement to casual entitlement to a panicked retraction. But I don't wait for her to reply. I turn off my phone and watch the storm roll in.

59

MARY ELIZABETH BURKE

JULY

My answer is yes.

Mary's text arrives while I'm on the train. I've been trying to take public transit more often. Cars waste both money and planetary resources, and riding in one increasingly feels like cutting myself off from the world in an unhealthy way. I want to experience everything life has to offer, even if that means smelling the sauerkraut armpits of the guy standing next to me.

I do a little shimmy of excitement and start typing a reply, but I'm only a few words in when I realize I don't really know what to say. *Thanks? Congratulations? Sorry?* I slide my phone back into my pocket, fully intending to respond later, when I can choose my words.

I get off the train in Mary's old neighborhood and make a quick stop at a bakery I fell in love with during the (mercifully) brief time I stayed in her apartment.

Rain's on the way, judging by the dark clouds and heavy stillness in the air. After waiting a few minutes for the bus, I give up and summon a rideshare. Environmental responsibility is all very well, but I'd rather not rock the drowned-rat look.

The building's lobby is squalid as usual, with the reek of something that must have crawled into one of the mailboxes and died. I'm mystified as to how Miguel can stand it here, rock-bottom rent or no. "I brought bomboloni," I say when he opens his door.

"Hi," he says. "I, um, didn't realize you were coming over." Even so, his arm finds its way around my waist, and our hello kiss is scorching enough to make me forget where we are.

A loud *boom* of thunder startles us apart. The rain comes in a patter I can hear through his closed windows. "I can't leave until the storm's over, so you're stuck with me. Hope you didn't have plans."

My cheeky grin pulls a smile out of him. "I was actually about to text you," he says.

"Looks like I read your mind, then." Closing the apartment door behind me, I set the doughnuts on the table where he puts his mail, then very deliberately remove his glasses and set them on top of the bakery box. A second later we're kissing. My back makes contact with the wall, then slides up it as he lifts me. My new body might not be as conventionally attractive as my old one, but I do enjoy being pocket-size. Getting carried to bed is just never not going to be hot.

Later, we eat bomboloni in bed, then order in for dinner. Dessert first—or at all—is a benefit of my newly high metabolism. I'd forgotten what I was missing since I turned thirteen and my mother started buying my clothes a size too small to "motivate" me.

After dinner, I have to leave. Jumbo needs his walkies. I try to get Miguel to come with me, angling for him to sleep over, but he claims he has to get some work done.

"Am I too much of a distraction?" I ask innocently.

"Sure are," he says, not even trying to sugarcoat it. He says he'll text me tomorrow, and I can tell he means it. He's not one to play who-can-seem-least-interested games. But I imposed on him today, so I'll let him make the next move. I still can't shake the feeling that he's with me against his better judgment. Not because he brings up my failings, but because I know what they are myself.

I am so incredibly lucky.

My new apartment is on a block of recently rehabbed buildings full of people like me: young and creative, childless except for our cats and dogs or, as in the case of my upstairs neighbor, a ferret. It's a nice enough place, though with none of the luxuries of my old house. I like it that way. I'd feel uneasy now, with that much empty space. I take Jumbo for a long walk, luxuriating in the poststorm coolness. By the time I get back, the light is fading and it's time to face down the night.

Too often when I sleep alone, I see Nate's face in my dreams. Not after I shot him, thank goodness—I closed my eyes when I squeezed the trigger—but before. His features distorted until I couldn't recognize the man I'd married.

My therapist has told me it's common to have lasting trauma after taking a life, even when it's justified. Nate would have killed me. He would have killed everyone in that room, and not just to cover up what he'd done to Lorne. He was going on pure rage. Maybe the person I thought was Nate was always an act.

I do some podcast research and writing, and record overdubs for the episode I'm planning to post tomorrow. Then I realize I still haven't replied to Mary's text. I'm willing to do just about anything to avoid going to sleep. I don't want a drink—I'd started doing more of that than I was comfortable with—so instead, I call her.

The call rings through to voicemail. What's so important that she can't pick up? It's not like she's living the influencer life anymore. That much is apparent from her ghost town of a profile.

I leave her a message. "This is going to be *so* amazing for both of us. Text me! We need to hang out soon." Like we're normal gal pals. But I want to be her friend again! I really do.

My apartment was advertised as having an eat-in kitchen,

though it's so small there's barely room for two chairs at the table. I stand on one of them to reach way back on the top shelf of a cabinet and take down a vintage hatbox. Before opening it, I make sure the curtains are completely drawn, no cracks around the edges.

Inside the hatbox is another, rectangular box, about the size of my hand. Inside *that* is a silicone wristband that could easily be mistaken for one of the knockoff wearables I see guys selling from fold-up tables on the street.

I run my fingertip over the text molded into the casing. *CONFLUENCE*.

The Empathyzer turned up in my mailbox the week after I met Mary for brunch. I don't know who sent it, but I'm betting on Hailey. Even if she's forgiven Mary and me for our parts in Garrett's downfall—which is doubtful—stirring the pot seems like something she'd do.

So I don't trust this thing, obviously, but that's not why I won't tell Mary about it. Nor are my reasons completely selfish, though I have my doubts that Miguel's and my connection could survive a change in bodies. After everything that happened with Nate and Lorne, I needed a fresh start. Mary has needed one for almost eight years. There's already enough uncertainty between us; I don't want to introduce any more.

I pour a glass of water from the fridge dispenser and take a sip, then set the glass on the table. The Empathyzer beside it looks untouched, like someone kept it squirreled away in a storage unit for years.

I pick it up, holding it over the half-full glass. I drop it in.

Mary might be the smart one. But when it comes to making sure we both live our best lives, I know better.

ACKNOWLEDGMENTS

There's a reason female friendship is written about so often. It's an ever-shifting, nuanced thing, and it's endlessly inspiring. I want to thank the girls and women who've been my friends on the various paths my life has taken. Whether you lifted me up or broke my heart (or both, at different times), you helped make me who I am today.

Second books bring into focus just how much support goes into creating them, and I've had a great deal of help along the way with this one. My editor, Jen Monroe, immediately saw the possibilities in my harebrained "*Single White Female*, but make it feminist" premise, and pushed me to make this novel the very best it could be, and Candice Coote provided valuable insights during the editing process. I am continually amazed that Claire Zion, Jeanne-Marie Hudson, Craig Burke, Ivan Held, and Christine Ball are on board to put my weird cross-genre stories out into the world and champion them, and I'm so grateful.

Colleen Reinhart created my perfectly creepy cover and found an image that captured Mary's soul, and I haven't been able to stop squeeing over the title page and interior book design from Alison Cnockaert. Zachary Vigna and Daniel Walsh have done their utmost to ensure I don't embarrass myself with continuity errors or get one of those reviews that read, "I wanted to like this book, but there was a typo on page 160." (If there's a typo on page 160, it's my fault.)

I'm especially thankful for the people who hype up my novels and help them find their readers. Hannah Engler and Lauren Burnstein—without you, I'd be lost in the noise. I so appreciate the sales team at Berkley and the booksellers out there, because as we learned during the pandemic, there's no substitute for books being in shops. Thanks to the Michigan Notable Books committee as well as everyone who has interviewed me, invited me to be on a panel or visit their book club, arranged author events, or shouted about my work on any platform. All the gold stars go to those authors who've been kind enough to provide blurbs for my books; an impressive amount of time and effort goes into those one to three sentences.

My agent, Joanna MacKenzie, has been the best partner I could ask for during this whole process. Angie Hodapp and Maria Heater gave me invaluable feedback and brainstorming help while I was drafting (and redrafting). Thanks to them and everyone else at Nelson Literary Agency—I feel so lucky to have landed there.

I would have disintegrated without the fellow writers who've listened to me whine (and whine, and whine) about how hard it is to do this thing we love so much. Berkletes and Shakespeare's Sisters—I love everyone in this bar. I'm especially grateful to Nekesa Afia, Olivia Blacke, Eliza Jane Brazier, and Amanda Jayatissa for workshopping help. Thanks to early readers Best Selling Brains, the Pod That Shall Not Be Named, and Lauren Beltz—you suffered through the parts that didn't need to be in the book. Audrey Burges and Katie Shepard offered pertinent legal insights, and B.C. Krygowski lent medical advice and a heavenly spot for a beach writing retreat.

Thanks so much to my family, immediate and extended, who've all supported me in so many ways. Claudia—you inspire me every day, even if I haven't put you in a book yet like you asked. (Horrible things happen to my characters!) Sean—with you standing beside me, I can do anything.

And finally, my readers. If not for you, I might as well keep my words on a cloud server somewhere. Thank you.

WHEN

I'M

HER

SARAH ZACHRICH JENG

READERS GUIDE

QUESTIONS FOR DISCUSSION

1. Which character did you root for more—Mary or Elizabeth? Or didn't you root for either of them? Did this change as the story went on?

2. If you had to choose, would you rather be isolated, as Mary was at the beginning of the novel, or surrounded by two-faced friends and admirers, as Elizabeth was?

3. Toward the beginning of the novel, it reads, "Girls become one another all the time," referring to the ways close female friends often take on similar characteristics. Do you think this is true? Do you think it's equally true for male friends?

4. Looking back on your life, if you've had a falling-out with a friend, was it more or less painful than a romantic breakup?

5. In the novel, a startup has created a wearable that lets people switch bodies as a way to increase empathy between them and improve their relationships. Do you think inhabiting someone's body for a short time would be the most effective way to see things from their point of view?

6. If such a device existed and you could try it without ill effects, would you? Would you stick to using it for its stated purpose (seeing things from a loved one's perspective) or would you be tempted to try "off-label" uses?

7. What do you think of Elizabeth's belief that her followers would judge her more harshly than they would Nate if her marriage were to fail? How are women evaluated differently from men, both in the public eye and privately?

8. What are your thoughts on the way male characters are portrayed in the book? Did you find some male characters more realistic than others?

9. Were you surprised by Mary's and Elizabeth's acceptance of their new circumstances at the end? Did you hope for them to resume a closer friendship?

10. Do you think Elizabeth did the right thing in the book's final scene?

BEHIND THE BOOK

When I was in eighth grade, there was a girl—we'll call her Veronica—who embodied everything I wished I could be and wasn't. Veronica's hair and clothes always looked right. She was a cheerleader and the whole school looked up to her. She was dating a boy as popular as she was. Most important, she had confidence and ease in social situations that I couldn't imagine ever possessing.

I have a vivid memory of going on a class trip, boarding the bus early because I always worried about things like where I would sit, and watching through the window as Veronica flirted with her boyfriend. And I thought: *What if I could* become *her?*

I imagined waking up the next morning in her body, while she woke up in mine. I'll admit I didn't spare much thought for poor Veronica, stuck in my life (which was difficult only in the sense of my being an awkward adolescent). I was too busy daydreaming about living hers. And I didn't take into account that even if I was her on the outside, I would still be me on the inside. But I understood that people are treated differently based on what they look like and their perceived place in the world.

Of course, the Veronicas of the world have their own problems, which is one of the main themes of *When I'm Her*. When I wrote the original synopsis for the novel, I knew that Mary, my main character, would figure out a way to switch bodies with Elizabeth, her much more successful ex-friend, in order to steal her "perfect" life. I also knew that Mary would have no idea what she was getting herself into.

Storytellers have long been fascinated by pairs of female friends. Thelma and Louise; Anne and Diana; Shug and Celie; Lila and Elena. All create their own realities where the other person is everything. Some pairings become more than platonic on the page or screen, while with others their queerness is a matter of interpretation. These relationships are ardent, consuming, and sometimes destructive. Women can be kind or cruel to one another, fiercely loyal or quick to betray, yet the ties between them remain even when stretched to the breaking point. While writing *When I'm Her*, I was inspired by these stories and others about friendship, as well as some of the novels about body swapping and impersonation you'll find on my reading list.

However, the two influences I kept coming back to were the Ingmar Bergman film *Persona* and David Lynch's *Mulholland Drive*. Each film has at its center a pair of women who quickly become bonded to each other. In both, this attachment leads to anguish and horror, yet endures in some form until the end. Every time I've watched these movies, I've been mesmerized by their haunting visuals and resistance to simple interpretation. Though directed by men, both films offer empathetic views into women's anger and self-destructive tendencies. The characters are allowed to make terrible choices, and they make them over and over. With Mary and Elizabeth, I embraced a similar approach of putting complexity before likability.

I also wanted to create some of the same nightmarish vibes. In *When I'm Her*, the lines between possible and impossible, real and unreal, are blurred. Technology exists that allows people to inhabit one another's bodies, but it works only some of the time. Mary experiences side effects that make her doubt her own perceptions. Her social isolation and naivete color her views of people's motivations and actions. She expects the worst from those who have burned her, while being oblivious to the faults of others until late in the game.

Making a character's reality subject to interpretation is a useful device in a thriller writer's toolbox, because we're all unreliable narrators of our own lives. We can't be privy to the motives and struggles of everyone around us, and research tells us that memory is impressionistic and frequently inaccurate. I'm sure Veronica from my eighth-grade class remembers her middle-school experience very differently than I do. In writing *When I'm Her*, I tried to inject that uncertainty of recollection into a story that would be thought-provoking but, more important, fun to read.

TEN BOOKS FEATURING BODY SWAPPING OR CHARACTERS WHO TAKE ON NEW IDENTITIES

THE TALENTED MR. RIPLEY BY PATRICIA HIGHSMITH

Tom Ripley doesn't switch bodies with his friend Dickie Greenleaf in Patricia Highsmith's classic "rags to riches to murder" novel, but after killing Dickie, Tom steps into his life of privilege without a hitch. Well, maybe a *few* hitches.

FREAKY FRIDAY BY MARY RODGERS

In this lighthearted switcheroo story that spawned several film adaptations, thirteen-year-old Annabel literally changes places with her mother and finds out what we all learn eventually: adulting is hard.

STRANGER WITH MY FACE BY LOIS DUNCAN

Lois Duncan was the queen of a popular subgenre of supernatural young-adult novels in the '80s and '90s. In this wild ride, teenage adoptee Laurie is haunted by a spirit who looks like her. It turns out to be her evil twin, Lia, who ultimately uses her talent for astral projection to take over Laurie's body and wreak havoc.

YELLOWFACE BY R. F. KUANG

The impersonation here is artistic and cultural rather than physical, but is no less shattering. After frustrated writer June Hayward witnesses the freak death of her friend Athena Liu, a bestselling author, she impulsively steals the manuscript of Athena's new novel. She gets it published as her own work—tarnishing Athena's legacy while "rebranding" herself as Juniper Song to head off questions of cultural appropriation.

TOUCH BY CLAIRE NORTH

Kepler is a "ghost": an entity that can transfer between people's bodies through a touch. Ghosts take over a body for seconds or years, and the hosts don't remember anything they did while possessed. Not every ghost is as careful with its hosts as Kepler is. Now ghosts are being hunted by a shadowy organization hiding an explosive secret, and Kepler is determined to survive at all costs.

MY SWEET GIRL BY AMANDA JAYATISSA

In this dual timeline psychological thriller, Paloma comes home to find that her roommate—who was blackmailing her with her darkest secret—has been murdered. Years earlier, growing up in an orphanage in Sri Lanka before being adopted by Westerners, she becomes convinced that she and her best friend, Lihini, are cursed. As malevolent forces close in, the book's protagonist will do anything—*anything*—to escape.

THIS BODY BY LAUREL DOUD

After Katharine dies of a heart attack, she wakes up in the much younger body of Thisby, an artist who has overdosed. Katharine must adjust to her new circumstances, including Thisby's struggles with addiction, and find a way to connect with the two children she left behind in her old life.

THE VANISHING HALF BY BRIT BENNETT

For Stella, a Black woman passing as white in the 1960s, pretending to be someone she's not is the only way to escape poverty and the lingering terror of having witnessed her father's lynching years before. But maintaining the deception weighs heavily and costs her her heritage and family—including her beloved twin sister, Desiree. This multigenerational story explores identity from several points of view.

GOOD RICH PEOPLE BY ELIZA JANE BRAZIER

Demi's at rock bottom when a chance meeting and a sudden death give her the opportunity to take over another woman's life. Squatting in the dead woman's apartment, Demi doesn't know that her wealthy new landlords have a game they play with their tenants. A game that ruins the tenants' lives. But Demi has struggled her whole life, and she won't be destroyed easily.

SOCIAL CREATURE BY TARA ISABELLA BURTON

Louise falls into a dizzying and toxic friendship with wealthy, mercurial Lavinia. One night, things go horribly wrong and Lavinia ends up dead. What's a striving young woman to do but assume Lavinia's identity? *The Talented Mr. Ripley* if Tom had social media.

Photo by Megan Brown

SARAH ZACHRICH JENG grew up in Michigan and always had a flair for the morbid and mysterious (for her dad's thirty-fifth birthday, she wrote a story entitled "The Man Who Died at 35"). She had a brief career as an aspiring rock star before she came to her senses and went back to school to become a web developer. Sarah lives in Florida with her family and two extremely hyper rescue dogs.

VISIT SARAH ZACHRICH JENG ONLINE

SarahZJ.com

🐦 SarahZJ

📷 Sarah_EZJ